THE REP

Terrence Damon Spencer

PUBLISHING

Dreams To Paper Publishing

INTRODUCTION

We've all felt it—the simmering frustration when confronted by a rude customer who aggressively berates and demands attention, resorting to insults, profanity, and threats to achieve their goals. While most of us manage these encounters with forced politeness, empathy, or simply the fear of repercussions, there's always an urge to respond more assertively.

Enter the turbulent mind of Tommy Thorpe, a collections agent trapped in a relentless call center in Milwaukee, Wisconsin. With each verbally abusive call, Tommy's grip on sanity loosens. Adding fuel to the fire are mounting pressures from his supervisor and a sudden plunge into financial hardship. As the stress intensifies, Tommy succumbs to his darker impulses, spiraling toward a horrifying solution to his mounting frustrations. Soon, the personal details he once collected professionally take on a sinister new purpose.

CHAPTER 1

FOOD FOR THOUGHT

"Eat it, eat it, eat it!" a chorus of fourth and fifth-graders chants, their voices shrill with excitement.

They form a tight circle around me and Dean Miller, whose body dwarfs mine by threefold, pinning me mercilessly against the cold playground asphalt. His knees grind painfully into my biceps, rendering me powerless beneath his weight. Dangling menacingly from his pudgy fingers is a plump earthworm, writhing desperately, clumps of damp mud clinging to its slimy skin.

"The only way you're gonna gain weight is if you eat. So, eat it, stick boy—eat it!" Dean sneers, smearing the squirming, filthy creature across my tightly sealed lips.

I twist my head side-to-side, frantic to avoid it, kicking and struggling to escape. But Dean's heavy ten-year-old frame pins my fragile nine-year-old body firmly in place. He twirls the worm teasingly above my mouth, until another child, impatient to witness the spectacle, lands a sharp kick into my ribs. Gasping in agony, my mouth springs open. Seizing the opportunity, Dean drops the worm directly into my throat.

I jolt awake, coughing and gasping, drenched in sweat as though the nightmare were real. It always feels real. I've lost count of how often I've had this same dream, at least once a week among other random ones that plague me. Despite Gram's, also known as my grandmother, insistence on therapy, I've learned to endure these nightly torments since they began about a year ago.

The chill of an early October morning drifts gently through my open window, a crisp reminder of winter's imminent arrival. My skin, dampened by cold sweat, shivers slightly in the breeze. I glance toward my feet, noticing the tangled heap of blankets gathered there—likely from thrashing around during my nightmare.

Sunrise barely creeps into the room, casting a dim and fuzzy haze across my surroundings. I fumble blindly for my rectangular black-framed glasses on the nightstand, sliding out of bed in my red and gray plaid boxers. Polishing away smudges with the corner of my bedsheet, I squint at the blurred digits glowing faintly on my alarm clock. They sharpen instantly when I push the glasses firmly into place: quarter after six. The dismal truth of another Monday morning settles heavily on my shoulders; God knows how much I despise Mondays.

Stepping up to the full-length mirror near my bed, I repeat a depressing ritual I began in childhood. I prod my exposed ribs, hoping futilely to awaken one day transformed into a stronger, more muscular version of myself. Yet, morning after morning, disappointment stares back at me from my reflection. At six-foot-two, my lanky frame defies the countless home workouts and endless consumption of calories recommended by questionable online advice. Now, at thirty-one years old, I remain trapped inside this skeletal curse.

I run my fingers through my dark brown hair, noting how desperately I need a trim. Typically, I prefer to keep it neatly cropped around an inch and a half, but lately, it's grown to twice that length, spiked and tousled from another restless night. My beard and mustache have grown thick and wild—deliberately fuller—to create an illusion of weight and strength. Occasionally, coworkers lightly tease me, affectionately dubbing me the anorexic version of "Grizzly Adams," a character from some forgotten 1970s television show. Whoever the hell that is.

Suddenly, a delicate sensation tickles my toes, swiftly followed by the gentle prick of tiny, sharp nails climbing cautiously up my leg. Glancing down, I find Tilly, my albino ferret, gazing expectantly up at me, her ruby eyes glittering patiently. It's her subtle morning plea for breakfast, but she'll have to wait.

I rescued Tilly from the shelter months ago, driven by loneliness in this cramped apartment. My landlord's strict "no dogs allowed" policy led me to search for a feline friend instead. But before I could reach the cat enclosures, Tilly captured my heart. She pressed her dainty paws against her glass enclosure, watching my every move, her silky snow-white fur and those mesmerizing crimson eyes drawing me irresistibly closer. It felt almost as though she was smiling at me, and I knew right then I couldn't leave without her.

At night, she glides about the apartment like a mischievous ghost, slipping silently beneath furniture and vanishing between shadows. My initial research indicated ferrets weren't nocturnal, which led me to expect quiet nights of mutual rest. Yet Tilly, ever the special case, defies expectations, racing joyously through rooms at midnight, springing onto my bed to curiously sniff my face in gentle reassurance of her playful presence.

(6:45 am)

This morning's steaming shower feels particularly comforting against my chilled skin. If I could linger in here endlessly, I surely would. But duty beckons, and on the most dreaded day of the week, no less, followed by four equally agonizing days. The thought alone fills me with unease, anticipating countless heated exchanges with disgruntled customers, while forced to maintain unrealistic standards and impossible goals at Easy Auto Acceptance Company.

Standing motionless beneath the hot, cascading water massaging my shoulders and back, my thoughts drift into a familiar existential spiral, questioning the meaning of my existence. Surely, everyone has a purpose, even if it's merely to serve another's ambitions. Yet, here I am, trapped—feeling cheated out of a more meaningful existence than these mind-numbing arguments over overdue accounts. My life cannot be reduced to something so trivial. Every day, I rise only to fulfill some CEO's grand ambitions, fattening their wallets while I'm left hollow and directionless. I'm instructed how to dress, where to stand, how to think and speak—as though my manager were puppeteering my every move, his hand firmly wedged up my ass. My soul aches from this emptiness.

I must have drifted in thought too long, for suddenly, the soothing warmth vanishes, replaced by streams growing colder by the second. Quickly, I lather and rinse before my morning ritual turns into an icy punishment.

(7:02 AM)

I reach for my neatly pressed red Polo shirt and khaki slacks, hanging ready from my closet doorknob, arranged meticulously the night before. Another habit borrowed from my father—always being prepared. Sometimes I wonder how much more he could've taught me, had he still been around.

Standing before the bathroom mirror, combing my hair neatly into place, I peer deeply into my own eyes, wondering what others perceive when they look at me. Too often I've heard phrases like, "You should smile more," or Gram's advice about always beginning the day with a grin, regardless of circumstance. So, I force a smile, as I do every morning—but it feels empty, never genuine, and entirely meaningless.

(7:20 AM)

Four slices of toast, thickly coated with strawberry jam and eight scrambled eggs overwhelm my breakfast plate. I hover above, silently hoping my daily intake of calories will eventually transform my body into something fuller and more muscular. As a child, eating even half this amount felt impossible, and as an adult, it's scarcely easier.

My mind drifts back to childhood dinners when my father patiently waited at the table until I'd cleared my plate, long after he'd finished his own. I would push aside the bits of unwanted meat sauce, leaving only bare spaghetti noodles behind. He always noticed. No matter how many times I tried, I never succeeded in slipping away unnoticed. Still, I would stubbornly turn my back, shielding my plate in hopes of swiftly emptying its contents into the trash before he caught on.

"Tommy, there are plenty of hungry kids around the world who'd love to have what you're refusing," he said, stopping me just two steps away from the dinner table. "Your mother made you an awesome meal, yet you're picking at it and frowning like she just handed you a plate full of poop." He glanced out from behind his newspaper.

I spun around reluctantly, setting my plate back on the table with a bit more force than necessary—but careful not to slam it. That would've guaranteed a whipping from the old man. A childish giggle slipped from my lips as I poked at the unwanted pieces of slaughtered cow with my fork. At six years old, hearing the word "poop" was irresistibly funny, though Dad failed to appreciate the humor. He slammed his fist down sharply on the table, jolting me upright.

"Damnit! Eat it, Tommy!" he shouted.

Immediately, I shoveled mouthfuls of the meat into my cheeks.

"You're never going to get bigger if you don't eat your protein, son. You'll just end up weak and sick. You don't want to be picked on in school, do ya?"

"Mo!" I mumbled, my words muffled by the stuffed mouthful.

"Then eat it, Tommy—Eat it!" he commanded. "And you better not throw it up again, cramming it in like that. We don't waste food in this house." His face vanished back behind the wall of newsprint.

At the time, I couldn't have guessed how much I would grow to despise that phrase later in life. "Eat it"—as if it were some magical, simple solution to my problems.

Snapping back to the present, I glance anxiously at the clock, quickly forcing down chunks of buttery toast and fluffy eggs. It's not just a race against time but also against my body's stubborn limits, urging me to stop as soon as it senses fullness. Just like that child in front of my father, here I am again, gulping down food frantically like a pelican determined to prove a point.

About halfway through my plate, an uncomfortable pressure builds rapidly in my stomach, climbing urgently toward my throat. Still, it doesn't deter me—not even when nausea threatens to force its way up. Pausing only briefly, I take a deep breath, forcing the food to settle again, then resume my frenzied attack, cutting massive bites of egg and toast before shoving them into my mouth.

I've read countless times online that if I consume enough calories, eventually weight gain would follow—the "eat it" mantra repeated again. It's the only affordable solution, compared to the pricey supplements others recommend. But clearly, that logic doesn't hold true for everyone. In a single day, I can devour five thousand calories or more—twice what that online calculator suggests. Yet here I stand, stuck in this thin, unchanged body. Why hasn't anything changed?

Someone once told me I just have a fast metabolism and should consider myself lucky for being able to eat whatever I want without consequence. They simply don't understand that I'd gladly give my left nut—hell, maybe both—just to have a bit more muscle, a little more substance to me. At this point, even some extra fat would be welcome if it meant hiding the bones protruding from this pathetic excuse of a body.

Before heading out, I pour Tilly's favorite meal into her bowl—cat food. I then crank the volume on my television up just past halfway—not loud enough to disturb my neighbors, of course, but sufficient to create the illusion someone might be home. With several recent break-ins reported on Milwaukee's north side—including some here in my building—I can only hope the sound serves as a deterrent, considering we have no alarm system or security to speak of.

"Stay away from the toilet paper, little lady; I don't want to find it shredded all over the living room again, okay?" I say affectionately, scratching the top of Tilly's tiny white head. Snatching my keys off the table, I hurry out the door.

Stepping through the rear exit of the apartment complex toward the parking lot, I catch a group of teenagers off guard, startling them enough that they frantically wave away clouds of pungent smoke. One boy leans casually against the back of my sky-blue pickup, while a girl and her boyfriend cling to each other nearby. Immediately, the thick, unmistakable scent of marijuana floods my nostrils.

"Do you mind? That's my truck!" I demand.

The boy leaning against it meets my gaze, pausing just long enough to send a defiant message. Without breaking eye contact, he casually extinguishes his joint on my polished chrome bumper. The trio moves slowly aside as I approach. Part of me would love nothing more than to confront him physically for the blatant disrespect, especially as he sizes me up. But he's clearly underage, and I know better—any confrontation would likely send me straight to jail. Besides, with my luck, he'd probably end up kicking my frail white ass anyway.

Despite these occasional irritations, my neighborhood isn't entirely awful. Forty-fourth and Hampton Avenue sits at an odd intersection between urban struggle and suburban quiet—almost a "ghetto suburb" of sorts. Just half a mile south lie the housing projects, and about the same distance north is one of Milwaukee's worst public schools. Unfortunately, many of the teens from those projects pass right by my complex daily, bringing along occasional fights, shouting, dancing, or idle loitering on the sidewalks and parking lot.

Heading eastward on Hampton Avenue for only a few blocks reveals progressively harsher realities. The lower the street numbers fall, the deeper you enter into more dangerous territory, with sidewalks gradually filling with small groups of suspicious-looking African Americans lin-

gering outside corner stores, seemingly searching for trouble or opportunity—perhaps both. I'm not racist, but I've lived here long enough to
know exactly who to avoid, particularly once the sun sets.

I pose no threat to anyone around here. I'm what people of color
would probably label your typical white dude—plain, unassuming, and
entirely forgettable. Fashion has never been my forte; designer labels,
expensive Jordans, or the latest trends hold no appeal for me. Most of
my wardrobe is sourced straight from Walmart or TJ Maxx clearance
racks. Sure, a few items carry a known brand name, but they're typically
outdated styles or have minor flaws, the very reason they're priced to fit
my modest budget.

Luckily, my company's dress code is strictly business casual—a re-
quirement many employees complain about, but one that's become second nature to me. Despite my lack of passion for the latest fashions, I
take pride in what little I do own. My slacks are pressed sharply, shirt
collars neatly starched, and shoes polished to a respectable shine. Gram
often remarks that I inherited my meticulous habits from my dad, who
always took exceptional care in his appearance.

Adjusting my rearview mirror to keep watch on the teenage potheads
still lingering behind me, I twist the key in the ignition. My engine roars
to life, shaking the pavement beneath it as it warms up. A satisfying puff
of dark gray exhaust suddenly erupts from the tailpipe, enveloping the
unsuspecting teens in a smoky cloud. Normally, I'd give the old V8 a few
moments to fully awaken, but with the irritated, coughing adolescents
now advancing toward my window after their taste of revenge smoke, I
had no such luxury. Not even time to clear the frost clinging stubbornly
to my windshield.

Quickly using the sleeve of my coat, I hastily wipe a small, blurry
patch clear enough to see, and then peel out of the parking lot. Just then,

something strikes the back end of my truck with a loud clank. Glancing anxiously into the rearview mirror, I catch a glimpse of the boy who'd leaned on my bumper, now standing defiantly in the street with his middle finger raised high. A fist-sized rock tumbles across the pavement behind me. I don't bother stopping to inspect any damage—this truck has weathered far worse in its long lifetime.

This sky-blue 1971 Ford F100 pickup truck belonged first to my grandfather before he passed. Gram gifted it to me afterward. Despite its age, the body remains sturdy, with little rust and just a few dents to prove its toughness. It's a resilient old beast, running smoother than most newer vehicles could hope for. I treat her well, keeping her polished and clean as best as I possibly can.

A sudden buzzing vibration jolts my attention as my cell phone rattles loudly inside the cheap plastic dollar-store cup holder hanging near my window. There's only one person who'd call at this hour—in fact, she's practically the only person who ever calls me at all.

"Hi Gram—how are you?" I say cheerfully, genuinely happy to hear her voice.

Glades Thorpe, my eighty-one-year-old grandmother, is the last person left in my life whom I truly love. Sweet, short, generous, and caring, she's everything you'd imagine an old-fashioned grandmother to be. Her shoulder-length, curly white hair frames a face accentuated by thick, burgundy Peabody-style glasses. Ever since Grandpa passed away a few years ago, she's grown more dependent on me, frequently inventing chores around her house just to draw me out to visit. Honestly, she needs me as much as I need her, especially living all alone out there in Oak Creek, Wisconsin, with her nearest neighbor almost half a mile down the road.

"Hi, Suga, I'm okay. But this doggone medication the doctor gave me for my hip ain't doing a lick of good," she says, her voice sweet yet trembling slightly with age and years of smoking. "You still planning on coming by to clean out that old shed? I gotta get rid of some of that junk your packrat Grandpa left behind."

"Yes ma'am," I reply warmly. "I can swing by before the end of the week. What about the wood chipper? Did you sell it yet—or do you still need me to move it?"

"Uh huh, could you, please? I wanted to put it on that internet thing, but you know I can't work that doggone computer to save my life. Hope it's not too much trouble for you, darling."

"Not at all, Gram, come on. You know whatever you need, I'm there. You know you're my sweetheart, right? Heck, I'll even post an ad online for you if you want."

She laughs softly, then pauses. I hear a faint struggle in the background, a scraping noise giving away whatever she's attempting to manage. A moment later, she inhales deeply, releasing a long, soothing exhale.

"I got some chicken, corn, and smashed potatoes here, sweetie," she says, chuckling. "You remember how you used to call 'em that when you were just a boy?"

"Yes ma'am."

"Oh, it was just the cutest thing. You should come by and get something to eat. I gotta feed you, you know? Always told your Momma, Lord rest her soul, she didn't feed you enough. That's why you're still so flipping skinny. And—"

"Gram, are you smoking?" I interrupt suddenly.

She hesitates briefly. I can almost hear the gears turning in her head as she searches for an excuse to give me.

"Well, you know Grandma, baby—I won't lie to you. Ain't got much else to look forward to since your Grandpa passed. Smoking helps me cope with things, okay? And what did I tell you about interrupting folks when they're speaking? It's just the rudest thing. Stop it, hear?"

"Yes ma'am. But come on, Gram, you don't need to smoke. You're gonna kill yourself with those things. And I still need you here with me."

"Baby, if the Lord hasn't called me home after eighty-one years, I ain't too worried about it. Grandma's had herself a long life. Smoking is the one small joy I've got left, so don't you take that from me."

"So, you're saying puffing on a cigarette gives you more joy than seeing me?" I tease, half-jokingly.

"If you don't quit nagging me about my cigarettes, then yes!" she retorts, laughing heartily.

CHaPTer 2

FIRST CALL

(7:59 AM)

I pull into the lot, the dull gray morning casting a faint pallor over the dark brown brick and black-glass facade of the call center. The building looms modestly, two stories tall, brooding and silent. As I glide past the Director's 2012 Acura TL, I give the throttle a sharp nudge, letting the deep growl of my 5.0-liter V8 rip through the stillness. The roar echoes off the walls, a tremor that rattles his tinted windows and, with satisfying precision, triggers his alarm.

In my mirror, I catch the dance of blinking amber lights, the rhythmic honking, and the shrill whine of protest from the Acura, all partially shrouded by the light-gray smoke curling from my exhaust. The mist clings low, a ghostly veil over the pavement and the surrounding cars.

Petty? Perhaps. But I've always believed in starting the day with a grin. And today, mine stretches wide, falsely innocent but wicked underneath. It's a small pleasure, but a pleasure nonetheless.

Inside, the call center hums with a quiet, early-hour energy. The reps are already busy, rifling through reports, seeking out the names of those who paid, and those who still owed. The low murmur of keyboards and printers is the only music in the air.

To my left, Freddie is at her usual station—the coffee pot—her tall, lanky frame leaning lazily as she waits for it to brew. At fifty-two, her curly brown hair is always a bit wild, her personality more so. Colleen, petite, in her thirties, listens politely, though I can tell by the tight smile that she's bracing herself. Freddie is recounting, as usual, the latest in her series of scandalous escapades—thus her nickname, "Freddie Cougar."

"So, we ended up back at my place for the evening," she purrs. "I wasn't ready to call it a night, so I offered him a drink. With arms that firm, I had to know what he was hiding under that red V-neck clinging to his biceps. He didn't hesitate—his eyes glued to my cleavage like a thirsty..."

Colleen catches my glance as I walk by, her eyes rolling skyward in a silent plea for deliverance. I offer a quick, knowing smirk, one conspirator to another, then carry on toward my desk.

Passing Mr. Gibbons' office, I spot him by the window, his figure stiff, staring down at the lot. His hand fumbles with the key fob, jabbing the button again and again, lips moving in what I can only imagine are muttered curses.

Amused, I linger for a moment behind the low wall of my cubicle, watching him through the glass. The signal never quite reaches from his office, which means he'll have to march out there to deal with it himself.

"Good morning, Mr. Gibbons!" I chirp, sweet as honey.

He doesn't answer, just storms past, trailing a faint breeze in his wake. I close my eyes, drawing in a breath of victory, small but satisfying.

But the moment is short-lived. A sharp, cheap perfume pierces the air, hijacking my senses before I can fully savor the triumph.

"Mr. Thorpe, log in and come see me before your first call, please," Kathy May says, her silver pen clicking rhythmically against the edge of my cubicle. The metallic tap-tap echoes in my ears like the ticking of a clock counting down to something unpleasant. Her face, weathered and deeply tanned, tightens with whatever storm brews behind her dark eyes. Long, bleached strands of hair cascade past her shoulders, curling inward like brittle fingers, framing her freckled chest, which strains against the low cut of her blouse.

"And bring your morning report," she adds curtly, turning with a practiced sway. Her blue skirt clings to her wide hips, which rock side to side with every deliberate step, heels clicking a sharp rhythm as she retreats.

Damnit! Here we go again. I haven't even had a chance to set my stuff down and she's already breathing down my neck.

I don't usually wish ill on anyone, but this woman tests every limit I have. Kathy May, the undisputed queen of micromanagement, grates on my nerves like sandpaper on raw skin. If she ever landed herself in the hospital, I swear I'd throw a party. A break from her constant barking of rules and policies would feel like a vacation in paradise. She sucks the life out of this place, draining morale with every clipped command, leaving no room for anyone to just breathe.

I let my backpack fall to the floor beside my chair with a dull thud, just as Kimmie's face slowly rises over the cubicle wall. Her wide, black-framed glasses magnify the concern in her eyes, soft with sympathy, like she's watching someone walk the last mile.

"Good luck, Tommy," she whispers.

"I don't need luck, Kimmie. I need a new damn job."

"That, we all do, buddy," she says, disappearing back into her seat like a groundhog retreating to its burrow.

Kimmie's a rare light in this dim place. Most of the women here seem to carry a chip on their shoulders, always ready to snap or complain about something—or everything. But not her. Kimmie's got a vibe, a kind of energy that fills the room, no matter what kind of day she's having. She's unshakable, always laughing, always finding the silver lining. She's got a flair too—her love for leopard print is legendary. You'll never catch her without it. Whether it's her blouse, her purse, or even her earrings, there's always a bit of the wild on her.

"If you ever see me without my leopard, lunch is on me," she once told me, grinning. "But don't hold your breath, baby."

I smile just thinking about it.

I'll never forget the time I almost killed her—well, not really, but close. She was standing in her cubicle, headset on, chatting away with a customer, her back turned. I'd dropped my report and bent to grab it, nudging her chair out of place without thinking. When I stood, I left it there—forgotten.

She turned, still mid-sentence, and went to sit. For a split second, it was like time froze. Her body paused, suspended in disbelief, eyes wide as saucers, realizing too late that nothing was there. She reached out, grasping at the air, at the cubicle wall, at anything. Papers tore, her calendar fell, and then—bam. The floor shook like a minor quake.

Even the reps across the room felt it.

They came running—drawn by the sudden commotion—her cries of shock tangled with bursts of laughter. A small crowd formed around Kimmie, kneeling to help her up, their voices a mix of concern and disbelief. And me? I just stood there like an idiot, clutching my report, my mouth slightly ajar, frozen between the instinct to help, the urge to laugh, or the fear of catching a well-deserved ass whooping.

I stammered out apologies, one after another, tripping over my own guilt. But Kimmie, true to form, just laughed—then and now.

"It's all good, Tommy, no worries," she'd say, waving it off like it was nothing. "With all this cushion I got back here, you'd think I'd bounce right back up. But no, my butt bone is killing me. You can get a sista some pain meds, though." And we'd both crack up, every time.

"Close the door, please," Kathy's voice cuts through, sharp as ever. "Take a seat."

I shut the door behind me and settle into the hot seat across from her desk, feeling that familiar weight in the room. The air always seemed heavier in here, like it carried all the reprimands and lectures of those who sat before me.

She doesn't look up. Her focus is on the papers spread before her, fingers tapping lightly as if keeping time to some internal rhythm. "I'm sure you know this by now, Mr. Thorpe, but your stats have dropped considerably."

Here we go.

"I know you're aware of the minimum requirements," she continues, tone flat, as though reading from a script. "You've got six new accounts at the top of your report barely making payments—or none at all. Two are on the edge of default. We're probably going to have to repossess those vehicles. You used to be my top guy. What's going on?" Her hand slips into the briefcase beside her, rifling through its contents.

I lean forward slightly, trying to steady the frustration building in my chest. "I need time to work these new customers. We just shuffled accounts this month, remember? Derrick got all my good payers, and I got stuck with his worst. Maybe if we—"

"No, no." She cuts me off with a quick wave. "Don't start blaming this on the company shuffle, Mr. Thorpe. We do this every year. Are you following company procedures when customers miss their Friday payments?" She pulls out a familiar sheet, the dreaded procedures, and slides it across the desk like a judge handing down a sentence. "Are you skip tracing? Calling their references?"

The paper feels like a slap in the face. Three years in this place, always near the top, and now I'm being treated like I just walked through the door. My hands twitch. I want to crumple it, throw it back, but I don't.

Instead, I glare at it, then meet her eyes. "You don't think it's strange that your top account manager suddenly tanks after a year?" My voice rises. "I had these customers from the start. I treated them like people, not just debts. I built trust, and they paid. Derrick? He talks down to them, harasses their references after a day late—anyone would be pissed. They're not paying because they want to spite him, not because I'm slacking."

I flip the paper she handed me face down, letting it lie there like an insult. "It's gonna take time to clean up his mess."

She's silent for a moment, elbows on the desk, fingers steepled under her chin, eyes narrowing in thought. Then, slowly, she reaches out, turns the paper face-up again, and taps the middle with one perfectly manicured nail.

"Follow these procedures," she says, voice cool but edged with steel. "Get them paying, or I'll take the next step. No more excuses, Mr. Thorpe."

"So, you don't think it's funny that the son-of-a... director of our fair company ends up with *my* customers and suddenly climbs to the top? One shuffle, and now he's the golden boy?" I snap, the frustration bubbling over. "Think about it. Mr. Gibbons favors him."

Mr. Brice Gibbons—the man behind the curtain. Director of this circus and, surprise, Derrick's loving stepfather. The same Derrick who seems to magically inherit my best accounts like clockwork at the start of each new month. Gibbons is the architect of it all. Tall, arrogant, and polished like a statue, he's an older black man with neatly trimmed salt-and-pepper hair and a goatee that he probably grooms more than he does his conscience. His shirts, always crisp Oxfords, look like they've never known a wrinkle, and his shoes—shined to perfection—seem to coordinate effortlessly with the belts that snugly hug his waist. He moves through the office with a lofty air, eyes half-lidded, as if we were all beneath the effort it takes to acknowledge our existence.

But of course, my little outburst lands flat. Kathy doesn't even flinch. It's like I'm invisible, my words vanishing into the stale air between us. She swivels away from me, back turned, already fixated on her computer screen as if I no longer exist.

I rise from the chair, the heat of anger still pulsing through me. I should walk away. But instead, I feel that familiar itch, that irresistible urge. My hand curls into a fist, and with a slow, deliberate motion, I raise my middle finger, just high enough.

"Don't push it, Mr. Thorpe!" she snaps.

I drop my hand like it's been burned, heart skipping. That's when I see it—a small mirror, tucked neatly to the left of her monitor. A paranoia trinket. She'd been watching me the whole time, eyes flicking from screen to reflection with the ease of a seasoned predator.

"Close my door on your way out," she says, a smirk tugging at her lips.

Flushed with a mix of embarrassment and irritation, I comply, easing the door shut behind me. The office air feels different as I step back into it, thick with curiosity. Eyes follow me as I walk, silent judgments and amused smirks. I ignore them, pushing through until I reach the small sanctuary of my cubicle.

Kimmie's head rises again over the wall, headset on, her fingers poised to dial. "Hey Tommy, do me a favor and turn around."

I narrow my eyes. "Why?"

"Just turn around. I wanna see something."

Confused, I oblige, giving her a half turn before glancing back. She's got one finger pressed thoughtfully to her chin, eyes focused on my backside.

"Damn. I can't tell," she mutters.

"Tell what? What are you looking at?"

"Well, you never had much of an ass to begin with, so I can't tell if she chewed any off," she laughs, her grin wide and wicked.

I shoot her a glare and give her the full extension of my middle finger, then sink into my chair, exhaling hard.

"So," she asks, chuckling as she adjusts her headset, "what was that all about?"

"My stats," I mutter, tossing the report onto my desk. "Apparently, they've tanked, and if I don't fix it, she's ready to take 'the next step.'"

"Seriously?" she frowns. "They just switched the accounts around. They expect you to work miracles in, what, a week?"

"That's exactly what I'm saying." I shake my head. "I told Kathy straight—Derrick got all my good accounts. I've been busting my ass to build them up, and now he's just handed the reward."

"What did she say?" Kimmie asks, her voice dipped in curiosity but laced with expectation.

"What do you think she said?" I exhale, rubbing a hand over my face. "The usual company bullshit—follow the procedures, hit the numbers, no excuses. After everything I've done with those accounts, you'd think I'd have earned at least a sliver of credit by now."

"I feel your pain, Tommy," she sighs, leaning against the cubicle wall. "Mine are just average payers, lucky for me. Low balances keep me under the radar. No one's breathing down my neck."

Her gaze shifts, sharp now, darting over toward Derrick's empty cubicle. "And where is this fool?"

"Your guess is as good as mine."

I'm about to respond further when the sound of the front desk clerk floats across the office, a cheerful greeting echoing toward the entrance. Kimmie straightens, squinting toward the front, and curls her lip in disgust.

"Well, speak of the devil," she mutters. "Here he comes, late again, like clockwork."

Derrick's entrance is almost theatrical at this point—a tired performance we've both seen too many times. He stumbles in, breathless, his face drawn into that same manufactured look of frustration, as if the universe conspires daily to make him late. He's perfected the art of appearing the victim of circumstance—power outages, traffic jams, flat tires, you name it.

Once, his antics were almost amusing, his excuses elaborate enough to spark a laugh. Now? They're just tiring. It's not funny anymore, not when it's the nineteenth time this month and no one dares call him on it. Anyone else would've been written up, or worse, shown the door. But Derrick? He's untouchable. Step-Daddy Gibbons sees to that.

Derrick Stevens is an okay guy at heart, but he's a walking disaster when it comes to self-care. His clothes hang off him like hand-me-downs from a giant, pants too long and frayed at the hem, streaked with grime from constant dragging. His shirts are oversized, usually stained or riddled with tiny holes, like he'd lost a fight with a moth colony. He lingers in the air with stale coffee breath and that distinct, sour underarm stench that hits you like a wall if you're unfortunate enough to get too close.

A self-proclaimed gamer, Derrick brags about owning every console known to man, sinking most of his paycheck into virtual worlds while neglecting the real one. We're the same height—six foot two—but that's about all we share. His unkempt, clumpy hair and sagging clothes give him the look of someone who might've wandered in off the street.

I rise from my chair, feigning a stretch just as he lumbers toward his cubicle.

"Sup y'all!" he calls out, out of breath, his voice deep and gravelly, like a knock-off Shaquille O'Neal. He tosses a plastic bag of snacks and a foil-wrapped breakfast burrito onto his desk with a thud, then sinks into his chair like gravity's playing favorites.

"Y'all won't believe what happened," he starts, already laughing. "Power was out this morning, so my alarm didn't go off. I think a transformer blew—whole block was dark. Then, of course, traffic was hell since none of the lights were working. That's how my morning starts."

Kimmie and I exchange a glance, her eyes saying what we're both thinking—here we go again.

"I see you had time to stop and get yourself some snacks," Kimmie cuts in, her voice sharp, slicing through the air like a blade. "I thought you said you used your phone to wake up."

"No, I didn't," Derrick mutters, eyes darting.

"Yes, you did," she snaps, her tone coiled tight. "You were just bragging about your new phone, remember? How the battery lasts forever? You even said you could finally wake up on time now." She leans, peering over the top of his cubicle wall like a cat stalking prey. "And what's that? Ninety-six percent battery left? So, how did you charge it, Derrick? We ain't stupid. Why you always lying?"

Derrick doesn't answer. He can't. His mouth opens slightly, but no words follow, only a hollow silence. I stretch my arms high above me, my joints cracking softly, and he glances up, eyes wide and desperate, as if drowning in the pool of his own lies, silently pleading for a lifeline.

"You always come in here every other day with a different story about how you—" Kimmie begins, but she cuts herself off, exhaling sharply as her eyes roll. Her headset chirps.

"Thank you for calling E.A.A.C., this is Kimmie, how may I help you?" she says, her voice suddenly sugar-sweet, vanishing below her cubicle wall.

I can't help but grin, glancing down at Derrick, who exhales as if a great weight's been lifted. The sharp interrogation paused, for now, saved by the rare grace of an incoming call.

"Sup, Derrick? How was the weekend?" I ask, already knowing the answer. More than likely, he'd been holed up in his dim gaming room, locked away from the world, diving deep into the two latest games that hit the shelves Friday night.

"Good—real good! And yours?" he replies, not really waiting for my answer, his fingers already hammering away at the keys. Then, suddenly, his arms shoot up, fists clenched in triumph.

"YES!"

"What's up?" I ask, wary. His excitement usually spells trouble for someone else—usually me.

"I made bonus—yes! That's gonna be an extra five hundred on the check coming up, bro!"

The words hit me like a blow to the back, a silent sucker punch that steals the air from my lungs. Bonus? Derrick *never* hits bonus. His accounts rarely come close. But now—now that he's got *my* accounts? That five hundred should've been mine. Mine for the late nights, the careful follow-ups, the respect I built with those customers. My jaw clenches, teeth grinding as an image flashes unbidden through my mind—me, lifting a desk chair high above his head, slamming it down, watching him crumple over his keyboard, dead weight, finally silent.

How dare he sit there, grinning, celebrating money he didn't earn?

A loud sneeze from another rep snaps me back, the violent sound like a gunshot in the quiet. Derrick, oblivious, stretches his hand over the cubicle wall for a high-five, expecting me to share in his victory.

I turn away, clutching the phone to my ear, pretending.

"Hello, Ms. Collins? Yes, ma'am, I was calling about your payment from last week for your car?"

It's the only escape I have—to fake a call, drown him out, and keep myself from losing control. From becoming that moment I'd just imagined.

CHAPTER 3

HIDDEN DESIRES

(11:30 AM)

"Can I speak to Darnell Stokes, please?" I ask, leaning back in my chair, eyes on the flickering screen, already bracing myself.

"This Darnell," comes the gruff reply, voice heavy with impatience.

"Hey, Mr. Stokes, this is—"

"Sup, Derrick!?" he cuts in, suddenly upbeat.

"No sir, this is Tommy from E.A.A.C. I'm calling about your car payment that was due on—"

"Where's Derrick at?" he snaps. "I don't like talkin' to nobody else about my account but him."

I sigh quietly, pinching the bridge of my nose. Here we go.

"I understand, Mr. Stokes, but I've been assigned to your account to help you get caught up. It looks like you've got a payment that was—"

"You should probably read your notes or talk to him, 'cause he knows how I am and what's goin' on. He knows my situation."

"Mr. Stokes, if you could give me just a moment to explain—" I push forward, trying to steady my voice. "I just want to help you get caught up, to avoid any further action."

"And how you gonna do that?" His voice rises, thick with sarcasm. "You gonna give me a month free, or throw a payment on the back end of my contract?"

"If your payments were on time, Mr. Stokes, I'd have more flexibility. But right now, you're almost eighty days behind. I'm sure the last thing you want is for us to have to retrieve the vehicle. I'm calling to help—"

"I always pay my note, late or not," he growls. "Y'all still gettin' your money. Times are hard, and Derrick gives me more time. He knows. I know y'all don't come for the car until I'm about three months behind, right? You just said I'm eighty days out. Last time I checked, three months is ninety days, bruh. So don't call me again 'til then."

My jaw tightens. I grip the base of the phone harder, knuckles white.

"So then, when *will* you be submitting your next payment, Mr. Stokes?" I ask, the frustration creeping into my voice despite myself. Derrick's been too generous, too open—now this guy knows our every move.

"When I can. I *said*. You death?"

"You mean *deaf*, Mr. Stokes?" I let out a dry snicker. "No, sir, I'm not. I heard you perfectly clear."

"So then why are we still talkin'?"

I sit there for a beat, staring at the screen, the silence between us thick as mud. Normally, threatening repossession gets me something—an excuse, a promise, *something*. But not him. Not today. Derrick's fingerprints are all over this mess.

Without another word, I hit the disconnect button, skipping the usual polite farewell. Policy be damned.

My frustration is a dull roar in my ears now, a pressure building behind my eyes. I can feel the heat crawling up my neck, fists clenched tight in my lap. It would feel so good—*too* good—to grab this flat-screen monitor and smash it against the desk, to take the edge off, to *feel* something break that isn't me.

Or better yet, swing it right into Derrick's smug face.

I log off my phone, the screen blinking back to its idle state, and push back from my desk. I need to cool off, fast. I head for the bathroom, each step heavier than the last, trying to lock the storm inside before it tears me apart.

"Mr. Thorpe! Come in here, please." Kathy's voice blasts from her office, slicing through the air just as I'm rising from my chair.

The sudden bark halts everything. Heads pop up over cubicle walls like prairie dogs, eyes peeking, curious and cautious. I pause, heart sinking, then pivot on my heel, heading reluctantly toward her lair.

"Close the door, please."

"Déjà vu," I murmur under my breath as the door clicks shut behind me, sealing me in with her.

"What the hell happened on that last call?"

The question stops me mid-motion, just as I'm about to sit. I hover for a second, stunned. Out of all the calls she could've monitored, of *course* it had to be *that* one. I've never caught heat for hanging up on a customer before, but with my luck today, I should've seen it coming. After our lovely chat this morning, I should've known she'd be gunning for me. The week's barely begun, and already my stats are in the dirt, and now she's got ammunition—a call that proves, in her mind, I'm not toeing the line.

All I can do is brace for impact, sit down, and take whatever storm she's about to unleash.

"This is *exactly* what I'm talking about, Mr. Thorpe. How in the *hell* do you expect to collect money if you're slamming the phone down on customers? We have *strict* policies about this—hanging up out of anger? That's strike *two* for you, Mister. If I—"

Her voice drones on, sharp and grating. But I'm not hearing it anymore. My mind drifts, dark and dangerous. I picture my hands, firm on the edge of her desk, and in one violent shove—with the strength of something primal—I drive it forward, crushing her against the wall behind her. I see her face, contorted in terror, eyes wide as ribs crack under the force. Blood spills down her chest, splattering those damned company procedures she worships. Her lips tremble, confusion mixing with pain.

"Thorpe!" she snaps, yanking me out of the fantasy like cold water to the face. "Are you okay? You're not on drugs or anything, are you?"

"What—no!" I shoot back, shaken.

"Did you even *hear* what I just said?"

"Yeah, I'm listening. Sorry."

She exhales sharply, eyes narrowing. "Let's get ourselves together here, okay? I don't want to hear anything like that on your calls again. Get your head out of your ass, and make some money."

———

(11:50 PM)

"Where you going for lunch, Tommy?" Kimmie's voice floats over the cubicle wall, a welcome break from the chaos.

"Just gonna stay here, hang in the break room. Think about some stuff. You?"

"My girl should be outside waiting on me. We're heading to UNO's pizza. Love that place."

"Have fun," I say, patting down my wallet and pockets, searching for enough dollar bills or loose change to feed the vending machine.

"You can come if you'd like," she offers, peeking over the wall with a sly smile. "I'm sure my friend won't mind. And she's cute."

"No, go have fun. I don't want to intrude. Besides, I don't really have the cash for that."

"Okay, friend. I'll see you in thirty."

Finally—lunch. After getting my ass chewed off by the Policy Princess, I need a moment. A moment to breathe, to collect whatever's left of my sanity. I log off my phone and head straight for the break room, leaving the wreckage of the morning behind me.

Inside the break room, the fluorescent lights hum softly above, casting a pale glow over the worn tables and scuffed linoleum floor. Two familiar voices fill the space—Claudia and Tim—locked in mid-conversation, their tones heavy with frustration. As I slip a few wrinkled bills into the vending machine and hear the satisfying clink of loose change dropping into the slot, I can't help but listen in.

Claudia's voice rises, thick with her strong Puerto Rican accent, her words sharp and edged with exhaustion. She sits with her back to me, fists clenched tight on the table, pounding it gently after every few words like a drumbeat of her anger.

"I *swear*, I should've listened to my sister and gone to da school for da nursing," she fumes. "Dis job works my nerves so much, Tim—I can't *stand* da stress. And these fuckers? So *rude*—dey don't wanna pay. Hell, we approve de applications for people on fixed incomes or welfare, and then press them with dis high-interest rate on a car that's way overpriced."

Her voice trembles as she continues, her frustration boiling over.

"And some of these customers, I *swear*," she pauses, her breath catching. "If I wasn't in my right mind, I'd *pay* them a visit and kick *der* asses. All de information's right dere on da screen for me to use, you know?" She exhales sharply. "Mr. Simpson called me an F'n bitch today. *Lord forgive me.* Why would you say dat, huh? I've done *nothing* to him."

I pass quietly behind Tim, nodding as I head toward the microwave with my arms full of cheap, desperate comfort—four hot pockets, the lunch of champions. I load them in, the hum of the machine filling the momentary lull.

"Hey, Tommy!" Tim calls out, breaking the tension, and Claudia spins halfway, her hand flying to her mouth in surprise when she realizes I've heard everything.

I shrug, indifferent. I'm no snitch, and truth be told, she's not wrong.

"What's up, Tim? How's your day?" I ask, setting the timer on the microwave, the first of my hot pockets beginning to spin lazily.

"Just having some rough calls, as you've probably heard," he says, glancing sideways at Claudia, his brows raised in a silent *damn.*

"Yeah, you and me both," I sigh. "Kathy's been riding me since I walked in this morning—tearing me apart over my stats. She just doesn't get it. We've had that stupid shuffle, and now I'm stuck trying to clean up after the mess Derrick made."

"You guys had an account shuffle?" Claudia asks, blinking in surprise.

"Yeah—hasn't everyone?" I pull the first steaming hot pocket from the microwave and toss it onto the table beside them.

"Not us," Tim says, shaking his head. "It's up to the managers now. It's not even required anymore."

Claudia nods, chewing thoughtfully on her sandwich, her eyes narrowing.

"Please tell me you're kidding." I glare, the heat rising in my chest again. "So I'm breaking my back for these deadbeats because someone's *daddy* decided to shuffle the deck anyway? And it's not even *required*?"

"Perks of being the son of the Director, I guess," Tim mutters.

"That makes me sick," I growl. "Now I've gotta straighten out a bunch of smart-asses and freeloaders. If I could just reach through the phone and strangle the crap out of one of them, just one..." I raise my hands and mime choking the air, fingers tightening in a slow squeeze.

They laugh, but I don't.

Instead, I sink into the chair, tearing into the coolest of the four hot pockets. It scorches my tongue, but I chew through the pain, letting the burn ground me, silent and seething.

(1:51 PM)

The clock on my screen blinks lazily, each minute dragging heavier than the last. I haven't touched the phone in over ten minutes—not a ring, not a dial tone, just the hum of fluorescent lights and the occasional low murmur of voices. Mr. Gibbons had sent out one of his infamous emails—mandatory office meeting at 2:00 PM sharp. The announcement had been met with collective groans, though unspoken. Meetings around here are little more than rituals of repetition—recycled policies, unresolved complaints, and the illusion of progress. Still, I'll take any excuse to step away from this desk. Even a mind-numbing meeting is better than being tethered to these cursed headsets.

From the other side of the cubicle wall, Kimmie's voice breaks the monotony.

"Oh my goodness—this fool," she huffs. "Tommy, can I ask you something?"

"What's up?"

"I just don't understand it. My boyfriend is trippin' lately, and I can't figure out why." She holds her phone up over the divider, the screen lit with a string of texts. "Here—scroll up a bit. Just read that convo."

I glance at the time. "We only got a few minutes before the meeting. Just hit me with the short version."

"Okay, look. I haven't given Jamal any reason not to trust me, right? But lately, he's been all over me about where I go, what I do. Just now, he texts me sayin' he doesn't believe I'm at work—and wants me to call him from the office phone."

"So call him and shut him up."

"That's not the point! He *shouldn't* be asking me to do that in the first place. He's supposed to trust me."

"How about we talk about it after the meeting? I gotta log off before—"

Chime.

The phone lights up with an incoming call, and my heart sinks. My first instinct? Kill the line—disconnect before it even starts. My finger hovers over the red button, ready to "accidentally" end the call. But just as I'm about to pull the trigger, I catch a glimpse of movement from the corner of my eye—Kathy May, creeping up like a vulture with perfect timing.

I pretend not to notice her, slowly shifting my hand away from the release button, sliding it toward the volume.

"I transferred that call to you," she whispers, her breath cold against my ear. "It's Ms. Baker—wants an extension again. You know what to do. I'll brief you after the meeting if there's anything worth mentioning."

I hit mute.

"You knew we had this meeting," I say, trying to keep my voice low. "Can't I just tell her we'll call back? Or better yet, *you* take the call and explain?"

Through the headset, Ms. Baker's voice cuts through, sharp and rising. "Hello? HELLO?"

"No," Kathy says flatly, already turning away. "You get that payment, Thorpe. Follow the procedure—just like we talked about."

Her heels click softly as she disappears down the aisle.

Kimmie taps her long, purple nails against the metal frame of my cubicle, catching my attention. "Sorry, Tommy," she says with a wince, before joining the rest of the reps, weaving through the narrow paths between desks, all funneling toward the conference room like cattle being herded.

There's no doubt in my mind—Kathy did this on purpose. One last jab before the meeting. As she settles into the conference room, she turns her head, eyes locking onto mine through the glass window. A small, smug smile tugs at her lips. She points at me, mouthing the words, *"Get the money, Thorpe,"* and then jabs her finger downward, commanding me to *sit.*

And I do. Clenched fists. Tight jaw. I sink back into the chair, seething, the headset pressing in like a shackle.

By now, Ms. Baker was in full swing, firing off a barrage of four-letter words into my ear like bullets, each one more abrasive than the last.

Her voice, shrill and relentless, echoed through my headset while a high-pitched yapping gnawed at the edges of her rant. That damn dog.

"*Shut up, Chilly—damnit!*" she shrieked, the sound of claws scrambling on hardwood in the background adding a frantic rhythm to the chaos.

I took a deep breath, steadying myself, lowering my voice to a flat monotone as I finally cut in. "Hello, Ms. Baker. How are you doing?"

The shift in her tone was almost surreal—like the eye of a storm suddenly rolling through.

"I'm not doin' good, honey," she cooed, her voice softer now, almost sweet, a jarring contrast to the woman who'd been cursing both me and her dog moments ago. "First off, my damn dog won't stop barkin', and second, y'all won't stop callin' me," she chuckled, though it sounded more like a cough twisted into a laugh, rough and dry. "I can't get no peace and quiet, so yeah, I'm a little upset right now. Your people call me *all* the time, but then when I finally get someone on the phone, you got me on hold for *forever and a day*. Simple solution to that, baby—call me when you're actually ready to talk, ya know?"

Her voice carried that kind of weary, well-worn Southern charm, laced with a bite she tried to soften.

"Well, we certainly hate to keep calling you like that, Ms. Baker," I replied, pressing my fingers to my temple. "What are we going to do about your payment so that we can get your account caught up and prevent any further calls? Would you like to set this up for automatic payment from your checking account? That way, it's all taken care of—no more calls—and you have proof right there on your bank statement."

"*Lord no!*" she snapped, voice rising again. "I don't need y'all in my banking like that. Takin' money that don't belong to you and all." She coughed, clearing her throat with a loud rasp. "Besides, with all the scamming goin' on nowadays, I'm a bit leery of doin' anything like that. You know, givin' you my personal info over the phone like this. I *remember when...*"

And then she was off.

Her voice became a steady stream, a flowing river of old stories and past betrayals—bad experiences with other companies, horror tales of stolen money, and mistrust. She veered off course like a driver lost on a familiar road, talking now about things that had nothing to do with her payment, as though I'd become more than just a rep on the line. Like I was someone who *cared*.

I let her go, nodding silently as the minutes ticked by, letting her fill the space. Five minutes passed, and still she rambled, her words circling around themselves. No end in sight.

"...since my last doctor's visit, so I don't know. My rheumatoid arthritis is actin' up, and the medication just don't seem to be workin'. It's kind of expensive since I haven't been approved for disability and..."

I cut in, firm now. "So then let's go ahead and set up a one-time payment using your credit or debit card, so we—"

"No-no, I can't even *see* the numbers on them things. If my daughter were here, I'd get her to read 'em off to you, but she's not. I *remember when* I used to read to her. Now she's gotta read to me like I'm..."

Her voice faded into background noise—just wahs and blahs, like that muted drone in a *Peanuts* cartoon classroom. I stared blankly at the screen, her words washing over me, nothing sticking, just sound.

And I was trapped.

The red release button pulses beneath my finger, glowing brighter, larger, with every second I stare at it. It taunts me, a siren's call promising freedom from the endless drone of Ms. Baker's voice. Each word she spills piles heavier on my shoulders, and all I want is the sweet relief that pressing that button would bring. Kathy May isn't listening, not now—she's tucked away in that meeting I'm supposed to be in.

And then, salvation—though not of my making.

Chilly, the dog, erupts again in another fit of yapping, slicing through her ramble. Then, a sudden yelp—sharp, quick—and silence.

"I'll have to call y'all back," Ms. Baker snaps, and the line goes dead.

For a moment, I just sit there, staring at nothing, stunned by the abrupt end. Slowly, I lower the headset to the desk, the plastic clacking softly against the wood. My hands run back through my hair, fingers tangled in frustration, and I let out a short, breathless chuckle.

Through the corner of my eye, I catch Kathy—watching me. She's turned in her chair, one hand on her hip, her gaze burning through the conference room glass like she can summon control even from behind walls. I don't give her the satisfaction. I walk past, eyes forward, letting her stare.

The bathroom's dull light flickers as I push in. The handicap stall's door, stubborn as always, won't budge. I shake it, one hand gripping the cold metal, the other bracing against the frame. One hard jerk, and it finally gives.

I don't like public bathrooms, never have, but when nature calls, there's no red button to save you. I start the ritual—no ass gaskets here, so strips of toilet paper are carefully laid, one by one, like building a shield. My pants drop just below the knees, and I settle in.

Sitting there, staring at the graffiti-scratched door, I let my mind drift. How did I end up here? This job, this life? I finished high school. Took some college courses. Knew my way around computers better than most. I wasn't supposed to be *here*. Somewhere along the way, I missed a turn—or maybe life just rerouted me without asking.

(5:10 PM)

After a few stubborn tries, the engine finally coughs to life. The steering wheel rattles under my hands as I press the gas, letting the engine growl awake. I sit there a moment, letting the warmth creep through the vents, replaying the mess of a day behind me. It's over now. That's all that matters.

Across the lot, I spot Derrick, swaggering to his black Dodge Intrepid—new to him, but used, of course—chrome rims gleaming under the fading sun, a spoiler slapped on the back like a badge of honor. He climbs in, carefree, not a worry in the world.

Figures.

I squint, wiping a sleeve across the foggy driver-side window to get a better look. The temporary tags taped to his rear window catch my eye. Fresh. Still got a couple of months before they expire. His loan must've just gone through—with *our* company.

Mine? Denied. Said they wouldn't finance employees anymore—*complications*, they called it.

"Son of a bitch!" I roar, slamming my truck into reverse. My foot hits the pedal hard, ready to rip out of this lot, tires screaming.

But the engine sputters and dies.

"Damnit!" My fists crash against the steering wheel, the horn whining in protest. I lean forward, forehead pressing into the cold vinyl, breathing hard, heat rising in my chest.

One more turn of the key, and the engine stirs again, grumbling to life. I don't peel out this time. No squealing tires. No triumphant exit.

Just a slow, bitter crawl through the lot—me, puttering toward the exit, head down, hands tight, anger simmering just beneath the surface.

On my way home, the traffic lights seem to mock me—merciless, unfeeling. Every single one, without fail, flickers from green to yellow, then red, just as I reach it, as if the whole damn city had conspired to drag this day out even longer. My patience, worn thin, frays further with each forced stop.

I head south, the road wide and open until it suddenly chokes to a single lane. Bright orange construction cones stand like sentries, stretching endlessly ahead, corralling traffic into a sluggish crawl to the far right. Not a worker in sight. Not a shovel turned. The pavement? Flawless. And still, they bottle us up for blocks, like cattle. I'll never understand it—this obsession with control, this need to manufacture chaos where none exists, especially at this hour.

My grip tightens on the wheel as the metallic herd in front of me inches forward at a torturous pace. My heart pounds, the pressure building in my chest. Enough.

I swerve suddenly, cutting through a gas station parking lot, the shortcut calling like salvation. A small Geo Metro, blue and battered, reverses from a space, and I nearly clip it. The driver slams her brakes, horn blaring like a wounded animal.

I don't flinch. I don't wave. I push forward.

As the sun sinks low, shadows stretch across the narrow side streets. The air cools, and dusk presses in. Up ahead, two small green orbs reflect in my headlights, hovering in the darkness. A black cat. It watches me, poised, tense, as I approach. I'm not one to believe in omens, but still—something stirs.

The cat darts out, crossing the road from the right. Fine. No threat there.

But then, it hesitates, turns, and bolts back from the left, aiming to cross my path again.

No.

Not tonight.

I slam the accelerator to the floor. Old Blue roars in response, tires screeching. The cat's eyes widen, claws scrabbling uselessly against a slick patch of ice. It slips, stumbles, and vanishes beneath the passenger side.

Thump.

I feel it—small and soft, crushed under the weight.

"Bad kitty," I mutter, voice low, as the truck lurches forward.

(7:00 PM)

"Keep the change," I grumble, snatching the bag from the short Asian man standing in the dim light of my apartment doorway. The scent of grease and spices drifts up, and I dig through the warm paper, eager for something, anything, to go right.

"Thanks."

I pause, pulling out a plastic container.

"Hey, wait. This is sesame chicken. I ordered General Tao's. And where's my egg roll?" I bark, my blood rising all over again.

"I'm sorry, sir. I can take it back and bring the correct order if you like," he says, reaching out.

I yank the bag close. "What—so I can wait another forty-five minutes for you to come back?" My voice rises, sharp, cutting. "No thanks!"

"Sorry, sir. I—"

"Don't *be* sorry," I snap. "Just give that chick that answers your phones some *Enguish ressons,*" I mock, twisting her accent, letting the words hang heavy in the air. "Maybe if she could understand what I was asking for—or if *I* could even understand *her*—this wouldn't be a damn problem."

And then, without another word, I slam the door. The frame shudders, the wall trembling under the force. A few crooked pictures fall, glass clattering on the floor.

I stand there, chest heaving. Maybe it was too much—probably way over the line. But after a day like this, it felt good to finally push back. People spit on me all day, every day. Sometimes, it's nice to spit back.

He'll have a story to tell, no doubt. One for the kitchen.

But I won't be ordering from them again.

Not if I know what's good for me.

Kneeling down to gather the fallen frames, I notice only one of them landed face up. The glass is smudged, but the image beneath is as clear as ever—*the* picture. The only one I have of my mother and father, frozen in a moment I've revisited more times than I can count.

They're on a beach in Florida, caught mid-embrace. My mother, always so small beside him, has her cheek pressed to his chest, her smile wide and radiant, like she'd just touched heaven. Her long, wet blonde hair cascades down her back, clinging to her skin, catching the light. My father towers over her, no smile, just that steady, solemn look he always wore. His dark eyes, shadowed beneath a heavy brow, seemed to see through the lens and into something beyond. His body, lean and carved like stone, held her protectively. The only flaw—if you could call it that—was the tattoo inked across his ribcage: a skeletal frog. A relic from his time as a Navy SEAL. A Frogman. Grandma always said I looked just like him—except for the muscles, of course.

This was the last photo they took together. The last memory before the plane crash that took them away, somewhere over the Gulf, returning home.

I remember the call.

I was six, sitting cross-legged on the floor of my grandparents' living room. Grandpa was in the kitchen, phone pressed to his ear, while Grandma stirred something on the stove. His back straightened, his hand froze midair. He didn't say much—just a single word, maybe two—before the receiver slipped from his hand, dangling on its pale blue cord, swaying like a hanged man.

He turned to her, slow, heavy, and took both her hands in his. His eyes were wide, glistening. I watched as he whispered the truth. Grandma crumpled before he could hold her. She dropped, soundless, her knees hitting the floor. Grandpa followed, folding himself around her as they both cried. I didn't understand the weight of it then—not fully. But I felt it. The sharpness of loss, even if I didn't yet know the shape of it.

I place the photo back on the wall, adjusting it gently, making sure it's straight. My fingers linger on the frame a moment longer than necessary.

Tilly's soft paws click against the floor behind me, and I glance over to find her perched on the couch, up on her hind legs, sniffing eagerly at the scent of Chinese food still hanging in the air.

"Not tonight," I say, pointing at her. "Go eat your duck-soup."

She tilts her head but doesn't move. Tilly's been under the weather these past few days—nothing serious, or so they say. The pet store clerk had waved it off. "A little digestive thing," they told me. "Mix her kibble with water, make a broth—duck soup, we call it." She barely touches it. Instead, she trails me to the kitchen, watching as I empty rice onto a plate and pour the creamy sesame chicken on top.

Tilly's like me in a lot of ways. High energy, high metabolism, needs constant fuel. I worry about her—more than I probably should. But that's just how I am. She sticks close, waiting, hopeful, always hungry.

I settle onto the couch, flipping through my old DVD case, one hand fending her off as she paws at the coffee table, licking her chops.

"No—no, get down," I say, giving the side of the table a light thump with my foot.

She drops back, tail flicking, but doesn't go far.

I slide *American Psycho* from its case, the disc cool between my fingers. I never made it through the first time—fell asleep sometime after those rich guys started comparing business cards like they were life or death. Maybe it was boring, or maybe I just wasn't in the mood. But tonight, it's the only thing left on the shelf I haven't already seen to death.

I pop it in the Blu-ray player and sink back, plate in hand, Tilly watching from the floor like she's waiting for me to drop something. I hit play. Let's see if this one keeps me awake.

As I finish two of the last few bites of my meal, the plate nearly licked clean, I glance down at Tilly, curled tight beside me, her small body warm against my leg. She blinks up at me, patient but hopeful, as if she knows there's still one morsel left. I pick up the last piece of chicken, now cool, and hold it out. She sniffs once, then snatches it gently from my fingers, tail wagging. Without a second thought, she darts off to her cage, eager to enjoy her prize in peace.

The credits roll on the screen, the faint hum of the television filling the quiet room. *American Psycho*—a bloody, twisted spectacle. Visually satisfying, sure, but the ending... it left me hollow. All that violence, all that chaos, and for what? For it to all unravel inside his mind? A fantasy? A delusion? At least, that's what it seemed like to me. The line between reality and madness was thin, blurred, and in the end, meaningless.

I stretch, standing slowly, the weight of the day pulling at my limbs. Time for bed.

Peeling off my clothes, I swap my work-worn jeans for a pair of loose shorts, an old t-shirt. As I fold the pants over, something stiff brushes against my fingers—a folded piece of paper, tucked into the back pocket. I pull it out, unfolding it slowly.

My customer report.

Rows of names, addresses, phone numbers—every account I've been chasing, laid bare in neat black ink. I must've stuffed it there after that lovely chat with Kathy, forgotten in the fog of the day.

I hold it a moment, staring at the list. Then Claudia's voice echoes in my mind, laughing with Tim, joking about paying her customers a visit, *"If I wasn't in my right mind..."* she'd said.

I smirk faintly and toss the paper into the trash, watching it fall like dead weight.

Done.

The covers are cool against my skin as I slip beneath them, the room dim and silent now, save for the soft rustling of Tilly settling in for the night. I close my eyes, letting the dark take me.

CHAPTER 4

STICKBOY

"Eat it—eat it—eat it!"

I jolt awake, legs kicking, heart pounding, dragged once more from the same haunting dream that refuses to let me go. My breath is ragged, chest heaving in the morning stillness. This damn dream again. I glance toward the foot of my bed, expecting Tilly's warm presence like always—but she's not there. Instead, she's in her cage, wide awake, her eyes locked on me, unblinking, as if she had been watching me wrestle with something unseen.

It's happening more often now. Three, sometimes four nights a week, like a ghost creeping in the dark corners of my mind, whispering the same cruel chant. I don't know why. I don't know what it means. But it lingers.

Sunlight pours through the blinds, harsher than usual, striking my face like a silent alarm. I turn, eyes darting to the clock—*7:41 a.m.*

My heart stumbles in my chest. Less than twenty minutes to shower, dress, and somehow make it to work.

"Shit."

I leap from the bed, fumbling for my phone, fingers shaky as I rush to the bathroom. The shower sputters to life, cold needles spraying wildly. One hand under the faucet, the other dialing the attendance line. My mind scrambles for an excuse—*any* excuse.

Derrick's voice echoes in memory. That bullshit excuse of his. Good enough.

"Yeah, um, this is Tommy. I'm gonna be coming in late this morning. Should be there at around 8:45 a.m. The power must've gone out in our building, so my alarm didn't go off. Ok, um, thanks."

I toss the phone onto the sink and step into the freezing water, flinching as the icy stream stings my skin like tiny blades. No time to wait. I lather up quickly, teeth clenched, muscles tense. The water warms, slowly, almost forgiving.

As I scrub, my mind drifts back—*the dream*. Dean Miller pinning me down, forcing that filthy, writhing thing toward my mouth. What does it mean? Is he just a face from the past, or something more? Some weight I haven't shaken? And the worm—could it be something I've buried, something festering, demanding attention?

I don't know. I'm no shrink.

But Gram's voice whispers in the back of my head, *"Maybe it's time you talked to someone."* Maybe she's right.

I pause, hands still, the soap turning soft, squishing between my fingers in warm, useless clumps. The water cascades over me, forgotten, as I stand lost in thought, unmoving, for what feels like forever.

Then—a thud. Loud. Sharp. Followed by the familiar crash of picture frames hitting the floor.

I snap back.

"Shit."

Grabbing a towel, I wrap it around my waist and creep to the door. I crack it open, the air outside cool against my damp skin. Tilly stands in the middle of the living room, her body rigid, eyes fixed on the front door, ears perked.

My heart races, each beat louder than the last.

Something's wrong.

I glance around for anything—anything I can use. My toothbrush? Useless. The comb? Pointless. My eyes land on the plunger, awkward but solid. Good enough.

I grip it tight, holding it like a bat, every step cautious as I move into the room. Tilly bolts past me, low to the ground, scrambling under the couch, her body wedged into the dark space.

I peek around the corner, plunger raised.

The door is closed. No one is there.

But the pictures—*again*—are scattered across the floor.

And the silence is deafening.

(8:42 AM)

The office buzzes with the usual morning chaos—keyboards clacking, phones ringing, voices overlapping in a steady hum of negotiations and promises. The low, constant drone of call after call fills the space like a restless swarm. I step into it, the fluorescent lights already too bright, casting their sterile glow across the rows of cubicles.

Derrick sits at his desk, hunched over, eyes glued to his screen, fingers dancing across the mouse with quick, mindless clicks. To my right, Kimmie's voice flows steady and professional, coaxing payment details from a customer, her tone smooth but firm.

"Sup!" Derrick calls, not bothering to look up.

"What's up, Derrick?"

"Nothing, man. Just gotta start calling some of these customers. They're slippin'—dropping their payments late and all that crap. I'm doin' a little skip tracing, hitting up references, seeing what I can find. You know how it is."

I nod, but my stomach twists. Hearing it out loud—*my* customers now tangled in his sloppy methods—sets my teeth on edge. The fallout is already here, only a few days in. I almost want to laugh. *Let it burn*, I think. Maybe this is exactly what I need—proof for Kathy May that he's sinking the ship faster than I ever could.

"I hate skip tracing," I mutter, shaking my head. "Especially calling people who ain't got nothing to do with the debt. Feels like harassment."

"You got that right," Derrick agrees, glancing at me briefly. "Looks like you got a late start today. Kathy told us you'd be rollin' in late, so she's already in the loop, huh? What happened?"

"Woke up late," I say, brushing it off. But something gnaws at me still. "But something's got me a little worried."

His eyes flick up, curious. "What is it?"

"I feel like someone was in my house, man."

Just then, Kimmie ends her call and pops up over the cubicle wall like a curious cat, eyes sharp, interest piqued.

"Hey, Tommy."

"Hey." I give her a once-over, eyeing her top, then leaning to get a look at her jeans, her shoes. "Ha, no leopard print. You *owe* me lunch!"

She grins, shaking her head. "No, Boo Boo, wrong again." She rolls up her sleeve, revealing a band-aid on her elbow—leopard print. "Told you it ain't happenin'. You'll *never* catch me without it, Tommy. You might as well give up now."

"Damn. One day you're gonna slip. I *will* get that free lunch."

"Y'all are silly," Derrick chuckles, spinning slightly in his chair.

"What's this I hear about you thinking somebody was in your apartment?" Kimmie asks, her tone shifting, serious now. "And yeah, I was eavesdropping."

I lean back, arms crossed. "I was in the shower when I heard my pictures fall—by the front door. The only thing that knocks those down is when the door gets slammed."

"Oh shit," Derrick says, leaning forward. "You think someone was in your house while you were in the shower?"

"That's scary, Tommy," Kimmie adds, brows furrowed. "Did you call the police?"

"I wouldn't've known what to tell them," I reply. "You know how Milwaukee cops are. I'd probably be the one endin' up in cuffs for something stupid. I don't mess with the police unless I have to."

"You should've at least told one of your neighbors, man," Derrick suggests. "Get somebody watchin' out while you're gone. I heard there's been a lot of break-ins around your area."

"Nah," I shrug. "I leave the TV on loud when I'm out. Whoever it was probably heard me in the shower and dipped out quick. I mean, I was home at a time I'm usually gone. Someone must've been watching me—or they know my routine."

The thought hangs there, heavy.

Kimmie shakes her head slowly, her eyes wide with a mix of concern and disbelief. "Scary, Tommy. *Scary.* Just thinking someone might've been in your house while you were butt naked and vulnerable..."

Before I can respond, Freddie suddenly freezes mid-step on her way to Mr. Gibbons' office, her heels clicking to a halt. Her head tilts, and with a nosy gleam in her eye, she tiptoes over like a child overhearing something they shouldn't.

"What!? Who? Where!?" she whispers, eyes darting, her curiosity almost tangible.

We exchange glances—Derrick, Kimmie, and me—all sharing the same half-amused, half-annoyed expression.

"Tommy had someone try and break in his house this morning," Derrick explains casually.

"Oh, *that's* it?" Freddie sighs, visibly disappointed. "I heard something about being butt naked and vulnerable, so, you know... just wanted to be nosey." She lets out a laugh, the kind that sticks in your throat, then struts off with a sway in her hips.

Kimmie scowls as Freddie disappears down the hall. "That nasty hoe. Always tryin' to get in somebody's business. She walks like her cookie hurts."

Derrick and I both wince, eyes darting, wondering if Freddie heard that last part—but then we burst into quiet laughter, unable to help ourselves.

(9:15 AM)

The whirr of printers fills the air as Derrick and I both head to the copy machine, reports in hand. As luck would have it, we arrive at the same time. He's already beside me, close—*too* close.

His scent hits first. A thick, raw staleness, like onions freshly cut and left to fester. It assaults my senses, drowning out the clean hint of Curve cologne I put on this morning. The air around him seems to warp, heavy and pungent. I instinctively hold my breath, subtly leaning away as he reaches past me for the stapler.

He turns his back to staple his report, and that's when I see it—something that freezes me in place.

A long white t-shirt, baggy pants sagging low, and those damn sandals he loves. But on the back of his shirt, there it is—a brown stain. Not just any stain. It's shaped like a crude lowercase "l," smeared in just the wrong place, perfectly aligned with the crack of his ass, had his shirt been tucked in. Coffee? Maybe. Chocolate? Possible. But this? This ain't no cola spill.

My stomach turns.

For a second, I'm stuck—caught between laughter and horror. Do I let it slide? Do I walk away, let him parade around with that grotesque mark for the world to see? Normally, I'd just laugh it off, chalk it up as the universe throwing me a bone on a crap day. But something stops me. Maybe pity. Maybe decency. Either way, I decide to save him from himself.

"Derrick! Dude, come here, man!" I say, waving him over, my voice low but urgent.

As he turns, I keep my eyes down, careful to avoid locking onto his. His smell is enough—I don't need the full force of his presence.

"Yeah?" he asks, confused.

"Man, I don't wanna sound like an ass, but I figured I'd tell you before anyone else sees it... You got a big brown stain on the back of your shirt. And from where it's sittin'... it looks like a doo-doo stain."

"What!? A *doo-doo* stain?" His head jerks back, eyebrows shooting up in disbelief, like I just spoke in another language.

Derrick reaches back without hesitation, pinching the fabric of his shirt between his fingers, twisting it forward until the stain is directly under his nose. He breathes in deeply, the sound loud and deliberate—then again, two shorter sniffs, like a bloodhound on a scent trail. His brow furrows, the lines on his face deepening with confusion.

"You're seriously smelling that? *Right here? Right now?*"

I can't help but grin, disgusted but amused, backing away slowly with my hands raised, as if surrendering to the absurdity of it all. Derrick doesn't answer. He just stands there, transfixed, eyes narrowing at the stain as if it holds some ancient mystery only he can unlock. His gaze lifts toward the ceiling, searching, thinking, trying to piece together some alternate truth. The color, the shape, the *placement*—and whatever godforsaken smell he's confirmed—it all speaks for itself.

I'm not sticking around for his epiphany.

Leaving him behind by the printer, I head to the restroom, needing distance and maybe a bit of sanity.

The lights flicker on automatically, humming to life as I step inside the darkened room. I take my usual spot at the center urinal, unzipping, grateful for a moment of solitude. The relief is just setting in when the door slams open with a burst.

"*Makeup!*" Derrick yells, breathless, as if he's uncovered some great truth. "My wife wiped her makeup off on my shirt!"

I glance at him from the corner of my eye, not turning fully, not needing to. A low chuckle escapes as I finish up. He's at the sink now, shirt twisted awkwardly around his body, desperately squirting soap onto the stain, scrubbing at it under the cold stream of water.

"So your wife always wipes her makeup off in a straight line... right where the crack of your ass would be?" I ask, dryly, as I wash my hands, smirking at him through the mirror.

"Yep! Crazy, huh?"

"You said it, bro. *Crazy.*"

He grins, as if proud of the explanation. "Oh yeah, by the way—Mr. Martinez is holding on the line for you. He called my line, but I told him you're his new account manager, so he needed to speak with you."

"Okay. Thanks."

Back at my desk, I pause, eyes narrowing. My headset isn't where I left it. My gut tightens. Derrick must've answered my phone. That's the kind of thing he'd do—no boundaries.

I glance at the phone, line one still blinking.

Mr. Martinez...

The name stirs something. I've heard it before—usually with Derrick complaining about how much trouble this guy gave him, always pushing back when payments were due.

I peek over my cubicle at Kimmie. "Can I use one of those desk wipes, please?"

She wordlessly hands one over, still deep in conversation. I wipe the headset thoroughly, the cool moisture biting at my fingers. I think for a second, weighing how best to handle this. Martinez's high balance could kill my numbers—or save them, if I play it right.

"Let's get to it," I whisper, slipping on the now-damp headset and pressing the blinking line.

"Mr. Martinez?"

"Yeah."

"Thank you for holding, sir. How can I help you today?"

"Yeah, I came up on a situation, and I need to put off my payment for a couple of weeks. I just can't do it right now."

Of course. I can't let this slide. Not with that balance hanging over me like a guillotine. Time to dig into the script.

"As you know, Mr. Martinez, we cannot allow your payment to go out that far. Is there any way you may be able to get a loan from a relative or friend?" I say, keeping my voice polite, steady.

Let's see how much of Derrick's damage I can undo.

"Don't be an insensitive ass, bro. I just told you I don't have it. I'm not about to go begging for money either. That's not my style."

His voice hits me like a wall, sharp and final.

"I'm not sure what to tell you then, sir," I reply, keeping my tone measured, but firm. "You're in a newer loan, and your late payment means you're going to be in default. Which means our company can legally collect on its property right away."

Silence.

A heavy, long pause fills the line, stretching out like a held breath. Collectors call this the "psychological pause," letting the weight of their reality settle in, giving them time to think—or sweat. I wait, fingers moving quietly over the keys, updating notes, pulling more info on him.

"So if I don't pay, you guys are going to come and pick up my car?" he asks, voice lower now.

"We really don't want to, sir," I answer, adding a hint of empathy, just enough. "But it is a part of the contract."

Another pause, but this one's shorter. Darker.

"Well, I tell you what, motherfucker—if any of you come on my property trying to get my car, I'll cut your balls off and hang them from my rearview. Now, I told you what I could do. You either take it or you don't."

The call just took a hard left—one I didn't expect, and definitely didn't want. But I can't afford to let this go. Not now. Not with my numbers hanging by a thread.

"Sir, if your payment is not made as soon as possible, we will have no choice but to send someone out for the retrieval of the vehicle, Mr. Martinez. I'm sorry."

"Well come get it then, *bitch*! If it's worth your ass getting kicked—come and get it," he spits. "You got all the info you need, I'm sure. Hell, I won't even hide my car. You heartless assholes better strap your balls on and come on over."

Click.

He hangs up.

I rip the headset off, tossing it next to the monitor, the plastic clattering loudly. My jaw clenches, a tight knot of frustration pulsing behind my eyes.

(5:57 PM)

The drive home is long, every stoplight another nail in the coffin of this godforsaken day. When I finally pull into the lot of my apartment complex, I kill the engine but don't move. I sit there, behind the wheel, hands slack in my lap, staring out at nothing.

The same thoughts circle, slow and heavy.

Quit. Walk away from all of it. But I can't. Not now. Not yet.

I lean back, staring at the sagging ceiling of my old truck, waiting for some kind of sign. Something from above, something divine. But all I get is the low hum of the engine cooling, the faint echo of a dog barking somewhere in the distance.

I sigh, push the door open, and head inside.

The elevator groans as I step in, its metal walls cool against my back as I lean into them. I jab the button for my floor. The doors stay open, stubborn, refusing to move. I press it again. Nothing.

Come on.

I press it once more, harder this time, the irritation crawling under my skin. Still nothing. Fine—I'll take the stairs.

But as I step forward, the doors suddenly slide shut with a soft *ding*, almost mocking. The box shudders, then lurches upward, the cables above me groaning and clanging like the whole thing might give out any second.

One day, this thing's going to kill somebody.

I lean back again, closing my eyes, willing the ride to end.

Relief washes over me as I reach my apartment door, key in hand, ready to escape the weight of this day. I fumble slightly, my aim off, the key missing the lock and striking the doorknob with a dull clink.

The door shifts—loose.

My heart drops.

The memory of the morning flashes back, sharp and unwelcome—the sound of falling pictures, the stillness that followed. I freeze, key still poised in mid-air, the tip hovering near the lock as fear grips me. The apartment is silent. Too silent. No hum from the TV, no noise at all. I swallow hard, throat tight, breath caught halfway between dread and disbelief.

I force myself to breathe, to move. One shaky step at a time. I draw in a deep breath and slowly push the door open. It groans against the frame, the wood near the lock splintering, flakes falling to the carpet like brittle leaves. The door had been forced.

I step inside.

The emptiness hits first—not just space, but *absence*. The hollow void where my most expensive things used to be. The weight in my chest sinks deeper, dragging me down. My book bag slips from my shoulder, landing on the floor with a soft thud as I make a beeline to the entertainment stand.

I drop to my knees.

Nothing. Just the dusty outlines of my television, my Xbox—ghosts of what used to be there. My fingers trace the vacant space as if they might suddenly bring it all back. I peer beneath the stand. DVDs, video games—all gone. I spin around, eyes locking on my desk. The laptop's gone. My programs, my mouse, the lamp, even the damn printer—*gone*.

I stare, fists clenched tight, rage and disbelief swirling, but held back, bottled up just below the surface.

I move to the bedroom, stepping carefully, afraid of what else might be missing. Tilly bolts from under the bed, scampering to my feet, pawing at my leg, her small claws hooking into my pants like she's clinging to something familiar—something safe. At least she's okay.

I kneel, running a hand over her soft fur. She trembles slightly, pressing into me.

I stand and return to the front door, examining the damage. The frame's split near the lock, forced open cleanly. Someone had to hear that. This hallway is quiet—always quiet. Someone must've heard something. Someone who's always home.

I cross the hall and knock hard on the door opposite mine. No answer. Then I remember—the place has been vacant for weeks. Useless.

Next door. The man I hear *every* day, when I leave, when I come home. He's always there.

I pound on his door, knuckles tight, urgency surging through me.

No answer.

I hit harder.

"*Hold on—damn it!*" A voice snaps back, muffled but rising, heavy footsteps following.

The door creaks open, just a crack, held tight by the chain. A shorter Hispanic man peers through, rubbing the corners of his eyes, squinting like I've dragged him from some dream. His hair's a mess, frizzy and dry, falling to his shoulders. His cheeks puff as if holding air, like a kid caught mid-breath.

"Sorry to bother you, man," I say, trying to steady my voice. "My place was broken into. Did you by any chance hear anything?"

He sighs long and slow, wiping his face with both hands, then without a word, slams the door shut.

I grit my teeth, jaw tightening, lips parting to spit out something sharp—when I hear the click of the latch.

The door creaks open again.

The door swings open fully now, and I get the complete picture.

He stands there in a stained, dingy white wife beater, stretched tight across a perfectly round belly, as if the fabric's one deep breath away from giving up. His black pajama pants are littered with bright green marijuana leaves, loud against the filth that seems to cling to everything but one thing—around his neck, a thin silver chain catches the hallway light, gleaming unnaturally clean. Hanging from it, an oversized silver emblem of an eagle, wings spread wide, frozen in flight. A symbol of pride, maybe, but lost on him. This walking mess, this caricature of apathy, could be Derrick's long-lost twin.

"Ah, shit dude, that sucks. I'm sorry to hear that." He scratches his stomach absently. "No—no, I haven't heard anything. I've been out on these meds all day, man. I don't hear shit after they kick in."

"Oh, okay. Sorry to bug you, man," I say, already regretting knocking.

"You know, I heard that shit's been goin' around, bro. Some other folks got broken into too. You should try leavin' somethin' on, so someone thinks you're home."

"Yeah, I know. I've tried that. It doesn't work, obviously."

"Oh." He shifts, scratching at his scalp with slow, dirty fingers. "Well, maybe somebody was watchin' you. Did you call the police?"

"No," I snap, voice tight. I don't want advice. I don't want conversation. It's too late for that.

"I'm surprised no one comes and gets my shit too, dude. I swear these meds have me in an entirely different place. You could walk in here, and I wouldn't even know it." He chuckles, eyes distant. "I'm surprised I even heard the door just now. I got this condition where—"

His words drone on, but I'm not listening anymore. Something inside me cracks, a quiet shift from frustration to something darker. My vision narrows, my hands tighten. I see myself stepping forward, grabbing him by that greasy hair, smashing his face into the wall until there's nothing left but spit, blood, and bone. I feel it—the release, the satisfaction.

But his sudden burst of laughter yanks me back.

"I have to go," I mutter, and before he can say another word, I turn, heading straight for my apartment.

"Uh, okay, bro. Hopefully you get your shit back," he calls out behind me, like that means anything now.

I slam the door—what's left of it—but it bounces weakly off the broken frame, refusing to close fully. I kick it in frustration, then drop to my knees, digging through my bag for my phone. My fingers find it, and without thinking, I dial.

911.

A woman's voice cuts through, brisk and emotionless.

"911, what is your emergency?"

"3825 West Hampton Avenue, Apartment 222."

"Not where, sir. *What* is your emergency?"

I grip the phone tighter, my jaw clenched. "Oh, my fucking apartment got broken into. Can you send the police, *please*?" I fight to keep my voice steady, but it cracks anyway.

"Okay, calm down, sir. There's no need for the profanity." Her voice stays flat, detached. I hear her typing, the clack of keys a cold contrast to the heat boiling in my chest. "I just have a couple of questions for you."

"How do you know your apartment was broken into?"

"Well, it's just a hunch, but seeing that my door is busted to shit and all my things worth stealing are gone... I'm kinda gonna go with burglary. Final answer."

She chuckles. "What is your name?"

"Thomas Thorpe."

"What is the number that you can be reached?"

"414-555-1777."

"Have you been hurt, or is there anything else you'd like to report?"

"No, thank you."

"Just sit tight at home, sir, and a police officer will be there shortly."
Click.

The line goes dead.

(7:23 PM)

Still no sign of the police. The apartment is heavy with silence, stripped bare of the noise I once took for granted—no hum of electronics, no flicker of a screen, nothing but the creak of the building settling and my own restless thoughts.

I sink into my leather recliner, the cold surface sighing beneath me. Leaning it all the way back, I stare at the ceiling, the off-white paint now a canvas for my frustration. My fingers claw into the armrests, knuckles pale, as images of faceless thieves dance through my mind—laughing, smug, enjoying what *I* worked for.

The recliner snaps back upright, the movement sharp, jerking me forward. I bury my face in my hands. My chest tightens, breath growing shallow. My stomach churns, but not from fear—from helplessness, from rage. My eyes sting as I squeeze them shut, willing the tears away.

I clasp my hands tightly, pressing them against my lips, and inhale deeply. The silence presses in closer. The weight of today, and all the days before, bears down on me. I begin to rock, slowly at first, but harder with each thought, each memory. The tears come fast now, carving hot tracks down my cheeks. I didn't want to break, not before the police came, but it's no use. The dam has burst.

Tilly appears from the shadows, her small frame brushing against my leg, her nose nudging gently as if trying to pull me out of the storm. Her tiny claws scratch at me, seeking attention—or comfort. I wipe at my face and push her aside, gently, but firm.

I can't take her comfort right now.

I stumble into the bedroom, the weight of everything dragging at my limbs. Sitting on the edge of the bed, I catch a glimpse of myself in the full-length mirror across the room. I hate what I see. The reflection stares back—eyes swollen, face hollow, glasses smeared with tears.

I yank them off and dry my face with my sleeves. But it's no use. I don't recognize the man in the glass.

Sad. Weak. Pathetic.

I stand, slow and deliberate, walking to the mirror, drawn to it like a moth to flame. I stare into my own bloodshot eyes, my lip curling in disgust.

Without thinking, without even breathing, I raise my fist and drive it hard into the glass.

The mirror shatters with a sharp crack. Splinters cascade to the floor, glittering like cruel stars, jagged and unforgiving. Larger shards slide from the frame and crash into the pile, a broken reflection of everything I've tried to hold together.

(9:08 PM)

A loud knock rattles the door, pulling me from a foggy sleep on the couch. My body aches, my hand throbs, and I have no idea how I ended up here. The room is dim, the only light a soft glow from the stove bulb in the kitchen.

"Milwaukee Police Department," a voice calls through the door, followed by another heavy knock.

"Alright, one second!" I shout, pushing myself upright, still groggy.

The room is a blur of shadows and sharp edges. I squint, trying to focus. The crunch of glass underfoot snaps me to attention, and I stumble, tripping over the overturned coffee table.

I reach the door, fumbling with the busted knob, and swing it open.

Two officers step in without pause, their flashlights sweeping across the room, cutting through the dark like blades. The beams stab into corners, then into my face, blinding me.

"Well, what happened here?" one officer asks, his tone almost amused, gum popping between his teeth. His dark skin gleams under the light, his bald head shiny, his expression twisted into a Cheshire grin.

"What's your name?"

Before I can answer, the other officer speaks, his voice calmer, more measured.

"Whoa. They really did a number on this place. What was taken?"

He pulls a notepad from his pocket, already scribbling. His hair is cropped in a tight, high-and-tight military cut, blonde against pale skin. He looks like he stepped off a recruitment poster—square jaw, broad shoulders, his uniform hugging muscles that don't fit the badge. His sleeves strain against thick, veined biceps, pulsing with authority.

"Well, from what I can see, they got my TV, my computer, and my Xbox," I say, my voice low, each word heavier than the last.

As I list off what's gone, the black officer—still chewing his gum with that obnoxious, wet smack—sweeps his flashlight up and down my body, slow and deliberate. His eyes narrow, lips curling into a sly smile like he's just solved some private riddle.

"How'd you get those cuts on your hands?" he asks, the light pausing at my knuckles.

I glance down, surprised to see the blood, seeping through the cracks in my skin, dried and fresh mixed together in angry streaks. I hadn't even noticed.

Thinking fast, I shrug. "I got them tryin' to pick up this broken glass, sir."

"Mm hmm," he hums, doubt thick in his tone, like he's heard better lies from junkies. "You're not on any drugs, are you, son?"

The question hits like a slap. Not the first time someone's assumed that—called me cracked-out, strung-out, worthless—but tonight? Tonight it stings deeper.

"No, sir," I say, lifting my hand, blood shining in the dim light. "I have AIDS."

"Whoa—whoa—whoa, buddy, *back up!*" he yells, stumbling back, his boot sliding on one of my muscle magazines, arms flailing for balance.

I can't help it—a laugh slips out, bitter but real.

"I'm kidding, sir. God just chose to bless me with this incredible physique you see before you." I stretch my arms wide, like I'm offering myself to an invisible crowd, center stage.

They exchange a look, eyebrows raised in quiet disbelief, then turn back to me.

"You mind if we look around?" the other one asks, slipping his notepad into his pocket.

"Not at all, officers. Go right ahead."

I step aside, watching them as they pick their way over the debris, muttering under their breath. The mess feels like part of me now—splintered wood, shattered glass, pieces of a life ripped apart.

Suddenly, Tilly darts out from the bedroom, a flash of fur weaving between the black officer's legs.

"Oh *shit!* What the fuck was *that?*" he shouts, flattening himself against the wall, one foot raised, flashlight trained like a weapon.

"It's a ferret, I think. My cousin's got one," the white officer says, crouching to get a better look. "Stinky little fuckers, but if you take care of them right, you can keep it down. Where'd you get him?"

"She's a ferret," I correct, scooping her up. "Her name's Tilly. Got her from a shelter."

The black officer pulls his partner aside, not bothering to lower his voice. "Jim, let's get this report and get the hell outta here. Stick Boy and his ghostly pet are givin' me the creeps."

Stick Boy.

The name cuts deeper than any broken glass ever could. A ghost from the past, wrapped in laughter and fists, in whispers and cruel jokes. It's haunted me for years.

I remember.

I was ten, sitting in front of Grandma's fireplace, the flicker of flames dancing in my eyes, the sharp sting of a busted lip fresh from another schoolyard beating. My tongue poked at the split skin, tasting blood and shame. I stared into the fire, wondering what it would feel like to burn, how long it would take before the pain disappeared, before I would disappear.

Even then, I hated what I saw in the mirror. Hated myself for what I was. And I hated God even more for making me this way.

"Sugar, you're way too young to have that look on your face. What's wrong?" Gram asked softly, easing herself into her favorite wooden chair, the one by the window where the light always seemed to find her. The chair creaked gently beneath her, familiar and worn like the hands that held the delicate china cup. She balanced it on the saucer with practiced grace, lifting it to her lips for a slow sip, the faint scent of chamomile filling the room.

"Nothing, Gram. Just thinking... and stuff," I mumbled, my eyes fixed on the crumpled piece of paper I'd pulled from the depths of my pocket. The corners were worn, the creases soft from being folded and unfolded too many times.

She didn't say anything right away. Just sipped, watching me over the rim of her cup, her smile as steady as the ticking of the old clock behind her.

"That's the same look your father had on his face when something was troubling him," she chuckled, a soft, knowing sound. "He was such a hard-headed little boy. And stubborn! Stubborn just like your Grandfather. I can see a lot of him in you, you know. Whatever's sitting heavy on that young mind of yours, there's no shame in it. Tell Grandma what's wrong, Suga."

I hesitated, fingers fumbling at the edges of the paper, the weight of embarrassment pulling at my chest. Slowly, I peeled it open, revealing the cruel simplicity of the drawing—a stick figure, thin lines hastily scratched in pencil, and above it, the jagged letters that screamed louder than any voice ever could: *STICKBOY*. A blot of red stained the center, small, but deep—blood from the fresh split in my lip, another gift from Dean Miller.

I didn't want to show her, but I did.

Her eyes widened, and she placed her tea down gently on the table, the clink of porcelain breaking the quiet. "Oh, my," she breathed, her voice heavy with something between sorrow and anger. "Who did this?"

"Just some kids at school," I said, my voice small, looking up at her, searching for something—understanding, maybe, or answers. "Gram, why is God so mean? He made everyone else okay, but makes people like me for others to pick on."

Her face softened, and she reached out, brushing a hand over my cheek, her touch warm and sure. "He isn't mean, sweetie. He loves all His children the same. And all of them—every one—are special in some way. We all have a purpose. You just have to trust and find yours. Follow your feelings, your heart."

I let her words sink in, heavy and confusing, as I watched her rise and move toward the old bookshelf that stood like a sentry against the far wall. Her fingers danced along the spines, pausing now and then, before she pulled a small book from the middle shelf, its cover worn with love.

"Here we go," she said, flipping through its pages with care. "Here's a story I think you'll appreciate very much. Come here on the couch with me."

"What is it?" I asked, climbing up beside her, curling into her side where everything always felt safe.

"It's a story about how the Stick Man helps Santa save Christmas."

"What? There's no such thing. You're making that up!" I laughed, shaking my head.

"No—no, I'm afraid not," she smiled, tapping the title with her finger. "Here it is, right here."

She looked down at me, eyes twinkling, and began.

"*Once upon a time...*"

CHAPTER 5

STICKMAN

(Friday – 6:25 AM)

"Stop it, Daddy, stop!" I scream through a flood of laughter, my voice bouncing off the walls as my father wrestles me down onto the couch. His big hands, rough and warm, slip under my arms with expert precision, wiggling at my ribs, then dancing down to my sides. I thrash beneath him, shrieking with the kind of wild, helpless giggle only a six-year-old can summon.

"Say uncle and I will!" he teases.

"No way!" I laugh, twisting, my elbows flailing to shield my sides, but his fingers—relentless and strong—easily bypass my defenses. The tickling intensifies. I can barely breathe.

"Say it!" he demands again, grinning with mock menace.

"No!" I gasp between giggles.

And then it happens—my knee jerks up instinctively, catching him hard in the chin. His head snaps back, and he stills.

The laughter vanishes from the room.

He brings a hand to his lip, inspecting the small split now trickling blood. My breath catches. My joy turns cold. Fear sets in.

"Sorry, Dad—Sorry!" I blurt, wincing, bracing for a punishment I've never received but suddenly believe is coming. A swat? A slap? Something?

He sits back, staring at me, jaw tight. For a breathless second, he looks almost angry—then his expression softens, and his lips twitch into a smile.

"Don't ever be sorry, son. Never. When life's got you down, and you feel like there's nothin' you can do... laugh and kick back. And kick hard. Just like you did to your old man just now, you hear?"

"Yes, sir," I whisper.

He leans in, pulling me into a hug—gentle at first. But it's a trap. His fingers return, merciless and quick, launching another tickle assault as he buries his face in my belly.

I squeal, trying to push him away, grabbing at his ears. My laughter is frantic, joyful—and then it freezes.

He lifts his face from my stomach.

His skin has gone pale.

In the span of a blink, his features begin to wither, flaking away like ash in the wind. My small hands clutch his head as it crumbles in my grasp, his flesh disintegrating, leaving only the bare gray skull behind.

I scream.

"Eat it, Tommy," he growls, voice no longer his—it's deep, guttural, something monstrous, something wrong.

I jolt awake, teeth clenched tight, clutching my blanket as if it *were* his skull. My eyes are wet with tears I didn't know I'd shed. This one... this dream is different! *Worse.* More vivid. More real. It lingers in my chest like smoke. Maybe it's time I actually listened to Gram.

Trying to shake it off, I head to the kitchen and crack open eight eggs into a bowl, the shells clinking like brittle bones. I whisk them with a handful of shredded cheese and pour them into the skillet, the hiss and sizzle giving me something familiar to focus on.

Then—*thud.*

A bump, followed by the low, dragging shuffle of something heavy in the hallway.

I turn down the burner and approach the front door. Since the break-in, I've shoved a dresser and a couple of weighted chairs up against it, turning it into a makeshift barricade. I kneel down and lean close to the splintered section where the lock used to be—my makeshift peephole.

Across the hallway, the door to the vacant apartment is open. I spot the edge of a brown leather couch being dragged inside, its base scraping across the floor with a muffled groan.

Curiosity anchors me. I squint through the gap, waiting.

Then, a voice—low, muffled, male. I can't make out the words. A shadow moves. He backs into the doorway, slowly, revealing only his torso. I watch, holding my breath.

"Hey, thank you so much for your help, I couldn't have gotten that damn thing up here without you," a sweet, melodic voice floats from just outside my door, muffled but close. She's just out of sight, hidden behind the shape of the man standing in front of my peephole.

"No problem, it was a good thing I was coming up when I did."

"Oh my God, yes," she laughs, light and easy. "Are you sure you don't want anything to drink? I have some soda, water, or juice."

"No, thank you. I need to be heading off, or I'll be late for work."

"Okay, thank you again, so much!"

"You are very welcome. I'm sure we'll see each other again. Hell, I'm only downstairs if you need me." There's a small pause, then, "Have a great day—and hope you enjoy your new place."

"You too!"

He steps away, and at last, the figure blocking my view moves. My breath catches.

There she is.

She stands framed in her doorway, hands resting on her hips, her chest rising and falling with the exertion of moving. A pink tank top clings to her, damp with sweat, and her jeans hug her petite, curvy frame. She's maybe five foot six, olive-skinned, with shoulder-length dark brown hair, damp and tousled. Her full lips are parted slightly as she surveys the hallway, eyes curious, absorbing her new surroundings.

I watch as a bead of sweat glides down her neck, slipping past her collarbone, disappearing into the delicate line of her cleavage.

Then—she looks directly at my door.

Directly at me.

Her gaze sharpens, drawn to the jagged hole where I peer from. My heart skips. She steps forward.

"Hello?" she calls softly.

I don't breathe. I don't move. My body tenses, willing myself invisible. The last thing I need is for her to think her new neighbor is some creep hiding behind broken wood. Even if, right now, that's exactly what I am.

She waits. I can see the hesitation on her face, the flicker of curiosity giving way to something else.

Then—*BEEP BEEP BEEP!*

The smoke alarm blares, slicing through the moment like a blade.

I whip around, eyes wide—the kitchen is hazy, filled with thick, gray smoke curling toward the ceiling.

I glance back through the hole. She's gone. Her door swings shut, soft and final.

I rush into the kitchen, grab the skillet—now spewing smoke and fury—and hurl it into the sink. The metal hisses as water blasts over it, steam billowing up in clouds. My eyes sting, my throat burns as I cough into my sleeve, stumbling toward the window. I throw it open, waving a kitchen towel, fanning the smoke like a man possessed.

Bent over the counter, I cough hard, eyes watering. The skillet, now cool, sits in a shallow grave of blackened eggs and cloudy water. My breakfast is ruined, and with it, the start of what could've been just a normal morning.

No time to make more. No time for anything now.

But, damn... she was *hot*.

(7:59 AM)

I slap two breakfast burritos and a bottle of orange juice onto the counter at the gas station, my stomach growling with frustration. If I'm already late, I figure I might as well eat. Something about taking control of *this* small thing feels necessary.

As the cashier scans the items, something catches my eye. A flash. A glint.

Hanging by the counter, a necklace—silver, delicate, but what hangs from it stops me cold. A stickman. Its face hollowed out, blank, like an empty soul trapped in metal. The tiny figure twists slowly on its chain, swaying back and forth, as though it's noticed me too.

It twirls, shimmer catching the overhead lights, pulling me into its rhythm.

For a moment, I can't look away.

"That'll be eight dollars and fifty-four cents, sir," the cashier says, breaking my trance.

"Wait," I murmur, eyes still locked on the twirling silver figure. "I'll take this too." I point to the necklace, unable to resist.

The cashier glances at it, then at me, a faint smirk tugging at the corner of his mouth. "Okay, that'll be twelve dollars and eighty-seven cents now."

I hand him the cash, fingers tingling as I scoop up my breakfast and the necklace, like I've just bought more than food—something symbolic, something... personal.

Back in my truck, I toss the burritos onto the passenger seat, but my focus stays fixed on the small, shining stickman in my hand. I loop the chain over the rearview mirror and let it hang, suspended, catching the morning light. It twinkles, swaying gently as I flick it with my finger.

For a moment, everything else fades.

I tear into the wrapper of one burrito, take a huge bite, and start the engine, never once taking my eyes off that little silver figure. It dangles there, calm and still, but something about it—about having it—floods me with a strange, sudden confidence. A weightless kind of power I can't explain.

I glance at myself in the rearview, just beyond the charm. My reflection grins back, cheek full of food, eyes brighter somehow.

I slam the truck into reverse.

(8:25 AM)

"You're late, Mr. Thorpe!" Kathy's voice slices through the air the moment I step in, sharp as ever from her office.

"For the second time in almost *two years*, Ms. May!" I shoot back, dropping my stuff to the floor without a care.

The floor shifts—conversations stall, fingers pause mid-type. For just a second, the usual buzz of the call center dips into something quieter.

I hear Kimmie's soft giggle from the other side of the cubicle wall, like she's trying to keep it under wraps.

"Hurry up and log in so you can get those numbers down, or you won't have to worry about what time you're coming in anymore," Kathy barks.

"Why do *I* get this kind of treatment when I'm late," I mutter, just loud enough for those around me to catch it, "but when others stroll in late, it's all good? Not naming names, of course."

I slam the login button as my eyes scan the room, searching. "As a matter of fact, where *is* he?"

Right on cue, I catch a glimpse of Kathy shutting her office door, cutting off any chance of an answer.

I stretch my middle finger up over the cubicle wall, aiming it in her direction with pride.

Today wasn't a *good* day—not by normal standards—but it sure as hell felt like something else. Something *better*. I didn't care about the mess, the smoke, the crap morning. I felt untouchable. Reckless. Like nothing could touch me, and no one's opinion mattered.

I just didn't give a damn.

(8:45 AM)

I watch the printer spit out my reports, still smirking. And there it is—top of the list, like a stain I can't scrub out. Mr. Martinez.

His balance is strangling my numbers, and I've had enough. I don't even think twice. I dial him, fingers steady, mind sharp. As it rings, I pull up his info, scanning for anything new, anything I can use.

He picks up before the first ring finishes.

"Good morning, Mr. Martinez. How are you today?"

"Look—look, man! Let's not start with this crap again this early in the morning. I don't know how many times I gotta tell you I'll pay when I get paid. Callin' me every damn day ain't gonna get shit done. You can't squeeze blood from a turnip."

"Well, that's a good thing, Mr. Martinez," I say, leaning into the sharp edge of my voice. "Because we don't give loans to turnips. And the last time I checked, turnips don't answer phones—or drive newly purchased vehicles. We provide loans to *people*, hard-working people like yourself, who understand the terms of a contract. People who know the consequences when that contract isn't honored. You are two months past due."

There's a silence, tight and bitter.

"You threatening my car again?" he snaps.

"No, sir. *You're* threatening your car—with your lack of financial contributions to your loan. Either pay your account, or forfeit the vehicle."

I know, of course, that technically the company won't lift a finger until he's over a hundred days delinquent. But this job? It's like poker. Bluff and hope they fold, or stand firm and risk the loss. Sometimes they call you out, sometimes they break. But if I don't push, don't pressure, I might as well kiss my own possessions good-bye.

I lean back in my chair, angling my head toward Kathy's office. Her door is wide open, but her seat's empty. A glance to my right—management huddled in the conference room, their voices a faint murmur.

Good.

No one's listening.

I grin, curling my lips around the mic, lowering my voice so the floor won't hear.

"This is the last time I'm gonna call you about your damn car, Mr. Martinez," I whisper, the words sliding out like venom. "Go to a pawn shop. Rob a liquor store. Shit—stand on a corner with a cardboard sign or sell your ass for all I care. But *pay* your fucking car, you broke bastard."

I can almost *feel* it—his rage, his disbelief, clawing through the line. I can picture him now, eyes wide, veins tight, fists curling around his phone.

"Who the hell do you think—where's your supervisor? I'm reporting you now!" His voice shakes, furious.

"Unavailable. What? You gonna tell on me?" I chuckle, low and cold.

"You're damn right I'm gonna tell on you! I know this is against your FCPCA or whatever it is. You can kiss your fucking job goodbye, asshole. I'm sure this call is being recorded."

"You mean *FDCPA*, the Fair Debt Collection Practices Act?" I say, savoring the correction. "And no, this call isn't recorded. We tell you when it is. Sorry to burst your bubble, but this isn't one of those times. Besides, who do you think they'll believe? Some broke-ass dude who's been ducking payments for months? Or me?"

Silence.

It hangs there, thick and heavy, until his voice returns—quiet now, but dangerous.

"Listen, you stupid, insensitive asshole. If you come anywhere near my garage, I'll castrate you. Come and get it if you've got the balls. *And I mean you. No one else.*"

Click.

He hangs up.

I sit back, the hum of the office creeping in again, softer now. My fingers hover over the keyboard, then move swiftly, typing out the *friendly* version of our exchange.

Mr. Martinez advised he is working on payment. Remains unwilling at this time. To follow up next week.

I glance down, eyes falling on the corner of my desk—a forgotten stack of business cards, bound in a thin, dust-covered rubber band. My name, my title, the company logo embossed in cheap gloss.

A spark flickers.

I pull one free.

My eyes shift back to the screen, landing on Mr. Martinez's name... and address.

An idea creeps in—dark, bold, and tempting.

Something I should have thought of before.

I highlight his information slowly, fingers tightening on the card.

CHAPTER 6

FOLLOW THROUGH

(7:45 PM)

I find myself lost again, leaning against the counter, eyes fixed on the skillet as the butter slides and swirls, sizzling softly, melting into itself like memories fading into the heat. The golden pool crackles, filling the kitchen with that warm, familiar scent.

My mind drifts—drawn back to simpler days, to the park with my parents. I see myself, small and carefree, swinging between them, their hands holding tight as they lifted me high, higher, laughing as I flew. My mother's camcorder capturing the moment, her voice light and full of love. My father chasing me through the wooden fort, growling like a playful beast, hands stretched out like claws. I ran, breathless with joy, until I stumbled—fell hard into the bed of wood chips.

She was there in an instant.

"Oh sweetie, you're okay. You're tough like your father!" she soothed, brushing the hair from my face, her long blonde strands falling like silk, tickling my skin. Her hands, gentle and sure, cradled my cheeks as I sobbed.

Pop.

A searing sting snaps me back. Drops of bubbling tomato soup leap from the pot, searing my forearm. I hiss, rushing to the sink, thrusting my arm under the cold stream. The chill bites into the burn, easing it slowly, grounding me.

The silence settles in again. The apartment feels hollow without the hum of the TV, without the soft background noise that used to fill the space, stave off the loneliness. I can't stand it.

I swipe open an app on my phone, desperate for a sound—*any* sound. I crank up some Dubstep, heavy and pulsing, trying to drown out the void. The bass thumps in my chest as I return to the stove, flipping sandwiches, stirring soup.

Tilly darts past, a crumpled piece of my newspaper clenched in her tiny jaws, the little thief doing her usual. I step forward, pressing down with my foot, but only manage to tear off a piece—the entertainment section, left behind like a clue. She vanishes beneath the bed with her prize. My eyes fall to the scrap left in my hand: *Take Control*, the bold headline shouts. A motivational speaker's mantra from a talk I'd ignored weeks ago.

I sigh, my gaze drifting to the blank space on the wall where my TV once hung, now just an empty canvas of nothing. I chew the last bite of my grilled cheese, the music pounding, repetitive, almost too much now. It's not helping.

I scroll for something else, something *different*. The first thing that pops up: Ludovico Einaudi. *A Fuoco*. I don't even know how to pronounce it. But I hit play.

The first notes of the piano spill out, soft and deliberate, like a whisper in a quiet room. The rhythm soothes something raw in me. The chaos fades, replaced by a strange, gentle stillness. My mind drifts again, but this time not to the past.

I'm in a car, sleek and quiet, gliding through city streets under the cover of night. Lights flicker past, windows sealed, the world outside blurred and silent. The music is the road, and I follow, aimless and at peace. I'm moving, but for once, not running.

Is this what meditation feels like? This stillness, this space where nothing matters?

For the first time in a long while, I just *am*.

I wonder why I can't stay here—why I'm always clawing, always pushing. Work, stress, noise. It's always about the bills, about survival.

They say, "Money doesn't buy happiness."

Bullshit.

That's just something people with money say to make the rest of us feel better.

I bend down, pick up the entertainment section from the floor, and tear carefully around the words that seem to speak louder than anything else in the room—*Take Control.* I place the rough-edged fragment in front of my empty bowl of tomato soup, letting the bold print stare back at me, daring me to act.

From my back pocket, I pull out the folded report, its creases softened from being carried, considered. Mr. Martinez's name sits there, waiting.

Maybe it's time I paid him a little visit.

(Saturday – 12:10 AM)

Milwaukee's night air is sharp, cutting straight through the layers of my coat like icy needles. I hunch forward, teeth clenched, as the cold settles deep in my bones. Old Blue groans along the narrow streets of the Eastside, her heater refusing to kick in, the windows fogging with each breath I exhale. I wipe the glass with the back of my hand, squinting through the mist, careful not to scrape the parked cars that line both sides of this tight one-way corridor.

Every few feet, I tap the heater's dial, willing it to life. Nothing.

The streetlights flicker overhead, casting long, crooked shadows on the pavement. My hands grip the wheel tighter. I remember his voice—*don't come near my garage.*

That's exactly where I need to look.

People always reveal too much when they're angry, when you let them talk. During that pause, that silence we're trained to give them, they vent, and their secrets spill. Mr. Martinez gave me more than he meant to, just like so many others. All I had to do was listen.

My GPS guides me to his street, and I slow as I reach the house. It's dark, still. No signs of life from within. Good.

I roll past, taking the corner slow, easing into the alley that slices through the block. The air feels heavier here, close. Garbage bins loom like silent sentries, their lids askew, trash scattered at their feet. I navigate Old Blue through the debris, tires crunching softly over bits of paper and glass.

Then, like something out of a dream, I see it.

Parked beside the garage, not hidden, not protected—just *there.* The green Ford Taurus gleams under a weak alley light, polished to a shine that almost mocks me. My heart thuds once, hard. This is it. The car he's trying to keep, the one he dared me to touch.

And it's just sitting there, waiting.

The heater in Old Blue finally sputters to life, blasting a wave of warmth across my face. I crank it up, letting the heat fill the cabin, thawing my numb fingers, steadying my breath. I stay there for a moment, watching the car, the way it gleams like an emerald dropped in the dirt.

He loves this car. Keeps it spotless, waxed, as if it's something sacred.

I pull closer, slow and deliberate, until I'm just a few feet away.

From my coat pocket, I pull the small stack of business cards, bound together with an old rubber band. I peel one free, running my thumb over the embossed letters. This is all it takes. One card. One reminder.

If I leave this on his windshield, he'll know—we're watching. And next time, it won't just be a card.

I scan the alley, eyes flicking to every window, every shadow. Nothing moves.

The air outside hits me like a slap when I open the door. I ease it shut behind me, careful not to make a sound. The latch clicks softly, not locked, just enough.

No need for noise.

No need for witnesses.

As I round the back of my truck, a flicker of movement catches my eye—a dim glow from the rear window of his house. Soft and brief, the light pulses in the kitchen, then vanishes. Maybe it was just the refrigerator door. Still, curiosity gnaws at me.

I can't help myself.

Stepping lightly, I creep through his overgrown backyard, the grass damp and wild against my legs. The night air feels thicker here, closer to the house. My breath slows, heart thudding in my ears as I near the window. Carefully, I rise just enough to peer over the sill, my glasses slipping down my nose. I push them up with a finger, narrowing my eyes to get a clearer look inside.

There he is.

Mr. Martinez, his back to me, clad in loose red shorts and a dark blue t-shirt. Oblivious. Relaxed. I watch as he prepares a midnight snack with the care of a man who's done this a thousand times. He peels the red skin from thick slices of bologna, stacking them between plain white bread, a smear of mayo holding it together. His drink of choice—a Corona—sits open on the counter, catching the faintest glimmer of light.

I rise a little higher, curiosity pulling me forward like a hook.

Then, *bam*—a sudden face, inches from mine. His Chihuahua, eyes wild, teeth bared, launches at the window with a burst of furious yapping.

"Shit!" I hiss, dropping like a stone.

In my panic, I crash into the metal tools propped lazily against the house—rake, shovel, garden hoe—all clatter down, vanishing into the thick grass. The noise cuts through the still night like a gunshot.

Frozen, heart pounding, I crouch low, scanning for a way out.

A light snaps on.

The kitchen flares to life again, washing part of the yard in a harsh, yellow glow. I press myself tight against the cold siding, breath shallow, muscles tensed. His shadow moves across the window, stretching long over the grass, his head tilted—searching.

I slide along the wall, inching into a darker patch, eyes darting back. His silhouette is gone.

Now. *Now.*

I bolt, legs pumping through the yard—but the grass grabs at my feet, and I stumble, crashing hard over the fallen garden hoe.

Another light flares—the back door.

Locks rattle.

I scramble to my feet, the sting of grass and dirt on my palms, and sprint the last stretch to Old Blue, diving behind her rear tire, crouched low, heart hammering.

The door creaks open. Footsteps.

From my hiding spot, I watch him step out.

He's not what I expected.

Average build, but there's something solid in his stance. His hair, long and silver, almost white under the porch light, frames a full beard. He has that clean-cut biker look—someone who's lived, maybe fought, maybe won. He scans the yard, eyes sweeping past me, resting briefly on his car.

I glance toward my truck—my door's still ajar, keys dangling in the ignition. If I'm quick, I could make it. Just slide in and take off.

The screen door slams.

Gone.

Relief floods me, and I let my back rest against the wheel, chest heaving, mind racing.

This was a bad idea.

I let out a breath, half a chuckle, half a curse. Here I am—crouched behind my truck, hiding like a kid caught sneaking out.

Screw it.

I'm dropping the damn card and getting the hell out of here.

I rise, brushing the dirt and panic from my clothes, heart still racing from the near miss. My hand reaches for the door of Old Blue, the cold metal grounding me, steadying me for just a moment.

But then—*crack!*

In the shimmer of the side mirror, I catch it—Mr. Martinez, shovel in hand, mid-swing, fury etched into every line of his face.

Instinct takes over.

I duck just as the shovel whistles past, slamming into the frame of my door with a thunderous clang. Glass shudders. Metal groans. I fall hard to my back, the wind knocked clean from my chest.

He's above me now.

Before I can scramble, the shovel's blade stabs into the ground inches from my face, throwing up clods of dirt and debris. His eyes gleam down at me, wild, lit with something feral.

"You drop something?" he sneers, holding up my stack of business cards. With a flick of his wrist, they rain down over me like a twisted confetti.

My heart pounds against my ribs, furious, panicked. His smile fades, twisted into a grimace, jaw clenched so tight I can see the cords in his neck.

Both hands grip the shovel handle.

He raises it high. No hesitation.

The flat side crashes down like a hammer, just missing my head as I roll, scraping myself beneath the truck. Sparks explode as the shovel grinds across the concrete, loud and sharp.

He drops to one knee, jabbing and swinging under the truck, shards of rock and sparks slicing toward my face, stinging my eyes, burning my skin.

I blink, blinded, heart roaring in my ears. I hear him shift, his boots scraping the ground, circling to cut me off.

"Come out from under there, motherfucker—so I can cut your balls off like I promised."

Another jab. The dull edge of the blade smacks into my ribs, the pain white-hot, sharp.

Gasping, I clutch my side, rolling desperately. I slip out from beneath the truck, forcing my body upright despite the stabbing ache. My hand lands on something solid—a brick, half-buried in the dirt.

I don't think. I *react*.

As he rounds the truck, I swing. Everything I have, everything I am, in that one blow.

The brick connects with the side of his face. A sickening thud.

He drops, knees buckling, flopping onto his side in a heavy sprawl.

I stagger, clutching my side, the brick still in my hand, slick with dirt and sweat. I hover over him, watching his body twitch, then go still. The world narrows—just me and the sound of my breath, raw and ragged.

Nothing else.

The silence rushes in, thick and deafening.

I glance around, heart hammering, eyes searching the shadows for witnesses—anyone. But the night is mute. The alley offers no judgment, only the cold.

My shirt is torn, blood seeping from my side, staining the fabric. I yank open the door to my truck, grabbing my red pullover from behind the seat. The weight of it, the warmth, settles over me like a shield. I pull the hood up, trying to steady the storm inside.

Breathe.

Inhale.

Exhale.

Slower now.

I turn, eyes locking back on him—still unmoving, sprawled in the dirt.

What if I killed him? What if I didn't? What if he wakes up and calls the cops?

I stand over him, heart pounding, head spinning.

What do I do now?

Endless questions spin in my head, looping faster with every breath. My hands, shaky, reach for his neck. I press two fingers gently to his throat, half-expecting the worst—but there it is. The pulse, strong and steady, throbbing beneath my touch. A shuddering breath escapes me.

Relief.

He's alive.

If he calls the cops—hell, if I call them first—this could still play out in my favor. It's self-defense, right? I wasn't here to hurt him. Just a business card. Just a message.

Maybe if I call it in... get ahead of it...

But before I can weigh that thought, a low rumble cuts through the night—the sudden growl of an engine behind me. I jerk my hand back as red light spills into the alley, harsh and accusing. The dark brown garage door behind us creaks open, yawning wide. Tail lights flash brighter, casting me and Martinez in an eerie red hue. Then the cold white of reverse lights snap on, flooding the alley like a stage, spotlighting my crouched form.

Shit.

No time to think. My hands seize his shirt, the fabric rough against my palms. I drag him, his dead weight heavier than I imagined, scraping across the ground as I haul him into the shadowed sanctuary of the backyard.

The car inches closer, breaking through its own cloud of exhaust. It noses toward the back of my truck, pausing, confused.

The driver throws it into park.

The door slams open, and a figure steps out—a young guy, face twisted in frustration. His eyes sweep the alley, land on my truck, then flick toward me. I freeze, hunched low over Martinez like a predator caught in the act, heart pounding so loud it deafens me.

But he doesn't come closer.

His gaze lingers, uncertain, then breaks away. He mutters something I can't hear and climbs back into his car. Slowly, carefully, he maneuvers out. His headlights pull away, shrinking, then vanish.

I let out a long, shaky breath, almost laughing.

But then—

A gasp.

I glance down—and Martinez is awake.

His eyes, wild with pain, lock on mine as his hand shoots up, gripping the front of my pullover with surprising strength. He pulls himself halfway upright, a desperate growl rumbling in his throat. I stagger, trying to shake him loose, but he clings, dragging himself with me. I haul him another foot, panic rising, then swing—once, twice—fists crashing into his face.

He drops.

Blood explodes from his mouth, hot and thick, splattering across my face, my glasses. I stumble back, wiping at the sting in my eyes. He blinks up at me, dazed, but alive.

Then—something shifts.

His eyes bulge, wide with sudden terror. His hands flail, clawing at my legs, grasping for something I can't see. He's choking, gasping, trying to speak but only blood comes out.

What the hell?

I step closer—and that's when I see it.

The rake.

Hidden in the long grass, the same rake I'd knocked over earlier. Its rusted metal teeth now driven deep into the back of his neck, curved prongs wedged near the base of his skull. The handle juts into the air, trembling slightly, like it too can't believe what's happened.

I watch, frozen.

He thrashes, weakly now, blood bubbling from his lips, fear flooding his face. He looks at me—*pleading*.

But there's nothing to be done.

He knows it. I know it.

This is the end. And I can't look away.

I wipe the blood from my glasses, using the inside of my pullover, careful, almost methodical. The smear clears just enough for me to see again, the world sharpening back into focus. I slip them back onto my face and kneel beside him, closer now, drawn in by something I don't fully understand.

I want to see. *All* of it.

His fingers twitch, weakly grasping at my shirt as I lean in. More blood gurgles from his lips, bubbling, spitting in erratic bursts. His grip, once fierce, fades with every shallow breath. The air is thick with iron and something else—something final.

Behind me, the high-pitched yapping of his little dog pierces the night, desperate and useless, muffled behind the screen door. But it's distant now, like everything else.

My mind slips.

I'm not here—not completely.

I'm in Grandpa's backyard, the air warm, heavy with the scent of cut grass and oil from old tools. My father's hands guide mine, both of us holding the worn stock of the BB gun we found in the garage. A rusted thing, but still working.

We laugh at first, shooting cans, watching them dance.

Then—a dove.

Perched, still, curious.

I pull the trigger.

The crack of the shot, the flash of movement. It falls.

But it's not dead.

It writhes, flopping helplessly in the grass, a small, pitiful thing with wild eyes and trembling wings.

"Put it out of its misery, son," my father says, pushing the barrel of the gun back into my hands, aiming it at the bird's bloodied head.

"But it's still alive, Daddy!" I cry, pulling away, horror settling deep in my chest. "We shouldn't have done it!"

"What's done is done," he growls, his voice hard. "The bird is dying—so end its suffering!"

I can't.

I drop the gun, the weight of it too much.

Disgusted, he snatches it up, takes aim, and fires.

The flopping stops.

He turns on me, eyes fierce, thrusting the gun into my chest. "If you're gonna do something, follow through. Take ownership. Finish the job."

I blink, pulled back to now—to Martinez.

His breaths are ragged, short. He's fading, yet still clinging, his hand trembling against my chest. The rake handle rises from his neck like a twisted flagpole, slick with sweat, with blood.

My fingers find the wood, sliding up its length, slow and sure, until they wrap around it tight.

He knows.

He *knows*.

His hand tightens, weakly, desperate. I slap it away, rising over him.

"All you had to do was pay for your car," I murmur, almost a whisper. "Now, look at you."

He stares up, eyes wide, glossed over but aware. I don't look away.

"Believe it or not, it wasn't supposed to be like this," I say, my voice steady, almost calm. "Doing this wasn't my intention. *This* is your fault—your fault that I'm here, your fault that we fought..."

I glance at my hand, gripping the handle tighter.

"And your fault that I have to follow through."

My pulse drums in my ears as I shift my weight, leaning in, pressing down with everything I have. The wood creaks, resisting, until the metal teeth tear through, bursting forward, breaking flesh and sinew. They pierce up through his throat, glinting faintly in the darkness.

His hands shoot up, fingers stretched wide, then curl—slow, tight, clawing at the air.

His legs jerk, stiffening, quivering.

Then still.

The flopping stops.

(12:52 AM)

I stare down at him—at what's left of him.

The barking, once just a dull echo, sharpens in my ears, piercing through the haze. It gnaws at me, tethering me back to the present. Back to this mess.

To my surprise, I feel... calm. Not numb, not panicked—just eerily, disturbingly calm.

I lift my hands, slick with blood, my palms open like I'm waiting for something to fall from the sky. The blood glistens dark in the moonlight, painting my skin in shades of red I never imagined. I kneel, wiping them against the tall, cold grass, the blades bending beneath the weight of this sin, this stain.

"What now, Thorpe?" I mutter to no one but myself.

No answers. Just silence, save for that damn dog.

I'm not a killer.

At least, I wasn't—until now.

My legs want to run, my body screams to get out of here, but my mind—my mind won't let me. I've seen too many crime shows, too many damn documentaries. *Leave it like this, and you'll be in cuffs by morning.*

Cover your tracks. That's rule number one.

First, the body.

But where? How?

A bloody mess sprawled out before me, soaking into the grass like spilled wine, and I'm standing in it, drowning in it.

Prison isn't an option.

I grip the rake handle, fingers tight around the slick wood, and drag him—heavy, limp—into the shadow by the fence. Out of sight, for now.

But I can't think straight. Not with that yapping. That shrill, frantic barking slicing through the quiet, calling out into the night like an alarm.

Change of plans.

First step—silence the noise.

I move toward the screen door, the dog's growls intensifying with every step. He senses me. Senses the blood. Senses the change.

Maybe I'll just let him go. He didn't ask for this. Just doing what dogs do—protect. Small dogs like this, they're all bark, no bite. Most run when faced with something bigger.

I crack the door.

He lunges.

Teeth snap into my pant leg, gnashing and pulling like he's trying to tear me apart. His little body shakes with rage, eyes wild.

"Son of a—"

I reach for his collar—*snap!*—he nips my finger, sharp, quick. Blood beads immediately.

He lunges again, but this time, I'm ready. I slam the door on him, trapping his squirming body between the frame and the weight of my foot. His yelps pierce the air, high and frantic.

Neighbors will hear.

I flip the back lights off.

My hand clamps around the scruff of his neck, lifting him like a soaked rag. He squirms, growls, but he's mine now.

The door clicks shut behind me as I carry him up the stairs, his tiny legs kicking, claws scrabbling.

"You see what you did, you little shit?" I hiss, holding him close, showing him my bloody finger. He snaps at it again, teeth bared.

The kitchen reeks—stale cigarettes, rotten trash, and something fouler underneath. My nose curls at the piles of dog crap scattered across the corner of the floor, dried and crusted like dirty little monuments. Some fresher, glistening, others pale and cracked like frostbitten earth.

Disgusted, I scan for a place to put him. Somewhere to shut him up.

The microwave gleams in the dim light, chrome and cold.

Without thinking, I shove him inside. His teeth catch my wrist—*again*—before I slam the door shut.

"Little shit—you're gonna pay for that."

The silence is instant, save for the frantic scratching from inside the metal box.

I grab a stiff, stained dishrag from the faucet, wetting it just enough to wipe the blood from my hands, from the tiny punctures along my wrist.

The dog doesn't bark now.

He just scratches.

Now that the first problem is contained—muzzled inside its gleaming metal coffin—I turn back to the real mess, the one lying in the dark, waiting for me.

The gravity of it pulls at me, heavy and relentless.

I move quickly, searching the house, opening closets until I find something useful—a dark brown blanket, thick and coarse, folded neatly as if it had been waiting for this very moment. Clutching it in one hand, I return to the kitchen, wiping the damp cloth over the microwave handle with mechanical precision. Small, deliberate circles, until I'm satisfied it bears no trace of me.

Then, I glance at the timer.

I turn the dial—*five minutes.*

My finger lingers a second longer, then presses *start.*

The microwave hums to life. I twiddle my fingers, slow, a mock good-bye to the frantic scratching within. The noise softens, fades, becomes part of the background.

There's no time to dwell.

I head outside.

The night air bites at my skin, sobering me, pushing me forward. The blanket unfurls in the bed of my truck like a burial shroud. I move fast, lifting his body—awkward, heavy, still warm—and lay him on the coarse fabric. The blood seeps through as I wrap him tight, pulling the edges together, cocooning him in dark wool.

No face. No form. Just weight now.

I don't stop.

The hose sputters, then comes alive in my hands, spraying a thin arc of water over the grass. The dark stains swirl, mixing with dirt, vanishing into the thirsty soil. I scrub with my boots, watching the red smear into mud, watching it sink.

Gone. Almost.

The garden rake lies abandoned, forgotten for a moment, until I grab it and fling it into the truck bed, landing with a dull *thud* beside him. Metal against metal, final and unforgiving.

I reach for the cab door and pull it shut, wincing as it groans and squeals like it's protesting, like it knows. The sound echoes down the alley, louder than I'd hoped.

Then—*boom.*

A muffled pop from inside the house.

Chapter 7

STICKS AND STONES

(2:36 AM)

I've been driving for what feels like hours—endless loops through the shadowed streets of downtown Milwaukee, circling like a vulture with no place to land. One hundred laps, maybe more. My mind churns, restless, scraping for an answer, a plan, anything.

The body in the back feels heavier with every mile.

Every squad car I pass seems to see *through* me—eyes behind glass, lingering too long. Parked in lots, crawling through intersections, idling just close enough to make my skin crawl. I swear I can feel their suspicion pulsing in my rearview.

I can't keep drifting like this.

I pull into a nearly deserted Pick 'n Save grocery store parking lot, tucked in the sleepy shadow of a local college campus. The lot is empty, save for a few scattered cars, forgotten under flickering lights. I kill the engine, resting my forehead on the steering wheel.

The lake?

No. Too risky. If they found him, and they *would*, forensics would peel me open like a book. They always find something—a stray hair, a fiber, a trace of sweat. This isn't the old days. You can't just toss someone in the water and expect them to vanish.

Not anymore.

I need something smarter.

Something final.

Across the street, movement catches my eye.

A garbage truck.

I watch as a trash man leaps from the back, latches onto a green dumpster, and tips it into the maw of the massive white beast. The tailgate lifts, grinding forward, crushing whatever's inside into compacted oblivion.

A slow smile creeps across my face.

(3:47 AM)

The sky is still dark, heavy with the last hours of night. I stand at the back door of Gram's house, pounding harder than I should. My breath mists in the chill, rising like smoke. I glance over my shoulder at the truck, at what waits inside, wrapped and silent.

The porch light flicks on, yellow and soft.

"Yes?" Her voice, groggy, thin.

"It's me, Gram."

A pause, then the sound of her clearing her throat.

"Oh! Hi Suga! Let me get the door," she says, warmth in her voice now. I hear the familiar clatter of deadbolts, one by one, then the old hinges groan as she opens the door wide. Her robe hangs loose, her gray hair in soft waves around her shoulders.

"If I'd known you were coming, I would've made you some sausage and eggs or something," she smiles, stepping aside. "You know you gotta eat."

"I know, Gram, but it's okay. It's way too early for you to be up cooking. I'm sorry I woke you. Just wanted to get an early start, get some things done."

She pulls me into a hug, and despite her age, her arms still have that familiar strength. My back cracks under the pressure of her embrace, grounding me for a moment.

"Come on in before we both catch a cold," she says, shuffling inside. "I got my robe, but couldn't find my slippers. This tile is so cold," she laughs.

I glance one last time at the truck, the quiet yard, the gravel driveway that leads nowhere. No sidewalks, no neighbors peering through curtains. Just trees and dark fields. Safe.

"I wanted to get started on that shelter today, if that's okay," I say, closing the door tight behind me.

She nods, already turning toward the kitchen.

"You don't have to work today?"

"No, Gram. It's Saturday. I usually only work Monday through Friday. I got nothing planned this weekend so..."

"Oh, okay, go ahead, honey. I'll get something on the stove for you."

"Gram, I'm serious, I'm not hungry at all." My voice is low, but firm, weighted with exhaustion. "I really don't have much of an appetite, so please—don't bother with that. Just go back to bed and get some rest. I honestly didn't want to wake you, but I don't have a key to get in."

She shakes her head, already shuffling toward the kitchen, her robe trailing behind like a cape. "Stubborn like your Grandpa," she says, her voice laced with warm amusement. "He always fought with me too, telling me to get some rest. But the second he smelled that sausage cooking, his attitude changed quick. He'd be right over my shoulder, sniffing around, asking how long before the food was done, drooling like a hungry wolf." She chuckles, that familiar sound, light as wind chimes. "Yeah... you wait till you smell the food, you'll eat."

She disappears into the bathroom, her bare feet slapping softly against the cold tile.

"Well, there my slippers are. I just don't remember putting them in here." A pause, then, "Baby, can you put my CD in the player for me? You know the one."

"Yes, Ma'am."

Of course I know the one. It's the only CD she owns. She plays it every day, like clockwork—while she cooks, while she knits or rocks in her chair by the front window, Grandpa's picture resting in her lap. If it's not that CD, it's some dusty old western flick humming from the little TV in her bedroom, her Bible and crossword puzzles never far from reach.

I gave her that CD for her birthday, after Grandpa passed. Edith Piaf. *La Vie en Rose.* The Little Sparrow. I didn't know who she was at first, but Gram told me about their first date, how they danced in the kitchen to her voice, falling in love one note at a time. After I did my homework, tracked it down, wrapped it in blue paper with a ribbon, it became the best gift I ever gave her.

I still remember her eyes welling with tears when she opened it—only for me to realize, in my oversight, she didn't even own a CD player. That was quickly remedied. She got two gifts from me that day.

Even now, before I've pressed play, I can hear her humming from the bathroom, catching the notes of that first song before it even begins. A tune stitched into her bones.

I slide the CD into the player, fingers pausing over the button, letting the moment breathe.

"Where is the wood chipper, Gram?" I call out, just as my thumb presses *play*.

"It's in that shed somewhere. You'll have to dig through all your granddad's stuff to get to it, sweetie." Her voice floats back, muffled by the door. "He was trying to fix it before he passed, but with his arthritis, he couldn't do too much with it. Got a big pile of sticks he was gonna get rid of in the back, that I can't do anything with now. It's there somewhere."

She pauses, then adds, "The key is under that rock by the wagon wheel."

The shed looms ahead of me like a forgotten memory—a small red barn with fading white trim, weathered but still standing proud. The tall shrubs behind it stretch like sentinels, separating her little world from the empty fields that roll beyond.

Next to the shed, just as she said, lies the pile.

A towering heap of sticks and branches, almost as tall as I am, sprawling wide, casting jagged shadows across the patchy ground. The remnants of the old tree Grandpa swore he'd tame. Most of it had warmed the house or the fire pit, but what remained lay here—lifeless wood suffocating the earth beneath, robbing the grass of sun, leaving it dry, brittle, dead.

I kneel, brushing aside the dirt-streaked rock by the wagon wheel, and find the key—cold and rusted in my hand.

I glance back at the house.

Piaf's voice drifts out through the walls, soft and haunting, the melody curling through the still morning air.

La Vie en Rose.

When I lift the rock by the shed door to grab the key, a monster of a spider—thick-legged and fast as hell—bursts from beneath it, darting towards a gap under the door like it's been waiting for this moment. My skin crawls as I watch it vanish, slipping into the darkness ahead of me. God knows what else is hiding in that shed. It's been sitting out here for years, left to rot and fill with creatures like the one that just skittered inside.

The doors groan as I pull them open, a puff of stale, musty air hitting me in the face, thick with the scent of old wood, rust, and time. A tangled wall of spider webs greets me first, clinging to my arms and face as I push through, the sticky strands catching in my hair. Behind them, a five-foot tall mountain of forgotten relics waits, coated in dust, the shadows playing tricks on the shapes. Piles of junk, broken dreams, and rusted-out projects loom.

My old bike, its chain snapped and a pedal missing, leans against Gram's sewing machine—another casualty of good intentions never finished. Tools, wires, scraps—each piece a testament to things my Grandpa once promised to fix, but never could.

There was nothing he couldn't repair, back when he was himself. Cars, furniture, radios—it didn't matter. His hands were magic, rough and scarred, but they knew the language of machines. He'd spend hours in here, swearing softly under his breath, busting his knuckles to breathe life back into dead things. But when Alzheimer's took hold, it stole those hands from him, one day at a time. It stripped away the man I knew—the craftsman, the teacher—until he became a silent shadow in front of the TV, staring at nothing.

God, I miss him.

Near the back of the shed, something glints faintly—like the last hand of a drowning man reaching out from under a sea of wreckage. The discharge spout of the wood chipper. It juts up from the pile, half-buried but unmistakable. My arms hang at my sides, heavy with the weight of dread. The thought of dragging that beast free, not even knowing if it'll run, nearly makes me turn back.

But I can't.

This is the only way.

(4:40 AM)

It takes nearly an hour—sixty long, breathless minutes of dragging, lifting, shoving—to clear a path through the chaos. The cold bites at my fingers, stinging with each piece I move. When I finally wrestle the crippled wood chipper into the open, I'm covered in dust and cobwebs, sweat soaking through my shirt despite the chill.

I stumble, knocking over an old rusted toolbox. The clang echoes in the stillness, tools spilling across the floor like a metal flood. Weathered screwdrivers, a busted pipe wrench, bits of scrap. But one thing catches my eye—the dull glint of something familiar.

An old blade, rough and dark, its handle still shaped from the head of a railroad spike.

Grandpa's.

I remember watching him, eyes wide, as he stood over the charcoal grill in the yard, tongs in one hand, hammer in the other. He'd work the metal, glowing orange in the coals, shaping it with steady blows. The flat of the spike would stretch into a blade, rough at first, then smoothed, sharpened, polished to shine like silver in the sun.

I pick it up, run my thumb along the edge, then wipe it down with a damp rag. The steel gleams beneath the grime. I find his old sharpening stone, add a little oil, and run the blade over it slowly. Back and forth. The sound is familiar, grounding. By the time I'm done, it hums in my hand like it remembers its purpose.

There's barely any light, but I don't have time to waste.

"First things first," Grandpa's voice echoes in my head. "Look for loose parts, oil leaks, broken hoses."

Right away, I see it—a fuel line hanging free. I reconnect it, fingers trembling, then spray the carb cleaner across the caked grime and rusted joints. The cleaner hisses, cutting through years of filth. I grip the pull cord, yank hard, and nothing. I adjust the choke, try again. And again. Twenty pulls, maybe more. My arm aches. My breath fogs the air.

Then, finally—it sputters.

The engine coughs, then chokes, then roars to life in a plume of white smoke.

I stand next to the rumbling beast, watching as it coughs out years of dust and decay, clearing its throat like an old man waking from a long sleep. My hands find their place on my hips, and for a fleeting second, I feel like a hero—like Grandpa when he'd finished a job he thought impossible. That quiet pride, the euphoria he used to call it, rises in my chest, warm and fleeting.

But I don't have time to stand here and soak in it. Not today.

I've got to finish this before Gram decides to come poking her head out, wondering why I'm still out here fiddling in the cold. I jog to the truck, climb in, and ease it slowly down the gravel drive. The tires crunch beneath me, each dip and rise of the earth making the truck shudder. As I glance into the rearview mirror, my eyes catch the lump in the bed, wrapped tight, unmoving. The blanket has shifted, ever so slightly, enough to make the shape of him more defined.

My stickman emblem swings wildly, catching light from the early dawn, a silver blur with each bump I roll over. I can't tear my eyes away from it as I park near the chipper, heart pounding, mind racing.

Then something catches my eye—a dark, slick puddle spreading on the driveway where the truck had been moments ago. Thick, almost black in the dim light, and glistening. It wasn't there before. My gut twists. It has to be blood. It must've seeped through the old rusted bed, spilling out onto Gram's driveway like an accusation.

Panic surges through me. I jump out, nearly slipping, and dash for the garden hose. My fingers fumble at the spout, cranking the old handle hard. Nothing. Just a dry hiss. My breath catches in my throat as I twist it again, harder.

A few pitiful drops fall onto the pavement, like the last grains of sand in an hourglass.

"Fuck!" I shout, my voice splitting the quiet morning air.

A gasp behind me stops me cold.

The slow, heavy creak of footsteps on old floorboards echoes above. Then the window, that damned squeaky window, groans open. I freeze, eyes wide, heart thudding in my chest like a trapped bird.

"Thomas Thorpe!" Gram's voice, sharp and fierce as ever, cuts through the air like a lash. "You watch your mouth, young man! You're not too old that I won't put a wooden spoon to your butt!"

"Yes, Gram, sorry," I call up, voice strained but respectful.

I don't breathe for a long second, waiting, praying she won't lean any further out, won't see the mess in the driveway or the mess in the back of my truck. Her sight's not what it used to be, thank God. The screen door slams shut, and I hear her shuffle away, her slippers slapping the floor.

I exhale, the weight of it nearly doubling me over. Think, Thorpe, think.

The hose. I shut it off for the winter, didn't I? To keep the pipes from freezing. I clench my fists, cursing myself, then climb back into the truck and park it right over the puddle, hoping to hide the evidence just a little longer.

From the pile of sticks, I grab a few thick branches, tossing them into the bed of the truck, covering the body the best I can. It looks rough, rushed, but it's better than nothing.

I head to the basement, the old wooden steps groaning beneath my feet. I grab the step stool, dragging it beneath the spigot. My hands are trembling as I twist the valve, and suddenly, I hear it—the hose outside jerking violently, sputtering to life.

"Ah! Thomas!" Gram's voice pierces the silence, sharp with alarm. My heart stops.

I nearly tumble off the stool, the blood draining from my face. She's found it. She's seen everything.

No—no, not like this.

I take the stairs three at a time, breath ragged, pulse hammering in my ears. I throw open the basement door—and there she is, standing in the doorway, soaked from head to toe, her robe clinging to her frail frame. She's holding a plate of food, scrambled eggs and sausage, the smell of it somehow cutting through the chaos like a blade. Her slippers squish with each shift of her weight, and the garden hose snakes wildly behind her, spraying the yard like it's lost its mind.

"If you didn't want breakfast, all you had to do was say so," she says, her voice trembling—not from fear, but from the cold. "Are you trying to kill your poor old Grandma?"

Her eyes, kind and tired, search mine. I nod, swallowing hard.

"No, Gram. I'm sorry."

"Oh my God, Gram, I'm sorry. I was just trying to—um," I stammer, my mind racing to pull together an excuse, something, anything to explain away the wild hose and her drenched frame. The truth, obviously, wouldn't do. "I needed the hose to rinse off the wood chipper—it's filthy."

I reach for her arm, instinctively wanting to guide her inside, to offer some small gesture of care. But she snaps her arm away from me like I'd stung her.

"I don't need your help—I'm perfectly capable—thank you," she snaps, sharp and proud. "You just hurry and finish so you can get some hot food in your system."

She squishes her way inside, slippers soaked, leaving behind a narrow, shimmering trail of water like some sad breadcrumb path. Her robe clings to her, dripping, and I feel that familiar weight of guilt, coiling tight in my chest.

I wrestle the hose into submission, its wild thrashing now reduced to a steady stream under my control. I flood the blood-stained gravel quickly, watching as crimson streaks thin and vanish into the dirt, leaving only the faintest blush of discoloration. Still, not good enough. I grab a shovel and scrape up loose gravel, spreading it thick over the damp spot until the driveway looks undisturbed, or at least, undetectable.

When I step back inside, Gram is already in the kitchen, dryer now, but still shivering. Another plate of food waits for me on the table, steam rising from it like a peace offering.

"Here you go, Suga. I hope that's enough."

"Yes, this is plenty, Gram. You really didn't have to."

"Nonsense," she replies, shaking her head, her teeth clicking softly like distant wind chimes. "Are you done now?"

I lean down and kiss her cheek, warm and soft against my lips. "Yes, Ma'am. I have to hurry though. I'll see you later, okay."

She watches me go, eyes tired but full of something that makes me hesitate at the door for a split second. But there's no turning back now.

Outside, I snap the latch of the wood chipper tight to the truck's hitch. Just as I'm about to shut the shed door, something catches my eye—Grandpa's silver hatchet, gleaming faintly from the cluttered shadows. Without thinking, I grab it and toss it into the bed with a dull thud.

***

(7:30 AM)

The early morning air clings to my skin, cool but not cold, and the sky glows faintly with the first light of day. I'm deep in Oak Creek now, the wooded bike trail beneath my tires crunching softly as I drive where I shouldn't. But here, in these parts, a man with a truck full of sticks and a trailing wood chipper doesn't raise eyebrows. Just another worker, clearing the trails, keeping nature tidy.

I veer off, finding a secluded nook by the water's edge. The creek rushes fast, churning with energy, free of ice. Perfect. I back the truck into position, the chipper's mouth aimed toward the flow, ready to swallow and send what's left downstream.

I strip the bed of the truck, tossing the sticks aside one by one, until only the blanketed form remains. He lies there, heavy and still. Grabbing his ankles, I pull. His body, lighter now, slides free from the truck and lands with a dull, muffled thump in the grass, still wrapped tightly. The blood's drained, taking some of his weight with it, leaving him almost... hollow.

I wipe my hands on my jeans, then grab the hatchet, its blade gleaming in the soft light. It's sharp—razor sharp—and will make quick work of what needs to be done. But first, I need to strip him bare. No sense hacking through layers of fabric, not when I need this to go smooth.

One by one, I peel away the blood-soaked clothes. The shirt, the shorts—they come off easy enough, stiff and damp in my hands. The last to go, his skivvies, I hesitate, grimacing. The sight of his lifeless body exposed to the morning light is enough to make bile rise in my throat, but I push it down. Can't run cloth through the chipper—not with elastic that might jam the blades.

I toss the garments into a black trash bag, cinching it tight. These will burn. Everything burns, eventually.

As I toss the bag of clothes aside, it lands with a dull thud in the tall grass, stirring up a faint cloud of dust and guilt. My eyes catch something brown just beneath where the clothes had been—his wallet, half open, waiting like a small trap for my conscience. I crouch down, wiping the sweat from my brow with the back of my hand before picking it up. The leather is worn but intact, soft in my grip. Inside, a photograph peeks out, catching the pale morning light.

A little girl, maybe six, clings to Mr. Martinez's back, her curly dark hair bouncing as she grins wide, eyes bright and full of trust. They're in a park, the sun shining down on them in happier times. His face is close to hers, cheek to cheek, smiling with a kind of ease that feels foreign to me now. I flip to the next photo—him again, feigning a choking expression as her tiny arms wrap tighter around his neck, both laughing. I slide the photo from its sheath, my fingertips trembling slightly. On the back, in the jagged scrawl of a child, it reads: *"Love you, Uncle Nemo."*

Something sharp tugs at the edge of my chest—remorse, maybe, or regret dressed in sorrow's clothes. My breath catches for just a second.

Then, I open the billfold.

Three crisp hundreds and four twenties sit neatly tucked in the wallet's folds. Enough to cover his car payment, enough to have spared me from standing here, covered in his blood, with his life seeping into the earth.

"Dumb fuck," I mutter under my breath, the sting of it snapping through me. I kick him hard in the ribs, the force jarring my leg, but giving no satisfaction. The cash finds its way into my pocket, smooth and cold against my thigh. My hand finds the hatchet next—solid, waiting.

I twirl it slowly, watching the light glint off its edge, now dulling with each breath I take. My eyes return to him, his naked body crumpled in the grass like discarded meat. All of this—every sickening moment—could've been avoided if he'd just paid. If he'd just shut up and let me leave that damn card.

But no, he had to fight. Had to run his mouth, threaten my job, my life. Now here he is—waiting to be chopped into digestible pieces, small enough for the chipper to consume.

I draw in a long breath, heavy with sweat and rot, then raise the hatchet high.

The blade slices through the air with a low hiss, thudding into flesh and bone. Blood arcs in a fine spray, speckling the grass and soaking into the earth. Over and over I swing, each blow splitting muscle, cracking bone, tearing him apart bit by bit. His arms first—shoulders to elbows, then elbows to hands. Each dismemberment jerks his body like a grotesque puppet, strings cut one by one.

The legs are worse—thicker, heavier. The blade resists now, dulled by the work, biting slower through the hips. I grunt, teeth clenched, sweat pouring into my eyes. Murder is not easy. It takes more than rage—it takes resolve.

The mess is worse than I imagined, blood pooling, tissue clinging to the grass. And time... time is slipping. The chipper's engine roars, a relentless beast, and I feed it quickly, desperate to silence the body, to erase him from this world. Bits of flesh, bone, sinew spray from the spout, caught in the current of the creek. The red mist settles on the water's surface, carried away like a secret.

The torso and head remain.

I kneel beside them, breath ragged, arms aching. His eyes are still open, glassy, staring through me—or at me. I place a hand over them, blocking out his gaze, pressing down until the lids close. My fingers tremble, but I reach for the hatchet again.

A few solid swings and the neck gives way, the head toppling free, rolling to rest on its side, mouth slightly open as if to speak.

I work quickly now, driven by instinct, by fear, by the strange calm that's overtaken me. The final pieces fall into the chipper, the machine snarling hungrily, spitting out what remains into the rushing creek. I stand, blood clinging to my hands, to my clothes, and stare at the head—the last remnant of Mr. Martinez—waiting.

What have I become?

Without daring to meet his eyes, I toss the head underhanded into the waiting mouth of the wood chipper. It spins through the air in a slow, deliberate arc, as if reluctant to meet its end. The head lands with a dull, fleshy thud, rolling lazily atop the grinder's teeth. It doesn't catch right away, just spins and wobbles like an unwelcome guest refusing to leave. I grab a thick piece of wood, and with one steady push, guide the last of my burden into the ravenous blades. A sickening crunch echoes out, followed by a fine mist that lingers too long in the air before being carried away by the creek.

———————

(9:54 AM)

I creep up to Gram's house, peeking through the side window like a stranger in my own skin. She's there, in her favorite chair, slouched and still, breathing deep in a slumber that seems untouched by time. Edith Piaf's voice floats through the air, soft and haunting, wrapping itself around her like a warm blanket while she dozes.

The back door gives easily under my hand, the old lock never turned. I move quickly, quietly, slipping inside with the trash bag slung over my shoulder—the bloodstained blanket, the clothes, the last remnants of what once was a man now gone. Each step on the basement stairs groans beneath my weight, as though they knew and didn't approve. I cringe, but Gram doesn't stir.

In the dim light of the basement, I find a dark corner and stash the bag there, behind a stack of old boxes and a broken chair. She never comes down here, not unless it's laundry day. For now, it's safe.

My eyes catch the small shower in the far corner—the one Grandpa started installing when he had big plans for this basement, before his body betrayed him. A man cave, he used to call it, smiling as he talked about pool tables, a bar, a place to breathe without Gram nagging at him. "The only place I can go poop in peace," he'd chuckle. But the stroke changed all that. After that, he hardly lifted a hammer again.

I flick the light switch in the bathroom. The bulb hums to life, casting a pale glow over dust-caked porcelain. Cobwebs string themselves from the ceiling to the corners, and everything smells of stale air and time long gone. I wipe the sink, toilet, and tub with a faded towel I find on the floor, stirring up the ghost of his efforts. The faucet coughs at first, then gives way to a stream of water, cold but steady.

Gratefully, I find clean towels in the dryer, soft and warm. I strip off my clothes—caked in blood and earth—and drop them in a heap. My eyes rise to the mirror. My reflection is a stranger, smeared with blood, haunted eyes hollow and dark. Red streaks cross my neck, my chin, ghostly fingerprints of a dying man. I stare, lost in the echo of his grasp, the weight of his last breath still clinging to me.

(10:31 AM)

Dressed now in Grandpa's old clothes, I step outside. His slacks hang too short, the fabric brushing just above my ankles, and the crotch rides high enough to make me wince. The khaki shirt is stiff and unfamiliar, carrying the faint scent of Old Spice and something deeper—something like him. I feel wrapped in his memory, and it presses heavy on my shoulders.

The fire pit calls to me, its embers still warm from the last time he lit it. I settle there, letting the heat lick at my skin, trying to find comfort in its flickering light. It's strange, wearing his clothes, walking in his steps. They don't fit, not just in size, but in spirit. I shift, trying to make peace with the tightness, with the weight of everything I've done.

I'm clean now, at least on the outside. But inside? I don't know.

The smaller, brittle sticks from the old pile catch fire with ease, crackling and snapping as they surrender to the flames. Soon, a fierce blaze rises before me, hungry and wild, sending waves of heat across my face.

I pull off my red pullover, its sleeves stiff with dried blood, and toss it into the fire. It lands with a hiss, the fabric curling in on itself as if recoiling from judgment. The flames devour it quickly, turning the evidence of my sin to smoke and ash. The hatchet is next, its worn wooden handle catching immediately, the flames licking up its length. The steel glows faintly, then brightens, red-hot and clean. I know it won't burn completely, but by the time I'm done, whatever it touched will be gone. When only the blade remains, I'll carry it to the lake and give it a final resting place in the deep.

(11:50 AM)

Inside, the world is quiet again.

Gram is still lost in sleep, her small frame curled gently in her chair, one hand resting on a faded photograph of her and Grandpa. Their smiles, frozen in time, radiate the kind of love that lasts beyond a lifetime. Her chest rises and falls slowly, peacefully, untouched by the storm that's raged in me.

I step softly across the room, careful not to wake her, and take her yellow knitted afghan from the back of the couch—the one she made herself, every loop and twist filled with care. I drape it over her shoulders, tucking it under her chin. Her lips part slightly, and she sighs, a quiet sound like the whisper of leaves.

Leaning in, I place a gentle kiss on her forehead, tasting the warmth of her skin, the innocence of her sleep. For a moment, everything stills.

The fire outside crackles faintly in the distance, and the air smells of ash and memories.

I stand there, watching over her, wishing I could borrow her peace for just a little longer.

CHaPTer 8

HOT STUFF

(12:43 PM)

When I finally pull into the lot and ease Old Blue into her usual spot, a heavy weariness settles over me like a thick blanket. I kill the engine, and for a long moment, I just sit there, slumped in the driver's seat, letting the silence soak into my bones. My lungs fill with a slow, deliberate breath, and I let it out through parted lips, tilting my head back against the worn headrest.

It's hard to believe it's already Saturday afternoon. The chaos of the night before still clings to me, like smoke in my clothes, refusing to let go. My body aches with a dull throb, and even the steady thrum of my heart feels like more work than it should.

Across the street, the neighborhood children are caught in their own carefree world, their laughter skipping through the air as they twist their ropes in rhythm, jumping and chanting, lost in that perfect simplicity I've long forgotten. The slap of rubber soles on pavement, the tick-tick-whip of the ropes—it all blends into a lullaby, a soft, distant hum.

Somewhere to my left, a plastic wheel rattles and roars, the unmistakable sound of a child's big wheel tearing down the sidewalk. That low, hollow rumble echoes in my head, dragging me backwards, further, until the weight of the present slips away.

My eyes flutter closed.

And just before sleep pulls me under, I drift into the memory of another time, another place, when life was smaller, and I was just a boy... riding that same familiar sound into the haze of childhood.

My orange flag whipped and snapped behind me, a blur in the wind as I flew down the concrete path in my Green Machine, the plastic wheels whining with every turn. I yanked at the long black handles, sending the back end fishtailing wildly, carving half-moons into the sidewalk. When I hit the corner, I'd slam on the brake, pull hard to one side, and spin in a tight one-eighty, the world tilting as the back end swung around. Then, without missing a beat, I'd launch myself in the opposite direction, the wind screaming in my ears, sugar rushing through my veins like jet fuel.

It was a Saturday, bright and warm, the kind that made everything feel endless. I was riding high on my fourth Rocket Popsicle, the last drips still sticky on my fingers, my blood practically glowing blue and red with syrupy energy. I was unstoppable.

From the porch of my parents' house, my audience watched—Grandpa, Dad, and Mom. I could hear the low hum of Grandpa's voice carrying on, probably in the middle of one of his wild stories, the kind I wasn't supposed to hear. Dad had his hand over his face, shaking his head like he always did when Grandpa went off the rails, but Mom? She was laughing so hard, she was clutching her side.

A few more laps and I was ready for the big show.

I'd seen the cinder blocks and that ragged piece of plywood near the neighbor's trash earlier, and now they called to me like a dare. Grabbing them, I set up my masterpiece: the blocks stacked tight, the plywood angled just so—my very own launch ramp.

I heard my Grandpa ask my Mother, who was still laughing, to go inside and get them some more beers. When I glanced back at them, my Grandpa and Dad were both smiling at me.

"You'd better get a move on," Grandpa said, pointing at the door behind him, as he drained the last of his beer and smiled at me, that crooked grin of his.

Perfect. They were watching now.

I straddled the Green Machine, rolled backward a few feet, then spun into position down the sidewalk. This was it. The moment. I had to make it count.

At the corner, I whipped into another one-eighty, facing the ramp, my heart pounding like a drum in my chest. In my mind, the front wheel spun like the tires of a race car, smoke curling from the tread, my little legs cranking faster and faster.

No helmet, no pads—nothing but my raw speed and the reckless courage that only a sugar-crazed six-year-old could possess.

The sidewalk cracks clicked beneath me, the sound speeding up as I tore over them, faster, faster, my body hunched low like a missile locked onto target.

Then Mom came back out, beers in hand, still smiling—until she saw the ramp. Her smile vanished, replaced by wide-eyed horror. She dropped the beers onto the porch with a clatter, her hands flying up as she bolted forward.

But I was already there.

The ramp loomed, and I hit it at full speed, the plywood flexing beneath me as I soared upward, my flag flapping madly behind. For a glorious, heart-stopping second, I flew.

My feet left the pedals, my legs kicking out wide. The front wheel kept rising, and I knew—too late—that this wasn't going to end the way I'd dreamed. My grin twisted into shock as gravity took hold. I let go of the handles, arms flailing out like wings that wouldn't catch the air.

The Green Machine vanished beneath me.

I crashed, hard, tailbone first onto the unforgiving concrete, the breath knocked clean out of me. I tumbled like a rag doll into the grass, ears ringing, world spinning. Somewhere behind me, I heard the plastic wheels clatter and the frame skid, then slam into a tree with a dull thud.

I lay there, the sky spinning above, wondering if I'd ever breathe again.

"Oh my God—oh my God, Tommy!" my mother cried, dropping to her knees beside me, her breath quick and panicked. Her hands, warm and trembling, hovered over my scraped palms, her eyes scanning my arms, my back, as if afraid to find something worse. Tiny pebbles clung stubbornly to the raw skin of my hands, embedded like little stingers, and she carefully brushed them away, her touch both gentle and frantic. She brought my hands to her lips, kissing them as if her love could seal the wounds.

"Why did you do that?" she whispered, her voice breaking, eyes wet. "You could've really hurt yourself, sweetie. I better get some peroxide—clean you up before this gets infected. Are you okay?" Her face was so close, her concern pressing down on me harder than the pain.

Before I could answer, Grandpa's gruff voice cut through her worry. "Aw, leave him alone, Allison!" he called out, strolling over from the porch with my dad in tow. His steps were slow, confident, like he'd seen it all before. "We all did stuff like that when we were young boys. It's all part of growing up. It'll make him a man one day."

"Yeah, if he survives," my mother shot back, her eyes narrowing, the corners of her mouth tight with anger. "That's just macho bullcrap. I can't believe you both just sat there and watched him do this. Why didn't you stop him?"

Dad crouched beside her, placing a steadying hand on her shoulder. "Baby, he'll be alright, don't worry," he said softly. "It's just a couple of scrapes." His voice had that calm edge, like he was trying to convince her of something he wasn't sure of himself. "Don't baby him."

"He's still a baby in my eyes," she said, her voice tender again, her eyes locking on mine, filled with love and frustration. She kissed my cheek, warm and soft. I couldn't hold it in anymore. The tears welled up and spilled over, hot and fast, as sobs shook my chest. The pain throbbed, but it wasn't the worst of it. What really ached was the humiliation—the crushing weight of what should've been my triumphant moment crumbling right there, in front of the two men I wanted most to impress.

"Aww, now look what ya done!" Grandpa barked, pointing at me with a huff of disapproval. "If you keep that type of crap up, Allison, you'll have the boy peeing glitter, shitting cupcakes, and farting rainbows before you know it."

Dad chuckled, shaking his head, then turned to me, scooping me up into his arms like I weighed nothing. "Come on—let's get you cleaned up, Mr. Evel Knievel," he said, carrying me towards the house.

And as I buried my face in his shoulder, I could still feel the sting—not just on my skin, but deep inside, where pride used to sit.

I'm jolted awake by the shriek of tires—rubber screaming against pavement. A flash of color catches my eye as a striped, multi-colored ball bounces out into the street, followed by a little girl darting after it, her tiny legs moving faster than fear. No adult rushes behind her, no panicked shout from a parent, just the silent gasp caught in my throat as the Buick barrels down.

I check my watch. 1:24 p.m.

Rubbing the sleep from my eyes, I scan the parking lot, cautious now, not of cars, but of eyes—watchful ones that might catch me in these ill-fitting remnants of my grandfather's closet. Satisfied the coast is clear, I clutch my backpack tightly against my chest and weave through the maze of parked cars like a fugitive dodging spotlights, heading straight for the back entrance of my apartment building.

The elevator greets me with a soft ding, its empty interior a small mercy. The hallway beyond is clear too, and I stride quickly, each step dragging these tight pants higher, sawing at me, wedging deeper into places I'd rather not think about. I move fast, each stride laced with discomfort, but fueled by hope that I'll make it to my door unseen.

And I almost do.

Just as I reach for my keys, they slip through my fingers and hit the carpet with a muffled thud. I curse under my breath, bending down swiftly to scoop them up before—

"Hi!" The voice behind me is warm, sweet—velvety. And perfectly timed to catch me bent at the waist, my bony ass shamelessly aimed in her direction.

I freeze for a beat, then slowly straighten, heart pounding, and turn to find her. The new neighbor. She's smoothing her dark hair into a ponytail, a few loose strands caressing her cheek. Her sleeveless crop top, a deep, rich purple, clings to her, just above the curve of her stomach. Jean shorts hug her hips, low enough to reveal that enticing V-shape that makes my mouth suddenly dry.

"Hey, umm... hi?" I manage, my voice betraying every ounce of awkwardness I feel.

"I'm your new neighbor, Tricia," she says with a smile, extending her hand like a peace offering.

I reach out, but the universe has one more jab to throw—my keys and backpack tumble from my arms again. I stoop to gather them, eyes landing on her perfectly painted purple toenails tapping lightly on the carpet in front of me.

Keys clutched, I rise, towering over her now. "I'm Tommy. Tommy Thorpe," I say, trying to sound composed as I take her hand, warm and small in mine.

"Well, hello Mr. Thorpe," she giggles, tilting her head. "You're awfully tall."

"Please, ju—just call me Tommy. All my friends do."

"Wow, you consider me a friend already? Careful, Mr. Thorpe."

"It's... never mind." I chuckle nervously. "Well, I hope you like it here. It was nice meeting you."

I turn, fumbling with the lock, desperate for escape.

"Wait—I was actually wondering if you could give me a hand. I have a fifty-five-inch flat screen that I can't get onto my TV stand alone. Would you mind lending me a hand?"

"No—not at all," I say, halfway behind my door now, peeking at her through the crack. "But if you don't mind giving me a few minutes?"

"Um, sure, that's fine. It won't take but a moment. I'd really appreciate it."

I nod, shut the door, and lean back against it, exhaling hard.

"You idiot. That was rude," I mutter, pressing the back of my head against the cool wood.

Tilly appears, slinking from the bedroom like a silent little judge. She plants herself in the center of the living room, rises onto her hind legs, and fixes me with a stare that speaks louder than words: Where the hell have you been?

"Oh crap, Tilly, I'm sorry," I say, dropping my backpack onto the floor. "Are you hungry, sweetie?"

I reach down, arms out, but she darts away, a flash of cream fur vanishing beneath the bed. Typical. I sigh, heading to the kitchen, grabbing her food dish, and filling it with dry kibble. The tiny clinks echo in the quiet room. No response.

Okay, plan B.

I grab the pack of Bandit Ferret treats from the cupboard, the crinkling sound enough to coax her most days. Kneeling beside the bed, I shake the bag gently, the treats rattling between my fingers like a peace offering. Her red eyes glint back at me from the shadows, unblinking.

"Come on, sweetie, I'm sorry. Will you forgive me?" I soften my voice, placing the bag just in view. "Look what I got for you."

She doesn't move, statuesque in defiance.

"Well, if you're not gonna come out, then I guess I'll just have to put these away," I say, slowly rising, retreating toward the door.

The rustle behind me is swift—her tiny feet scurrying out, standing tall on her hind legs, expectant.

"That's my girl." I smile, pouring a small handful of treats onto the carpet. She dives in eagerly, crunching away.

Now that the cold shoulder has thawed, I can turn to more pressing matters—like getting out of these clothes and lending a hand to my new neighbor before she recruits someone else. My stomach growls, a hollow ache reminding me I haven't eaten, but I ignore it, stepping into the closet.

Jeans, a plain white T-shirt—simple, safe. I reach for my shoes—

"Tilly, no!"

She's already snagged the last of her treats and vanished under the bed again, leaving behind a pair of once-white tennis shoes, now ragged and frayed, chewed at the edges like they'd been through a wood chipper.

(1:59 PM)

I knock lightly, just enough to be heard. Her door swings open almost instantly, and there she is again—Tricia, glowing, with a soft vanilla scent that wraps around me like a subtle charm.

"Hi again!" she says, her eyes flicking over my change of clothes, then down to my feet. "Oh my. What happened to your shoes?" She giggles, covering her mouth.

I glance down, the mangled sneakers glaring back at me. "It's my punishment for neglecting a certain friend."

"Looks like a rat got ahold of them."

"Close. My pet ferret."

Her face lights up. "You have a ferret? Oh my God, I love animals! They're so cute. I've thought about getting one, or maybe a guinea pig, but the smell's too much for me."

"There are things you can do to keep it under control. Honestly, they make great pets."

"Nice! You'll have to introduce me to your roommate someday," she says, flashing a smile that sends a ripple down my spine. "Oh, I'm sorry, come on in. You'll have to excuse the mess—I just moved in."

"Well, yeah."

I step inside, expecting the chaos of moving boxes. But her place is surprisingly neat—minimal boxes, but the walls are alive with bold, raw paintings. Nude figures, their bodies swathed in impossible shades of blue, red, orange. They seem to pulse with emotion, untamed and wild.

One painting in particular stops me—a striking blue, well-hung man, muscular and lean, holding the hands of a smaller green woman, her curves exaggerated, both of them unapologetically bare.

"Nice."

"You think so? Not many people do."

"No, I like it a lot," I say, still admiring the raw energy in the brush strokes. "Why are all the characters in your paintings different colors? Like... the colors of the rainbow?"

She steps closer, her arms folding loosely across her chest. "The colors of the rainbow are natural, just like us. But mostly, it's because I think color shouldn't matter. Skin, race... all of that. It's just a shell. And as you can see, I'm not really into clothing either." She smiles, half-playful, half-serious. "We should all be natural. The way God intended."

"I can understand that. But what about people who have, you know, defects, or body shapes, or skin conditions they don't want to show? Clothing gives them a chance to hide that, to feel... normal. Free from judgment."

"Maybe," she says with a shrug, brushing a loose strand of hair behind her ear. "I'm just saying—people who want to walk around naked should be able to, without being ridiculed. They do it on beaches in California, Europe... and think about it, no place to hide weapons, no massive bills for clothes." She laughs lightly, tapping her bare shoulder. "It's simpler."

"And what about winter?" I smirk.

She rolls her eyes dramatically and turns toward the TV stand. "Alright, philosopher—are you strong?"

"Define strong," I say, stretching my arms. "Because I haven't eaten all day, and I might just pass out right here."

"Oh God, don't mention food." She pats her flat stomach. "All I've got is ramen noodles and a loaf of bread. If I don't get groceries soon, I'll probably die of sodium overload."

I step closer. "How about a suggestion?"

She grins. "Lay it on me."

"After we tackle this big-ass flat screen, we order food. My treat."

"That sounds amazing. I haven't had Chinese in ages."

I hesitate, the memory of the Red Dragon delivery flashing in my mind. "Uh, yeah, about that... only one place delivers Chinese here."

"Oh, cool—let's call them."

"Actually... let's go with pizza?" I offer, hopeful.

She tilts her head, considering. "Eh, okay. I can do pizza."

"Awesome," I say, pulling out my phone. "POP?"

"Yep."

As I scroll through my contacts for Prince of Pizza, she leans on the TV stand. "So, what do you do? For work?"

"I'm an Account Manager at Easy Auto Acceptance Company."

She raises a brow. "That sounds... official."

"More like officially stressful."

She laughs softly, then sighs. "I'm a file clerk. Law firm. Or was. Might not be come Monday."

I glance up. "Why? What happened?"

She shifts her weight, the smile fading. "Got into it with this chick who's been riding me about how I dress. Too casual, too revealing, not 'professional' enough. I finally snapped and cursed her out. Right there. Clients and all."

"Damn."

"Yeah," she says, running her fingers along the edge of the stand. "Called off to move in here, and my friend tells me they were talking about firing me. She's been there forever, so they'll probably keep her."

"That sucks. Maybe they'll surprise you and dump her instead."

"Doubt it." She shrugs. "It's whatever. I've been talking to this guy about some... alternative work. Serious money. Not the nine-to-five grind."

I glance up, curious. "Yeah?"

"Yeah. His eyes are freaky—like ice blue. Almost too perfect. But he seems legit."

(3:03 PM)

I'm wedged tight between the wall and Tricia's TV stand, the last speaker wire pinched in my fingers, when a sharp knock echoes from her front door.

"Yes! Pizza time!" Tricia jumps up from her fold-out chair, nearly knocking it over in her excitement. "Give me the money; I'll get it."

I reach into my pocket and pull out a crumpled handful of bills—tainted spoils from Mr. Martinez. My fingers instinctively sort through them, my pulse ticking up as I spot faint red smudges staining the edges. Without a second thought, I swap out the bloodied bills for the cleaner ones and hand her a crisp twenty.

"Thanks. Did you want to tip the pizza guy?"

"Yeah, just give him the whole thing."

She beams and turns for the door. I can't help but watch her move, her hips swaying gently beneath her shorts, a soft rhythm to her step. As

Grandpa used to say, "She's got an ass that wiggles like stale Jell-O on a warm day." The thought almost makes me smile.

She exchanges the money with the delivery guy, rising up on her toes, her face lit with joy as she takes the steaming box and a bottle of root beer.

"Hot-hot-hot!" she laughs, rushing the pizza to the coffee table, fanning the box open. The scent of melted cheese and spiced meat hits the air, curling into my nostrils.

"How much was it?"

"Special—$9.99. Came out to $10.14 with tax."

"What?"

She giggles, tossing her hair over one shoulder. "The pizza dude looked like you just made his week. That was one hell of a tip. You could've bought another pizza."

"Guess I'm feeling generous today," I say, half-joking, as I tug myself free from behind the entertainment stand. "Alright, I think that's the last wire. Got a DVD? Let's give this setup a test run."

"I don't know where they are—still packed. Just grab something from your place?"

"Sure, easier than digging through boxes."

"Oh, and grab some plates too?"

I nod, leaving her door open as I slip across the hall to my apartment. I grab the first DVD I lay eyes on—"The Boogieman"—and snatch two mismatched plates from my cabinet. My place still reeks of smoke and stale memories, so I'm quick to head back.

When I step inside, she's focused on her phone, her brow furrowed, muttering curses under her breath. Her thumb freezes on the screen, and with an exasperated sigh, she tosses the phone onto the counter.

I take a step forward.

"Holy shit!" she gasps, clutching her chest. "What are you, a fucking ninja? You scared the crap out of me." She laughs, and I join her.

"Sorry. Here—plates." I hand them over and move to the TV. "I'll pop this in to check everything."

"What'd you bring?"

"Boogieman."

Her eyes light up, curiosity flickering. "Never seen it. Mind if we watch while we eat?"

I've been hoping she'd say that.

"I'm good with that."

———

(5:24 PM)

The pizza didn't stand a chance. Between the two of us, we polished it off, save for a few lonely crusts I'd tucked aside for Tilly. The room now hums with a soft, content silence, the kind that settles after a good meal and better company. Tricia is curled up beside me, cocooned beneath a blanket, her breathing slow and steady, her head resting lightly against my shoulder. She's completely out.

The movie fades into its credits, the flickering light painting the walls in shadows as the room grows dim. Her phone buzzes softly on the table, the screen flaring to life for a brief moment. My eyes catch it before it locks again.

"They've already cleared your desk. If you want, I can bring your stuff to you. Or they will leave it at the front desk with security. I'm so sorry."

I glance at her, still asleep, blissfully unaware. Her lips are slightly parted, her brow peaceful. Carefully, I shift, easing myself from the couch, doing my best not to disturb her. She stirs a little but doesn't wake.

At the kitchen counter, I find a marker. The pizza box is still open, the scent lingering in the air. I flip it closed and write in bold, simple strokes:

"Didn't want to wake you. Thanks for hanging out with me. Call if you need anything, anytime. Tommy 414-555-1777."

I set the box down gently, casting one last glance her way before slipping quietly out.

CHaPTer 9

SOUP OR SALAD

(Monday 2:37 AM)

I woke up in a way I hadn't in years—quiet inside my head. No screaming dreams. No sweat-soaked sheets clinging to me like a shroud. Just me and the low hum of silence.

Tilly was curled up tight against my side, her little nose jammed into the sweat-soaked hollow of my armpit. I peeled myself up slowly, my mouth dry as ash, my eyes crusted shut with sleep grit. I wiped at them with the heel of my hand and sat there for a moment, letting the darkness settle around me.

First thought in my head wasn't about the time, or work, or even what I'd done. It was her—Tricia. I hadn't heard a thing from her all Sunday, even though her door opened and slammed more times than I could count.

My body felt strange—well-rested but hollowed out. Like something important had been scooped out of me when I wasn't looking.

Still dark outside. No rush.

I grabbed my phone off the nightstand. Dead. Just a black slab. Figures. I tossed it on the charger and shuffled into the kitchen, my stomach gnawing at itself.

Two slices of stale bread, smeared with peanut butter thicker than I needed, folded in half and devoured in seconds. I rinsed it down with the last gulp of lukewarm milk, straight from the carton, like some feral animal.

Still wasn't enough.

Dragging my blanket from the bed, I collapsed onto the couch and let the TV flicker silently in the background. Just a little more sleep before reality came calling again.

(7:25 AM)

By morning, I was a ghost, moving on muscle memory. I gassed up Old Blue at the corner station, blinking against the grimy sunrise.

Mud caked every inch of the truck's undercarriage, slathered up the sides like dried blood after a long kill. Ten bucks more for the "Ultimate Wash." Small price for a clean conscience.

I pulled up to the car wash bay where some old-timer in a sun-bleached ball cap waved me forward with a half-smirk. His boots crunched on the concrete as he circled the truck, whistling low through his teeth.

Then he stopped, just out of sight.

"What did you kill?" he asked, appearing in my window like some goddamn ghost, hand out for my receipt.

My spine locked.

"What!?" I barked, voice cracking a little too sharp.

He chuckled, easy and slow. "That's a lot of blood back there, son. Buck, maybe? My old man used to clean his deer the same way. Little advice—throw a tarp down next time."

Relief tasted bitter on my tongue. I laughed it off, casual. "Oh—yeah, thanks. Appreciate that."

"She's a beauty," he added, stepping back. "With a little work, you could sell her for a pretty penny." He pantomimed counting bills, grinning like we shared some private joke. "Just roll onto the tracks, kick it into neutral. She'll be clean as new in no time."

"Thanks," I said again, hollow. "I'll remember."

The machine grabbed my tires and pulled me forward into the dark mouth of the wash.

Before the brushes started spinning, I glanced back over my shoulder—and there it was. Clear as day.

A dark, dried pool right in the center of the bed.

Panic cracked through me like a whip, but before I could think—before I could even move—the back window disappeared under a coat of pink, blue, and white soap.

Washing it away. Like it never happened at all.

(7:45 AM)

I sit tucked away in a booth at McDonald's, staring down at the unexpected blessing the cashier gifted me. I only paid for one sandwich, but somehow two ended up on my tray—nestled between my hash brown and the large orange juice sweating against the plastic. Hunger gnaws at my gut hard enough that my conscience doesn't stand a chance.

I tear open a ketchup packet and squeeze the thick red stream onto my sausage and egg biscuit, using the crumpled wrapper to smear it around. The sight triggers something deep and unsettling—reminds me too much of that scene by the creek. The hatchet. The splattered grass. My hands soaked and dripping.

I shake it off, replace the top half of the biscuit, and notice I've lost track of myself again. I've dumped way too much ketchup, drowning the sausage in blood-red. I stare for a second before biting deep into the sandwich anyway. It oozes from the sides, dripping onto the wax paper in slow, viscous blobs.

My phone vibrates harshly across the table, loud against the laminate. I lunge to catch it just as it's about to hit the floor.

"Good morning, Gram!" I say, forcing some cheer into my voice.

"Hi, Suga," she answers, her voice thin and frail.

A knot tightens in my gut. "Hey... what's wrong?"

"Nothing, I'm okay. Just... wanted to hear your voice."

I frown, glancing out the window at the orange-pink smear of sunset over the parking lot. "You sure that's all?"

"Yeah. Well... you could've come to see your Grandmother this weekend. Usually you stop by. This time, nothing. Not even a phone call."

I blink hard, caught off guard. "But Gram, I was there. You don't remember? Saturday morning, I cleaned out the shed? You made breakfast and everything."

Silence hums over the line, stretching thin.

"I know it was early," I add, feeling my chest tighten, "but you—"

"Oh my!" she laughs suddenly, a brittle, embarrassed laugh. "You're right, Suga. I'm so sorry. You know my memory ain't what it used to be. You'll forgive your old Gram, won't you? Maybe I caught that disease your Grandpa had. Is that contagious?"

I chuckle lightly, but it feels hollow. "No, Gram, it's not contagious. Don't even start that. You just lost track of the days, that's all. And I'm sorry I didn't stay longer. I'll make it up to you, I promise."

"No, no, don't worry about it," she says, her voice softer now. "Just don't forget about me again. It gets lonely, sittin' in this big ol' house by myself."

I sigh under my breath, already bracing for it.

"Y'know," she continues, "I have two empty bedrooms here. You could save yourself a lot of money if you moved in with me."

"Gram..." I say, dragging the word out. "You know you live too far. Driving that gas-guzzling beast back and forth would kill my paycheck. And no offense, Gram—" I pause, smiling faintly at my half-eaten sandwich, "—but I love my privacy too."

"You have no idea what it's like to be alone, truly alone, Suga," Gram says, her voice softer now—fragile, like a thread unraveling. "To wake up every day without the man you've spent your life growing with... loving. My bed used to be warm with him beside me. Now it's just cold and far too big. The only thing left is the faint smell of his cologne. And I cry, baby. I cry every time I have to wash the sheets because I know I'm scrubbing away another piece of him I'll never get back." She pauses, her breath catching. "So his pillow stays right where it is. Unwashed. Untouched."

I press my fingers against my eyes, exhaling slowly, already knowing what she'll say next.

"You know... the other morning, I woke up in my chair with the blanket from the couch laid over me." Her voice wavers. "Your Grandpa used to do that—rather than wake me, he'd just cover me up and let me sleep." A beat of silence. "I wondered how it got there. You didn't do that, did you?"

I hesitate, then lie. "No, Gram. I left, remember?"

"Hmm." A soft hum follows, almost wistful. "Maybe your Grandpa paid me a visit... maybe he was letting me know I'm not as alone as I feel."

"Maybe," I whisper, the guilt thick in my throat. "I'm sorry, Gram. I've felt lonely too, ever since Mom and Dad died."

"I know you did, sweetie... but this is different." She breathes in, the sound of her lighter flicking follows. "It's not a loneliness that fades when the house gets busy or when someone calls. It's something that lingers—settles in your bones. You can't understand it unless you've lived it."

The sound of her puffing on a cigarette filters through the speaker, fragile and rhythmic.

"It doesn't help that my health is slipping," she adds. "And I don't want to be put in a home, Tommy. Promise me you won't send me to one of those awful places."

"Never, Gram," I say quickly. "Why are we even talking about this? I'd never..." My eyes drift to my watch—8:14 a.m.—and panic squeezes my chest. "Gram, I'm so sorry, I have to go. I'm late for work. Can I call you later?"

"I guess, Suga..."

"I love you."

She doesn't respond before I end the call. I grab my things and bolt from the restaurant, brushing past two teenage girls with a polite nod and a quiet "Excuse me."

(8:35 AM)

As I make my way through the call center, something feels... off. The usual smiles and casual greetings don't meet me today. People glance up, but only for a second before their eyes dart away, like I'm carrying something contagious. As I approach my desk, I feel their stares crawling across my back. But the moment I spin around to catch them, they snap back to their screens like synchronized dancers in a cheap routine.

The room feels like an aquarium, and I'm the bleeding fish in open water. They're the ones hiding in the coral, watching something unseen circle above me.

"Thorpe!"

Kathy's voice cuts across the floor like a whip crack, snapping everyone out of their fake focus. My heart drops into my gut. The walls feel like they've closed in an inch. I grab my notepad, shedding my coat slowly, trying to keep my face unreadable.

There's no way she knows anything about Martinez. Not yet. It's too soon. Isn't it?

As I step into her office, she's already leaning back in her chair, elbows resting on the arms, chin perched on her laced fingers. Her mouth is pursed like she's tasting something sour, and her eyes are slit thin—calculating.

"So, we just show up late for work and walk in like nothing's wrong now?" she says coldly.

"I called into the attendance system to report that I would be late this morning, but the line was busy," I say, the words tumbling from my mouth before my mind can properly process them. I already know—every rep does—that if the automated system doesn't pick up, protocol demands a call to your direct supervisor or the front desk. No excuses.

Kathy doesn't say a word. Her expression is unreadable, carved from stone. The silence between us is suffocating, and I can almost hear the gears turning behind her narrowed eyes.

"You do realize a 'no call no show' is grounds for automatic dismissal?" she says at last, pulling the thick company handbook from her desk drawer as if it were a sword she intended to wield.

"No call no show? But I'm only thirty minutes late. I'm just... tardy, not a no show."

She exhales sharply and leans forward. "Mr. Thorpe, it's Tuesday morning! Where were you on Monday?" Her voice rises like a gavel striking down.

My brow furrows in disbelief. "What!? Tuesday?" I blurt out, as if the very word were poison on my tongue. "It can't be Tuesday."

But even as I protest, uncertainty creeps in. I reach for my phone like a lifeline and wake the screen.

Tuesday.

A chill settles in my chest. It *is* Tuesday. The realization spreads through me like a slow leak. Somehow, I've blacked out a full day and a half. That gnawing hunger I felt earlier, Gram's confusion on the phone, the double order at McDonald's—they all make terrible sense now. It wasn't kindness or coincidence. It was "Twosday"—the promotion where they serve two breakfast sandwiches for the price of one.

And now, here I am, committing one of the most cardinal sins in the call center world—no call, no show.

I glance over my shoulder, half-expecting Human Resources to be at my cubicle, boxing up what little pride I have left. But my desk remains untouched. For now.

"Thorpe!" Kathy snaps, yanking my attention back like a leash. "You need to go over these policies—because you're on a very thin line. Lucky for you, the rule recently changed to *two* no call no shows instead of one. But between your attendance issues and your numbers? You're still dangling."

She leans back, then forward again, resting her chest on her forearm. Her pen, previously clenched between her lips, now twirls idly in her fingers as her eyes drop—not to the papers on her desk, but lower. Far lower.

Her pale cleavage, dotted with freckles, pushes up softly between her forearms. Her biceps squeeze gently against them, making the effect... pronounced.

"Give me a good reason why I shouldn't fire you," she says, her tone sweetened with something I can't quite name.

I blink. My gaze lingers a little too long—then shifts quickly upward in guilt. Confusion wells in me. Was this... intentional? Was I seeing this right? I tilt my head slightly, unsure if I'm reading too deeply into things or not deeply enough.

Kathy's eyes drop again—this time to my lap. She draws her pen from her lips with a slow, deliberate motion, letting it roll between her fingers like a cigarette in a noir film.

I don't know what's happening.

And yet... I do.

"Ever heard of quid pro quo?"

Her voice glides across the desk like a velvet ribbon, soft but deliberate, wrapping itself around the moment. She doesn't blink—just watches me, expectant. I hesitate, caught between instinct and uncertainty. My mouth is dry, but my body is very much alive—responding to her gaze in ways that betray me. A certain part of me, long neglected and never touched by anyone but myself, now stirs like it's waking from a long sleep. The slow, aching swell moves downward, pressing against the inside of my thigh.

"I think I've heard about something like that, in my sexual harassment class," I manage.

She smirks. "So then I don't need to explain to you, correct?"

"Um... I'm not sure what to say exactly."

"Say what you feel," she says, her voice low and smooth. "It's just you and I in here, Tommy."

Tommy. Not *Mr. Thorpe.* Not even *Thorpe.* The way she says my name—like she's already tasted it—sends another jolt through me. This feels surreal. It's like something out of the adult films I used to hide behind—the cheap ones with bad acting and worn-out DVDs that skipped just when things were getting good. But this? This feels dangerously real. Like I've wandered into a scene I was never meant to be part of.

"I guess I'm willing to do whatever it takes to keep my job. I need the money."

I brace for her to rise, to walk around the desk and perch herself in front of me, legs crossed, skirt rising high like some soft-core fantasy. But that doesn't happen.

"Stand up," she says, her tone suddenly sharp, a command cloaked in silk.

"What?"

"I said, stand up."

I fumble slightly, shielding the obvious rise in my pants with my notepad as I rise from the chair.

"Move that," she gestures, swiping the air like she's clearing her own desk.

"What?"

"You're suddenly hard of hearing, aren't you? I think you heard what I said. Do it!" she snaps, tossing her pen to the desk with an impatient clatter.

I move the notepad, slow and unsure, like peeling off a bandage. Her lips curl into a slow grin of satisfaction.

"Judging by what I'm seeing, you know exactly what you need to do to keep this job, Tommy. And it looks as though you're willing to do it. Or at least a part of you is."

My face burns. I cover myself again and slowly sink back into the chair.

"I'll text you tonight and tell you where to be. Don't respond. You just be there at the time I say. *Capiche?*"

"What?"

"Oh my God. Do you understand? *Comprende?*"

"Yeah. Sure."

She scribbles something on a scrap of paper, tears it cleanly, and slides it across the desk toward me. "Here is my number. Be certain you program that into your phone so you know it's me when I send that text."

I sit frozen, unsure if I should speak or simply vanish. But she's already turning away, rifling through a stack of reports like I never happened.

"You can go now," she says, not even sparing me a glance.

"Oh. Okay."

I stand, fumbling with my pen and notebook, then reach for the door. As it opens, I'm met by a sea of curious eyes. Heads turn quickly back to monitors, pretending they hadn't been watching. I lower my notepad once again to shield the lingering evidence of our conversation and quietly walk back to my cubicle.

(8:32 PM, Friday)

"...eighteen, nineteen, twenty," I count, my breath ragged, sweat dotting my forehead and darkening my shirt. My arms tremble slightly as I push off the floor and stand, catching my reflection in the darkened window.

Without my electronics to distract me, working out has become my new evening ritual. Push-ups. Sit-ups. More push-ups. A routine to anchor me. A punishment. A release.

I'd read up on it at work—ways to build strength without bulking up. My metabolism runs too fast. If I don't eat enough, my body devours muscle and fat alike. Tonight, I feel hollowed out but wired. Like a machine on low battery, still trying to run full speed.

Maybe it's guilt. Maybe it's adrenaline. Or maybe it's just hunger—hunger for more than food.

After a sixty-second breather, I drop back down onto the floor for another round—twenty more push-ups to clear my head and wear down the nerves. Just as I hit fifteen, my phone vibrates like a wasp against the glass on the coffee table. I pause, muscles tight, breath shallow, and glance over. A single text message lights up the screen:

"Sunrise Inn by the airport, 10:00 pm, room 113."

"Here we go," I murmur aloud, breath catching in my throat.

Some part of me had hoped she'd changed her mind. That she'd rethink whatever this was before it became real. But another part—a darker, more curious version of myself—wondered what it might be like to follow through. How many chances like this does a guy like me ever get?

I know what she's doing is wrong. Morally. Legally. It could cost her career. And me? I could report it, twist the whole thing into a case, maybe even walk away with money. But let's be real—I'm a guy. And a lonely one at that.

In the shower, I let the water run hot, longer than usual. I lather soap between my palms until it foams, then take extra care washing the space between my legs, preparing for scrutiny I've never had to consider before. As I glance down, I cringe at the tangled thicket I've neglected. Short curls, springy and dense—like a little overgrown forest at my beltline.

With no shaving cream, I make do—soap and slow, delicate strokes with a cheap razor until everything is smooth, bare, and painfully unfamiliar.

I press a crisp white shirt with thin blue pinstripes and tuck it into a pair of khakis. The belt buckle aligns perfectly with the fly and the center seam of my shirt—what Dad used to call the *gig line.* Military precision. I knot my flat black tie into a tight Windsor, then spritz Curve on either side of my neck.

Finished, I stand in front of the mirror. Not smiling. Not frowning. Just... blank. Staring at a man who doesn't quite recognize himself anymore.

(9:37 PM)

The air is cold and clean as I drive beneath a sky full of stars, windows fogged lightly at the edges. I make a quick stop at Smucker's gas station and grab a single rose from the cooler near the door. It feels like the polite thing to do. Something old-fashioned. Gentlemanly. A token gesture to soften the shame.

The guy at the counter looks eerily like Ice Cube and greets me with an amused smirk that sticks even after I hand him the cash.

"Everything okay?" I ask, trying to read his expression.

"Yeah bruh," he says, eyeing my tie. "Nice outfit though."

I pause, glancing at the faint reflection of myself in the window beyond him.

"Is there something wrong with it?"

"Nah. Nothing—if you're going to church or a job interview, maybe." He slides my change across the counter. "Thirty-five cents. Have a great night."

He turns to restock a shelf, and I catch him in the reflection again—still grinning as I push through the door.

———————

(10:05 PM)

Room 113. The brass numbers glint in the amber glow of the parking lot lights. I walk slowly, deliberately, heart pounding harder with each step. My brain churns through every possible scenario: candlelight, silk sheets, leather restraints, a whip, some cliché from the countless films I've seen alone in the dark. Something daring. Something surreal.

I raise my hand and knock gently three times.

Silence.

I check the number again, then glance at my phone. Right room. Right time.

I knock again—and before the second knock lands, the door swings open.

She's wearing the same outfit she had on earlier that day at the office. Blouse. Skirt. Hair still pulled back in that same taut bun. Just like that, the fantasy cracks and falls away, the latex dominatrix fading into dust.

"Well," I whisper to myself, "guess we're doing this the real way."

Nevertheless, I knew it wouldn't be long before she revealed all she had to offer.

She leaned against the doorframe, her gaze sweeping from my shoes to the part in my hair before curling into a smirk. It was the same look the cashier gave me earlier—like she knew something I didn't. I cleared my throat and extended the single rose, a small, stiff gesture meant to show some semblance of class.

"Hi," I said, quietly.

"You're kidding me with the rose, right?" she laughed, then grabbed my wrist and pulled me inside without another word.

The door clicked shut behind me. She flung the flower toward the bed like it was nothing more than a paper napkin. Her hands were on me in an instant, tugging at my tie with abrupt confidence. The knot slid loose, and she tossed it to the floor. Her fingers went to the top of my shirt, unbuttoning the first two fastenings, then yanking the hem free from my waistband. I didn't move. I stood there and let her dress—or rather, *undress*—me to her liking, like a mannequin being tailored for a window display.

She stepped back and gave me a final once-over. "That'll have to do," she muttered, already halfway to the bathroom. "Make yourself comfortable. There's cheese and wine on the dresser. I'm gonna change. Be out in a minute."

I turned toward the makeshift spread she'd laid out—three glasses around a tall, dark bottle of merlot. Two were already poured. I picked the clean one beside the glass with faint lip prints on its rim. The wine hit my tongue bitter and dry, an acidic warmth trailing it down. Not exactly my drink of choice, but I needed something to settle the nerves. I swallowed the whole thing, grimacing, then poured another, chasing it with sharp cubes of cheddar and soft clusters of red and green grapes.

A black briefcase sat at the center of the bed, its metal latches cracked just wide enough to tempt a glance. Something pink peeked out from its edge. Grapes in one hand, I crept closer. With my index finger, I eased the lid upward for a better look.

My stomach gave a small flip.

Inside, nestled among velvet lining, lay two enormous dildos—one pink and shaped like a missile, the other jet black with veiny detail and a wrinkled set of testicles sculpted onto its base. My hand hesitated, then opened the case a bit farther. Handcuffs. A leather riding crop. A coil of thick rope.

The bathroom door creaked open suddenly.

I jumped, snapped the case shut, and slid down to the corner of the bed, wiping my palms discreetly on my pants.

"You like?" she asked.

She stepped out into the room and slowly turned to give me the full view. The red-and-black leather ensemble hugged her thick curves tightly—corset laced up the front, thighs poured into glossy boots. The freckles that dotted her chest spread like constellations down her arms and over her back.

It wasn't what I had imagined. It was... more.

She turned again, slowly, and I caught a glimpse of the tattoo on the lower cheek of her left buttock—what looked like a pair of red lips, stretched and dimmed by a web of cellulite.

Still, I found myself hard.

"Well, say something," she demanded, irritation rising in her voice.

"You look good," I said, still unsure if I was breathing properly.

"Good?" she scoffed, striding toward the mirror and adjusting her cleavage. She gave them a dramatic lift, then checked the shine of her corset under the light. "I think I look *fucking fabulous.* Something's wrong with your eyes. *Good?* Really?"

After a few final adjustments, she tossed her hair to one side and turned toward me, her eyes scanning me with a predator's patience. I swallowed the last of the grapes in one dry gulp, shifting awkwardly on the edge of the bed.

She smirked, her gaze dipping low. "Wow. Well, someone thinks I look better than good, don't they?"

I instinctively leaned forward, trying to cover myself. "Sorry. It's just... it's been a while since I've been with anyone."

"Don't be sorry." She stepped closer, her voice smooth as velvet. "You're not a virgin, are you?"

"No," I answered a bit too sharply. "I've had sex. Just not in a long time. But I'm not a rookie."

"Didn't mean to offend you, Mr. Experience," she teased, letting the sarcasm linger as she retrieved something from the dresser.

By now, the Merlot had done its work—my limbs relaxed, my nerves dulled. I kicked off my shoes and leaned back onto the bed, eyes closing for what I thought would be just a moment. When I opened them again, she stood before me with two wine glasses, one nearly filled to the brim.

"Here you go," she said, handing me the fuller glass. "To better days."

"To better days," I echoed, and our glasses clinked softly in the dim light. She took a delicate sip, while I drained nearly half my portion in one go. The bitterness clung to my tongue, but I welcomed the warmth that spread through my chest.

She sauntered closer, setting her glass aside. With a graceful tug on my wrist, she brought me upright at the bed's edge, then turned and pressed herself against me, moving to some silent rhythm. Her curves swayed and dipped, her body heavy with intention. I tried to stay composed, sipping the last of my wine, but everything began to blur at the edges.

Then she turned, her hands roaming up the insides of my thighs, her gaze locked onto mine. I felt the zipper on my pants slide down slowly. She leaned in, nearly touching her lips to mine.

"How do you feel?" she asked.

"You tell me."

That's when it hit me. A queasy wave surged through my gut, and the room shifted—tilted—spun. Her weight pressing down made it harder to breathe, harder to focus. The shadows around her face blurred and doubled, and I struggled to lift my arms, my voice, anything.

She slipped off me. My body went limp against the sheets.

Somewhere at the foot of the bed, voices emerged—hers, and someone else's. A man. The words were muffled, echoing like I was underwater. I tried to speak, to move, to rise—but nothing responded.

My body had become a locked box. And I was still inside.

(8:37 AM Saturday)

A low, throbbing ache blooms across my skull as I stir awake, the muffled drone of the Weather Channel filling the room. Some over-enthused forecaster goes on about an approaching snowstorm, but his voice feels distant, hollow, like it's coming from the bottom of a well. My face and chest cling stubbornly to the bedsheet, stuck by a thin sheen of sweat or something else. With a wince, I peel myself free, the fabric making a soft tearing sound against my skin, and roll onto my back.

The room feels different—hollow. Empty. Only a sliver of morning light sneaks in through the crooked curtains, casting long, tired shadows across the floor. The air is heavy with the stale scent of old carpet and something sweeter... baby oil?

A knock rattles the door.

"Housekeeping?"

The voice is muffled, but sharp enough to jolt a deeper awareness into me. My body tingles, pins and needles stabbing into my limbs as sensation slowly returns. A deep, searing pain throbs in my lower back—no, lower than that. I wince, reaching behind to investigate, and my fingers come away slick with an oily residue that glistens under the weak light.

Another knock, louder this time. "Housekeeping!"

Panic surges up my throat. My memory is a blank slate after the wine—the last clear image I have is the click of our glasses. After that, only fragments. Blurry movements. Muffled laughter. Darkness.

I shift clumsily to sit up, but everything aches. The cold air brushes against my bare skin—only then do I realize I'm completely naked. The oily scent clings to me, sticky and sour, making the anger rise in my chest like bile.

The door clicks and swings open.

"Housekeep—" she gasps, her eyes wide as saucers at the sight of me sprawled naked across the tangled sheets.

"Fuck off!" I bark, my voice rough and alien to my own ears.

She recoils immediately, slamming the door shut so hard the walls seem to tremble with the impact.

I sit there for a moment, breathing hard, the sting of humiliation mixing with the gnawing confusion eating at my mind.

Something happened last night.

And whatever it was, it sure as hell wasn't what I had expected.

CHAPTER 10

BREAKING POINT

(12:30 PM Sunday)

I've been keeping my promise to Grandpa—dragging myself to church with Gram at least once a month. A ritual wrapped in loyalty more than belief. Truth is, I find the place stifling—thick with the scent of old wood, perfume, and the quiet perfume of hypocrisy. Everywhere I look: smiles that don't reach the eyes, praise sung from lips that spit gossip the moment they leave the pews. Liars in Sunday best.

The congregation belts out *"We've Come This Far by Faith,"* clapping in rhythm, eyes closed and swaying like the Spirit was truly moving them. I just stand there, hands at my sides, aching slightly as the hard wooden pew presses into my still-tender backside. Gram elbows me softly in the ribs, urging me to sing, to clap, to play along. But my mind is elsewhere—still trapped in that hotel room, replaying fractured images and unanswered questions.

The collection plate makes its third round—three times, like we're paying rent for salvation. It's passed like a hot stone, avoided by most with murmured apologies or polite smiles. But not Gram. With quiet dignity, she places a crisp ten in the center like she's feeding something sacred. Her eyes close briefly as her hand lingers, and she smiles like it's her small offering to keep the world spinning.

After a long, winding prayer, the benediction finally rolls to a close. The congregation rises like released captives, flooding toward the doors in a slow-moving wave. Outside, the sun blesses my face with its warm touch, the air cool and clean. I pause on the front steps, half-listening to Gram still chatting inside with a group of silver-haired saints. Her voice floats up among the others—laughter, gossip, the latest sickness or grandchild born.

Around me, groups of members share too-wide smiles, embrace with exaggerated warmth, then roll their eyes the moment backs are turned. It's all a cycle. Come in broken, sing like saints, leave unchanged. Their salvation is performative, like Sunday scrubbing makes up for the filth of the week. I've had enough. I head to the truck.

Later, back at Gram's place, the house quickly fills with the familiar, mouth-watering scent of garlic, simmering tomatoes, and herbs—the unmistakable aroma of her homemade spaghetti sauce. She moves like clockwork in the kitchen, filling pots and humming softly. She always makes too much, still cooking like the house is full—like Dad, Mom, and Grandpa will walk through the door at any moment. She says it's habit. I think it's hope.

As the sauce bubbles, I make my way to the bathroom, more curious than concerned. I turn on the light, drop my pants halfway, and crane awkwardly at the mirror, trying to inspect the source of that lingering sting. As I reach for the cabinet, a tube of ointment tumbles out and lands in the sink with a dull clink.

And just like that—one scent, one sound—I'm ten years old again, eavesdropping in the kitchen while Grandpa entertained my father.

"...heck no! That boy's only talent was fiddlin' with himself. Caught him jerkin' it in outhouses, on scaffolds, in the damn utility trucks. Hell, he'd probably go at it mid-lunch break if you turned your back too long!"

Dad was doubled over with laughter, and Grandpa wasn't done.

"Word was, he picked up some fire-crotch disease from a two-dollar street gal and still didn't slow down. Got caught again in the warehouse, pants down, goin' to town with a Costco-sized tube of Neosporin. He was healin' and gettin' off at the same time!"

Grandma slammed her knife down on the cutting board with a sharp thud that startled even the walls. "Richard! That's enough. Your grandson is right there," she barked, voice sharp enough to slice through the room on its own.

"Oh, baby, he don't understand a lick of what I just said. He'll be okay," Grandpa replied, laughing through his words like it was nothing more than harmless mischief.

The memory fades as the present reclaims my attention. I'm back in the dim bathroom, standing in front of the mirror, jar of ointment in one hand, a dull ache still lingering where pain shouldn't live. I hear Gram's muffled voice calling out from the hallway, words distorted by the steady stream of water still blasting into the sink. I shut it off, silencing the rush.

"What, Gram!?" I shout through the door, my voice sharper than intended.

She doesn't miss a beat. "Don't you yell at me, young man—I'll still put one on ya!" she growls.

I exhale and lower my tone. "I didn't mean any disrespect, Gram. Sorry, I had the water going."

"I asked if you enjoyed Pastor Reed's sermon today," she repeats, calmer now.

"Yes, Gram. Did you?"

"I did," she says, her voice drawing nearer, "but I figured you'd enjoy it better, seeing as you're into debt and bills and all that."

I open the bathroom door just in time to catch the tail end of her smirk.

"But I'll be honest with ya—I was finding myself dozing off at the sound of his voice. He's just so damn boring at times. One day your Grandma's gonna fall asleep in that church and be gone for good," she chuckles, shaking her head.

"Don't say things like that, Gram," I reply, the words coming out a bit too harsh, touched with worry.

"Well, it's true," she says with a shrug. "And you wouldn't have far to go. I'll already be in the house of the Lord, so just throw me in a box and say a few words." She laughs again, the sound fuller this time, like it comes from a place she's made peace with.

I don't laugh. I just stand there, arms crossed, the hallway light painting shadows under my eyes. She sees it in my face—knows I'm not a fan of these little jokes she makes about death. She gives me a gentle pat on the chest before shuffling off to the kitchen, her slippers dragging against the old hardwood.

But I know the truth behind her words. I see it in her eyes when she thinks I'm not looking—how much she misses Grandpa. How every casual joke is a whispered wish to be with him again.

Funny thing is, Pastor Reed's sermon actually hit home for me. As much as I normally tune him out, something stuck this time.

"The wicked borrow and do not repay. But the righteous is gracious and gives."—Psalm 37:21

He said it like he was talking directly to me, like maybe God was watching me and nodding in approval. Maybe what I did to Mr. Martinez was divine justice. Maybe I wasn't just a killer—I was a vessel. A sword in the hand of something higher.

(7:25 AM Monday)

There's a buzz under my skin this morning. A nervous charge I can't shake. Part of me wants answers. The other part wants to stay blind. If I confront Kathy, I risk knowing the truth—one I might not be able to stomach. But if I don't... it'll gnaw at me forever.

I burst from my apartment and make a sharp turn down the hallway, nearly colliding with the elevator doors just as they open. Out steps Tricia.

She looks... different. Pale. Withdrawn. Her black skirt clings to her hips, and a cropped leather jacket hugs her frame. She doesn't even meet my eyes. Slipping out of her heels, she lowers her head and shields her face like she's afraid to be seen.

"Hi, Tricia," I offer softly.

"Hey," she mumbles, barely audible.

She doesn't stop. Doesn't slow. Just keeps moving like she's late for something—or running from it.

"Are you okay?" I call after her.

She fumbles with her keys, her back still to me. I hear it then—a quiet sob, a break in her breath that confirms what her body already betrayed. She bumps her shoulder against her door once, twice... and finally it swings open. She vanishes inside, the door closing just slow enough for me to second guess whether or not to follow.

I want to knock. Ask. Say something. But I'm already late.I press the elevator button, watching the numbers descend, and leave her pain behind me in the hallway.

(7:57 AM)

As the glass doors sigh closed behind me, the scent of burnt coffee and industrial cleaner greets me like a familiar but unwelcome handshake. Jessica looks up from the front desk, her smile cheerful but thin, like she's already over the day.

"Good morning, Tommy," she says.

"Hey, good morning Jessica. How are you?"

"I'm good. Hey, so you'll be reporting to Mr. Gibbons today."

That name alone makes my spine stiffen. "Mr. Gibbons? Why is that?"

"Kathy's out for the day. She called off just a few minutes ago."

"What?" The word falls out of me like a brick. "She didn't say why?"

"Nope," Jessica shrugs. "Just said she was taking a day off. So your whole team has to meet with Mr. Gibbons to go over your reports sometime today."

I groan and let my bag slide from my shoulder with a thud. Leaning on the counter, I press the heels of my palms to my forehead like that'll somehow help keep my frustration in. "I don't have time for this crap this morning."

"I know, I know. Happy Monday, huh?"

"Yeah. Happy freak'n Monday," I mumble, dragging my voice like dead weight.

I head toward the break room, the weight of the day already pressing on me before it's even properly begun. There's a strange conflict brewing under my skin—relief that Kathy isn't here, and a twinge of disappointment too. No sideways glances. No cryptic comments. No tension thick enough to slice with a box cutter. But still... it's like a page is missing from a chapter I need to finish.

Inside the break room, Freddie is at the sink, swirling her mug under the stream. Bold gold letters stare back at me from her cup: *QUEEN OF FUCKING EVERYTHING.* She throws a glance my way, then returns to her scrubbing like I'm just another stain she'll eventually wipe off.

I stuff my plastic bag into the fridge—three peanut butter sandwiches stacked in a paper towel, a pint of milk, and a sad apple rolling free. Then I head to my desk without ceremony. Kimmie's already at hers, peering at her screen with the usual "I-told-you-so" aura.

"You got about twenty-five seconds, Tommy. You better hurry," she says, tapping her watch like she's auditioning to be a timekeeper in a boxing match.

"Okay."

But I don't pick up the pace. Honestly, one minute past the hour is treated like a felony here. Thirty seconds, thirty minutes—it's all the same in their book. So I move like I've already been convicted.

"Did you make it?" Kimmie asks as I finish logging in.

I glance at the screen. 8:01:03. Of course.

"Nope," I say, flat.

"You know they can write you up for that? And Kathy ain't here to buffer it. Mr. Gibbons is gonna be all up in our ass. When he sees that you're one minute and three seconds late, he's gonna—"

"I don't care, Kimmie!" My voice punches through the cubicle wall louder than I intended, loud enough that a few heads lift and swivel toward me.

Her eyes go wide and her mouth opens in offense. "Excuse me?"

"What's going on over here?" The voice cuts in from behind, smooth and cold like a scalpel. Mr. Gibbons.

Kimmie and I freeze. She looks at me like *you're on your own,* and I stare at him without offering an explanation.

"I need you both to print off clean copies of your reports and come to my office, please," he says—calm, but sharp. Sharp enough to bleed you with a compliment.

We both nod and turn like children dismissed from the principal's door. As we fumble with the printers, Derrick comes trotting in, huffing like he ran the last block from his car. He dumps his usual gas station haul onto his desk—chips, a soda, and something that looks like a breakfast burrito.

"Sorry y'all. I had to get some gas or I wasn't going to make it in. Good morning!" he chimes, way too cheerful for this environment.

"Hey," we mutter in unison.

Derrick squints at us. "What's wrong with y'all?"

"Nothing," I mutter.

"Nothing," Kimmie echoes, clearly not in the mood to explain. "Mr. Gibbons wants us to print our reports and head to his office."

"Why, what's going on?" he asks, his smile fading.

Kimmie shrugs and casts a glance toward me. "Your guess is as good as mine."

(8:15 AM)

The silence in Mr. Gibbons's office is stiff, like the starched collar of a cheap dress shirt. The three of us sit rigidly around his oversized desk, the air dense with expectation. He clicks and scrolls, the soft hum of his computer the only sound in the room besides the faint groan of his leather chair as he shifts his weight.

Finally, he leans back, fingers interlocked beneath his lips in a contemplative steeple.

"Kimmie, how long have you worked here?" he asks, his eyes never leaving the glow of his monitor.

"Three years," she replies, her voice even but clipped.

"Tommy, how about you?"

"Two and a half years, sir." I sit up a little straighter, unsure why he's asking but already bracing for impact.

"Derrick?"

"Since before we moved to this new location. I'd say about six years, sir."

There's a pause—one of those long, weighted ones where you know the next sentence won't be good. Gibbons's stare remains locked on the screen, but his words come sharp.

"So, with all of your experience and time with this company, you all still can't seem to get this location under control. These numbers are terrible."

He swivels the monitor toward us, the bright spreadsheet like a crime scene photo. "All of these figures here are in the red, people. All of them."

"But my individual numbers are meeting standard, Mr. Gibbons," Derrick blurts out, too quickly.

Gibbons lifts a brow, voice syrupy with sarcasm. "Oh, I'm sorry Derrick, you can go ahead and go back to your desk."

Derrick, oblivious, gathers his things and begins to stand. "Uh, Derrick?"

"Yes, sir?"

"Sit your ass down, please," Gibbons says, calm as ever.

Derrick hesitates, then slinks back into his chair with the grace of a deflated balloon. Kimmie and I lock eyes for a second—she's chewing the inside of her cheek, trying not to laugh. I look away, swallowing a smirk.

"This is a team effort," Gibbons continues, his tone now clipped and direct. "And your numbers alone don't accomplish the goals. All of your numbers, as a whole, have to be meeting in order for the North Milwaukee accounts to meet their required standards."

He scans the room. None of us speak. We just trade glances like we're passing around a hot potato of guilt.

"Okay," he says, leaning forward, "well I have a suggestion. As of today, we are going to back each other up by calling on one another's accounts. That way, the customer hears a different voice, a new approach. I want urgency—push the payment today. And don't get soft on me."

He leans back again, eyes narrowing.

"You know as well as I do that North Milwaukee is the toughest account we have. They will walk all over you if you let them. Stick it to them—or get a talk off if you need one. Does anyone have questions or anything they'd like to say?"

Derrick, this time more cautiously, raises his hand.

"So because my numbers are meeting, you just want me to call on some of their accounts then?"

Gibbons nods once. "That's my point, son. Yes."

"Oh. Okay."

He claps his hands once, loud and final. "Alright. Well, if there aren't any more questions—get back to work, my friends."

The three of us rise in near-unison. No one speaks. No one looks at one another. Just the quiet shuffling of paper and the squeak of chairs pushing back into place, as we head back to the floor to face our phones—and whatever kind of Monday this was shaping up to be.

(10:34 AM)

The day is dragging, and with it, my patience. I've only managed to squeeze a couple of payments from low-balance accounts—barely enough to nudge my numbers in the right direction. I've already combed through my entire list once, so I decide to switch gears and target the high-balance accounts. Might as well try swinging at the heavyweights.

First up: Carmen Bridges.

I've run a little skip tracing on her in the past, dug up a few alternative numbers—one of which I'm about to test.

The phone rings twice before a sharp voice cuts through.

"Hello?"

I sit up straighter, smoothing the edge of my desk with my fingers as I answer in my most composed, professional tone. "Hello, may I speak to Ms. Carmen Bridges please?"

"She ain't here. Who is this?" she snaps, her voice raspy, tired, and defensive.

"This is Tommy with—"

"Oh, is this about my car payment?" she interrupts, already exasperated.

"Well, is this, or is this not Carmen Bridges?"

"Yeah, it's me," she sighs, the fire in her voice dimming just slightly.

"Yes, ma'am. I was calling to see when you planned on coming in with your payment. Your account is over sixty-seven days past due."

"I don't have the full payment right now," she blurts, her words tumbling out. "My paycheck's being garnished for my student loans, so I'm not getting paid what I used to. Can I ask—how did you get this number?"

I skip past her question. "Well, you said you don't have the full payment. How much *can* you come in with today?"

"Nothing!" she barks, her tone flaring up again. "I need my money. Could you answer my question please?"

"It's a number we've had on file for you, ma'am," I say, even though we both know that's probably not true. "Look, I know your car's important to you. I'm trying to help you keep it, but we're reaching a point where I may not be able to stop the repossession."

There's a beat of silence. Then:

"You know what?" she says sharply, then pauses as if trying to rein in her temper. "First of all, you don't have my number on file. I *never* gave this number out to anybody. Second, I work hard—I work *really* hard for what I have. Can't you just give me an extension or put the payment on the back end or something?"

I keep my voice even, but firm. "That's not how the loan works, Ms. Bridges. I'm sorry. We have to do something to get your account current. You've had over sixty days—that's two months. With a balance this high, I'm honestly surprised they haven't picked up your car already."

More silence.

"Ms. Bridges?"

Her voice returns, but it's no longer angry—it's wounded.

"You people are the devil—the *devil*," she hisses. "I work the second shift, Monday through Saturday, doing security at the hospital. I got one day to myself, and that's barely enough to breathe. Sometimes I do odd jobs just to make ends meet. I live alone. No help. No support. The *Lord* knows I'm a good woman, and I do what I can to survive—*legally*. I will *not* let you devils get ahold of my heart and make me something I'm not. I will not be a slave to this debt."

She pauses, then with a voice full of fire and faith, she adds, "*'The rich rules over the poor, and the borrower is slave to the lender.'* That's *Proverbs 22:7*, from the Good Book. You should read it sometime."

"Ms. Bridges, did you know it's also a sin to owe a debt and not repay it? *'The wicked borrow and do not repay, but the righteous is gracious and gives.'* That's Psalm 37:21, straight from the Good Book, ma'am."

She doesn't miss a beat. "Young man, *Romans 13:8* says, *'Owe no one anything, except to love each other, for the one who loves another has fulfilled the law.'* I've done no wrong by God or man," she fires back, her voice full of righteous heat.

I take a breath, trying to meet her fury with a thread of patience. "What can I do to help you get this caught up then, Ms. Bridges?" I ask, softening my tone in an attempt to show what the company calls *empathy*—that performative balance between compassion and duty.

"You can get off my motha-fuckin' back, that's what you can do!" she spits, voice jagged and crackling with rage.

"I'm not riding your back, ma'am," I reply, measured and tight. "Just simply trying to help you."

"All you're doing is stressin' me the hell out, Tommy. Your momma and daddy ain't teach you no better manners than to bother a good, honest, hard-working Christian woman?"

Her words hit like a slap.

"Please don't refer to my mother and father, Ms. Bridges," I say, jaw tightening as I clutch the yellow highlighter in my fist.

"Well *someone* needs to address their sorry asses, 'cause they raised a disrespectful son-of-a-bitch like you. Probably some meth-heads. Or pot smokers—or *somethin'*. You over here worryin' me about a damn payment like it's coming out of *your* pocket. I got enough stress in my life without this mess!"

It's like something shifts inside me. I feel it—a slow burn that becomes a blaze. My heart begins to hammer in my chest, so hard I can hear it in my ears. Her words are still coming, still tearing at me, but all I can feel is this weight pressing down—rage, sorrow, confusion—twisting into something I don't recognize.

I don't know why she's affected me this way. I've dealt with worse. I've had men curse me out, women threaten to "find me," and once, a caller just screamed into the phone for thirty seconds straight. But this? This hurts.

The insult to my parents—a wound she couldn't see, but opened wide with every careless word.

My grip on the highlighter tightens until my knuckles ache. I imagine her neck in my hand, not the plastic tube.

The pain from her words cuts deeper than I expected, dragging out something old and raw. My right eye twitches. My jaw pulses. And then, without even thinking—*snap*—something breaks inside me.

A single teardrop rolls down and lands on my report, darkening the paper like spilled ink. And that's all it takes. One teardrop too many.

Suddenly, I'm a boy again. That stick figure drawn on lined paper, red ink scribbled where a heart should be. *Eat it.* The laughter. The fists. Dean Miller's sucker punch to the mouth. That hot, copper taste.

The phone, the paper, the highlighter—*everything* on my desk explodes to the floor with one wild sweep of my arm. The crash of it turns every head in the room.

But I don't care. I bury my face in the crook of my arms, curling in on myself like a clenched fist, and I cry. Quietly, bitterly, my teeth clenched, tears sliding sideways across my cheeks.

I know they're watching—Kimmie, Derrick, probably half the damn floor—but I can't stop. I don't know *why* this hurts the way it does. I only know that something broke loose in me, and I can't pretend it didn't.

Not this time.

Kimmie rushes around the cubicle divider like a gust of wind, dropping to her knees beside me. Her hands scoop up the fallen items from the floor—my pen, my notepad, the crumpled report—placing them gently on the desk as Derrick joins her in silence, helping without question. When the last of it is gathered, Kimmie stands behind me and lays her palms softly on my shoulders.

The moment her fingers make contact, it's as if something within me unravels. The pressure I'd been holding behind my ribs lets go all at once, and my tears return—hot and relentless. I try to catch them, try to steady my breath, but it only makes it worse. Her touch is kind, human, and unintentionally hits some hidden panic switch.

"You should go outside and get some fresh air, my friend," she says gently, like she's coaxing a frightened animal.

I inhale through trembling lips, forcing down the ache in my throat. A few deep breaths help me lift my head. My sleeves are damp from wiping at my face, but I still use them again, rubbing my cheeks and eyes until I can halfway see straight.

"Come on," she says. "I know you don't smoke, but you might need one of my filtered cigars to calm your nerves. I'll grab a couple."

As I push myself up from the chair, the world tilts slightly, but I find my footing. My eyes scan the carpet and land on one last item they'd missed—a yellow highlighter lying just beyond the chair leg. I stoop to pick it up. Its plastic feels warm in my palm from the floor's low-grade static.

My hands still shake as I turn my report over and stare at the highlighted entry: Carmen Bridges.

Her full name, date of birth, address, phone number, Social Security, place of employment—laid bare in bold black ink, as if daring me to do something more. I uncap the highlighter with a snap and press it down on her name. The felt tip squeals against the paper as yellow floods across her information. I don't stop. I press harder, dragging the pen across her details again, and again—until the paper wrinkles, the ink soaks through, and the contact information beneath becomes a fluorescent smear of uselessness.

(11:55 AM)

"Hey, Tommy, are you almost done with that call?" Kimmie peeks over the top of the cubicle wall.

I nod, phone to my ear, as I leave a generic message asking a customer to return my call.

"Okay," she says, her voice lighter than before, trying to steer things back toward normal. "We're going outside to eat, if you want to join."

I hang up and exhale. "Yeah, I'll meet you out there. Just give me a minute to grab my lunch."

I log out of the phone system, then lock my computer. As the screen goes black, it reflects a distorted version of me. No features, no eyes—just the silhouette of a man backlit by office fluorescents. But even in that faceless mirror, I can still see the heat in my stare. Rage, dulled but simmering beneath the surface like coals waiting for a breath of wind.

My coworkers shuffle out in clusters, heading toward the cafeteria and front doors like ants following a familiar trail. I don't follow. I wait, letting the swarm pass. I'm not ready for their glances, their half-hearted sympathy or quiet speculations. I'd rather hide in the shadows for now, with only my thoughts to keep me company.

I lean back in my chair, still staring into that dark reflection, and it pulls me backward—into memory.

I was maybe ten years old, sitting in the dollar theater with my father. The movie was some action flick I barely remember, but the noise behind us was unforgettable. A group of two young men and two women sat just a row back, laughing too loudly, making jokes through every scene.

My dad turned around, cool but firm. "Could you please keep it down? My son and I are trying to enjoy the movie."

There was no answer. Only a snicker from one of the women, the kind meant to provoke.

"What the fuck are you laughing at?" the man beside her hissed, his thick Russian accent cutting through the darkness.

My dad looked over at me then, his hand resting gently atop mine. He didn't say anything else. Just returned his eyes to the screen.

But then, the man kicked his feet up onto the seat next to mine—his heels thudding close, too close, to my head.

I turned my eyes upward, slowly, already knowing what I'd find—my father's expression, sharpened by anger that hadn't yet found its way into words.

He turned back to the man once more, lifting his eyebrows with calm insistence. "Do you mind?"

"Why no, I don't mind at all," the man replied coolly, his feet still firmly propped up on the seat in front of him, as if my father hadn't spoken at all.

Without a word, my father took my hand and guided us down the row to a cluster of empty seats, farther away from them. The group burst into snickering behind us—mocking laughter, the kind that prickled the back of your neck. I glanced at my father's face. His jaw was tight, his nostrils flared ever so slightly, but his composure held. That same quiet discipline I'd seen when he ironed his uniforms or lined up his boots just so. He didn't say a word.

Then something small and sharp struck the back of my head. I winced, startled. My father, ever observant, caught the movement.

"What's the matter?"

"Nothing," I muttered, trying to shrink into my seat.

I didn't want to tell him. Maybe it was just one time. Maybe they'd stop. I just wanted to enjoy the movie with my dad, even if it was already starting to feel ruined. Actually, if I was honest with myself—I just wanted to go home.

But moments later, something else hit me—this time in the neck. It tumbled down the back of my shirt and landed in my lap. I reached for it with trembling fingers. A Raisinet. I held it up for my father to see.

"What?" he asked, voice low, already reading my expression.

"Someone keeps throwing these at me," I whispered, my eyes beginning to sting.

His gaze darkened instantly. Without hesitation, he rose from his seat, turning fully toward the group. His movement was fluid, quiet, but every muscle in his body looked coiled, ready. The man's date fumbled quickly, snatching the box of Raisinets from his lap and stuffing it into her purse. The man didn't bother to deny it. He only stared at my father—and smiled.

"You want to throw shit at my son?"

"I don't know what you're talking about," the man replied, smug. "Sit the hell down."

My father stood there for a moment, unmoved. A few others in the audience joined in, urging him to sit. Reluctantly—almost painfully—he obeyed. His eyes twitched, and I saw the fire simmering just behind them. His fists were clenched, knuckles white. Without a word, he reached down and grasped my wrist, guiding me swiftly up the aisle and out of the theater.

Rain fell hard and fast as we burst through the exit doors, the wind slapping water across our faces. My father's grip on my wrist was iron-tight as he dragged me through the maze of parked cars, my feet slipping on the slick asphalt.

"Let's go! Hurry!" he barked over the downpour. *"You're gonna get drenched and catch a cold. Your mom'll be pissed."*

He yanked the back door open and buckled me in with the speed of a soldier disarming a bomb. Then he rounded the hood of the car and slid into the driver's seat.

But he didn't start the engine.

We sat in silence. The sound of rain hammering against the windshield filled the car like static. I fidgeted in the back seat, twisting my Rubik's Cube slowly, trying to find patterns in the chaos of colored squares. My dad, on the other hand, never took his eyes off the glowing entrance of the theater. He stared, unblinking.

Minutes passed. Maybe more. Then, without a word, he finally turned the key in the ignition and the engine rumbled to life.

We drove through the city without speaking. The windshield wipers made their rhythmic sweep, slicing through the water, and the tires hissed with each puddle we passed. I didn't know where we were going. It didn't *feel like home. All I knew was that a red car had appeared ahead of us, and my father seemed to follow it with a quiet purpose.*

I barely noticed. My focus remained on my Rubik's Cube—the yellow side was almost done. Just one more twist. One more perfect alignment.

We rolled to a stop a couple of car lengths behind a red sedan, idling in front of a worn-down apartment complex. The rain was falling in thick, slanted sheets, and the windshield was dappled with droplets that shimmered against the glare of oncoming headlights. Visibility was poor, but I caught sight of a figure stepping out of the sedan's back seat—a man who looked eerily similar to the one I'd noticed behind me at the movie theater. I couldn't be certain, not in this weather, not from the backseat.

"Can we get an ice cream, Dad?" I asked hopefully, clinging to the thought of something sweet and normal.

"Not right now," he replied, his tone firm but not unkind. "I need to take care of something. I may be awhile, son, so take a nap. And if anyone tries to get in this car, you lean on this horn. You hear me? I promise—by the time you wake up, we'll be somewhere that's got a cone with your name on it."

I nodded and laid down across the back seat, the leather cold beneath me as he closed the door with a thud that felt heavier than usual. But sleep didn't come right away. I sat back up just in time to see him slip through the front entrance of the apartment, the same one the man had gone into.

I returned to my puzzle cube, trying to make sense of the green center on the yellow face. It wouldn't line up—nothing would. Fifteen minutes passed. Maybe more. The windows began to fog from my breath and the car's warmth, so I leaned into the front seat and cracked the driver's side window for some air. A wave of damp air swept in, making me shiver. I curled up again, using my jacket as a blanket, and finally drifted off to the lullaby of thunder and rain pattering against metal.

A violent crack of lightning snapped me awake.

Still no Dad.

The rain now felt biblical—monsoon-like. Thick drops slammed the roof like fists. I crawled into the front seat, wiping away the fog on the glass with my sleeve, and peered out toward the apartment building. Just as my anxiety began to spike, the front doors burst open and there he was—moving fast. I scrambled to pretend I was still asleep, slumping low in the passenger seat and shutting my eyes tight.

The car door creaked open. The scent of rain and sweat swept in with him. I could feel it before I saw it—his presence, heavy, pulsing. Through the narrowest slit in one eye, I watched as he adjusted the rearview mirror, angling it until his bloodied knuckles came into view. He wiped his face with the back of his arm, smearing something dark across his shirt sleeve, then stared at his own reflection. He didn't blink. Just stared. That cold, hollow look in his eyes that night... it's the same one I catch in myself sometimes now, staring at my own reflection in the glow of this monitor.

The office is quiet, humming with the occasional voice of a collector stuck on a call. Lunch is winding down. I gather my things and leave my desk, not particularly hungry, but knowing I could still eat. And truth be told, I don't mind having lunch with Kimmie. Somehow, she always manages to carve out a sliver of light in my otherwise overcast day.

I reach into the fridge for my lunch and immediately notice the knot in the handles of my plastic bag has been undone. When I open it, my gut twists. Two of my sandwiches are gone—and my apple, the one I'd picked for its perfect shine, has a massive bite taken out of it.

(5:36 PM)

When I step off the elevator and into the hallway, the first thing I see is Tricia—curled up on the floor, her knees tucked to her chest, her face hidden in the crook between them. Her entire posture radiates defeat. I drop to a knee beside her and gently place a hand on her shoulder.

"What's going on? Are you okay?" I ask, my voice low.

She lifts her head slowly, revealing a bruised and swollen eye. The discoloration stretches down to her cheekbone. "I'm okay," she murmurs.

My stomach tightens. "Oh no. What the hell happened to your face?" I reach toward it instinctively.

Before I can touch her, she catches my wrist and holds it still. "It's okay, I said. Don't worry about it."

"Who did this to you?" My voice sharpens despite my efforts to stay calm.

"Nobody. Just had an accident, that's all."

Even though it's obvious she's not telling me the whole story, I let it go. I'm no stranger to secrets. I've buried enough of my own.

Setting my bag down by my door, I ease down beside her. We sit in silence, the hallway around us filled with background noise—faint TV chatter behind one door, an argument muffled by another wall. Then it all fades to quiet.

Her hand rests on the floor next to mine. Small, soft-looking. Nails painted the color of rose petals. I hover my hand just above it, hesitating, thinking maybe this is the moment. But before I can act, the sound of scratching at the base of my apartment door breaks the silence.

"Sounds like your roommate knows you're home," Tricia says, glancing toward the noise.

"I think you're right. Want to meet her?"

She sits up straighter, her voice lifting. "Sure."

When I open the door, I brace it with my foot to keep Tilly from bolting out. She doesn't give up easily, though, squirming and clawing until she squeezes her little body past me.

"Tilly!" I exclaim, stumbling over my bags as I try to catch her. But instead of darting down the hall, she makes a beeline for Tricia, stopping right at her feet.

"Well hello, Tilly," Tricia says with a soft smile, crouching to greet her.

"She doesn't get much company. She's mostly cooped up in the apartment while I'm working."

"Aww, poor thing. You want some friends, don't you?" she coos, running her fingers through Tilly's fur.

"She's probably starving. Can you grab her and bring her in? If I try now, she'll vanish under the couch."

Tricia lifts her effortlessly. Tilly melts into her arms, burying her nose under Tricia's chin like they've known each other for years.

"Wow, you smell pretty good, little Tilly. Daddy takes good care of you, doesn't he?"

"Ha—if she could talk, she might say otherwise. Been stressing lately... forgot a few feedings here and there. Not on purpose."

"Mind if I feed her?"

"Go for it. Her bowl's on the kitchen floor, food's in the bottom left cabinet."

I start toward the bedroom as she heads into the kitchen. "She mostly sleeps all day anyway—eighteen hours or something like that."

"I remember reading that ferrets need a buddy. They're social. Not meant to be alone," she calls out.

Then comes the sound of a bag hitting the floor, followed by a cascade of kibble scattering across tile like marbles.

"Oh no—oh no! I'm so sorry!" she shouts from the kitchen.

I dart into the kitchen to assist her, nearly slipping as I round the corner. Tilly is in full-on feeding frenzy mode, her tiny body lunging and lunging again to scoop up as many scattered cereal bits as she can before we intervene. I snatch up the closest pieces just in time, before she can claim them and stash them in one of her many little hoarding nooks I've stumbled across over time. Still, she manages to snatch a few and dash away with them puffing from her mouth like trophies.

"She's fast," Tricia says with a quiet giggle.

"You have no idea."

Together we sweep the remnants into a dustpan, a synchronized rhythm forming between us—one holding, the other dumping. As I empty the last collection into the open bag she's holding, I notice her gaze through my peripheral—steady and searching, as if she's reading something etched beneath my skin.

"So what's your deal?" she asks.

I glance over, brow furrowing. "What do you mean?"

"I mean, what's your story?" she says, folding the top of the bag neatly. "I can see it in your eyes. The stress. You're a pressure cooker, Tommy. A cork ready to pop."

"You think so, huh? And what makes you the expert?"

Just as I finish speaking, her sleeve slips back slightly while she bends to tuck the bag into the cabinet. A pale scar, faint but unmistakable, crosses her wrist like an old truth that refuses to fade. My father once told me—side-to-side meant a cry for help. But lengthwise? That meant someone truly meant to say goodbye.

She catches me staring, but says nothing about it. Instead, she closes the cabinet softly and stands upright again, brushing invisible crumbs from her jeans.

"I've had my fair share of stress in my twenty-eight years. Name a bad situation, I've probably lived it—or something close." She meets my eyes. "But don't change the subject. I want to know what's eating at you. Why are you so... wound up?"

I shift my weight. "I really don't want to go into it."

"It's just us here." Her voice is gentle, not prying, but full of honest concern. "I want to help before something in you snaps. People who bury that kind of anger too long—either they hurt someone... or themselves."

"No, it's really okay," I say, my voice sharper than intended. "Can we talk about something else? Maybe not my anger."

She rises fully now and wipes her palms on her thighs, the softness in her face dimming just a little. "You don't have to bite my head off. I was only trying to help. Sometimes talking's the only way to make the weight go away."

I look at her—really look—and point toward the fading bruise beneath her eye. "Don't you think that's a little hypocritical of you to say that? I'll talk... if you do."

Before she can reply, three slow, deliberate knocks echo from across the hall. We freeze. Our eyes lock.

Then—three more, heavier than the first. A rhythm that demands attention.

Tricia gasps softly, fumbling her phone from her back pocket like it might confirm a fear. "What time is it?" she whispers. "Oh God... it's after six already?"

"Why are you whispering?"

She doesn't answer. Instead, she tiptoes to the front door and presses her cheek to the peephole, silent, unmoving. Whatever—or *whoev-*

er—she sees, she doesn't say. Her palms stay planted on the wood like she's bracing for a storm.

Another round of knocks. Louder. Angrier. Then retreating footsteps, fading into the hallway beyond.

She cracks the door, just enough to peer out.

"I have to go," she says in a whisper that feels heavier than any shout.

"Yeah," I mutter, sarcasm slipping in before I can stop it, "you really have a lot of explaining to do now."

She doesn't dignify it with a response—just casts a sharp look over her shoulder, full of disappointment... maybe even a little hurt, before vanishing through the door and softly clicking it shut behind her.

CHAPTER 11

CLEANSING OF THE WICKED

(8:16 PM)

Only two small, shriveled curly fries remain—cool and forgotten—at the bottom of my number three meal from the burger joint just down the block. I lounge on the couch, lost in thought, replaying the last conversation I had with Tricia. There was something unsettling about how effortlessly she peeled back my layers, reading the chaos in my eyes like a roadmap. Her words lingered, heavy and accurate. Maybe she had solved the riddle I couldn't decipher—what had truly set me off at work today.

While I drift in my own mind, Tilly seizes the moment. With a swift motion, she plucks the fry right from between my fingers, then springs from the couch and darts out of the room, her claws clicking against the floor like a mischievous warning bell.

It's only a quarter after eight, yet it feels much later. I'm restless. I stare at the empty patch of my nightstand where my electronics once lived—the things that used to fill the silence, keep my mind at bay. If I could just get my numbers up, hit that bonus, I could start replacing what I've lost.

I reach for a copy of my report and skim the details on Ms. Bridges. Late shift worker—won't be home until morning. That works in my favor. I could leave a card on her doorstep about the vehicle and avoid the kind of drama I dealt with from Mr. Martinez. No confrontation. No shouting. Just in and out. Easy. Like taking candy from a—

(1:15 AM)

I sit idle at a red light on Twenty-Seventh and Wisconsin Ave—famously the slowest signal in the city, or so it feels. My eyes wander to the corner store across the street where two homeless men are locked in a noisy spat over a battered paper bag. A pair of prostitutes work the far end of the block. Life churns here, even at this hour.

Out of the shadows, a tall man draped in a hood crosses the intersection with a pitch-black German Shepherd trotting beside him. Without pause, they melt into another alley across the way, as though swallowed by the dark itself.

I catch the faint shimmer of my stick-figure ornament swinging gently from the rearview mirror. In its reflection, a police cruiser creeps into view, slipping out from a side street and settling in just behind me. Lately, the sight of those red and blues has been enough to churn my stomach—and with good reason. I stay still, cautiously pulling the seatbelt over my shoulder and fastening it with deliberate care.

Suddenly, the squad car lets out a couple of sharp chirps from its siren and flashes its lights before shutting them off again. A hand appears from the driver's side window, gesturing impatiently for me to move along. In my focus on him, I hadn't even noticed the light had changed.

I ease forward, making a slow turn onto the next block to put distance between myself and the patrol car. But then, just as I think I'm in the clear, those lights erupt behind me again. My pulse hammers in my throat. But instead of pursuing me, the officer veers hard toward the sidewalk, hopping the curb to break up the two men still wrestling over their mystery bag.

A rush of relief floods my chest. I accelerate a little too aggressively, my back tires spinning on a hidden sheet of ice. The truck fishtails before straightening out with a shriek of rubber. Stupid. I'm lucky he didn't see that.

Finally, I roll into Ms. Bridges' neighborhood. The street is silent—no sign of movement, no flicker behind curtained windows. I kill the engine and sit for a moment in the hush, letting the stillness settle before I move.

I need something subtle—just enough to let her know we mean business—without crossing the line into anything that could land me or the company in legal trouble. On the back of a standard business card, I scribble *Call ASAP!!* in bold strokes. Without lingering on the ethics of it, I slide out of the truck and approach her front door with casual, practiced ease. I'm dressed in all black—long-sleeve tee, jeans, and sneakers—not by design, but the effect is just intimidating enough. I wedge the card into the screen door near the handle. Clean. Uncomplicated. Purposeful.

As I step off her porch, satisfied with the message I've left behind, something catches my eye—a large box propped against the green dumpster on the side of the house. I veer toward it, drawn by instinct more than intention. The glossy image on the front shows a sixty-inch flat screen TV, the kind that costs more than some used cars. Interesting.

My curiosity sharpens. I drift over to the front window and peek through a sheer curtain that offers little in the way of privacy. Inside, the new television rests like a crown jewel atop a sleek glass-and-wood entertainment stand. Below it, a Blu-ray player, a Wii console, and surround sound speakers are arranged with meticulous care. A plush, chocolate-brown leather couch and matching loveseat sit in front of it all, like a showroom frozen in time.

That itch for more details pulls me farther along the house. I move quietly toward the rear, mindful of each step. The kitchen curtains are wide open, the light above the stove casting a warm halo over stainless steel appliances that gleam like they've never known a dirty dish.

From there, I ease over to the back door and glance through the small windowpane. Her dining room comes into view—impeccably furnished with a dark wood table topped with mint-green marble so polished it almost glows. Six padded leather chairs surround it, matching the living room's theme with a designer's precision. If she's struggling, she hides it better than most.

"Greedy bitch," I mutter, my breath fogging a soft patch of the window.

I shift slightly, trying to get a better view of the hallway. I press against the door, just enough to tilt my head—and hear the unmistakable *click* of the lock giving way. The door creaks open an inch. My heart skips. I immediately retreat into the shadows beside the garage, crouching low between a cluster of bare bushes, eyes locked on the door and kitchen window. No alarm sounds. No lights flicker on. No barking. She told me during our last exchange, "I live alone, with no one to help me."

I repeat her words silently, studying the stillness.

The door swings slightly in the breeze, hinges moaning faintly with each sway. I rise from my crouch, the brittle twigs behind me scratching against my neck. My curiosity digs in deeper, sharper than before. I know I shouldn't, but I can't help myself—I slip toward the entrance and push the door open with slow, deliberate pressure.

It gives, releasing a drawn-out whine as it moves. The moment I step inside, I'm struck by the scent—soft vanilla intertwined with lavender, like a whisper wrapped in warmth. Enya's *Only Time* plays gently in the background, each note lingering in the air like a secret. A water fountain trickles peacefully in the corner beside the fireplace, casting soft reflections across the room.

As I step into her living room, the warm fragrance of lavender still hanging faintly in the air, my eyes land on a tidy stack of envelopes resting dead center on the glass coffee table. The pile sits like a silent confession, and though what I've already seen confirms plenty, I can't help myself—I need more. I crouch down and begin flipping through the stack, one envelope at a time, as if peeling back layers of a lie.

E.A.A.C. is stamped across the first envelope. Behind it—Red Mountain Gas & Electric, Stone Cutter's Jewelry, and a few bearing the insignia of Sanford Security, her listed employer. Could be check stubs. I slide my thumb beneath the flap of one and tear it open with practiced ease.

Inside is a recent stub, dated just last week. I remember Ms. Bridges mentioning wage garnishments for student loans, but this paper tells a different story. There are no deductions beyond the standard medical and dental. Her year-to-date 401(k) contributions top five thousand dollars. Her take-home pay? Seven hundred twenty-three dollars and thirty-two cents.

"Do not say to your neighbor, 'Go, and come again, tomorrow I will give it'—when you have it with you," I murmur, quoting aloud. "Proverbs 3:28, Ms. Bridges." With a flick of my wrist, I toss the stack of mail back onto the table where it lands with a papery sigh.

A wicked thought takes root—harmless, but unsettling enough to leave a mark. I walk through her house, quietly resetting every clock to 3:28. The wall clocks, the one on her microwave, even the analog alarm clock by her bed. Then, I remove the batteries, freezing time in place. I twist the dial on her alarm clock to set the wakeup chime—right at 3:28—but I don't activate it. I just leave the setting where it is, like a whispered threat only she will understand.

For the final touch, I take the Bible resting neatly on her end table and open it to the verse I quoted. Just so she knows someone's been here... someone who reads between the lines.

That's when it happens—a flash of headlights glints across the living room wall. Instinctively, I drop to the floor. The rumble of a car engine rolling up the driveway confirms my dread: Ms. Bridges is home. Early.

Panic crackles in my chest. I scramble to the front door, certain she's still in her car, still out of view—but the knob won't budge. My fingers twist and jerk at the handle, but it's locked tight. A double cylinder deadbolt. Keyed on both sides. No way out.

"Shit, Tommy! Think—think—think," I whisper harshly to myself, heart galloping.

I sprint back toward the kitchen, gently closing the rear door before she steps inside and realizes something's off. The jingle of her keys cuts through the tension like a blade. Then, the telltale squeal of the back screen door—long and metallic, like brake pads worn to the bone.

No time. Nowhere to go.

I rush down the hallway and duck into the back bedroom. With no better option, I drop to the floor and shimmy beneath the bed, my body low and flat, feet angled toward the headboard. I gather the clutter around me—shoes, scattered clothes—and pull them close, letting them shield me like debris in a storm.

She enters moments later. Her steps are deliberate, each one mapped by the groaning wood floor beneath her. My ears tune in to her position as though I've lived here for years. Then comes the flick of a light switch. The room glows. Her shiny black shoes appear right in front of my face as she kicks them off, unknowingly blocking my view.

I hold my breath.And wait.

The pungent scent of her damp, worn shoes assaults my nostrils, sharp and musty, laced with an undertone of something fouler—human waste, faint but undeniable. I wince and instinctively raise my hand to cover my nose, then gently nudge the shoes aside to clear my view.

From beneath the bed, I catch glimpses of her white socks as she moves. The hem of her gray slacks sways slightly with each pass—part of the standard security uniform I'd seen before in my report. She paces the room, breathing heavy from what I assume was a long, stressful shift.

Her phone rings, shattering the hush.

"Hey, Momma," she says, still winded. "Yeah, I'm home now... Cutter let me go home early because of it, so I'm okay." She exhales deeply, the weight of her day clinging to every word. "No Momma, I'm not gonna quit my job unless you're gonna help pay my bills for me." A tired laugh follows. "Well, the guy could've had a knife or a gun though. I'm kinda glad it was just a bag of shit he threw... Sorry, Momma. But okay, I'm home so you can stop worrying. I'm gonna take a shower and throw this uniform in the washer. love you too. Bye."

I hear the soft squeak of the bathroom door as it opens. A moment later, the water hisses on, echoing through the pipes like distant static. I watch as she peels off her socks, then unbuttons her slacks and shrugs off her shirt, letting them fall in a loose pile at her feet. With a rustle of the shower curtain, she steps into the tub and disappears behind a wall of water and steam.

Now. This is it.

I move quickly, brushing aside the shoe fortress I'd used for cover and crawling out from under the bed with all the caution I can muster. I rise to my feet in one fluid motion, aiming for the door, but my foot catches on the slender cord of the lamp perched on her nightstand. The base tips. I lunge—too late. The glass shatters against the floor with a crash that splits the silence.

The singing from the bathroom cuts off mid-note. The water stops.

Then comes the sharp rasp of the curtain rings being pulled back.

I freeze.

In the soft glow cast by the hallway light, she appears in the bathroom doorway. Her full, naked silhouette stands in stark contrast to the surrounding dark. The towel clutched to her chest does little to hide her shape. Her breathing is loud and uneven—through both her nose and mouth—as she scans the room, trying to pierce the shadows with narrowed, fearful eyes.

"Hello?" she says, her voice small and trembling.

I don't move. I don't breathe. I hope—foolishly—that she'll write the noise off as nerves or paranoia, and return to her shower. But she doesn't. She lingers in place, her body rigid, eyes fixed on the darkness that conceals me.

Then, slowly, she crosses to her dresser—positioning herself directly between me and the only exit. She picks up her phone and begins tapping the screen, her thumb gliding in frantic, uncertain swipes. If she calls for help now, I'm done.

I don't give her the chance.

I break into a full sprint, rounding the bed with the speed and focus of a defensive end locked on his mark. Her eyes flare wide, lips parting in a gasp, but there's no time to scream. I crash into her like a wave, knocking her off her feet and sending her flying backward into the hall. Her soaked skin squeals as it slides across the polished wood, her towel twisting loose and left behind like a flag of surrender.

She tries to scream, but only stammers, choking on breath and panic. Her limbs flail wildly as she scrambles to rise, slipping again and again on the slick floor.

The terror in her eyes is raw, unmistakable, as she glances back at the darkness she was hurled from.

She bolts, crawling and clawing her way toward the living room.

And I follow.

As I round the corner from the hallway into the living room, I find her still crawling, struggling to slide her glasses back onto her tear-streaked face. She fumbles, the lenses crooked, her fingers shaking. The moment her eyes rise and meet mine, she lets out a terrified scream that pierces through me like a jagged blade.

I strike before she can move—an instinctive, reckless haymaker that lands square on her jaw. Her head whips to the side, and her body drops flat to the floor, motionless.

My chest heaves, lungs fighting to keep pace with the hammering in my chest. The room feels as though it's tilting, shifting under the weight of what I've just done. My fists clench and unclench at my sides, buzzing with adrenaline. I force my eyes shut and inhale deep, trying to steady myself—trying to think.

I need to make sure she's still alive. That I haven't taken this too far. Again.

I crouch beside her, gently removing the bent glasses from her face. Her skin is warm, her breath faint against the silence. I press two fingers to her neck.

Her eyes snap open.

I jolt back, nearly falling. But she doesn't move. Doesn't flinch. Her eyes are wide and vacant, fixed on something beyond me—staring through me as if I were nothing more than a shadow. There's no focus in them. Just... stillness. Something eerie coils in my gut. I rise, unnerved, and back slowly into the kitchen, never taking my eyes off her.

She remains there, limp and staring.

In the dim light of the kitchen, I plant my palms against the counter-top, trying to catch my breath. Sweat slides down my nose, pools at my chin. I wipe it away with trembling hands, drying them on my jeans. I need to think. Fast.

There should be a towel around here. I pull my sleeve over my right hand and search the counter, then the drawers. Finally, I find a small hand towel folded near the sink. I begin wiping down the inside door-knob of the back entrance—just in case.

But the moment I finish, a sound slithers behind me. The metallic whisper of steel against wood.

I freeze.

"Get out of my house!" Her voice shakes but rises with fury. I turn slowly. There she stands, about ten feet away, clutching a knife pulled from its holder. The blade quivers in her grip, catching a glint of light from the stovetop. She holds it tight with both hands, just beneath her chest, pointed straight at me.

"You got five seconds to leave, or I'mmo kill you. I swear to God, I will. Just go!" she cries.

I don't move. Don't speak. We stare each other down across the small, cluttered kitchen. The air is thick with tension, her panic radiating in waves. I watch the tremor in her wrists, the wild fire in her eyes.

Could she identify me later?

I take a slow step forward.

She tightens her grip on the handle. Her breathing is quick, sharp—blood stains her lips, and she licks them reflexively. Her body shifts back, but she's not retreating. No—her knees bend, her heel bracing against the base of the cabinets like a sprinter preparing to launch.

Then, she screams—and charges.

She comes at me like a freight train, the knife thrust out like a rhino's horn, barreling through the kitchen with blind rage. I snatch a ceramic plate from the place setting on her table and raise it like a makeshift shield. Her feet slide out from under her on the slick tile, and she stumbles, swinging the blade wildly as she falls forward.

I pivot, just in time. Her swipe misses me by inches.

Her head cracks against the sharp edge of the marble tabletop with a dull, sickening thud. She collapses, her body seizing violently on the floor, limbs flailing, her breath stuttering through clenched teeth.

And then—silence, save for the low hum of the refrigerator and the dull ringing in my ears.

Only Time still echoes softly from the stereo, haunting the air with its melancholic melody. It must be looping on repeat—either that, or time itself has fractured, bending around the chaos I've found myself in. Everything feels slowed, surreal, like I'm wading through a dream stitched together with dread.

It takes nearly all my strength to roll her over. She's heavier than she looks, limp and unresponsive. As her body turns, my eyes lock on the hilt of the very knife she'd raised against me, now protruding from her abdomen. Blood oozes from the wound, dark and thick, sliding down her side and soaking into the fabric beneath her.

Her eyes are partly open, glassy and unfocused. She stares through me—or maybe into me—like a mirror reflecting every reckless decision I've made.

Suddenly, I'm back with Mr. Martinez—his gurgling cough, the crimson bubbling from his lips, the way he looked at me just before the end. That same helpless defiance. That same mess.

I rub my eyes hard, as if I can wipe the memory away, erase the echo. But when I look again, she's still here. Still bleeding. Still real. And I'm still the one who did it.

"Damnit!" I shout down at her, fury building behind my clenched teeth. "Why did you come home early? You should've stayed at work, Ms. Bridges, and none of this shit would've happened!" I drive my foot into her ribs—once, then again, harder. "Stupid! Why couldn't you just pay your damn bill!?"

I run my fingers through my hair, yanking it back as I pace from the kitchen to the living room and back again, stepping over her body like she's nothing more than debris. My mind races in circles, no answers, only panic and shame twisted up with rage.

She's too big to move. Not like Martinez—he was small, wiry. Disposable. Ms. Bridges is solid. There's no way I'm lifting her into the truck without being seen or throwing out my back in the process.

Frustrated, I yank out one of the chairs at the head of the kitchen table and drop into it, breathing hard. She lies just below me, a tangle of blood and breathlessness.

"Why couldn't you just pay your bill?" I ask again, softer this time, my voice frayed. I lean down, peering at her through narrowed eyes. "Hmm? All this nice stuff... all this luxury you can't afford. Why do people like you reward yourselves while others scrape by? Why do people like me have to come chase what's owed? Why must we suffer so you can pretend you're something you're not?"

I sit back upright and drum my fingers along the edge of the table, the rhythm matching the pulse in my temple. My anger rises again, boiling through the cracks.

"And you had the audacity to talk about my parents. *My* parents." I grit the words. "Who the fuck are you to do that? You don't even know them. Hell, *I* barely knew them."

I glance down at her one last time. Her chest no longer moves.

"You know what you are, Ms. Bridges?" I whisper, venom lacing each syllable. "You're a selfish, bible-thumping, hateful, arrogant, lying bitch."

With both hands, I grip the edge of the heavy marble tabletop—cold, solid, absolute—and heave it forward. It crashes down onto her head with a sickening, wet crack, silencing the room for a moment as *Only Time* continues to play, soft and steady.

I drop into my seat again, spent.

Her blood, now pooling around the shattered ruins of her face, begins to spread across the tile, inching toward my feet. When it gets close enough, I see my reflection rippling in its surface—my shadowed silhouette staring back at me like an echo I can't shake.

A darker version of myself. Watching. Waiting. Approving.

CHAPTER 12

THE DEVILS REWARD

(Two weeks later – 6:35 AM)

I'm halfway through my fifth set of push-ups—twenty-five reps per set—my palms pressed into the worn-out carpet, the rhythm of my breath syncing with the rise and fall of my body. A dull ache burns in my shoulders, but I welcome it. It's proof that I'm growing stronger. The ten-inch tube television—an ancient relic I picked up off Craigslist for next to nothing—sputters static before settling into the morning news. The screen flickers, casting a faint blue glow across the room.

Ever since the incident with Ms. Bridges, I've realized just how fragile I really was—physically, mentally. That revelation pushed me into a daily regimen of at-home workouts. My frame is still lean, wiry, but there's definition now—tightened muscle clinging to bone, and a core strength I hadn't known I was capable of.

From the tinny speaker, the voice of Conzuelo Valdez cuts through the air like a blade:

Newscaster (Conzuelo Valdez): "Police are still asking for leads on the murder of Milwaukee resident Carmen Bridges, who was found dead almost two weeks ago in her home. Detectives have discovered some possible clues that could help in the investigation. Investigators did mention that all of the clocks and digital devices in her home were adjusted to 3:28. Later, detectives made another discovery in relation to this number when they found the victim's Bible opened to Proverbs 3:28, highlighted in her own blood. The scripture relates to debts owed by the wicked, so police believe this to be drug or gang related. If anyone has any information pertaining to this case, please call Crime Stoppers at 1-800-55CRIME."

Conzuelo Valdez (continued): "Also, police would appreciate any information on a man who has been missing for a few weeks."

Her voice softens as a photograph fades in—one I know all too well.

Valdez: "Mr. Nemo Jose Martinez, age thirty-seven, has not returned to his home or visited any relatives, which, according to his family and friends, is highly unusual. Police suspect foul play after discovering his pet dog... dead, inside the microwave."

I pause mid-rep, my chest hovering above the floor, sweat trailing down my temple. The muscles in my arms tremble slightly as I push upward, finishing the set in silence. The TV drones on, but my focus sharpens like a blade.

I've been watching the news religiously since that night—not out of guilt, but out of strategy. A hunter listening for movement in the tall grass. So far, they haven't deviated from the script. The details are vague. Theories scattered. The anchors keep circling the same points, offering nothing new. Which, frankly, is good news.

I made sure to leave no loose ends. No fingerprints. No shoe treads. No stray hairs. I scrubbed the scene of my sins with methodical care. And as the days have slipped by, the sharp edge of my paranoia has dulled, replaced by something new.

Confidence.

Control.

Something inside me has shifted. The anxiety that once gnawed at the corners of my mind has grown quiet, and in its place... a strange, intoxicating calm. A cocky version of myself, rising with each clean morning, as though I've not just outrun the storm—but mastered it.

(8:00 AM)

"Well, thank you for showing up on time today, Mr. Thorpe!" Kathy calls out from the depths of her office chair, watching me with her usual blend of sarcasm and smug authority as I drop my bag at my cubicle.

I offer no reply—just a smile tight enough to be polite, loose enough to betray how little I care for her morning games. It's the end of the month, and I can already sense she's sharpening her claws, ready to tear into my performance stats.

Derrick's cubicle, a few paces away, comes alive with his usual symphony of low muttering and rustling paper. His curse words spill out in clipped bursts. Typically, I let his tantrums fade into background noise—he throws fits like this every other week. It's either bad numbers, or his wife riding him for wasting another paycheck on video games or new headphones.

But something about the weight in his voice this morning pulls at my curiosity. I lean over the divider. "What's up, bro?"

"Nothing you need to concern yourself with... Mr. MurderRoute," he mutters, eyes locked on his screen.

My chest tightens. "Mr. MurderRoute?" I echo back, lowering my voice. "What the fuck is that supposed to mean?"

Without looking at me, he hands me a report over the cubicle wall. "Check the stats and find out for yourself." When he finally meets my eyes, his expression is more wounded than angry. "Two high balances dropped off your route. That alone pushed your numbers into the green. So guess who's suddenly getting the bonus this month?"

I take the report from his hand, stunned. He's right. My delinquency rate has dipped below team average, which pushes me into the top slot. And it doesn't take a genius to realize which two names are missing—Mr. Martinez and Ms. Bridges, both of them formerly albatrosses on my balance sheet. Gone.

I flip through the notes with shaking fingers. Martinez's vehicle was returned. Carmen's account is now marked "Deceased." And oddly enough, my initials as the account manager have vanished, scrubbed clean. Only the echoes of our conversations remain in the logs.

A smile creeps across my face. It starts in the corners and stretches, slow and steady.

"Yeah, enjoy that while you can," Derrick growls, snatching his report back.

"What's that supposed to mean?" I ask with a chuckle. "You gonna steal my route again?"

No response. Just a shake of the head, heavy with resentment.

"Thorpe! Come in here please," Kathy calls out, her voice a little too satisfied.

Damn. I exhale through my nose and rise slowly, my report and notepad in hand, steeling myself for whatever theatrics she has planned. But really, what can she say? I've hit the numbers. If anything, she ought to say, "Congratulations."

I step into her office with my chin slightly raised and the barest hint of a smirk. She adjusts her glasses, eyes dancing over the pages in front of her as I settle into the chair.

"Sit down," she says, flipping through the report like she's searching for a mistake.

Then, after a long pause: "Wow. You are one lucky son of a gun, Thorpe. How the hell you've managed to benefit from someone else's tragic loss like this is beyond me. I hate to say this, but you're at the top of the team now and haven't done a lick of work to get there."

"That's not true," I say, my tone rising with conviction. I scoot forward, lay my report flat on her desk, and start pointing out names. "I've busted my ass getting these smaller balance accounts in order. Look here—and here. Most of them are on time now. My high balances are few and far between. This is the route you assigned me, and I worked it exactly how I was supposed to."

"Do you really think you deserve this bonus, Thorpe?" Kathy asks, slowly removing her glasses, letting them dangle in her hand like some sort of verdict.

"Are you kidding me?" I snap back, my voice louder than intended.

And there it is—the glint in her eyes I've come to recognize. That thin, gleaming veil of manipulation, masked in professionalism. It's the same look she gave me when she first made her indecent offer—draped in suggestion, wrapped in power.

"Your performance was lacking this month, Thorpe. You've been late. You've neglected your route. You haven't followed company policy. I could still fire you," she states, matter-of-factly, her fingers laced neatly beneath her chin like she's playing chess and has just whispered the word *check* across the board. "Mr. Gibbons will back me if I say you're undeserving of this bonus."

"You would take my bonus away, Kathy?" I ask, trying not to let the disbelief twist into something worse.

"In a heartbeat... unless..." Her grin curves upward, slow and smug.

"Unless, huh? Unless what?" I lean forward, though I already know the game.

"Well, it is Friday. I could use a little company tonight. Are you free?"

I feel my throat tighten. "Well, I figure if I'm going to keep my bonus this month, I better be. Right?"

She smiles. That same knowing, predatory smile that had haunted my thoughts since the first time. It's been weeks since that night, and though I've tried to scrub it from my memory, the ache it left behind—both physical and psychological—has lingered like a bruise that refuses to heal. What stings more is knowing exactly why I felt that pain.

I want to say something now. Lay down rules. Draw a line in the sand. But I don't. Not yet.

Instead, I keep the calm mask in place.

"Do I need to remind you what you need to do?" she teases, biting her lower lip.

"No. Just wait for a text, I suppose?" I say flatly. My voice gives nothing away, but the disgust coils behind my ribs like smoke.

"Good boy." She reaches for her phone and leans back into her chair. "Now get out of my office and make some money," she says, waving me off like a dog who's done his trick.

I stand. But this time, I leave with a smile of my own—slow, creeping, and razor thin.

As I return to my cubicle, I catch Derrick watching me from the corner of his eye. He's scanning my face, trying to decipher what just went down behind that office door. He's waiting for a clue. If I came out looking pissed, he'd pounce with questions. But a smile? That keeps him in check.

"Hey," he calls carefully. "What was that all about?"

"Oh, she just wanted to congratulate me on my bonus for this month, that's all. And for taking the lead on the team."

"Oh." He sounds unconvinced. "I'm surprised they let you keep it, since two of your high balances were write-offs. But... that's cool."

"Whatever they are, man, it's still five hundred extra dollars in my pocket."

His lips pinch together like he's holding something back—anger, jealousy, maybe both. I sit at my desk, calmly logging into my system, pretending not to notice the weight of his stare boring into the back of my head.

From the other side of the cubicle, I hear Kimmie snicker under her breath.

Yeah. Everyone's watching now.

(7:42 PM)

The pile of sticks in Gram's backyard is massive—dry, ashen gray, and brittle enough to snap beneath the weight of my boots. They crunch like old bones as I break them down and load them into the bed of my truck. Each splintered limb stirs an unwelcome memory of the last time I ran that wood chipper. I still hear its grinding teeth, still see what was left of Mr. Martinez churned into a slurry of blood and bone. I have no desire to hear that sound again.

While I'm stomping the load flat, balancing myself in the bed of the truck, the back door creaks open behind me. Gram steps out, her house slippers scuffing the porch as she makes her way over, holding a plate wrapped in tinfoil and grinning like she's about to scold me with love.

"Oh, thank you so much, Suga, for clearing that all out for me," she calls out, shielding her eyes from the dying sunlight. "The yard looks so much better now. I'm gonna have to throw some grass seed over there, since those damn sticks killed off my lawn. Come on down here."

I hop down with a thud and land beside her, brushing bark and dirt from my pants. "You're welcome, Gram. Anything for you," I say, leaning in to plant a kiss on her soft, powdered cheek.

"Gram, you didn't have to bring me any food."

"I know what I have to do, young man, and it's to feed you," she says, nudging the plate against my chest. "So go ahead and take it now. You know you're not gonna win here."

I smile, defeated. "Yes, ma'am," I say, placing the warm plate on the passenger seat of the truck.

"Now what are you going to do with all of that in the bed of your truck?" she asks, glancing over my shoulder.

"I'm just gonna burn it up, Gram. I know a spot I can do it. I took those two old aluminum gas cans from the shed to use. Hope that's okay."

"Well, baby, just don't blow yourself up, hear?" she warns, only half-joking. "You make sure that you come and see your Grandma this weekend? You seem a little distracted lately."

"Okay, I promise. I'll pick you up Sunday at nine o'clock in the morning for church."

"Lord willing. I may be with your Granddad by then."

"Come on, Gram! Please don't start that," I say, half-laughing, half-scolding.

"Well, I'm just preparing you for when that day comes, sweetie. You just never know when it will." She gives me that soft smile, the kind only a woman who's lived through storms can give, then leans in to kiss my cheek.

"Go get some rest. And eat, for God's sake."

I climb into my truck, and she stays planted there in the gravel, hands on her hips like she's watching her world roll off again. I give her a warm smile, start the engine, and roll down the window.

"Love you, Gram!!"

"Love you too, sweetie," she calls back, blowing me a kiss that floats on the breeze.

(9:31 PM)

The flickering shadows of *Nosferatu* dance across my walls, casting long, exaggerated shapes that stretch like clawed fingers toward the ceiling. My thrift-store DVD player hums softly as the grainy black and white film sputters on. I drift in and out of sleep, lulled by the eerie silence that punctuates the vampire's slow ascent up the staircase, his silhouette looming with every measured step.

I should feel on edge, but instead, I float in that half-sleep state where time has no real meaning—waiting, unwillingly, for a text I hope won't come.

But it does.

The sharp buzz of my phone against the table jolts me upright. My heart jumps. For a second, I pray it's not her.

"Room 237. Same location. 11:30 PM."

Short. Cold. Businesslike.

I stare at the message as if it might rewrite itself if I give it long enough. Part of me wants to ignore it. Lie. Say I'm sick. Say I'm out of town. Say I'm dead. But that other part—the part that can't let things go, the part with something to prove—knows I'll go. Not for her, but for me.

(11:05 PM)

The dark jeans fit snug and straight. My black T-shirt clings just enough to the chest to make me look like I might've been hitting the gym. I spike my hair with a little mousse, tousled in a way that says I didn't try too hard, even though I clearly did. One last glance in the full-length mirror—clean, sharp, presentable. I hit myself with a quick spritz of Curve cologne and pocket my keys.

The deadbolt jams again. I jiggle the key, grunt under my breath, then kick the door in frustration just as I hear her voice behind me.

"Well hey there, stranger."

I turn, startled. Tricia stands outside her door in a loose t-shirt and faded shorts. Her skin catches the low hallway light, and I notice the faint purple shadows of bruises along her arms and legs.

"Hey," I say. "It's not me who's the stranger. Where've you been all this time?"

The bolt finally gives with a reluctant *click*.

"Here and there," she shrugs, leaning against the wall like she's melting into it. "Just kind of keeping to myself, you know. Where are you headed so late? Smelling like trouble. Hot date?"

"No," I lie. "Just the store. Tilly's running low on food."

She grins knowingly. "You lie."

"What makes you think that?"

"Never mind."

We stand in silence—her toe looping over the other like she's tying knots with her feet. There's something heavy hanging in the air between us. Not romantic. Not even tension. Just a weight neither of us is ready to lift.

"What's going on?" I ask, resting my back against the door. "What's wrong?"

"Nothing. I'm all right."

"You lie."

She laughs softly, then sighs. Her foot fans out, toes spreading, as if she could ground herself through the linoleum.

"It's just hard sometimes, you know?"

"What do you mean?"

"Struggling all the time. Just... I don't know. Life's just fucked up."

"Ain't that the truth?"

"I wish there was no such thing as money," she says, voice low. "No clothes, no cars, no stupid TVs. The world would be better without all of it. People might actually be decent for once. I hate the world. I hate my life."

I look at her—really look at her. Despite the tired eyes, the worn voice, she's still beautiful in a bruised kind of way.

"You're a beautiful woman," I tell her. "And you seem like you've got a lot going for you. Why would you hate your life?"

She lets out a bitter laugh.

"You know how many guys have said that to me? That I'm beautiful, that I could have anything I want?" She shakes her head. "I wish it were that easy—to just bat my eyes and have everything I need handed over. But guys... they'll say anything. It's always the same in the end."

Her words hang there—quiet, aching, familiar.

"I'm not trying to get into your pants. I was just..."

She tilts her head toward the ceiling, letting the harsh white light spill across her face. Her eyes shimmer, beginning to pool with tears that glint like glass.

"I'm sorry. I'm sure you have things to do, and here I am holding you up."

"No. You're not holding me up at all. But I don't know what to say, or what I can offer to make you feel better."

She turns her gaze to mine, and something in her expression softens—vulnerable, desperate in the gentlest way. "Can you just, be my friend? I don't have very many of those anymore. You seem like a nice guy."

"What? Of course." I extend my hand, trying to anchor the moment. "I don't have many friends myself. As a matter of fact, Tilly..."

But before I can finish, she rushes into me, her arms wrapping tightly around my waist in a sudden, trembling embrace. I barely have time to respond, my arms just starting to rise—when she pulls away just as fast, turning and darting through her doorway. The door slams behind her, leaving the air thick with everything unspoken.

I stand there, frozen in place, my hand still awkwardly extended—no handshake, no goodbye. Just the echo of her retreat. And yet, what she gave me in that fleeting moment meant more than any handshake. It was a rare thing. A gift. Something I've never really had before. My heart pounds, not from dread or adrenaline—but something warmer. Something that feels... good.

(11:21 PM)

I pull into the gas station just like before. The place hasn't changed—the same pale fluorescent hum, the same sleepy-eyed clerk perched behind the counter. The rhythm of it all hits like déjà vu, echoing the last time I stopped here before seeing Kathy.

He lifts his head and smiles as I walk in.

"You guys have any rope or bungee cord?" I ask.

"Go straight down that aisle to your left. I should have a few on the bottom shelf."

He leans over the counter with both palms flat, his eyes tracking me as I move. I'm the only one here, so I guess I've become his entertainment for the moment. I grab the rope and bring it to the counter, tossing it in front of him.

"Did you find everything okay?" he asks.

I chuckle. "Yeah, thanks."

"Is that gonna be all for you then?"

"No, I'll take this pack of gum," I reply, digging into my back pocket for my wallet. "Oh yeah, and let me get two gallons on pump three."

"Big plans tonight?" he asks with a smirk.

"Nah, just hanging out. Have to burn those sticks in back of my truck, but I need to tie them down 'cause they're blowing all over when I drive."

"Nice." He scans my items. "You were here the other night a few weeks or so ago, weren't you?" He hands me my change. I say nothing. "Yeah, you were dressed a little differently too, but I remember. Much better look, bro—much better."

"Thanks."

"Yep, have a good one. And be careful out there, the streets have been crazy lately."

(11:27 PM)

I sit behind the wheel outside the hotel, the engine idling while my thoughts spiral. The lot is anything but quiet. A couple argues a few cars down—his voice sharp, hers raw with betrayal. A second girl climbs out of the passenger side, slamming the door and storming away. It doesn't take much guessing to know what just went down.

All around them, doors open and curtains part. The hotel guests become spectators, eyes flickering with judgment or boredom, maybe both. I stay where I am, tucked in the shadows of my cab, watching, waiting—trying to sort through my own storm before stepping into another.

There's way too much chaos unfolding out here. Voices rising, doors slamming, fists threatening to fly—it's all too exposed. Something about it feels off. Wrong. Like a current pulling me toward something I shouldn't be near. I trust that feeling. So instead of stepping out into the open, I reach for my phone and send Kathy a quick message.

"No thanks! I just can't do this. If this is what I have to do to keep my job, then you can fire me Monday? Find someone else to play your bedroom games tonight. I'm done."

I sit in the truck a moment longer, watching the drama play out across the lot. The guy now stands between the two women, his arms raised in some desperate, useless attempt at peacekeeping. His girlfriend lunges past him, her hand drawn back to strike the other girl—the mistress, by the looks of it. The air buzzes with anger and confusion, a crowd gathering like moths to the flame of conflict.

Then I spot it: a narrow, dimly lit stairway at the back of the hotel, well away from the commotion.

I crank the engine, keep my lights off, and ease the truck around to the rear lot where I park beside a massive dumpster. No one in sight. No cameras I can see. Just the soft hum of the building behind me and the rustling of wind through chain-link fencing.

Taking the steps two at a time, I make my way to the second floor. The corridor is silent, shadows clinging to the corners as I locate room 237. I knock three times, firm and deliberate.

The door jerks open just enough for Kathy to wedge her body into the frame and lean out. Her breath hits me like a wave—sharp and sour with liquor.

"Right on time, baby. What, no rose this time?" she slurs with a lopsided grin. "And I'm guessing you've quickly changed your mind after that text you just sent."

She's clearly been drinking heavily. Her speech is slow and unsteady, and she's gripping the door like it's the only thing keeping her upright. Past her head, I spot movement—faint, subtle. The bathroom door shifts slightly, casting a sliver of light across the worn carpet before slowly narrowing again.

Looks like our friend is here again.

"You're looking hot in your little dark get-up," she adds, swinging the door open farther. She steps back to drink in the sight of me as I cross the threshold.

"Thanks."

"I need to go to the bathroom to change, but first let me get you something to drink."

"I could use a drink."

"I hope you like E&J, 'cause that's all we got. No grapes or cheese this time. Well, that and that bottle of wine in my purse, but we forgot the corkscrew, so..."

"Who's we?"

She hesitates, just a flicker. "Well, you and me, Tommy—who else."

I watch her carefully as I sit on the edge of one of the two beds, the one closest to the bathroom door. Her movements are clumsy, exaggerated by drunken sway. She fumbles with something near her purse, her flabby upper arm wobbling as she shakes—what, a powder? A dropper? I can't see clearly, but I've seen enough.

She's trying to drug me again.

"Here you are," she says, handing me a short glass filled with amber liquid. "And I'll be right back. Bottoms up, buttercup. Oh, and you see that big-ass bottle over there? There's plenty more, so help yourself."

The moment the bathroom door clicks shut behind her, I move quickly.

I crouch and pour the drink out beneath the bed, letting it soak into the ugly motel carpet. Then I grab a corner of the sheet and wipe the inside of the glass until it's bone dry. I move with precision—quiet, deliberate—then pour myself a small splash of the E&J from the bottle, just enough to make it look like I've taken a few casual sips.

Let her think she's ahead of the game.

Let her feel like she's winning.

A few minutes slip by. Then, at last, Kathy emerges from the bathroom, pulling the door closed behind her, though the fluorescent light within still spills out beneath it. She's changed—or rather, undressed—now wearing a red lace bra and a matching thong that vanishes between the folds of her oversized, dimpled backside. Her pale, freckled skin almost glows beneath the harsh motel lighting, the crimson fabric drawing stark contrast against it.

She teeters forward in a pair of black stiletto heels, each step unsteady, her balance clearly compromised by the alcohol. She heads straight for her cell phone, her back to me, swiping at the screen with clumsy determination.

"What are you doing?" I ask.

"Trying to find some music for us. What do you like?"

"I don't know. You have any Enya?"

"Oh my God no! Are you kidding?" she barks out a laugh. "Do you really listen to that?"

"I've kinda grown to like it recently."

The haunting beat of *Sweet Dreams*—Marilyn Manson's version—slinks from the phone's speaker, dark and brooding. Seemingly satisfied, she turns her attention to me, staggering with intention as she approaches, deliberately swaying her hips with each unbalanced step.

She stops just inches away, locking eyes with me as she begins to move with the rhythm—gyrating slowly, sensually. Her fingertips travel lightly across her belly, up over the curve of her chest, then glide over her shoulders and into her tousled red hair. With practiced seduction, she massages her scalp and lets the strands fall in waves across her eyes. Her gaze never leaves mine.

One hand twirls a few strands of hair lazily between her fingers, while the other glides between her thighs, tracing invisible paths. She turns slowly, her back now to me, and bends slightly at the waist—offering a full rear view, then casting a look back over her shoulder, lips parted in a coy, silent invitation.

Surprisingly, I find myself reacting more than I anticipated. There's something almost hypnotic in the way she moves, but the illusion is fleeting. I remind myself—*he's still here*. The man behind the bathroom door. Watching. Waiting. This performance isn't just for me. It's a countdown. She's buying time, waiting for the drug she thinks I drank to hit.

Keeping my expression neutral, I lift the glass of E&J and knock back the last swallow in a single gulp, then slam it down hard on the nightstand.

She grins. "Let me get you another one," she says, voice eager, and snatches the glass with practiced speed.

With her back turned, I stand and approach slowly, soundlessly. She's focused on the drink—dropping what looks like powdered sugar into the fresh pour, then swirling it gently with her pinky finger. I slide up behind her, pressing my body close, letting her feel the full pressure of my presence. She startles, and the glass tumbles from her hand.

"Oh damn! Damnit, Tommy; look what you did." She bends to retrieve it, swearing under her breath. "You can't just sneak up like that, sweetie. That was a perfectly good glass of liquor."

As she scoops up the scattered ice, I reach casually into her open purse and pull out the unopened bottle of wine. It's heavier than it looks. Cold.

She begins to rise, and just before she straightens fully, she catches a flicker of my reflection in the mirror.

Too late.

I bring the bottle down with swift, brutal force. It cracks across the back of her skull with a dull, wet thud, and she crumples to the floor like a marionette with its strings cut.

"Yeah I know, I'm sorry," I say loudly, pitching my voice toward the closed bathroom door. "I really want to try that wine again though. I have a tool in my truck to open that up if you like. I'll be right back."

I drag Kathy's limp, heavy body across the worn carpet, her arms flopping uselessly beside her. She's dead weight—literally—and I can only pull her so far before my muscles start to burn. I manage to wedge her between the two beds and lay her out face-up, her mouth slack, eyes half-lidded. No time to second-guess. No time to breathe. I need to move before the creep in the bathroom grows impatient and comes out looking for her.

I slip out the door, closing it quietly behind me, and make my way back to the truck.

Inside, I grab the two aluminum containers of gasoline, the dustpan, and the rope I picked up earlier. The night air feels colder now, heavier. Purpose sharpens everything. Once I re-enter the room, I move quickly, efficiently.

I head straight for the small sink just outside the bathroom. Its porcelain basin is cracked and stained from years of use, but it will serve. I crouch beneath it, tying one end of the rope securely around the U-shaped trap under the sink. The other end I stretch to the bathroom door and tie with a mover's knot—tight, but not too tight. I leave enough slack to crack the door open, just enough to make my move.

The bucket of ice in the sink gets dumped without hesitation. I pour a generous amount of gasoline into it, letting the strong, nauseating fumes rise around me. My pulse is steady. Focused.

I ready the bucket, draw in a deep breath, and open the bathroom door.

Sitting on the edge of the tub is a middle-aged man with stark white hair. He's dressed in nothing but powder-blue boxers, black dress socks pulled tight beneath his knees, and a thin white t-shirt stretched across a soft gut. His fingers are fiddling with the straps of a leather mask. His voice is a quiet rasp.

"Hell, it's about time."

He stands—slowly, almost relieved—but his expression shifts the instant he sees me. Shock drains the color from his face.

In a sudden burst of panic, he lunges at the door, slamming his shoulder into it, trying to force it shut. His sock-covered feet slide uselessly across the slick tile floor. I shove back, harder. He grunts, loses traction, and collapses to his hands and knees.

I drive the door into his face with brutal force. There's a sickening crunch. Blood spills down from a fresh gash on his forehead, trailing into his eyes and over the bridge of his nose. He stares up at me, dazed and drenched in fear.

"So you like to screw dudes in the ass while they're unconscious?" I say coldly. "You should burn in hell for that sin."

He tries to speak, but only manages a stuttering breath. I raise the bucket and douse him with the gasoline. He sputters, gasping as the liquid splashes over his chest and down his legs. I slam the door and, without hesitation, yank the knot tight.

"What the..." he sputters, breaking into coughing fits as the fumes hit his lungs. "What the fuck is this? Jesus!"

The doorknob rattles. He's trying to open it—yanking, shaking, kicking. The rope holds.

I drop to one knee and slide the dustpan under the base of the door, then slowly pour the remainder of the gasoline from the first container onto it. The liquid funnels cleanly beneath the door.

"Hey, no—what are you doing?" he cries, pounding the door with both fists. "Please don't do this. I didn't do anything wrong. I'm sorry. Hey man, answer me, please! Hey!"

I pause. "If you didn't do anything, why are you apologizing?"

His silence is short-lived—replaced by more begging, more pleading. I don't respond.

I take the thin plastic liner from the ice bucket, stretch it across the lone smoke detector in the room, and snap a rubber band over it to keep the seal tight. The cheap hotel isn't built for safety anyway, but I'm not taking chances.

From my pocket, I retrieve a small cardboard matchbook. I strike one.

The tip bursts into flame, a slow, flickering burn that crawls up the stick like a fuse. The air is thick now with gasoline and fear, the pounding on the bathroom door growing more frantic.

I wait.

Just a moment longer.

Just before the fire reaches my fingertips, I flick the match toward the door. The moment the flame meets the air thick with fumes, the gasoline ignites in a violent burst—an explosion of heat and light that blooms outward like a fire-breathing beast. It erupts before the match even touches the floor. The bathroom door, thankfully hinged to open inward, absorbs the blast. It trembles, quivering under the pressure, but holds fast.

From inside comes a guttural scream, raw and piercing. I hear the man thrashing, the metallic rings of the shower curtain screeching as he pulls it down in his panic. The sound claws at my nerves.

I wince, instinctively stepping back, my eyes darting to the walls as if expecting someone to burst through them. The walls are thin. Paper-thin. I can only pray no one in the other rooms is sober—or curious—enough to check.

I grab a few thick, scratchy bathroom towels and begin wiping down anything I may have touched—doorknobs, light switches, surfaces. When I'm satisfied, I drench the towels in water from the sink and wedge them tight under the base of the door, sealing in the smoke, the screams, and the growing inferno behind it.

Kathy remains sprawled between the beds, her body still and heavy, unmoved since I laid her there. That blow to the head, coupled with the alcohol, has her under deep. She'll be out for a while yet.

I turn my attention to the briefcase they brought with them—its contents now laid bare on the bed like a perverse inventory. Dildos, handcuffs, lotions, whips... tools of indulgence and control. But one item in particular draws my attention. I don't touch it. Just stare. Then I close the case, leaving the rest of their twisted toolkit scattered across the comforter like discarded toys.

Standing over her, I speak aloud without expecting a reply. "Now what do I do with you?"

It takes everything I've got to wrestle her weight back onto the bed. She's limp and uncooperative, a burden of flesh and regret. I bind her wrists and ankles with the same rope from earlier, securing each end to the heavy legs of the bed frame. Once I'm sure she's going nowhere, I grab the now full ice bucket and return to her side.

Hovering above her, I tilt the bucket and let the water pour slowly over her face—targeting her nose and mouth. The shock is immediate. She jolts, gagging and choking, her body bucking against the restraints. Her eyes shoot open wide, wild with confusion and fear.

I reach for the bunched-up bed sheet near her head and gently dab the water from her eyes.

"Thorpe!" she snarls, yanking at the ropes. "Fucking untie me now, or I swear to God you're screwed."

I lower myself to the edge of the bed beside her, my expression unreadable.

"Did you fucking lose it, Thorpe? Untie me now!" she shouts again, pulling harder. The rope digs into her wrists, biting deep until her hands flush a vibrant purple.

"Oh my God. Chad!" she cries, her voice cracking as she turns her face toward the bathroom door. "Chad!"

"So that's his name?" I ask.

She stops, her head snapping back to me. Her eyes narrow, confused, terrified.

"Well, I don't think Chad will be helping you anytime soon."

"What... What did you do to him? Where is he?" she demands, voice high and strained.

I close my eyes for a moment and inhale through my nose, slow and deliberate, lifting my head as I savor the scent.

"Ugh... so that's what burnt human flesh smells like. Do you smell that? Kinda nauseating and sweet at the same time. Somewhat... steaky, with a hint of burnt hair. Hell, you can almost taste it."

"Thorpe," she says, and her voice falters—cracks. "Please tell me you didn't. This is a fucking joke, right? Let me go—let me go now, Thorpe, and I won't say a word to anyone."

I lean in just slightly, not to intimidate her, but so she can't mistake what I say next.

"You see, even now—with you tied to a bed, completely at my mercy—you still don't get it. You still think you're in charge. That you can give orders. That you're owed something."

Her eyes go wide. Her breathing ragged.

"God, you crazy son-of-a-bitch!"

"That surely won't help you any," I say, staring down at her, my voice low and steady. "So tell me... that first night we were together—what exactly did you let that burnt piece of shit do to me?"

She doesn't answer, but she doesn't have to. Her eyes betray her, wide and glassy, fixed on me with mounting dread.

"I mean, I woke up feeling... off. Less than myself. Sore as hell. Something happened. God only knows what you two did to me."

I reach across the bed and pick up one of the larger toys from the cluttered mess they brought. I don't use it—I just let it hang from my hand above her face, letting the weight of the unspoken accusation sink in.

"Was this it? Sure as hell felt like it."

Still, she stays silent. Her breathing grows faster, more ragged, and she twists at her restraints, wrists pulling hard against the rope. The panic rising in her is nearly palpable.

"Oh, now you've got nothing to say? That's funny. You always had something to say at work—giving orders, making threats, playing games with people's lives. All that talk, and now you're mute. Because of your bullshit... that's three now. Three."

"Three?" she whispers, voice cracking with desperation. "What do you mean, three?"

I smile coldly.

"Well, I did tell you I had to work hard to get that route down. What, you thought it was just luck something happened to my top two competitors? You think the world just clears a path like that by accident?"

Her expression changes—jaw trembling, lips parting in disbelief. The fear in her eyes sharpens into something raw and shaking. Then come the tears. Loud and broken.

I climb onto the bed, straddling her waist. She thrashes, trying to buck me off, but the panic robs her of coordination. Her strength fades fast. I place a firm hand under her chin and press her mouth closed.

"Are you done?" I ask.

She sobs harder, each breath more hysterical than the last. And the more she cries, the more that quiet rage I've carried builds. It claws up my spine, begging for release.

I grab the dildo and try to shove the head of it in her mouth. She clenches her jaw and screams through her tightened lips. I smack her across the face numerous times until her mouth tires and finally falls open. Quickly, I grab her by the throat, press my palm on her Adam's apple, and then jam the head of the dildo into her mouth. Little by little, I twist and turn it further in; her eyes rolling upward.

"Good girl, eat it, eat it."

Vomit begins to seep from the corners of her mouth, thick and lumpy like curdled cream, sliding down her cheek in slow, sick globs. Her face—once flushed with a feverish red—starts to shift, darkening to a dusky, bluish hue. Her neck bulges grotesquely, stretching unnaturally as the shape forces its way farther down, distorting the soft lines of her throat. Her feet quiver behind me as the balls of the nine-inch dildo, touch her lips.

Her arms thrash against the restraints, muscles straining in desperation. The rope on her right wrist stretches to its limit—then snaps with a sharp, sudden pop. Her freed hand shoots upward, fingers clawing weakly at my shoulder. But there's no strength behind the motion. The effort drains from her just as quickly as it rose, her grip slipping like water through my shirt.

She collapses beneath me, her body sagging into the mattress, breathless and spent—limp as a ragdoll.

My arms quiver as I use all my strength to force the toy further down her throat and hold it, just to make sure.

The adrenaline in my arms is still burning, making my fingers twitch.

What have I just done?

I look down at her body, bound and broken. My heart pounds, but not with fear.

I check my watch. Not even an hour has passed since I arrived.

It feels like a lifetime.

I climb off of Kathy, her body unmoving beneath me, and drift toward the window with quiet, measured steps. The weight of the air around me feels heavier now—thick with smoke and consequence. I reach for the curtain and peel it back slowly, just enough to cast a narrow slit through which I can study the world outside.

Nothing.

The parking lot lies empty, cloaked in shadows. No footsteps echo. No headlights sweep across the concrete. It's calm—too calm. Still, I can't just walk out the front door and hope the night continues to look the other way. There's too much of me in this room—too many fingerprints, fibers, careless imprints of my presence. One wrong move, and this place becomes a confession.

The smoke above me begins to gather near the ceiling, curling in lazy, ghostlike tendrils. It sparks a thought.

My eyes shift back to the bed.

There, folded neatly beside Kathy's corpse, is something that hadn't caught my attention before: a sleek, black nylon bodysuit, clearly part of their briefcase of indulgences. I step over, strip away my clothes, and slide into the outfit. The fabric is cool and tight against my skin, hugging every angle of my lean frame from toe to throat. A faceless nylon mask completes the look—anonymous, empty, void.

For a moment, I stand over her, holding the full can of gasoline. I wonder what I look like now—a shadow given shape. A figure birthed from smoke and vengeance.

I begin to pour. The liquid cascades over her body, drenching her in silence. I move methodically, soaking the beds, the floor, the memory of everything that happened here. Then I strike a match, watch the flame breathe to life, flick it toward her, and then leave quickly before the blaze draws attention.

(1:12 AM)

I step quietly into my dim apartment, the stale hallway light fading behind me as I close the door. The black costume remains tucked beneath the clothes I wore before, still clinging to my skin like a second layer of shadow.

Tilly's soft white fur glows like a halo in the low light. She's curled in the corner of the couch, but her head lifts the moment she hears me. Without hesitation, she trots over and paws at my pant leg, rising onto her hind legs in greeting.

I feed her.

Then, wordlessly, I begin to undress, stripping away the outer layer without removing the nylon beneath. I crawl under the covers, the sheets cool against me, the night still pressing in through the walls.

Lying there, I stare at the full-length mirror across from my bed. My eyelids are heavy, slipping. But just before they fall, I see something faint—thin, black, and still—standing within the reflection.

It watches me.

But I don't feel fear. Not anymore.

CHapTer 13

CHECK PLEASE

(8:10 AM Monday)"Good morning, BigMoney!" Derrick's voice calls out behind me, loud and grating. I don't bother turning to face him—just nod once, curtly.

"Shit, so what you gonna spend the big bonus check on?" he asks, his tone dripping with curiosity and that familiar edge of envy that always clings to his words.

For reasons I can't explain, his voice is even more irritating today than usual—like a buzzing in my ear I can't swat away.

"I don't know yet. Probably a new television or something. It depends on how much I get."

"You don't know how much you're getting? I would have thought you'd have your check laid out on the desk by now."

I pause my typing, rest my hands on either side of the keyboard, and slowly ball them into fists. A long breath filters through my lungs as I resist the impulse to snap.

"It's still early, Derrick, so Mr. Gibbons hasn't given me my check yet. It's only ten minutes after."

Just then, Kimmie pops up over the divider like a curious prairie dog. "What's up y'all?"

"Hey, Kimmie!" we both chime, nearly in sync.

"Y'all ready for this Monday morning bullshit?—I know I'm not," she says, a groan laced in her voice.

"I'm ready to get my check and leave, to be honest. I don't feel like dealing with these customers today and their snotty 'I'll pay when I want to' attitudes. But my route is starting to come around and pay off," I reply, eyes still on the screen.

"Mine would too if a couple of my top balances got murdered and fell off my route," Derrick mutters with a laugh that doesn't quite land.

"One is missing; the other was murdered," I snap, turning toward him now. "I work my route and don't need any outside help—like some people."

"Oh? So what you trying to say?" Derrick's voice rises, laced with challenge.

Kimmie cuts in before it escalates. "Seems to be a lot of killings going on lately. Got me kind of scared. And right before Thanksgiving too. I hate hearing about deaths around the holidays."

"There's no need for you to be scared, Kimmie. I'm sure you've done no one wrong," I say, glancing up at her. "It's the people who are doing wrong that should worry, you know?"

That's when Mr. Gibbons rounds the corner, arms folded, expression sharp. "It's almost fifteen minutes after the hour. Shouldn't you all be on a call or something by now?"

None of us reply. Instead, we exchange sheepish glances, like three school kids caught talking in class. We quietly sit.

"Thorpe, come see me in my office, please."

"Yes, sir."

I rise and follow him down the hall, my mind spinning with possibilities. Each step feels heavier, and before I can land on a reason that makes sense, we're already in his office.

"Hey, sit down, Thorpe," he says while rifling through a stack of envelopes. He plucks two from the pile and lays them neatly in front of me.

"Looks like you lucked out on this one, man—you think?" he adds, pushing both envelopes toward me. One is the standard paycheck. The other, unmistakably, is my bonus.

"But policy is policy, and rules are rules. And since your numbers did meet; you got your check."

"I don't know about luck, Mr. Gibbons. I worked hard on this route, despite the unfortunate happenings of my top two delinquent accounts. Don't forget, this was Derrick's old route—I needed time to get things down."

"If you say so," he responds coolly, fixing me with an unblinking stare.

The silence stretches. His eyes don't waver. It's stiff, uncomfortable—like he's waiting for something more than what I've offered.

"Did you have something you needed to talk to me about, Mr. Gibbons?" I finally ask, cutting through the silence.

He leans back in his chair, the worn leather groaning beneath his weight. "Oh—oh yeah. Let me ask you something, Thorpe. Do you like it here? If so, where do you see yourself going with our company?"

He asks it like he's the CEO of some towering empire, not the supervisor of a cluttered office in a fading call center. The way he peers over that desk—chin high, eyes narrowed—you'd think thrones were involved.

"Umm, actually, I don't know, Mr. Gibbons."

"You don't know if you like it here?" His brow furrows, his tone cooling a few degrees.

"No, I mean—I like it here. I just want to do well and get my bonus. Not really looking at becoming a manager or anything. I like what I do."

He shifts his gaze toward the office door just as Derrick appears, peering in through the glass like a child begging permission to enter a grown-up's world.

Derrick opens the door without waiting. "Dad, can I speak to you for a minute?" he asks, barely containing his urgency.

"Yeah, I was just finishing up with our top performer here. That's all I have, Thorpe; you may leave now," he says, dismissing me with a tone fit for royalty brushing off a servant.

I'm not sure what drove the impulse—maybe instinct, maybe something sharper—but I let the envelopes in my hand slip as if by accident. They flutter to the floor just beyond their view. As I kneel to gather them, I unlock the note app on my phone and quietly tap record. With care, I slide the device just beneath the lip of Mr. Gibbons's desk, angled out of sight.

Rising smoothly, I turn toward the doorway. Derrick avoids eye contact, fixated instead on the paperwork in his hand.

"Okay, thanks, Mr. Gibbons. Excuse me, Derrick," I say, stopping squarely in front of him—waiting. Daring him to meet my eyes. He doesn't. He sidesteps without a word.

(8:37 AM)

The silence of the office is broken by a sudden rhythm—heavy boots striking tile, the jingle of keys, and the garbled crackle of a two-way radio.

I rise from my chair, heart tapping against my ribs, and glance down the aisle of cubicles.

Two law enforcement officers approach—one tall male in plainclothes with the weary eyes of a detective, the other a uniformed female officer trying to match his long stride. Our admin clerk walks briskly ahead, guiding them straight toward Mr. Gibbons's office.

My stomach knots. There are a hundred reasons why they might be here. But I know better than to speculate. The only thing that matters is keeping my composure.

Kimmie is the last to notice, rising from her chair just enough to block my view as she peers over the wall.

"That can't be good," she murmurs. "Anytime you see those blue uniforms in a call center, you have to assume the worst."

Moments later, Derrick steps out of the office, face drawn, brows lifted in confusion.

"Don't even ask, 'cause I don't know either," he says, brushing past us and heading toward the bathroom, leaving a wake of questions behind him.

(9:10 AM)

Mr. Gibbons steps out of his office with the two officers flanking him. His composure is cracked—there's a tightness in his jaw, a faint tremble in his hands as he shakes theirs. After they exit through the front entrance, he exhales and wipes his face with both palms, as if trying to erase what just happened. Then, with a resigned posture, he plants his hands on his hips and raises his voice.

"If you are not on a call, I need you all to go to the back conference room immediately," he announces. "Team Leads, please make sure all reps are off their calls and in the conference room within the next ten minutes."

I log off and join the slow-moving stream of employees, each of us weaving through the maze of cubicles like cattle headed for the unknown.

"Oh man, I wonder what's going on," Kimmie murmurs behind me, her voice laced with unease.

"I have no idea," I answer. "I saw those cops talking with Mr. Gibbons, then next thing I know, he's calling this meeting. He definitely didn't look calm."

The conference room quickly fills with restless bodies. Some remain standing, leaning against the walls, while others settle into chairs toward the back, deliberately avoiding the empty row of seats up front. Mr. Gibbons enters last, sealing the door behind him with a quiet finality.

"Everyone, please have a seat. Fill into the front," he instructs, massaging the corners of his eyes between his thumb and forefinger before lowering his hands.

"I have some alarming news to inform you all of," he begins, pausing only a second, though the silence stretches like wire. "As you all are aware, I was just visited by two Milwaukee Police Officers, who informed me that our very own Kathy May was found dead this weekend."

Gasps ripple through the room like aftershocks. One woman lets out a choked sob. Others glance around in disbelief, lips parted, eyes wide. All except me.

I remain by the window, still. Detached. My gaze drifts beyond the glass, out to the woods surrounding the building. The wind stirs the naked branches into a slow, haunted sway. To drown out the murmurs and grief rising behind me, I imagine the sound of that wind slicing through the brittle trees, with me standing beneath their skeleton limbs.

"What happened to her?" Freddie asks, voice fragile. "Was she murdered?"

"I'm not sure what happened," Mr. Gibbons says. "Someone found her and another man in a hotel room—burned."

"Oh my God!" Kimmie gasps, her hand flying to her mouth.

"To show respect," Mr. Gibbons continues, "we are going to close down E.A.A.C. for the remainder of the day. After this meeting, you all can gather your belongings and go home. Tomorrow will be business as usual."

I pull myself away from the window and speak plainly. "Is that unpaid?"

The room freezes. Every head pivots toward me, stunned. Their eyes bore into me, as though I'd shouted profanity at a funeral. Some look offended. Others—quietly—seem to appreciate the bluntness of the question and turn back to Mr. Gibbons, waiting for his reply.

He doesn't hide his disdain.

"Yes, Thorpe," he says, the words soaked in contempt. "It will be paid."

(9:25 AM)

The moment I push open the front door of the call center, a sharp winter wind cuts across my face like a slap. I wince, then dig into my coat pocket and pull out my knit cap, tugging it down over my ears as I step into the gray parking lot. The cold feels deeper than usual—heavier, somehow.

Behind me, hurried footsteps pound against the concrete.

"Tommy—hey, Tommy, hold up a minute, man!" Derrick calls out, breathless.

I turn, my boots crunching to a stop. "What's up?"

"You dropped your phone in Gibbons' office." He hands it over, the screen still dark.

"Oh, thanks." I take it and slip it into my coat pocket, nodding without much warmth.

We fall into an awkward stride toward the lot. I lengthen my pace, hoping he'll veer off toward his own car and let the cold silence settle back in. But he keeps up, his breath puffing beside me in faint clouds.

"Damn, it's cold out here," he mutters, shivering.

"Yeah, I've noticed that. Where's your jacket?"

"In my car. I was running late this morning and left it when I jumped out, trying to get in here on time." He jams his hands deep into his pants pockets, shoulders hunched.

There's a pause before he speaks again. "Hey man, I just wanted to apologize to you."

"For what?"

"You know, all of the tension between the two of us. Well, at least I feel the tension—and I can't work like that, you know? We have to see each other every day, so we need to get along and be cool."

I slow to a stop and turn to face him. "I hear you, man. No hard feelings at all." I extend my hand. "It's all business, right?"

"Sure is," he says, shaking my hand with a firmness that feels forced. "If I remember correctly, you said you're a gamer?"

"I used to be. Can't get on anymore."

"Why not?"

"I got robbed, remember?"

"Oh yeah. Oh shit, I forgot about that, dude—I'm sorry." But the look in his eyes tells a different story. He didn't forget. He just wanted to remind me.

He shifts quickly. "We should get together and play that new game that came out. Not sure if you've heard of *Dark Rain*?"

"Yeah, I've heard of it. You pair up with someone and search the city for clues leading to a serial killer?"

"That's it!" Derrick exclaims, perking up.

"Yeah, I'm down for sure. Let me know when. I'm pretty much free anytime."

"Will do. We'll talk about it later and plan something." He backs away with a grin and throws up a peace sign.

I return the gesture—with a middle finger.

When I reach my truck, I climb inside and pull the door shut. The cab muffles the outside world in a cocoon of cold quiet. I retrieve my phone and check the recording. It had been running long—fifty-one minutes and three seconds. My pulse quickens.

I scroll to the start and hit play.

Me: "*Okay thanks, Mr. Gibbons, excuse me, Derrick.*"-*The door closes.*-

"*Dad, could you loan me a couple dollars or give me some cash until next payday?*"

"*What's going on now, Derrick? You spend all your money on them damn video games or another flat screen?*"

"*Nah, I gotta catch up the rent, Dad. You know Stephanie lost her job last week, so I gotta do something about the bills. I wouldn't be asking if Tommy didn't beat me out on that bonus. I was really actually counting on it.*"

"*How about you sell some of that shit you got, Derrick? You have to have thousands of dollars' worth of electrical crap and video games.*"

"*Yeah, but that would take me a minute to sell, Dad. Come on, help me out. I just need about five hundred dollars to get me to where I need to be.*"

"*Damn boy, that's a lot of money. I want this money back within the next two checks this time, ya hear? I can't keep doing this. You're a grown-ass man, Derrick. A grown-ass man that's married to my daughter.*"

"*I know—I know. Can I ask you something?*"

"*What, Derrick?*" Gibbons' voice snapped, rough with impatience.

"*When are you going to do another shuffle of the routes?*"

There was silence. Long, weighted. I could just make out the faint clicking of a keyboard in the background.

"*I'll shuffle the route one more time at the end of this month. But any more than that and people will start getting suspicious. Derrick, it's time you start pulling your own weight, boy. I don't want my daughter married to someone that can't do for himself. And clean yourself up.*"

"*That's cold, Dad. You should know me better than that. But okay.*"

"*That's why I'm saying what I'm saying. I know what she tells me. And I know you do nothing but game all day. You need to start taking care of yourself, son, and put them damn games behind you, or there's no doubt in my mind that you'll lose Stephanie.*"

A knock came faintly through the speakers, followed by the creak of a door opening.

"*Yes?*" Gibbons' voice called out.

"*Excuse me, Mr. Gibbons,*" said a woman, likely Jessica. "*But you have a couple of police officers who would like to speak with you.*"

"*Oh, come in, officers. Derrick, I'll talk to you later.*"

"*Good morning, Mr. Gibbons,*" a new voice said. "*I'm Detective Clemens, and this is Officer Wright.*"

"*Good morning,*" Officer Wright added.

"Good morning," Gibbons replied. "And how can I help you? Please, have a seat."

"Thank you. Well, Mr. Gibbons, we aren't here for your help, sir. Actually, we're here to bring you a bit of bad news. I'm not exactly sure how to tell you this, so I'm going to just come right out and say it. You have a Kathy May that works here, correct?"

"Yes, we do have someone that works here by that name. She hasn't made it in yet, though. But I'm assuming that's why you're here."

"You would be correct in assuming that, yes. Kathy isn't going to be making it in today. Or any other day for that matter."

I listen intently as the recording continues to play, my heart thudding against my ribs, the faint echo of voices filling the quiet cabin of my truck.

"What's going on?" Gibbons asks, his voice already taut with concern.

"She's dead, sir," the detective says plainly.

"Jesus, what? Dead?" Gibbons gasps, the disbelief cutting through his words.

"Please, keep your voice down, Mr. Gibbons," the female officer urges calmly.

"She was murdered," the detective continues. "Now, the details of the case I cannot disclose at the moment, but we know for sure that there was foul play involved from the evidence found at the scene."

"You can't tell me anything besides the fact that she's dead? Where was she found? Can you tell me that?"

"She was found in a hotel room. Burned, Mr. Gibbons. Burned, with an object lodged in her throat."

"Dear Lord." He exhales like the wind's been knocked out of him. "Who could do something like that? She was such a sweet lady. Have you notified her family?"

"Yes, we have. And we plan on finding out for sure who did this. That's one of the reasons we're here. I may return soon to question some of your employees—if that's okay?"

"Sure."

"There are a few leads already. We have a possible witness who may have seen something."

"I hope they can help with this. Is there anything I can do?"

"Do you think you may know of anyone who'd want to harm her? Someone she might have wronged?"

"I don't think there's anyone she's wronged... well, not really—to the point where they'd want to kill her."

"Who?"

"Well... she is—or was—a supervisor. Who knows? She had a life outside of this office. It could be anyone."

"You'd be surprised, Mr. Gibbons. Murderers come in all different shapes, sizes, and mentalities. They all just need a reason to start—something to trigger the inner desire."

The recording goes silent. For nearly twenty seconds, only the ambient hum of the office carries through faintly in the background.

Finally, Gibbons speaks again. "Well... I'm going to have to break this horrible news to my office. Is there anything else I can do for you fine officers?"

"No, sir. But here's my card. If you come across anything—anything at all—don't hesitate to call. In any case, I'll be seeing you again soon."

With that, I tap the screen and stop the playback at 00:34:13.

Satisfied.

(5:11 PM)

The crawl home is agony. I'm locked in the far right lane, inching forward at a pace fit for funerals. My truck growls beneath me, its gas gauge balancing just above empty, threatening to quit at any moment like a weary old dog. Every tap of the accelerator feels like a gamble I can't afford.

But what truly grates on my nerves isn't the traffic—it's the van directly ahead.

I can see the reflection of the woman driving, a classic soccer mom, lit by the glow of her phone screen. Her eyes are glued to her device, thumbs dancing mindlessly as traffic clears in front of her. She doesn't notice. Doesn't care. In the backseat, two children bounce around unrestrained, laughing and climbing over seats like a jungle gym on wheels. No seatbelts. No discipline. No concern.

I press my horn—long and deliberate. The sound tears through the stale air and jolts her from her digital daze. She stomps the gas and the van lurches forward, launching her hyperactive offspring over the back seat. One of them smacks the rear window face-first. Under different circumstances, I might've laughed. Today, I barely manage a twitch of the lip.

Eventually, I pull into the lot of a corner gas station, the truck heaving slightly as I roll to a stop beside a pump. As I climb out and swipe my card, something catches my eye.

There—leaning against the side of the building by the ice freezer—is Tricia.

She's dressed like temptation on a tired afternoon: red skirt just above the knee, tall heels, a short black leather jacket clinging to her like attitude. A cigarette dangles between her fingers, smoke curling lazily from her lips as she takes sharp, impatient drags. She shifts her weight from one foot to the other like the clock is ticking too slow for her.

Moments later, a sleek black Chrysler 300 glides into the lot, near the bathrooms. Its dark tinted windows gleam like polished obsidian. The headlights flicker once—just a flash.

Tricia sees it.

She inhales twice, fast and deep, then flicks her cigarette away without a second thought. It spins across the asphalt in a tiny arc of dying embers. She approaches the car, leans in, says something to the driver. The window opens just enough to trade words, and then she slides inside.

The pump clicks. My tank is full.

As I replace the nozzle, the Chrysler rolls past me without a sound. Through the driver's side window, I catch a glimpse of the man behind the wheel. An older white guy, late fifties maybe, pale skin and unnaturally light blue eyes that lock onto mine—cold, penetrating. He watches me as the tinted glass creeps upward, slowly severing our brief and uneasy connection.

I watch the car disappear around the corner, the unease trailing it like exhaust.

Chapter 14

WHAT'S MINE IS YOURS

(8:05 AM Tuesday)

The day after the news of Kathy's murder settles over the office like a damp, heavy blanket. The air inside the call center is thick with silence, broken only by the steady drumming of rain against the ceiling—nature's own eulogy. Outside, the sky weeps with relentless fury, its torrential downpour matching the somber mood within.

But me? I'm quietly thrilled.

The stillness, the lack of chatter, the blessed absence of managerial eyes watching every move—I soak in the peace like sunlight. For once, the world around me matches the calm I feel inside.

Mr. Gibbons' head suddenly appears around the corner, eyebrows arched with purpose.

"Hey Team North, don't log in yet. I need to talk to you all in my office for a moment," he says, then disappears again just as quickly.

Once he's gone, the three of us glance at one another with wide-eyed caution, each silently hoping someone else might know what this was about. No one does.

Derrick's the last to step into the office.

"Shut the door, please," Mr. Gibbons says, his tone clipped. He begins handing out the new North Milwaukee route assignments.

My eyes drop to the paper, and almost immediately, I see the numbers—my percentage. It's jumped from last month's seven-point-forty-two to a staggering fifteen-point-ninety-eight. Well beyond what the company considers acceptable. Kimmie's reaction mirrors my own—her face scrunching as she pulls the sheet closer, disbelief etched in every line. Derrick, though? He shows nothing. Just leans against the wall like a bored observer, staring out the window behind Mr. Gibbons.

"Since you're all on your own now without a manager—at least until we find a replacement—I'll be stepping in as your temporary manager," he announces. "I've gone ahead and reshuffled the routes, tried to even out the account load. We're coming up on the beginning of the month, so you've got time to work things down. Don't get discouraged."

His eyes flick back and forth between me and Kimmie, almost daring one of us to argue.

"Does anyone have any questions?"

Silence.

"No one has anything to say? Amazing! So then I have your commitment to focus hard on your new routes this month?"

Still nothing.

"Derrick?"

"Committed as always, sir," Derrick answers with robotic enthusiasm, like some fresh recruit at roll call.

"Kimmie?"

"Yeah, I guess."

Then Mr. Gibbons turns his attention to me. No greeting. No name. Just a long, steady stare.

"I'll work my route down like I did my previous one, Mr. Gibbons," I say, voice flat but pointed.

He chuckles softly.

"My boy, you just benefited off of someone else's misfortune. That was hardly worked down at all. But I admire your determination—and I hope to see you succeed with that."

After the meeting, we head back to our cubicles. Derrick lingers just behind us.

"Hey y'all," he says, "I just wanted to say I had nothing to do with this shuffle. I know that's what y'all are thinking—but I didn't."

"Okay Derrick, nobody accused you of anything," Kimmie replies, her voice calm, maybe even tired.

I don't say a word.

I just sit, resume my work, and let him stew in the silence. The nerve of him—trying to play innocent. If he only knew what I've heard on that recording. Selfish. Disgusting. Greedy bastard.

From his office, Mr. Gibbons' voice cuts through the hush.

"Hey, I need those originals back. One of you can make copies for yourselves."

"No worries, you guys. I got it," I say, collecting the reports without missing a beat.

(9:35 AM)

I stand in my cubicle, holding a printed email in my hand, feigning interest in its faded ink as my eyes shift occasionally toward the hallway. Just enough to keep my act believable. Derrick reaches over to grab his cigarettes from his desk drawer, his movements casual and familiar.

"Break time?" I ask, keeping my tone light.

"Yeah, I'll be back. I need to run to my car too."

He disappears down the corridor, unaware of the opportunity he's just given me. The moment his figure vanishes from sight, I rise slightly and peek over the cubicle wall. Sure enough, his screen glows in idle anticipation—still unlocked.

Without hesitation, I step into his space and slide into his chair like I belong there.

(9:45 AM)

"Hello?" a groggy male voice answers, thick with sleep and suspicion.

"Good morning, is Mr. Rodger Brown available please?"

"Yeah, this is..."

"Hi, Mr. Brown, this is Tommy with E.A.A.C. Calling about your first car payment that was due two weeks ago."

"Oh shit, I was gonna call you guys. Hey look—I lost my job, man, and I need a little time to get things together. My Human Resources Department told me it's going to be a couple of weeks before I see a check. If you can give me a couple of weeks, I'd appreciate it."

His tone is desperate, each word trembling between truth and performance.

"Unfortunately, Mr. Brown, I wouldn't be able to give you a couple weeks; seeing as this is your first car payment. Usually, when your first payment is late, we require the recovery of the vehicle until payment is made. When would you like to bring the car in? We can hold it for you until then."

"I'm not bringing shit in, bro—how the hell am I supposed to get to work? I mean, listen to yourself. How does that sound, dude? You want me to bring my car in until payment is made? Does anyone really do that?"

"Yes, they do, sir."

"That's bull, bro!! Look, I'll be working here in a couple weeks, and I'm sure it's gonna take that long, if not longer, for me to get my check. I'm good to people and pay my bills. You will get your money, I just need time—and I need my car."

"Mr. Brown, you just said you would have a check in a couple of weeks. Now you're telling me you won't be working for a couple of weeks? I don't know what to say to you, sir. I mean I'd like to help but this—"

The line goes dead.

Without wasting time, I head to the file room. The walls are lined with alphabetized drawers like vaults of half-truths and overdue promises. I find his file. His application is still crisp—recently submitted. But according to him, he's already unemployed. Curious.

Everything I need is there. Employer information, contact names, a supervisor listed under Milwaukee Transit. Perfect.

I return to my desk, lift the receiver, and dial.

"Milwaukee Transit, this is Rebecca," a receptionist answers.

"Good morning Rebecca, can I speak with your HR department please?"

"Yes sir, one moment."

A soft click, then hold music—brief and forgettable.

"Human Resources, this is Karen."

"Hi Karen, my name is Tommy from E.A.A.C. I was calling to confirm employment for a Mr. Rodger Brown. He has you listed on his application as his employer."

"What is the last four of his social?"

"Eight-six-nine-eight."

"Okay, one moment please while I pull him up in our system." A pause, then the sound of typing. "Okay yes, Mr. Rodger Brown has been employed with us for several years as a bus driver and is still currently an employee," she answers with bureaucratic cheer.

"Thank you very much, Karen. I hope you have a pleasant day," I say with a smile, even though she can't see it.

"Well thank you—you as well, sir."

I waste no time dialing Mr. Brown back, eager to press my newly uncovered truth into his ear like a burning coal. I already know how this conversation will end, which is why I reach into my drawer, retrieve my highlighter, and cap it with a casual flick. The phone barely rings once before it's snatched up.

"Look, this is harassment, bro. You guys aren't supposed to call me twice in one day. That's against your regulations—I know it."

"The call disconnected, sir; I thought maybe one of us had lost the connection. The law permits us to follow up if a call ends unexpectedly," I reply, letting a sly grin curl at the corner of my mouth. "Besides... I just had a lovely conversation with Milwaukee Transit. And guess what? You got your old job back!" I exclaim, layering my voice with artificial cheer and a healthy dose of sarcasm. "Turns out they never removed you from payroll. You're cleared to start immediately. Karen, from your Human Resources Department, says 'hi.'"

Just as I deliver that final barb, movement catches the edge of my vision.

A detective strolls past my cubicle—not the one I'd seen before. This one's older, with neatly trimmed white hair and a shiny dome forming at the crown of his balding head. He's average in height, clean-shaven, and dressed in a salmon polo shirt tucked into tan khakis. His badge glints from his belt like a silent threat with each deliberate step. He glances my way—brief, unreadable—before Jessica leads him toward Mr. Gibbons' office.

Then Mr. Brown's voice explodes through the receiver, filled with venom. He unleashes a barrage of rage and filth, spitting accusations and racial slurs so vicious they leave a bitter taste in my mouth—even though I'm the one being targeted.

"If I had you in front of me right now, my nigga..." he rants. "Guys like you talk tough over the phone. I'll sue you for harassment, for calling my job. You're screwed, brotha. You'll hear from my lawyer."

I remain perfectly still, my voice cool and unfazed.

"Well, that's where you're wrong, sir. First, I'm white. Second... you've got money for an attorney but nothing for your car payment?"

Click.

The line goes dead.

"Hey, did you see the news last night?" Kimmie's voice drops down into my cubicle, her head peeking over the divider.

"No, why?" I ask, swiveling slightly in my chair.

"They were talking about Kathy's murder. The manager of the hotel—some old lady—said she saw a stick figure running through the parking lot the night she was killed." She chuckles, then immediately covers her mouth. "Sorry, that's not funny. But... she must've been drinking or something."

"A stick figure?" I laugh. "What the hell was she smoking? People will say anything to get on TV."

"That's what I was telling my boyfriend," she says, shaking her head. "It was late when she saw it. Even the news anchor was trying not to laugh. The old lady looked sweet though. She said, 'Oh, I don't know. I was telling my husband to get up and come to the window. I could barely see it 'cause it was dark, but I know what I saw. It was a stickman—long and black, running through the parking lot. Scared the bejesus out of me.'"

I smirk as Kimmie mimics the news anchor's reaction.

"Then she says, 'Well, there you have it folks—a possible killer stickman on the loose in Milwaukee.' But the look on her face was priceless—like she was thinking, *Really, lady?*"

Shortly after Kimmie's lighthearted reenactment of the news broadcast, Mr. Gibbons rounds the corner once more, his expression unreadable. He points directly at me, then curls his index finger inward in a slow, deliberate motion, beckoning me to follow.

"My office, please," he orders, his tone clipped.

Oh shit. What now?

I rise from my seat, offering Kimmie a quick glance. Her brows knit together, clearly puzzled as I trail behind him down the corridor. The walk feels longer than it is—every step echoing louder in my head than in the hallway. When I step into the office, the detective rises from his chair in a fluid, practiced motion.

"Tommy Thorpe?"

"Yes?" I answer, wary but composed.

"Hi, I'm Detective Bedwell with the Milwaukee Police Department." He offers no badge, but his presence is official enough. "Mr. Gibbons, do you mind if we have a moment alone in your office? I promise you, this will only take a few minutes."

"You gentlemen take your time," Mr. Gibbons says before easing the door shut behind him.

"Okay, Tommy, please—have a seat." Bedwell gestures toward the chair across from the desk, then circles around and lowers himself into Mr. Gibbons' seat with casual authority.

"I just have a couple of questions for you, sir, if you don't mind."

"Not at all," I say, masking the churn in my stomach. Inside, it feels like a mosh pit of butterflies, each one with razor wings.

"As you're already aware, Kathy May was murdered this past weekend, correct?"

"Yes."

"Okay, well during part of our investigation, one of the items we recovered from the scene was her cell phone." He studies me now—not just watching, but *measuring*. "And I'm sure you can guess what I found after pulling her text messages."

"My text message, I'm assuming?"

"You assume correct, Mr. Thorpe. Do you mind if I read it back to you?"

"Well, I know what it says..."

"She gives you the location of the hotel room, and you reply, *'No thanks! I just can't do this. If this is what I have to do to keep my job, then you can fire me Monday? Find someone else to play your bedroom games tonight. I'm done.'*"

He sets the phone down on the desk, his eyes never leaving mine.

"I can't find anywhere else in her messages where the conversation builds up to that kind of response. You want to tell me what this is all about?"

"I don't have a problem with that," I begin, keeping my tone level. "Kathy would text me to meet her at a hotel to play... with her and her friend. In return, I got to keep my job, which she reminded me of constantly. So I did what she asked. But that night, I was fed up. I didn't want to do it anymore. Told her to find someone else."

Detective Bedwell's stare hardens slightly as he reads me again, searching for cracks.

"So you didn't go up to see her that night?"

"No."

"Were you attracted to Kathy at all?"

"Not at first. But I'm not exactly a looker, so I went for what I could get." I shrug slightly. "It was a change from jerking off to online porn—you know what I mean? But I didn't know her male friend would be involved. He was always there, watching. Doing things in the background. It was creepy. He even tried to join in."

"Did you allow him?"

"To a certain extent, yes."

"What did you allow him to do?" he asks, his voice cutting the air like a blade.

I pause, uncomfortable. "Well... I'm not too sure I'm comfortable telling you that, Detective Bedwell. I don't see what that has to do with Kathy being murdered."

"I'm sure you're not comfortable, Mr. Thorpe," he says, leaning in slightly. "Every man wants to preserve or protect his manhood. But what if I told you we have blood and semen samples on a couple of the toys found at the scene?"

His words hang in the air like smoke—thick and suffocating.

"Would any of those be yours?"

"Could be possible. Last time I was with them was a couple of weeks ago. I would have hoped they washed those things off by then. But who knows."

"Yeah, who knows, right?" he says, lingering on the thought before shifting gears. "Do you mind telling me a little bit about yourself, Mr. Thorpe?"

"What would you like to know, Detective? Can I ask—am I a suspect in this case?"

"No—no, you're not. I just wanted to ask a few questions, is all." He gives a tight smile, one that doesn't quite reach his eyes. "Actually, I think I have all I need for now. I'll keep in touch with you. And if you come across anything—or just want to talk—feel free to give me a call."

He extends a business card between two fingers. I take it, noting the slight tension still lingering in his jaw despite the polite words.

He's frustrated. I can see it. He's walking out of here with more questions than answers and probably needs time to regroup. Maybe he thinks I came off too guarded—defensiveness being a red flag in his line of work. But he has nothing concrete. Just a text message and some innuendo. If there was something more... anything solid... he wouldn't be playing nice. He'd be slapping cuffs on me instead.

I shake his hand—firm, brief, deliberate. He nods, thanks Mr. Gibbons on the way out, and slips through the main office doors without so much as a glance at the employees now staring after him.

Then, like a wave rolling across the floor, every curious eye turns to me.

"Okay, Thorpe. I don't pay you to stand here. Get to your desk and get those customers paying, sir," Mr. Gibbons barks.

"Sure, Mr. Gibbons," I say, slipping the detective's card into my pocket as I head back to my cubicle.

(10:25 AM)

"Good morning, may I speak to Mr. Donte Stevens please?" I ask, dialing the next number on my list.

"Who dis?" the voice on the other end snaps, instantly defensive, like I'd just woken him from a nap he wasn't supposed to be taking.

"Hi, this is Tommy Thorpe with E.A.A.C. I was looking for Mr. Stevens."

"Dis him. How you get my number?"

"It's what we have here in our files, sir."

"Nah, it ain't. Y'all must've called one of my references or something—'cause don't nobody have this number, playa. Besides, I'm at work right now and ain't got time for this here."

"Well, Mr. Stevens, I'm calling about your car payment, sir."

"What—that Buick? Man, I don't even have that car anymore. I gave that to my cousin a while ago. I ain't got it. Y'all need to talk to him if you want it back. He was supposed to do the payments."

His voice is cocky, self-satisfied. And behind him, I can hear a chorus of snickers—co-workers or friends egging him on, enjoying the performance.

"Mr. Stevens, it is still your vehicle. So may I ask—when can we expect the payment?"

"Bruh," he says, stretching it out like it's a punchline, "I'm gonna quote D.L. Hughley on this one— *'Hello... you can expect payment whenever you want, sir!'*"

The laughter behind him swells, louder now. He's putting on a show. I've had enough.

Without another word, I end the call and lean back, exhaling sharply. I grab my highlighter, press it firmly at the start of his name, then drag it angrily across the rest of his information, the ink bleeding thick and heavy across the page like a final judgment.

***

(6:43 PM Wednesday)

The day before Thanksgiving. The call center is winding down, and the energy feels electric—not from the work, but from the shared anticipation of escape. As the clock strikes the end of the day, a tidal wave of voices surges toward the front door. Laughter, handshakes, and hurried goodbyes spill into the parking lot, where cold breath curls into the night air like tiny ghosts.

Above us, the sky is painted a deep velvet blue, scattered with more stars than I've seen in months. They glitter in sharp contrast to the silhouettes of snow-dusted pines in the distance. There's a rare stillness tonight, the kind of peace that only comes with crisp air and silent roads. The scene feels... almost majestic.

Driving home, I lose myself in the rhythm of the tires on asphalt and the memories that begin to surface. The few Thanksgivings I got to spend with my parents before they were gone... they play like warm, fading reels in my mind. Gram used to make us go around the table and say what we were thankful for before we could lay a finger on the feast she'd spent hours preparing.

And Grandpa—God, he could never just play along. While the rest of us muttered about family or good health, he'd sit back with that mischievous grin, waiting for his turn like a performer prepping for curtain call. One year, he said he was thankful not to be his best friend,

Corporal Greg Shamrock—then proceeded to tell the infamous story of *The Ether Bunny*. According to Grandpa, Greg's barracks roommate had regular access to ether and a twisted sense of opportunity. The guy would wait until Greg fell asleep, then slip a rag over his nose and...

Well, let's just say the story ended with laughter so hard it left Grandpa wheezing, despite Gram's repeated kicks beneath the table. She scolded him every year, but he'd never stop. I used to think that story was hilarious—until recently, when its dark edge hit a little too close to home.

By the time I pull into my driveway, the nostalgia has faded into a numb quiet. I walk inside and drop onto the couch, letting the silence of the apartment settle around me like a blanket.

Then—*knock knock*.

It's soft. Timid. I freeze for a second, waiting to make sure it's actually my door. *Knock knock*—again, a little firmer this time.

I push myself up and glance through the peephole.

Tricia.

She's standing there in the porch light, waving her index finger at me like a slow-moving metronome, a small, uncertain smile on her face. Without hesitation, I swing the door open.

"Hey, are you busy?" she asks.

"No, actually, I just walked in the door. What's up?"

"Nothing really. Was just bored and thought I'd come and say hi. I haven't talked to you in a while."

"So you only talk to me when you're bored now? I thought we were friends." I offer a playful smile.

"No, it's not like that," she sighs, her voice dipping. "It's way more complicated than you know, Tommy."

"No need to explain yourself. I get busy too. You want to come in?"

"Sure, but I know you just got home, and I don't want to impose. I can come back later if you want to get some rest."

"No, not at all. Do you want something to drink?" I ask as I head into the kitchen.

At that moment, Tilly bounds out from my bedroom, a streak of white fur across the hallway. She runs straight to Tricia's feet, tail wagging with approval.

"No—no thank you; I'm okay." She bends down and strokes Tilly's head gently, her voice softening as if she were speaking to a child. "Hi, Miss Tilly! How are you today?"

"You sure? I've got 7-Up, sweet tea, ice-cold water..." I offer, still half-leaning into the refrigerator's glow.

"No, it's okay, really. I'm not thirsty at all."

I close the refrigerator door with a soft thud and make my way back to the couch. The cushion shifts slightly as I sit beside her.

"So, what have you been up to?" she asks.

"Just working," I reply with a shrug. "Trying to get my life together. What about you?"

"Same. But the more I try to get my life together, the more things seem to fall apart. It just keeps getting worse and worse."

"What do you mean?"

"It's complicated," she sighs, her eyes searching the carpet as if answers might appear there. "I got myself into something I shouldn't have. I just have to figure out how to get out of it, is all."

"Anything I can do to help?"

"Sure," she laughs, eyes flickering with something deeper than humor. "I just need you to kill a few people."

The laugh lingers only a moment, but it's clear she's deflecting—same as always. The more I try to draw her out, the more she dances just out of reach, like steam curling from a kettle. She's like me in that way. A bottle trembling under pressure, just waiting for the cork to snap free.

"I saw you at the gas station the other night."

Her hand freezes mid-stroke on Tilly's back. She turns to face me, eyes narrowing slightly. "What? When?"

"I think it was Monday night. I was pumping gas, and you were standing outside."

"And you didn't say hi?"

"I would have. But you jumped into a black car and rode off. I'm surprised you didn't see me—you drove right past. Who was that guy, anyway?"

She breaks eye contact, lowering her gaze as she resumes petting Tilly, who has now settled comfortably beside her.

"Just a friend, that's all."

"Well, your friend looks pretty damn mean. And those eyes—wow. He looked like a damn vampire..."

"Can we talk about something else?" she cuts in quickly.

"Um, yeah. Of course."

A silence settles between us—thin and awkward. I scan the room for something to say before she decides the quiet is reason enough to leave. My eyes fall on the turkey symbol printed in the corner of a report lying on the coffee table.

"So, what are you doing for Thanksgiving?"

"Probably just hang out at home," she says with a small shrug. "I don't really get into the holidays anymore. What about you?"

"Doing what I always do—eating at my grandma's house. You're more than welcome to come, if you'd like."

"No, I'll be okay. Thank you, anyway."

"Gram cooks way too much food," I say with a grin. "We end up freezing half of it or tossing it out. Besides, we'd both love the company."

She glances at me, hesitating. "Are you sure it's okay?"

"Trust me—it's okay. I'll call Gram and tell her to set another place."

(1:25 PM Thanksgiving Day)

I stand outside Tricia's door, dressed in a black collared shirt, gray slacks, and polished monk-strap shoes. The afternoon air is crisp, but not cold—just enough to carry the distant scent of chimney smoke and roasting turkeys.

I glance down and notice a few of Tilly's white hairs clinging stubbornly to my shirt. With a quick brush of my hand, I sweep them away and knock again.

"Just a minute!" she calls from inside.

I hear the rapid click of high heels on hardwood as she rushes to the door. When it opens, only her head peeks through—diamond earrings catching the light like tiny stars, her hair pulled back into a smooth, curly ponytail.

"I don't know if I should go," she says, smiling nervously.

"What? Why?"

She hesitates for just a beat, then opens the door wide, revealing the full effect of her outfit. A form-fitting, full-length dress clings elegantly to her figure, with long sleeves that kiss her wrists and a soft sheen that catches the hallway light. Black heels add height and grace, and a delicate silver necklace rests just above her collarbone, like a thread of moonlight draped around her neck.

She looks breathtaking—like a femme fatale from a classic Bond film, exuding mystery and allure in equal measure.

"Close your mouth," she teases, giggling as she catches my dumb-struck expression. "You don't think this is too much, do you? I really didn't know what else to wear."

"Um, I'm not complaining at all. You look good—great. I mean... beautiful. I mean..."

"I know what you mean. Thank you, Tommy." She smiles softly. "Are you ready to go?"

"Yes, I am. And I hope you're hungry," I grin. "I also hope you brought a change of clothes—because after eating at Gram's house, you're definitely gonna pop out of that dress."

(1:36 PM)

On the road to Gram's house, the cab of my old truck feels strangely balanced—like beauty and rust holding hands. Tricia sits beside me, quiet, her perfume barely noticeable but somehow comforting. I keep catching glimpses of her from the corner of my eye, stealing moments without turning my head. It's hard to believe someone who looks like *her* is riding shotgun in *my* beat-up truck.

Since leaving her place, we've exchanged only small talk—remarks about the weather, how grateful we are for such a beautiful day. Now the silence lingers, not uncomfortable but thoughtful, as she gazes out the window, and I keep my eyes on the road.

Then she catches me.

"Stop it," she says, smiling at her own reflection in the glass. "I can see you watching me. You're embarrassing me."

"No, I'm not," I lie, chuckling. "I was just making sure you had your seatbelt on, is all."

"Really, Tommy?" She shakes her head, amused. "So... have you always spent Thanksgiving with your grandmother?"

"Yes. Every single one since I was born."

She doesn't answer right away. I see her faint reflection in the passenger-side window—her smile fading, her eyes softening with something more fragile. She rummages in her purse and pulls out a pair of oversized sunglasses, slipping them on with a quick, practiced motion.

"You're very lucky," she says quietly, settling back in the seat.

"Why am I lucky?"

"You just are. Don't you think you are?" she asks, turning to face me.

"No, actually I don't," I reply. I tighten my grip on the wheel. "I believe you make your own luck."

She doesn't argue. Instead, she shifts her gaze to the open road ahead.

"You want to know a secret?" Her voice is lighter, but there's weight beneath it. "This is the first time I've ever gone to a Thanksgiving dinner."

I glance over, puzzled. "What do you mean? You've never been invited to someone's house?"

"No, I mean ever. I've never had Thanksgiving dinner."

"You're kidding, right? I mean, come on..."

Slowly, she lifts her sunglasses just above her eyes, and what I see silences me. Her eyes are red, the rims swollen, threatening to spill tears that she's clearly trying to hold back.

"Does it look like I'm kidding?" she asks.

"...No," I say gently, adjusting my own glasses to avoid staring too long. "Forgive me, but... do you mind if I ask why?"

She slides her shades back down, pressing them into place with a single finger. Then she turns back toward the window. For a moment, the only sound is the low hum of the engine and the faint rustle of wind through the slightly cracked window.

She breathes in slowly, then exhales hard through her nose, as if trying to exorcise something old and stubborn.

"It's a long story."

"You always say that," I reply, not unkindly. "We've got a pretty long drive to the country. Talk to me. I think it's about time you open up a little. Since we are friends and all."

There's a pause. Then she shifts in her seat, just slightly.

"You first," she says. "I think I'd feel more comfortable if you told me a little more about *you*. I mean, how you were as a kid. How were your parents? Where did you grow up? Stuff like that."

"I grew up here in Milwaukee. My parents died in a plane crash when I was six-years-old. My grandparents raised me after that. I've been skinny like this all of my life. For the majority of my childhood, I've been picked on because of my appearance. I can't gain weight for the life of me, and I'm a virgin." Her mouth drops open. "How's that for opening up?"

"I'm really sorry about your parents Tommy. That had to be hard on you as a child. And kids can be cruel, we all know that." She leans forward to look me in the eyes. "You're seriously a virgin?"

"Yes. Well, no. Well, I once had a girl in high school kiss me while giving me a handjob. Does that count?"

She shakes her head no.

"I didn't think so. So yeah, I guess I am. Okay, now it's your turn." I find myself growing angry after hearing my own short pitiful description of my life.

"I don't know, Tommy. You're just so lucky to have at least *some* memories of your parents. I have nothing. I don't even know who they are, what they look like; if they are dead or alive—nothing. I don't even know where to start if I wanted to look for them."

"Then you don't have family? But, who raised you?"

"I've spent most of my life in the foster care system. From as far back as I can remember, I was always around different children, adults, and homes. I've always received visits from time to time by people with badges or identification cards hanging from a lanyard around their neck." She fiddles with a tassel hanging from her purse as she continues. "When I got older, the more frequent my change in scenery became."

"Why?" I ask

"No one wanted to adopt an older child. And I was becoming a little rebellious. A damaged child they called me."

"That's crazy."

"I remember when I was nine years old, one of the fathers used to want me to massage his feet every evening after dinner. I would eat after their biological children were finished, and after I'd completed my chores. They owned some chickens in the backyard and would always tell us not to let them out when the dogs were out in back playing. They had a pit-bull and a black lab. One day, I had finished massaging the father's feet, fed the chickens and was on the way to take out the trash. I was so hungry Tommy. I looked at the food that was to be mine. Two huge meatballs and some spaghetti. I licked my lips and dragged the full trash bag to the dumpster.

When I had returned, the oldest, Stacy, was shoving the last meatball in her mouth with a fork. She knew it was my dinner and already had her fill. She just smiled at me and ran off giggling. I screamed, loudly. The foster parents became angry because of my screaming but did nothing to their daughter. They then sent me to the basement without dinner. I laid in bed, crying in the little room they build for me with the spiders and potato bugs. They made me go to sleep without dinner that night.

I couldn't sleep of course. Instead, after Stacy let the chickens out, they all went to sleep. I snuck upstairs, grabbed a bowl of cereal and some milk, then binge ate for about thirty minutes straight on other things in the kitchen. Their dogs were under me, wagging their tails frantically, hoping I was gonna give them something to eat. So I did, and let them out with the chickens."

"Holy shit, what happened?" I laugh, but it falters the moment I catch the look in her eyes.

"I got beat up by the oldest, which was ordered by the father. Social services came the next day to remove me since the parents complained of my behavior."

Her words land like a blow. I'd been expecting some kind of silver lining—a turn for the better. Instead, her story ends like a door slammed shut.

"I'm sorry," I murmur.

"Don't be."

Silence settles between us after that. Not the awkward kind, but the kind that's shared. Understood. The hum of the engine is the only thing that speaks for us as we finish the drive.

(1:58 PM)

"Well hello there, stranger, come on in!" Gram greets us with arms wide and a grin that warms the doorway.

"Stranger?" I chuckle, stepping forward.

"And who is this lovely young lady?"

"Hello, Ma'am," Tricia says politely.

"Gram, this is Tricia. Tricia, this is my Grandma, Glades."

"My, my—you are such a gorgeous creature," Gram says, eyes twinkling as she steps aside to let us in. "Come on in, you two. Just toss your coats on the couch. Oh, listen to me, talking like you've never been here before, Tommy. It's been so long I'm treating you like a visitor. I'm surprised I still know your name," she adds with a playful chuckle.

"Gram, come on. Stop," I say, smiling as I peel off my jacket. "You know I've been really busy with work. I'm not trying to ignore you."

She turns to Tricia, as if letting her in on a long-standing inside joke. "He used to call me every single day to ask how I was doing. Now, I'm lucky to get a call once a week. Or I just have to pick up the phone and call him myself."

As she opens the oven door to check the turkey, a rush of rich aromas fills the room—seasoned warmth that smells like childhood and comfort.

Tricia smacks my shoulder lightly. "You should call your grandmother more often. You're lucky to have her."

"Hit him again!" Gram calls out.

She does—and they both laugh, their voices mingling in the kitchen air.

(3:17 PM)

By now, I've cleared my third plate of food, stuffed to the gills and leaning back, while Gram and Tricia are still working on their first—talking between small, careful bites.

"Oh yes, a garden would be lovely," Gram says, dabbing her mouth with her napkin. "I'm just having some complications and can't really tend to one. All that bending down and pulling weeds—my body just wouldn't be able to take it."

"I would love to have my own garden," Tricia says, her eyes lighting up. "Everything fresh from the earth and unspoiled. If I had a backyard like yours, I'd already have a spot picked out. I'd grow tomatoes, peas, corn—whatever I could manage."

"I had one once," Gram says with a satisfied sigh. "And let me tell you, sweetie, it's hard work—but well worth it." She takes the final bite from her plate. "So what is it you do for a living, Tricia?"

"Oh, I do customer service now. I was a file clerk before that."

"For a call center? I hear you need the patience of a saint for that kind of work. I'd hate answering phone calls all day."

"So do I," Tricia mutters with a crooked smile. Then, suddenly brightening, she adds, "Wow, Mrs. Thorpe, that was a fantastic meal. You sure know how to cook."

"Why, thank you," Gram beams. "Comes from years of practice, my dear. I wasn't always good in the kitchen, you know."

"Gram, you were always good in the kitchen," I say. "She's just being modest. She can cook just about anything. If Grandpa were still around, he'd tell you."

Tricia wipes her mouth, then leans forward slightly. "So, I have a question—and I'm sure it's probably obvious—but what started you calling your grandmother 'Gram'? I'm guessing it's just short for Grandma, right?"

Gram laughs, her eyes crinkling as she reaches for her napkin again. "Sweetie, it all started when Tommy was just a toddler..."

"Oh God," I groan, burying my face in my hands.

"He loved his little snacks in that Tupperware bowl his Momma would pack in his diaper bag," Gram says with a sparkle in her eye. "She'd fill it with Cheerios, little squares of cheese, grapes—just finger foods a toddler could manage."

Her hands move in slow, illustrative gestures as she speaks, reliving the memory like a cherished photograph come to life.

"Well, one day, his Momma forgot the snack bowl when she dropped him off at my place. All I had in the cupboard were these big square graham crackers, so I broke them up into little pieces. He took one bite and—oh, his little face just lit up with joy."

She chuckles, a deep, genuine sound, like the memory still warms her from the inside out.

"He was so adorable. Could barely talk, hadn't even started calling me 'Grandma' yet. But he knew what he wanted when he came to my house. And he knew the face that gave it to him. So the first thing he'd say when he saw me..."

"Gram!" I interrupt, smiling wide.

"Oh my God, how cute!" Tricia gasps, clasping her hands to her chest.

"Yes, yes it is. I love that little story." Gram stands to gather our empty plates, a playful glint in her eye. "Now you two have a choice to make."

Tricia and I exchange confused looks, brows raised.

"It may be too soon," she continues, "or you may not want them at all..."

My stomach knots and I can see the color drain from Tricia's face. We both brace ourselves, half-expecting a conversation about babies, marriage, or some painfully awkward blend of the two—especially after all this toddler talk.

"Gram, wait," I blurt out, hands raised. "Tricia and I are just friends."

Gram freezes mid-step, then sets the plates back down with dramatic flair. She turns to Tricia, locking eyes briefly, then swivels her gaze toward me with a slow, theatrical arch of her brow.

"Okay, Suga. But what does that have to do with you eating chocolate cake or pumpkin pie?"

***

(6:14 PM)

The truck idles softly beneath us as twilight folds over the parking lot. Tricia's head rests against the door, her body curled up like something fragile and forgotten. My pullover serves as a makeshift pillow beneath her cheek. One hand clutches her earrings loosely, as if they'd slipped off mid-dream.

I watch her breathe, the rise and fall of her chest calm and rhythmic. In this moment, she looks untouched by the weight of the world—a sharp contrast to the scar along her wrist that I can't seem to forget. That mark whispers of a history I don't fully understand, a depth of pain I can only guess at. And yet, she's still so kind... so sweet.

"So are we going to get out, or are you just going to sit there and stare at me all evening?"

Her voice startles me. I straighten up fast, eyes snapping forward as if I'd been caught doing something wrong. "I'm sorry, I was just..."

"I know—I know. Making sure I had my seatbelt on, right?" She laughs, pulling on her shoes. "It's okay. How long have we been here?"

"I don't know. Maybe a few minutes."

She rummages through her purse and retrieves her phone. The moment her eyes land on the screen, her expression shifts. The smile fades, replaced by a sudden sharpness. She looks around the parking lot, her movements quick and searching.

"What's wrong?" I ask.

"Nothing. I have to get to my apartment though. It's getting late," she says, her tone clipped and eyes distant as she gathers her things.

"Late? It's barely after six."

She climbs out of the truck abruptly, slamming the door without another word. I follow her, confused, watching the anxiety play across her face like a stormcloud as we step into the building.

We ride the elevator in silence. She won't meet my eyes, and I don't press her. The tension feels too real now—too thick to cut through with words.

As soon as the elevator dings, she slips out before the doors have fully parted. But then she halts. Dead stop. I peer around her and see them—two men, dressed in dark clothing, posted in front of her apartment door like sentinels.

"What?" I ask. "What's wrong?"

She spins toward me, her face a mask of casual irritation that doesn't reach her frightened eyes.

"Just play along, okay?" she whispers through barely parted lips.

"No, I said!" she suddenly snaps. "I have a boyfriend already. Now get off of me."

With a shove, she pushes me backward into the elevator and hisses under her breath, "Go!"

The two men begin to advance, fast and silent. I lurch back and hit the first-floor button. The elevator begins to close just as Tricia positions herself to block their view.

And just before the doors seal us off completely, I catch a flash of something too familiar—eyes, an unnatural shade of blue, locking with mine for the second time.

Chapter 15

VALENTEEN'S DAY

It was an urge...a strong urge, and the longer I let it go the stronger it got, to where I was taking risks to go out and kill people—Edmund Kemper III.

(Friday, 7:14 AM)

The day after Thanksgiving—Black Friday. For most, it's a well-earned day off. For my company, it's just another name for Friday. Business as usual. And heaven help you if you try to call out—they'll dock your holiday pay faster than you can sneeze. Screw it. I'll take the hit. My bonus check's already burning a hole through my wallet, and there's an empty television stand begging for attention.

I stand in front of the bathroom mirror, stripped down to nothing but my underwear, trying to piece together a halfway believable excuse. Something that'll get me out of work without too much scrutiny. If I call now, I'll get the voicemail and be spared the performance. Any later and I'll have to deal with Mr. Gibbons himself—his sighs, his lectures, and that same tired guilt trip about being dependable. I've heard it all before.

I go straight to voicemail and leave a long, meandering message. There's a small thrill in it—the quiet satisfaction of reclaiming the day, of pulling the covers back over my life for just a moment longer. No one can touch me now. My time is mine again.

I mentally scroll through my list of errands, things I told myself I'd get done. But they can wait. Right now, the only plan that matters is sliding back into the warm imprint of my bed, planting my face deep into the pillow, and vanishing beneath the blankets like a ghost gone to rest.

(6:24 PM)

The hallway is dim as I make my way back to my apartment, arms sore from errands and arms full from my "Black Friday miracle." From the other side of my door, I can already hear the unmistakable hum of my new TV. It's louder than I'd usually allow, just brushing the line between enjoyment and disturbance. Not that it's truly *new*—just new to me. A pawnshop special: a secondhand flat screen paired with a used Xbox 360. It works. That's enough.

I picture Tilly—my cat—probably curled up in the quietest corner of my room, ears folded back from the sudden volume spike.

With everything I lost now back in place, and the threat to my job removed, I've abandoned the last two names I'd marked for follow-up. There's no longer any reason to chase ghosts. My life is patched back together. Good enough.

As I pass my neighbor's door, it swings open abruptly. A wave of foul air hits me in the face—something like overcooked cabbage left too long in a humid room. I wrinkle my nose and cover it instinctively.

"Hey bro, I see you got new stuff," he says, scratching lazily at his stomach while leaning into the doorframe. His pajama pants—bright green and patterned with marijuana leaves—complete the usual ensemble.

"What do you mean?" I ask, pausing just short of my door.

"You got jacked a while ago, but I hear a television going in your apartment. Did you have insurance coverage or something?" he presses, now fiddling with the shiny eagle pendant hanging from his neck.

"No. I had no insurance," I answer plainly.

"Oh," he says, nodding slowly. "Then you must've come up with some money to replace all that stuff, huh? What all did you get back?"

His tone shifts—nosy, probing. I don't like the way his eyes hold mine for too long, waiting. I narrow mine in return, but say nothing. Instead, I push my door open and step inside, leaving him there with his question floating unanswered in the stale hallway air.

(10:15 PM)

The evening passed in a blur of outdated shooter games and forgettable movies—just like old times, before everything got turned upside down. But now, even with the glow of the screen and controller in hand, I can't shake the restlessness settling over me like dust.

Four hours of digital escape later, I'm no longer entertained—just buzzing with nerves and weighed down with boredom. The high has worn off, and the silence feels louder than the TV ever was. I scroll through the DVD shelf without much thought, grab something mindless, and drop it into the tray.

A little solo relief session. Just something to clear my head and kill the tension.

The flickering screen casts a soft glow over the room as I sit there, watching some cheap, low-budget porn. I work my nearly limp package with less enthusiasm than before, my mind already drifting. The images onscreen blur—fake moans, mechanical thrusts, sterile lust—and even as I try to picture Tricia in those same twisted positions, wearing the skimpy outfits, arching her back just right, nothing stirs in me the way I thought it would.

Her body, her voice, her curves... even the fantasy falls flat.

Then, a girl appears in the scene—tight cutoff shorts, a crop top clinging to her frame—as she starts raking dirt in her garden. But it's not the girl that grabs my attention. It's the rake. Just like the one Mr. Martinez fell on. The memory punches through the haze—those metal spikes piercing his neck. Blood. Convulsions. Silence.

The scene fractures. Now it's Ms. Bridges—her skull catching the full force of the stone table as it slammed down. The sharp, wet crunch of it. And then Kathy... her legs trembling violently as I forced the dildo deeper into her throat.

I'm suddenly hard. My leg shakes, involuntarily, right on the edge of something sharp and terrible. A climax looms, but it isn't the porn fueling it—it's the blood, the violence, the control. I feel possessed, overtaken by something darker than fantasy.

I stop. I breathe hard, trembling. What the hell is wrong with me?

I already know the answer, though.

This—*this*—is sicker than anything I've ever admitted, and yet, it's more intoxicating than any fantasy or skin flick I've ever seen. It fills me in a way pleasure never has.

So I let it happen. I finish.

(11:12 PM)

I wake up on the couch to the low hum of voices just outside my door—two men, their tones sharp and heated, though their words are hard to catch. My body is still groggy, my mind slow to catch up.

A knock hits the door—loud, firm, and then... nothing. Silence.

I rise slowly, heart thumping, and peer through the peephole. No one. But across the hallway, Tricia's door hangs wide open. No lights. No sound.

Something doesn't feel right.

"Tricia?" I call, easing my door open to get a better look.

That's when they move.

Two figures flank me in a flash, one on each side—the same two men from yesterday, the ones who showed up after Thanksgiving dinner like shadows from a darker world.

The older one steps forward from the left, casually pulling a green sucker from his mouth. His freakishly pale blue eyes lock onto mine, unblinking.

"Hello, my friend," he says, the thick Russian accent curling through his words like smoke.

I barely have time to retreat before the second man grabs me. I'm slammed hard into the hallway wall, his forearm pressing into the base of my throat, firm and immovable.

He smiles. It's the kind of smile that makes you feel like prey.

"Where are you going in such a hurry, my friend?" he asks. "We just want to have a talk with you. Seems we have some business to discuss."

"Business? What business?" I manage to say, my voice tight under the pressure.

The older man pops the sucker back into his mouth, pacing slowly.

"Well…" he muses, then pulls the candy out again, sticky and wet. "First, before discussing any business, I think it is formal—and polite—for one to introduce themselves. Yes?"

I don't answer.

The one pinning me shoves harder. "*Answer him!*" he barks, his accent just as heavy.

"Yes," I grunt. "I suppose."

"Good." The older one nods, pleased. "I am Valentin. And please, the pronunciation is *Vah-lyen-TEEN,* not *Valentine* like the holiday. I fucking hate that fucking holiday, so please do not get it confused."

He resumes sucking on the candy, pacing slowly in front of me.

"My friend here, the one you're so close with at the moment—that's Boris. He's very strong, as you can tell. Boris likes to break things. Dishes, chairs, arms, legs… maybe a neck or two. So he's very handy when it comes to discussing business."

Just then, a couple turns the corner into the hallway.

Without missing a beat, Boris releases his grip on me, casually dusts off my shoulders, and adjusts my shirt like we were old friends sharing a laugh. Both men put on friendly faces, nodding politely at the unsuspecting couple as they pass. Their act is disturbingly natural—like flipping a switch.

Valentin waits until the elevator doors swallow them up before shifting his gaze to Boris. His tone hardens.

"Take him inside."

Boris grabs a fistful of my shirt and hurls me through the doorway of my own apartment. I hit the floor hard, catching myself just short of the corner table. The door slams shut behind them, rattling the walls—so hard it knocks down the framed photo of my parents. It hits face-down on the hardwood.

"Do you mind getting to the point?" I bark, breath short. "I have no idea what this is all about."

Valentin exhales slowly, then grins like a man preparing to deliver bad news over coffee.

"Well, let's see. Where were we? Ah yes, my name is Valentin, and this is Boris. Your name, please?"

"Tommy."

"Okay, Tommy. Nice to meet you. So now we can discuss our business, now that we are past that. Yes?"

"Get to the point," I snap, pushing myself up.

Boris answers with a sudden, brutal kick to my chest that slams me flat again. Air punches from my lungs.

"Show some respect," he growls.

"To the point, yes. Let's do that then," Valentin continues, calm as ever. He crouches beside me, tapping his sucker toward my face like it's an extension of his finger.

"You are acquainted with our friend across the hallway?"

"Who, Tricia?"

"Yes, Tricia. You spent some time with her on your Thanksgiving Day, correct?"

"Yeah, so what? We had dinner at my grandma's house."

"Well, Tommy..." Valentin rises and begins pacing, his shoes silent across my floor. "There is where we have the problem. And where we must now discuss our business."

He bites down on the sucker with a satisfying *crunch*, chews thoughtfully, and then drags the empty stick through his teeth.

"Mmm. Bubble gum. Green apple. I love these things. Green is my favorite." He smacks his lips with exaggerated delight. "Delicious."

Then, without pause, his tone turns sharp again. "Anyways, since you've spent so much time with her—my business associate next door—it has cost us lots of money. I need her when I need her, you know? And it just so happens I needed her on Thursday... when you decided to have a lovely dinner with Grandma."

"Needed her for what? She said she works in customer service."

Boris chuckles under his breath, but Valentin doesn't join in.

"Shut up," he snaps. Boris obeys instantly.

"You see, she is correct, my friend. We have *customers*, and she provides a *service*. A service that costs our clients one hundred dollars per hour."

The pieces snap together in my head like broken glass reassembling—and cutting me on the way in.

"Tri... Tricia's an escort?"

"He is smart one, huh?" Boris says with a smirk.

"Why are you acting surprised, my friend?" Valentin asks, his brow raised. "She says you already knew this."

"What? No!" I say, my voice sharper than I intend.

"Well, nevertheless," Valentin says, brushing it off, "I take her word over yours. I need my money for the time you spent with my merchandise. She says you knew, so—you pay. And with the amount of time you've spent with her, it comes out to around five hundred dollars."

"I didn't know. And besides, I don't have that kind of money."

Valentin pauses, tilting his head.

"Oh... so she is lying?"

I don't answer. The air thickens.

"Okay, then this means I must take the missing money out on *her*." He sighs, shaking his head slowly as if burdened by his own cruelty. "I really hate doing this kind of thing. Last time a girl owed me this much money, she was not able to work for a couple of weeks."

He clicks his tongue. "It is not good for business. But my girls... they must learn a lesson. Do you agree?"

He doesn't wait for an answer.

"Boris. Let us go, my friend."

"Wait. Just—wait," I say, pushing myself up on one arm. "Give me some time to pay it, and I'll get you your money. Just leave Tricia alone."

Valentin tilts his head, the hard edge of skepticism already etched across his face. "I'm not sure I can do that."

"You can hold me entirely responsible for you not having your money. I'll pay. You have my word. Just give me a couple of weeks to do it. That's all I ask."

The two exchange a glance, wordless but weighted.

"Excuse me for a moment," Valentin says.

They step away, just far enough to murmur among themselves, their voices low and fast in a language I can't understand. As they confer, I scramble through desperate possibilities. I could return the TV and the Xbox. Maybe pawn a few other things. If they gave me a month, I could stretch it—make something work.

"Okay," Valentin says at last, chewing his gum loudly, his mouth half-open like it's all just a minor inconvenience. "I'll give you one week."

"One week!" I echo, stunned. "Are you kidding me? I can't come up with that in less than a week."

He shrugs. Boris smirks.

"Looks like it's your problem and not ours," Boris says, holding the door open for his boss with a smirk that grates like sandpaper.

As Valentin steps forward, his boot nearly crushes the picture frame still lying face-down on the floor. He stops, stoops down, and picks it up.

"Who are these people?"

"My parents," I answer flatly.

"Hmm. I feel like I know these faces."

"You don't," I say. "They died in a plane crash when I was a child."

"A plane crash, huh? Ah, okay." He sets the photo gently on the wall, then adjusts it with a strange reverence. "I will see you next Friday, my friend Tommy... uh, what is last name?" he asks, pausing just beyond the threshold.

"Thorpe. My name is Tommy Thorpe."

He turns slowly, casting a final glance at me where I still sit on the floor—his eyes void of warmth, unreadable and cold. He reaches into the inside pocket of his coat.

My breath catches. I raise a hand instinctively, heart punching my ribs, vision narrowing in panic.

In a swift motion, he pulls something free—just another green sucker. He unwraps it with precision, spits his gum into the wrapper, and pops the fresh candy into his mouth. Boris chuckles under his breath.

"The flavor in the gum never lasts with these things," Valentin says, smacking his lips. "But I still love them. You have a good day, my friend."

And just like that, they're gone—walking down the hallway, their voices fading into hushed Russian as they head for the elevator.

The door swings shut behind them, and the quiet is thunderous.

Furious, I kick the door with the heel of my foot, slamming it shut. I stand slowly, chest heaving, jaw tight. My fists clench until my knuckles ache. There's a fire behind my eyes, swelling up from somewhere deep—hot, raw, and choking. My vision blurs as tears threaten to spill, my rage and confusion folding into each other like storm clouds.

Is it what just happened? Or what I've learned about Tricia? Maybe both.

My breath comes hard through flared nostrils as I explode.

I drive my fist through the plaster of the living room wall with a sharp grunt, the drywall giving way like paper. The coffee table is next—splintering with a single angry kick. I storm into my bedroom, red with fury, and shoulder the tall dresser onto its side. Drawers spill open, their contents scattering. My mattress follows, flipped up against the wall with one violent heave.

Below me, I feel the angry thumping from my neighbor—his fists beating against the ceiling, but I don't care. I don't stop.

I spot my clothes iron on the floor and snatch it up, turning toward the full-length mirror, ready to shatter the only thing still standing.

But I freeze.

There it is again.

That dark, slender reflection—impossibly still, impossibly familiar—staring back at me from inside the glass.

I drop the iron with a metallic thud, breath caught in my throat. The rage melts into silence. A strange calm settles over me as I lock eyes with what shouldn't be there.

My reflection—no longer mine—slowly raises a long, thin finger and points to the floor beside me.

I follow its gesture and spot the paper—the folded report from work.

The one with two names highlighted.

I pick it up, unfolding it slowly, almost reverently.

When I look back to the mirror, the reflection is gone.

But the message is clear.

So is the answer.

(12:43 AM)

I've already slipped through Mr. Roger Brown's partially opened window like a shadow on the breeze. He's stretched out on the couch, half-conscious beneath the flicker of an action movie, his snoring nearly as loud as the bass rumbling from his surround sound system. The steady rumble grants me cover—no need for finesse or silence. I move like mist through the frame and now stand behind the couch, just inches from him.

Clad in my nylon costume, I loom over the sleeping figure—muscular, broad-shouldered, his skin pale against the dim light of the screen. His bus driver uniform is still half on, shirt unbuttoned to reveal thick pectorals and a sculpted abdomen that rises and falls with every slow, heavy breath.

I tap the flat edge of the railroad spike blade—my latest find from the old shed—against my thigh. The metallic *ting* echoes faintly through the room, drowned beneath the booming soundtrack of the film. My thoughts churn with every insult and lie this man spat at me through the phone, and now, here he is—helpless.

Do I wake him? Confront the arrogance head-on?

Or do I simply end it here—quiet and clean—while his body rests?

I lean in close, positioning the blade beneath his throat, pressing just enough to feel the warm pulse against the metal. One single, swift slice. That's all it would take.

But fate intervenes.

He snorts—chokes on his own spit—and bolts upright with a hacking cough. I recoil like a shadow, melting back into the deepest corner of the living room before his groggy eyes can focus. Hidden in the veil of darkness, I watch as he stumbles to his feet and lurches toward the bathroom, sputtering mucus and slapping at the walls for balance.

He flips the light switch on his way past, and for a moment, the room fills with harsh white light. I hold still—breath shallow—as it passes over everything but me.

He slams the bathroom door behind him.

No, I can't take this guy head-on. Not in a fair fight. I need an edge. Something clever. Something quiet.

I move quickly while I can.

A tap of the blade against the light bulb, and it bursts with a soft *pop*, drowning the living room in blackness. Then to the kitchen—another bulb shattered. The bedroom follows. I weave through the shadows like smoke, silent and surgical. Finally, I reach the entertainment system and yank its power cord free from the outlet, letting silence swell where cinematic chaos once played. The room goes utterly still.

Then, I return to my corner.

Moments pass.

The bathroom door swings open abruptly, stopping short as his face peeks out into the void. The faint yellow light behind him casts a weak glow into the living room, but it barely reaches past the threshold. As the door opens wider, I can see him fully now—his movements cautious, his breathing shallow.

He starts creeping through the darkness, one foot sliding tentatively in front of the other. His fingertips brush the coffee table as he fumbles his way toward the kitchen. A metal door creaks open—fuse box. He's checking the obvious first.

With the bathroom empty, I glide inside. One quick tap of my blade, and the final light dies.

"What the shit, bro!" he yells, voice echoing from the kitchen in raw frustration.

He's close to figuring it out. The fuse box won't tell him anything. It won't be long before suspicion turns to fear. I retreat once again, sinking into the same corner, still and breathless.

I hear him shuffle back toward the living room, dragging his hand across the furniture to guide him. Then, a faint *click*. The screen of his cell phone springs to life, casting pale blue light across the floor. A second later, the flashlight flicks on, cutting a narrow beam through the dark.

His hand follows the unplugged cord along the carpet. He squats, examining the disconnected entertainment system like he can't believe what he's seeing. A quiet panic swells in him.

The flashlight starts swinging—jerky, uncontrolled. He waves the beam across the room, searching every corner but the one behind him.

Where I stand.

Watching.

Waiting.

I have nowhere else to go. No shadows left to disappear into. So I stay frozen, breathing shallowly, waiting for the right moment to strike.

Step by step, I creep toward him—my body tight, movements slow and deliberate. But then... *pop*. A floorboard beneath me betrays its age with a sharp crack.

He spins around instantly, flashlight beam slicing through the dark like a blade. It lands square in my face.

Instinct takes over.

I surge forward and slash across his chest. The blade tears through his shirt and into skin—deep and fast. A flash of red. A scream. He stumbles back with a howl, tripping over the arm of the couch. His body crashes down onto the coffee table, shattering it into splinters beneath him. His phone slips from his grip and skitters across the carpet, vanishing beneath an end table.

"What the fuck—what the fuck, man!" he screams, scrambling backward through the debris, kicking at shards of wood as he goes. "Who's there!?"

He begins hurling broken table legs and splinters in my direction. They bounce harmlessly off walls and furniture as I close in, step by step, the spike blade still warm in my hand.

On all fours, he crawls fast toward the glow of his phone's screen. I'm nearly on top of him when he reaches for it. I slash downward, catching the back of his hand with a sharp slice. Blood sprays. He shrieks, but he doesn't stop. He lunges forward again, grabs the phone, and kicks out with full force.

The heel of his foot crashes into my midsection.

The wind rushes from my lungs as I collapse backward, skidding across the floor.

By the time I sit up, groaning, he's vanished—retreating into the closet and slamming the door behind him.

Still shaken from the kick, I rise slowly and approach the closet door with cautious steps. I press my ear to the wood. On the other side, Mr. Brown's panicked breathing is shallow and fast, his voice trembling as he fumbles with his phone.

I feel the pressure of his body leaning against the door—his weight heavy and desperate. I raise the blade and press the tip gently against the wood, aiming just where I think the center of his back would be. I steady my breath, preparing to drive it through.

Then his phone rings.

"Jarod—Jarod, bro, call the police!" he hisses. "Somebody's fucking in my house, dude... Fuck no... Just head over now, bro, *please!*"

I hear the beep as he ends the call and immediately punches in three numbers. A sigh escapes me. I'm disappointed. Deeply.

For all his bravado—his trash talk and threats over the phone—he's just another coward with muscles. A man who could overpower me in an instant, now trembling behind a thin door, whimpering like a child.

"I'm calling the police! You better get the fuck out while you can!" he yells, voice cracking.

"911, please state your emergency," the operator says, her voice filtered and calm through speakerphone.

"Hello—you guys have to hurry and get someone here quick," he blurts out.

"What's your emergency, sir?"

"Somebody is in my fucking house," he sobs.

"Are you in a safe place, sir? Are you injured?"

"I think he's still out there... and yeah, he's got a knife. I got cut a couple of times—so I'm bleeding like a bitch. Send somebody quick?"

"Yes, sir, I'll have a unit on the way. Just stay put, okay?"

"Yeah—just hurry!"

"Now, can you describe what the intruder looks like?"

"No, he has a mask on."

"What kind of mask? Ski mask, hockey mask...?"

"No—no, it was blank. Nothing. Just black. He looked like..."

There's a pause. I lift the blade slightly, adjusting my aim to where his voice is coming from—closer to the back of his head.

"Sir?"

"You're gonna think I'm on crack or something."

"Just tell me what you saw."

His voice drops to a shaky whisper.

"It's dark in my house—but he had all black on, and a mask. He looked like... like a damn stickman."

That's when I drive the blade forward—hard and fast—into the wood, angled upward.

A sharp *crack* as the spike punctures through, followed by gurgled choking and violent thrashing of his body against the inside of the door. The phone clatters to the floor, the call still active, the voice on the other end calling his name.

"Sir—sir? Are you still with me? Sir?" the 911 operator calls out, her voice now muffled, seeping from beneath the closet door where the phone had landed.

Blood oozes from the jagged hole where my blade punched through the door—thick and dark, trailing in a syrupy thread as it snakes its way down to the carpet below. The door groans under the weight of his body as I begin to pull it open, slow and deliberate. His heels scrape across the floor, resisting only by the slack drag of death.

Through the widening crack, I catch a glimpse of the aftermath—my work in full, grotesque display. Still impaled and upright, Mr. Brown hangs there like a coat on a hook, supported only by the blade buried in the base of his skull.

He doesn't move.

He won't.

The spike had entered the base of his skull and exited clean through his open mouth—forced wide around the dark metal like a grotesque puppet. Yet... he's still breathing. Barely. His eyes flutter beneath half-closed lids, blood spilling from his lips in lazy drips.

"You should really be careful of the people you threaten over the phone, Mr. Brown," I murmur. My tone is calm—collected—as if offering advice rather than vengeance. "All I asked for was a simple car payment, and you threaten to kick my ass... then call me the 'N' word?"

I shake my head slowly, more disappointed than angry.

"Look at you now. What a shame."

His bloodshot eyes meet mine with a weak, stuttering awareness, then slowly roll backward. His limbs twitch once, then go limp. Silence follows—thick and final.

I stare at the massive man crumpled behind the door, once loud, now quiet, his bravado dissolved into a pool of blood and shame. A beast brought down not by brute strength, but precision. Fear. Control.

There's something awe-inspiring about it. The sheer improbable nature of it all.

I know I'll never kill someone like this again—not in this exact way. So I take a breath and commit it to memory, etching it deep into my mind like a photograph hung in a gallery. A private collection. A trophy no one will ever see but me, on a shelf in my mind.

Company will be here soon—flashing lights, boots on floors—but I can't leave without leaving something behind.

A mark.

Both of his clocks—one in the kitchen and one in the hallway—are set to the same time: 2:10. Ten minutes past two. A moment preserved. A final, personal note scrawled in the language of obsession.

I crouch and attempt to retrieve my blade. It's wedged deep into bone and wood. I tug, twist, strain—but it's no use. It won't budge.

Fine. There's still a bucket of railroad spikes waiting in the shed. I'll make more.

I wipe down the handle to remove any evidence, then reach for the Bible I brought with me. Carefully, I dip my finger into the blood streaking down the door and use it to highlight a passage—*James 2:10*: *For whoever keeps the whole law but fails in one point has become accountable for all of it.*

Let that be his sermon.

———————

(10:13 AM — Sunday)

The sun cuts across the windshield as I coast through familiar neighborhoods, cruising past addresses connected to one name: *Donte Stevens.*

I nearly call it off—too many false leads—until something catches my eye.

A car. The same make and model from the file, but instead of the bright red listed, this one's been covered in a dull, uneven coat of black. Spray paint. Sloppy. Rushed.

I slow for a closer look.

The cover-up is amateur. Overspray clouds the windows, and along the lower panels, the original red still peeks through in forgotten patches. He didn't even bother to peel off the company bumper sticker—just sprayed right over it.

No need to check the VIN. This is him.

The street is crowded—vehicles parked bumper to bumper on both sides. Perfect. My own car blends into the background like another commuter left behind for the weekend.

So I wait.

———————

(11:20 AM)

It only takes an hour before I spot him.

Short, bald, Black male in neon orange and yellow—colors so loud they practically announce him from half a block away. He moves with a kind of swagger, but there's tension in his stride. Urgency. He heads straight for the Buick.

He yanks the door open, throws himself inside, and fires up the engine before even closing it. No patience. No caution. Just instinct and panic.

He throws it in drive, lurches out of his spot, and nearly clips a man stepping out of his own vehicle. Horns blare behind him.

I slip into gear and follow, steady and invisible in the sea of Sunday traffic.

For the entire drive, he gives no indication that he's noticed the bright blue truck shadowing him. From where I sit, tucked a few car lengths behind, I watch him through his rear window—his attention glued to his phone, thumb scrolling, eyes occasionally flicking up to check traffic. Oblivious. Predictable.

I stay close as he weaves through the city, trailing him for several miles until he finally pulls into a Village Inn parking lot. But instead of heading inside, he scans his surroundings with a twitchy kind of caution, then ducks into the alley behind the restaurant.

His neon clothing works against him—orange and yellow practically glowing in the gray morning light. Even from the main road, I can trace his movement, catching flashes of him slipping between fences and sheds, weaving through the backs of quiet houses like a man with something to hide.

I pull out the folder from my passenger seat and flip through his references. One address stands out—just a few blocks from where he vanished. Rather than tailing him on foot, I take the smarter route, circling the block and parking two houses away from the listed residence.

Five minutes pass.

Then I spot him.

Mr. Stevens emerges from the backyard, dusting his hands off as he approaches the door. He fishes out a set of keys, but before he can sort through them, the door swings open.

A short, curvy Black woman steps outside, her stance hard and unwelcoming. She's dressed in light blue pajama bottoms and a white bra, her hair wrapped in a red bandana. Arms crossed tight over her chest, lips curled with disdain, she plants herself firmly in his path.

He tries to speak, but she silences him with a single palm to his face—again and again, shutting him down before he gets a word out.

Still, he persists. After some hushed back-and-forth, she finally moves aside and lets him in.

That's all I need.

This is definitely his place.

And now that I know where he sleeps... I'll be back.

———————

(7:31 PM)

The scent of Gram's special spaghetti sauce has been teasing me for the better part of an hour—its rich, savory aroma curling through the air like a warm embrace. My stomach growls, helpless under its spell, as I sit at the table watching her move with practiced grace between the stove and the counter.

Finally, she places a generous plate in front of me, the steam rising in swirling waves. The thick, red sauce clings to the tender noodles like it knows it's something special. She follows it with a tall glass of lemonade, so cold the condensation's already pooling near the base of the cup.

"Eat up. You know your Mom would never forgive me—letting you get all skinny like you are, Honey," she says with a smile, setting the crystal pitcher gently on the table beside us.

"I like being skinny, Gram. But you don't have to worry about me eating today—I'm starving. I could eat three plates just like this one. I swear, your cooking gets better every time. There may not be any leftovers when I'm done," I grin, then dive in, twirling the noodles and slurping them with abandon. Sauce splatters. A few strands flick the sides of my face.

"Mind your manners, Tommy!" she snaps with mock horror.

"Gyes Gam!" I mumble, mouth packed full of pasta.

She rolls her eyes and turns back to the sink, shaking her head while running the water for the dishes. I hear her mutter something under her breath about raising me better than this.

"You're not gonna eat?—Come on, Gram, sit down with me," I offer, nudging the chair beside me outward with the side of my foot.

"No sweetie, I'm not hungry. I made that for you. I already ate earlier and don't have much of an appetite right now," she says with a light laugh. "Besides, your Granny needs to lose a little weight, so it's best I don't."

"Nooz neight...what!?"

"*Thomas Thorpe!* If you don't chew your dang food before talking to me..."

I rush to swallow, nearly choking. "Who said you need to lose weight?"

"The doctor. Don't worry about it though. I've been having some pains in my legs, and Dr. Strauss thinks it would help if I lost a little weight," she says, nodding down at her swollen ankles.

She gives me a look, then shifts the conversation. "How long you think before you're all finished with that shed? You've been working on it for a long time now."

"It shouldn't take long, Gram. Why don't you have a seat? You've been on your feet all afternoon. You should rest."

"I guess I can go in the living room and watch my news for a little bit. Then finish this later."

"Don't worry about the dishes, Gram. I got them."

"No—no—no, I'll get them. I just need to get off my feet for a moment," she says, drying her hands on a faded kitchen towel. She shuffles gently toward the living room, hand on the wall for balance.

"Okay. I'll come join you when I'm done," I call after her, already reaching for my glass.

(8:13 PM)

After finishing another overflowing plate of Gram's homemade magic—stuffing, candied yams, and the juiciest turkey this side of Heaven—I quietly ignore her standing rule and begin washing the mountain of dishes stacked beside the sink. The clatter of pots and glass, along with the hiss of running water, makes it impossible to conceal my rebellion.

"Sweetie, you better not be in there washing those dang dishes!" she hollers from the living room, her voice both stern and filled with love.

I don't answer. I just smile to myself and keep scrubbing.

A short while later, I step into the living room. Gram is in her favorite chair, her patchwork afghan tucked around her legs. She's sound asleep, her head tilted back, mouth slightly open, completely still.

The sight tugs at something deep in my chest.

She's been talking more and more lately about "going soon," like the idea has already settled somewhere inside her. And people always say that when one passes, the other follows not long after. Gram and Grandpa had that kind of love—steady, unconditional, rare. The thought of losing her too...

My fingers are still damp from the sink, and without thinking, I slip them gently under her nose.

A soft breath.

She's still here.

Carefully, I pull the afghan up over her shoulders, tucking it beneath her chin. Then I lean in and kiss her forehead, her skin warm and familiar.

"Love you," I whisper.

(10:24 PM – Sunday Night)

"I'm serious, Donte. I'm tired of this shit!"

"I told you I ain't going anywhere. Stop tripp'n!" Donte Stevens barks, his voice rising through the bedroom window I've crouched beneath, hidden in the thick hedge line outside.

From where I'm concealed in the dark, I can see just enough. He's seated at the edge of the bed, glued to the television, a game controller clenched in his hands. His girlfriend stands in the bedroom doorway, wrapped in a towel, her face flushed with frustration. The uniform folded neatly at the foot of the bed suggests she's getting ready for a late shift.

"Can't you turn that down some?" she snaps.

"Damn! Is everything I'm doing messing with you?" he shouts back. "Go take your shower and close the door."

She sucks her teeth and stares him down, eyes sharp, jaw tight. He doesn't flinch—yet—too caught up in his game. But her presence unsettles him. You can see it in the way he tenses, just a little, when she walks past.

"Your lazy ass needs to get a job or something. This laying around the house shit ain't gett'n it done, Donte. And I *dare* your ass to leave for some bitch's house while I'm gone."

"Psh, wow," he chuckles dismissively, eyes never leaving the screen.

"I'm not playing, Donte. Let me find out you did, and see what happens."

He rolls his eyes again, this time more forcefully. Then she reaches for the remote beside him, and his body jolts—just for a moment, like a dog that's been kicked before. She clicks the volume down hard, each push of the button echoing like punctuation marks on her anger. Then, with deliberate defiance, she tosses the remote beside him and storms off toward the bathroom.

Donte doesn't say another word. Just resumes playing, shoulders tight with irritation.

Earlier, I scoped out the perimeter—doors locked, windows sealed. There's no clean way in.

If I come back later, odds are he won't be here. From the sound of their argument, he's got a wandering eye and an even lazier sense of loyalty.

I circle the house once more, keeping to the shadows, each step slow and silent as I wrestle with how to approach this—how to catch Donte Stevens alone and vulnerable. Just as I'm about to abandon the idea for the night, something catches my eye: the main fuse box near the rear of the house.

An idea sparks.

I stoop and pick up a palm-sized stone, just heavy enough. A sharp clang breaks the quiet as I knock the lock loose. Inside, the switches are clearly labeled—kitchen, bedroom, bathroom. Doesn't matter. I flip them all.

Within seconds, the house is swallowed in darkness. From inside, a shriek echoes through the walls—his girlfriend, caught mid-shower. The sound is sharp, frantic, echoing just long enough to draw a grin to my face. I retreat into the corner just beside the fuse box, vanishing into the dark.

The back door bursts open. Donte steps out, swearing and shivering, a small flashlight trembling in his grip.

"I knew I should've saved my game," he mutters, hugging himself against the cold. "Now I gotta do that shit all over again..."

He pauses, his breath curling like smoke in the frigid air, eyes dropping to the rock I left beside the broken fuse box. I watch him closely from the shadows, seeing the realization begin to bloom in his expression.

Slowly, his gaze lifts—first over his shoulder, then snapping sharply around with a sudden twist of his body. The narrow beam of his flashlight cuts through the dark, wavering as he tries to steady his hand. His breaths grow quicker, more visible, like fleeting ghosts pushed from his lungs.

His beam finds me as I step forward from the shadows—calm, silent, deliberate.

The flashlight slips from his grasp, clattering to the ground as his hand trembles. He doesn't move. Can't. His body locks in place, stiff with fear, eyes wide and glassy under the pale moonlight.

Frozen.

Just the way I wanted him.

Before he can bolt, I close the distance. The move—just like Boris taught me—is swift and practiced. I pin him against the siding with a forearm to his throat.

"You really ought to watch who you mouth off to, Mr. Stevens," I whisper. "You had so much to say over the phone. I figured I'd come hear another one of those D.L. Hughley quotes in person. Kings of Comedy, right?"

I act quickly, silencing him with one hand as I finish what I came to do. I thrust the blade of my newly crafted knife upward and under his breast plate, pressing my hand harder over his mouth, muffling his scream. He raises to his toes and grabs my shoulders. His eyelids flutter like my last victim, then roll upward. I jabbed him two more times, in the same manner, twisting my knife deep. The blood from his mouth finds its way between my nylon-covered fingers. One last jab and his body almost instantly loses what little fight it had left, and he collapses to the ground.

It's over before he fully realizes what's happening. His body slumps, the light fading from his eyes as the cold night swallows him whole.

Time is short.

I drag his body inside through the still-open back door. The shower is still running. Her voice echoes down the hallway—completely unaware.

"Donte! Hurry up and fix that mess—I can't see a damn thing! I need to get ready for work! If you weren't running all those damn electronics—"

I prop his body on the couch and straighten his head. No power means no digital clock. No calling card.

I slip back outside, reset the switches. Lights blink back to life inside the house.

And she keeps shouting.

It should buy me just enough time.

"Thank you!" she yells.

I need to move quickly. My hands tremble slightly as I rush from room to room, adjusting every clock to read ten minutes to six. There's already a Bible open on the kitchen table, the thin pages fluttering from the breeze slipping through the cracked window.

I settle on Ecclesiastes 5:5—*It's better not to make a vow than to make one and not keep it.* The hour and verse don't quite align, but it's the best I can manage with the time I have.

With deliberate care, I drag a thin smear of his blood across the passage, the crimson streak sinking into the page like ink.

A short note comes next, hastily scrawled but clear. I place it where she's sure to see it—should she bother to look. Then I kill the lights in the living room, letting the darkness settle like a shroud before slipping out the front door.

I linger just beyond the window, watching.

She emerges slowly, wrapped in a mint green towel that glows faintly against the deep warmth of her skin. Her footsteps are cautious, hesitant. She approaches the light switch and flicks it on.

Donte is seated on the couch, his back to her.

She stiffens, senses it—something's wrong. Her breath catches as she inches forward, rounding the couch.

Then it happens.

A scream tears from her throat, raw and piercing, as she sees my knife still buried in his chest. Panic grips her, and she bolts for the door, flinging it open and crying out even louder into the night for someone—anyone—to help.

I shake my head, more annoyed than satisfied.

She didn't even read the note: *Find yourself a new man. As you can see, this one is no good.*

CHaPTer 16

LOST AND FOUND

(6:14 AM, Monday)

This morning, I pushed my limits, surpassing my usual "300 workout" and stepping into the pain of a "400 workout," all while the morning news droned in the background. Sweat clung to my skin, and my muscles burned, but I welcomed the distraction.

(Newscaster Lovanda White):

"This weekend, two more individuals were found dead in their Milwaukee homes. Authorities remain tight-lipped regarding the victims' identities, but they've confirmed there are leads—and similarities—linking the recent string of murders.

In a chilling twist, one victim managed to place a 911 call moments before his death. Due to the active investigation and the disturbing nature of the recording, we are unable to air it. However, sources say the victim described his assailant as 'faceless... tall and thin... dressed entirely in black.' Sound familiar? Last week, a woman reported seeing that exact figure leaving a hotel parking lot shortly after another homicide.

Is the so-called 'Stick Man Murderer' real? Authorities seem to think there's substance behind the rumors. Milwaukee residents are urged to stay alert and keep all windows and doors locked—especially when home."

(8:12 AM)

The office buzzed with its usual Monday inertia when Kimmie's voice lifted me from my thoughts.

"What's up, Tommy?" she chirped, beaming brighter than her usual sunshine self.

"Hey, Kimmie! What's got you so happy?" I asked, pausing my shuffle through the morning reports.

"Oh, nothing." She rested her hands on the cubicle wall and gave her fingers a playful wiggle.

"Okay..." I replied, puzzled—until the light caught something glittering on her left hand. My eyes widened. "What!?"

"Yep!" she squealed, grinning like the Cheshire cat as she bounced on the balls of her feet. "He asked me during dinner—right in front of his parents! Tommy, I was sweating my ass off. I was happy and nervous as hell. I wasn't expecting anything like this so soon."

"Well, what did you say?"

She stared at me with exaggerated disbelief, lips twisted as if I'd just asked if the sky was still blue.

"Oh no—shit, right! That's awesome, Kimmie!" I quickly corrected, catching myself.

She laughed and tilted her head. "What's on your mind?"

"Nothing really," I lied. "Just gotta get these numbers down, that's all. You know... same old crap." I rifled through my papers, pretending to care.

She nodded. "Yeah, they are coming down hard on us."

She wasn't wrong. My head was definitely elsewhere. I kept darting glances toward the front desk, half-expecting Detective Bedwell to come strolling through the doors again. With the recent wave of killings, it was only a matter of time before he returned. But I couldn't let Kimmie sense the tension bubbling beneath my surface.

"Did you set a date yet?" I asked, feigning curiosity.

"No—no date yet. We want to get our finances in order first. Maybe a couple years from now. Who knows?" Her smile broadened. "I'm just happy Greg finally committed. It's proof he really loves me."

Her teeth sparkled like they belonged in a toothpaste commercial.

"Sup y'all?" Derrick's voice broke through the moment.

"Sup, Derrick?" I called back.

"Hey, Derrick," Kimmie chimed, then proudly displayed her ring again, repeating her little finger dance with twice the enthusiasm.

All I could do was smile—and hope I wasn't next.

Both of them launch into a nearly identical conversation to the one I'd just had with Kimmie moments earlier. Their voices rise and fall with excitement, but mine—my mind—wanders once again to the front entrance. I can't keep doing this. I know I've cleaned up every trace, erased every breadcrumb, yet the thought of a surprise visit from Detective Bedwell keeps digging at my nerves like a splinter under the skin. This kind of unease festers. And I know better—worry breeds doubt, and doubt invites panic. Panic... will land me in a cell for the rest of my life if I don't get my head straight.

I need to pivot. Now.

"So Derrick, did you get that new game *Drafted*?" I ask, cutting clean through their chatter like a blade through fabric. Kimmie throws me a glare—sharp and unamused—before ducking back behind her cubicle wall, out of sight.

"Oh yeah, I'm picking that up Friday, man," Derrick replies with genuine excitement. "That's the new first-person shooter, right? Supposed to make *Call to Arms* look like child's play. The AI is next-level, and the campaign? Supposedly endless. A world of missions you can't even finish."

"Yeah, that's what I've heard. If you're not tied up, maybe I'll swing by when you crack that bad boy open."

"Ah yeah, that'd be cool. My wife's outta town this weekend, so I'll be just chillin'." He brings a finger to his lips and leans in. "Keep that on the low though. She thinks I'm going fishing with her dad. He already canceled, but I didn't tell her. I just don't wanna go to Cleveland to see her damn family—can't stand her sister, her brother, her mother—none of 'em. Always whispering, throwing shade. Nah, I'm not about to subject myself to that mess. You feel me?"

"Loud and clear," I say with a chuckle. "So, Friday release. But let's be real, you're not gonna wait 'til Saturday to play it."

He grins. "Hell no. But come by Saturday, man. That'll give me a little head start to get used to it. Then I can properly whoop your ass."

I laugh, slipping my headset on. "If you say so, man. You're gonna need that extra day, though. I catch on fast."

"Whatever!" he calls out.

(8:13 PM)

The cold metal of the elevator button presses in with a soft click as I arrive at my apartment complex. I lean against the wall, the weight of the day—and the dark thoughts lingering behind it—still clinging to my shoulders. I find myself running through imaginary conversations with Detective Bedwell. What I'd say. How I'd say it. The tone. The posture. The lies, polished to shine like truth.

I press the button again. Nothing. No familiar whir, no mechanical hum. Just silence.

With a sigh, I pivot to the stairwell. My legs feel heavier with every step.

As I push the door open to my floor, something pale and twitchy darts across the hallway—erratic and quick, like a ball of static come to life.

It takes a second, but I recognize her. "Hey! What the hell—how did you get out here, Tilly?"

The little furball bolts toward me, her snowy coat bouncing with every springy movement like a living slinky. I crouch, scooping her into my arms as she reaches me—her tiny frame trembling with excitement. But as I rise and approach my door, a queasy, queasy lurch swells in my gut—sick and sudden, like that dreadful second before a rollercoaster plummets.

Something's wrong.

There—right at the threshold—wood chips scattered across the hall-way floor. The door isn't closed. A warm sliver of light spills through the narrow gap where it hangs slightly ajar.

I stare at it for half a second too long, then drop Tilly to the ground before the fury and fear inside me cause me to squeeze too hard and crush her by mistake.

My heart races—each beat louder, faster, heavier—thundering in my ears like distant drums of war. As I push the door open, a few more splinters of wood break free, drifting down like brittle snowflakes onto the floor. The moment is eerily familiar, but this time, the feeling of intrusion cuts deeper. The air feels colder, the silence sharper.

"How could this happen," I whisper, barely recognizing my own voice.

Once again, I'm staring at the dusty imprint where my new television used to rest, the ghost of its weight still etched into the stand. The shelf where my Xbox sat now gapes open like a mouth mid-scream. It's all gone. Again.

Everything I worked so hard to reclaim—vanished in the blink of an eye. A sick, hollow ache swells in my chest. Powerless. Frustrated. Fury rising like bile in my throat.

Just as rage threatens to take full control, a glint near the back of the TV stand tugs at my vision. Something metallic, small, and reflective catches the lamplight and tosses it back like a signal flare. I step closer, cautious but drawn.

And there it is—two tiny silver wings, outstretched like they're poised to take flight. The eagle pendant dangles from a broken chain, the clasp snapped clean. I don't even need to turn it over. I know exactly who this belongs to.

The same bastard who looked me dead in the eye the last time and told me—without flinching—that he hadn't heard a thing.

My jaw tightens. I close my hand around the necklace, the little eagle swinging from my clenched fist.

Without another thought, I storm down the hallway toward my neighbor's door. The urge to pound it into splinters floods through me, but I stop myself. No—he's listening. He's always listening. Probably grinning on the other side of that door, waiting for me to lose control.

I hear the faint creak of floorboards. The soft shuffle of footsteps retreating. He's moving away.

I smirk and knock gently. Just enough to let him know I'm here.

"Hold on!" he calls, his voice casual and unbothered.

When he cracks the door, I'm greeted only by the sight of his bare neck and a smug, too-relaxed expression.

"What's up, bro?" he says, his tone coated in false innocence.

I keep my hands behind my back, clutching the evidence of his lie.

"Did you by any chance hear anything next door?" I ask, voice even. Controlled.

"No, bro, why?"

I narrow my eyes, my gaze cold and slitted.

"I got robbed again. Someone took my shit, so I was wondering if you saw or heard anything."

He shakes his head, his eyes wide with feigned surprise. "Nah, not at all. I've been asleep most of the day, bro, so I don't know what to tell you. Damn, that sucks. Again!?" He opens the door a little more.

I tilt my head slightly. "Hey... what happened to your necklace? You usually have it on when I see you."

His eyes drop to his chest, fingers patting at bare skin.

"Damn. I have no idea. Maybe they got my necklace too?" he laughs, forced and hollow. "Nah man, it probably fell off on the bed or in the couch when I was takin' a nap or something. It'll turn up."

I raise my hand, letting the necklace dangle in front of him like bait on a hook.

"Sooner than you think. I found it for you. It was behind my TV stand."

His eyes widen, panic flashing across his face. He jerks the door, trying to slam it shut—but he's too slow.

I drive my foot forward with all the strength I can muster. The door slams back open with a violent crack, smashing into his face. He stumbles, his pudgy frame wobbling like a struck jelly mold before he topples to the floor.

A sharp, startled fart escapes him on impact—like a trumpet announcing the fall of a pathetic little king.

I step inside and quietly close the door behind me. The air inside is thick—rank with the stench of old weed smoke and rotting garbage. Empty beer cans rattle under my foot, and greasy pizza boxes lie collapsed and sunken like miniature coffins on the stained carpet. It's a pigsty, every square inch of it. And somehow, this degenerate manages to outdo Derrick in pure filth. I didn't think it was possible.

"Where's my stuff? I'm only gonna ask once," I say, voice cold and firm.

Blood streams from his crooked nose, dripping onto his already stained shirt. He tries to scuttle away without uttering a word, but I kick at his feet, knocking him further off balance. Still no cry for help—no yelling, no threats, no calls for mercy. That silence screams guilt. He knows better than to bring the law into this. Guys like him, the ones with skeletons packed into every closet and warrant-shaped shadows crawling behind them, would rather take a beating than risk the cuffs.

The necklace still clutched tightly in my left hand, I raise my right and unleash my anger in a flurry. My fist finds his face again and again—each strike snapping his head to the side, each blow fueled by more than just this moment. His thick arms rise in a weak attempt to shield himself, but I'm quicker. My reach curves around his defense like a whip finding cracks in armor. He grunts, groans—until eventually, he gives in. His arms fall. His body slumps. Unconscious.

But I don't stop.

I keep going.

The room narrows to the sound of knuckles hitting flesh, over and over. I want to kill him—but I won't. I can't. It's too close to home.

Then I feel it—something shifts beneath my fist. A crack. A bone gives. I pause, breathing hard. My hands are sticky with blood, fingers tingling and numb. I rise slowly, hovering above the mess I've made. His face is a swollen ruin of bruises, blood, and busted skin. His lips barely move, but after a moment, he groans—alive. Barely.

He opens one eye—the other is completely sealed shut. He turns his head to cough, spitting out a tooth like a chipped pearl, and winces as he sees it lying on the floor.

"Where's my stuff, bro?" I ask, mimicking his usual drawl. "Answer me, dude, or I'll jack you up some more."

He doesn't speak—just lifts one trembling hand and points with a shaky, half-curled finger toward the back room. It's a weak gesture, but it's enough.

I make my way down the narrow hallway, stepping over clutter and beer bottles until I reach the back room. A black bedsheet covers a lumpy mound of what looks like electronics. I pull it off.

There it is. My things. All of it. My old TV. My Xbox. And a whole pile of other stolen gear—DVD players, flat-screens, game systems. He wasn't just a thief. He was running a whole damn racket.

This is where most people would call the cops. But I'm not most people. I know better. I'm no saint. In fact, I may be worse than him, depending on how you look at it. The law isn't something I can afford to invite into my life.

So, I gather my things—my property—and prepare to leave. I return to him one last time, kneeling beside his head. His one good eye follows me weakly, swelling creeping around it like a tide.

"Listen to me," I say quietly.

He can barely lift his head, his face so bloated and bruised it looks ready to split.

"I could turn you in for all that shit you've got back there. You'd go away for a long time. Or..." I pause, making sure he's listening, "I could take a few things, mine included, and we call it even. No cops. What do you think?"

He stares at me with that one puffy eye, then slowly nods.

"Good," I say. "Now, if you ever step foot in my apartment again, the outcome won't be so pleasant. I'm going through enough shit already, and you—you're just piling it on."

I stand.

"Now stay on this floor until I'm finished."

Chapter 17

FOOD FOR THOUGHT

(4:30 PM – Friday)

"Good night!" Kimmie calls out, already halfway through the log-off process as her fingers dance across her keyboard. She grabs her bags in a flurry and makes a beeline for the exit, barely managing to juggle her purse and coffee cup without spilling either. She doesn't look back—not once.

Friday has finally arrived, and the energy on the floor shifts like a breeze through an open window. Everyone's ready to escape, their minds already clocked out and on their way to weekend plans. Derrick, true to form, had called off—again. Anytime a major video game drops, you can bet your last dollar Derrick will be "sick." His absence didn't surprise anyone. It never does.

As for me, there's no celebration waiting at the end of my workday. No couch, no game controller, no cold beer. Just a looming meeting with Valentin and his oversized shadow, Boris. I'd managed to scrape together the five hundred—and then some—by selling off a few "bonus items" I acquired from my thieving neighbor. Craigslist made it easy. No questions asked. No serial numbers checked. A haven for quiet desperation.

Since Derrick never gave me his contact info for our Saturday gaming plans, I helped myself to it. A quick peek into our company's vehicle account, and just like that, I had what I needed. He should've known better.

I log out of my computer, toss my bag over my shoulder, and make my way to the exit with purpose. A breath of relief escapes my chest. No angry customers. No Detective Bedwell. A clean Friday—for the most part.

But my peace is fleeting.

The moment I step outside, the cool afternoon air brushes my face, and there he is. Leaning casually against his navy blue, unmarked vehicle, peeling peanuts and popping them into his mouth like he's on a picnic. That damn complacent smirk resting on his face like it belongs there.

"Well hey there, Mr. Thorpe," Detective Bedwell says, brushing peanut crumbs from his hands as he straightens up. He extends one toward me.

I force a smile, play dumb. "Hey, what's up, Detective..."

"Bedwell. Detective Bedwell," he replies, coolly unimpressed by my charade.

I snap my fingers and point at him with mock realization. "Oh yeah, that's it."

He lets the pause hang for a beat.

"Heading home for the evening?" he asks.

"Evening? I'm headed home for the *weekend*. It's been a long one." I chuckle, casual, trying to keep the air light as I continue walking toward my truck. Maybe he'll let it go.

I hear the faint crinkle of plastic behind me as he crushes his empty peanut bag.

"Just so you know," he calls, "we're real close to finding that killer. He's gonna slip up soon. I can feel it."

"That's awesome, Detective," I say with a wave, not bothering to look over my shoulder. "Let me know how that goes."

"Oh, I will," he says, his tone suddenly sharper. "I can honestly say... you'll be one of the first to know, Mr. Thorpe. And hey—nice emblem in your rearview mirror, by the way."

I freeze for half a second but say nothing. His words cut deeper than he lets on, and he knows it. They weren't casual. They were a warning.

I swing the driver's side door open, climb in, and slam it shut harder than necessary. My hands grip the steering wheel, but my eyes find the emblem he mentioned—dangling from the rearview, catching the last sliver of daylight. My reflection stares back at me—tense, grim, eyes burning beneath furrowed brows.

The engine growls to life, and as I rev it, the rearview mirror trembles violently—jittering with each growl—shaking the image of Bedwell into a blur.

As I pull out of the lot, I catch one last glimpse of him through the passenger side mirror. His smirk fades, replaced by something far more serious. A look of resolve, cold and focused. He tosses the peanut wrapper to the ground and wastes no time climbing into his car.

He's not just sniffing around anymore.

He's hunting.

As I make my way home, the reflection of Detective Bedwell lingers in my rearview mirror—three car lengths back, his vehicle trailing me like a shadow. I don't speed. Don't swerve. There's no need. If he had something concrete, we'd be having a very different conversation. He's not chasing. He's watching. Stirring the water, hoping I'll ripple.

But just under a mile from my place, he veers off onto a side street, vanishing without ceremony. Just like that. No sirens. No lights. Just quiet retreat.

(5:35 PM)

I sit motionless on the couch, the glow of the blank TV screen staring back at me like a mirror reflecting my nerves. A soft stream of classical music hums from my phone, each note carefully selected to dull the edge of anxiety. Tilly rests beside me, curled like a warm comma in my otherwise tense paragraph.

On the coffee table in front of me, the unsealed envelope waits—stuffed with five hundred dollars, give or take. I've kept it tidy, crisp bills tucked neatly as if presentation might make the situation feel less grim. We never set an exact time for this little exchange, but I know better than to expect punctuality from men like Valentin and Boris. I just want this part of my life done with. Paid. Closed. Forgotten.

(6:41 PM)

Tilly's beneath my hand, melting into the rhythm of my fingertips behind her neck. Her body stretches, soft paws rising in surrender as she rolls onto her back, silently demanding belly rubs. Within moments, she's dozed off completely—breathing slow and deep, lost in the kind of peace I can't seem to find for myself.

She's got it easy. No threats. No debts. No Russian muscle knocking at the door. Just naps, food bowls, and my hands.

The apartment is still, silent enough that I catch the distant chime of the elevator as it opens down the hall. Muffled voices drift closer—low tones, rhythmic and calm. The voices stop directly in front of my door. Then:

Knock knock... knock-knock... knock.

That old Shave and a Haircut rhythm. Always missing the Two Bits.

I scoop Tilly up, gently cradling her in my arms. She stirs but doesn't fuss. I place her in her cage and close the latch, giving the door an extra tug to ensure it's locked.

Three more knocks—this time firmer, sharper. Less playful.

"Hold on!" I shout, voice firm as I snatch the envelope from the table and slide it behind me, tucking it at the small of my back.

Through the peephole, I spot Valentin—stone-faced, impatient. Boris stands just out of frame, to the right, a looming presence like a thundercloud at the edge of vision. Valentin glances directly at the peephole, eyes narrowing as if he could see through it.

"Are you going to open the door or just look at me all day?"

I unbolt the deadlock and twist the knob—no more hesitation.

The moment the door cracks, Boris surges through like a battering ram, shoving me aside to clear the way for his boss, who steps in with the air of a man arriving at his rightful throne. Boris flicks on the lights without asking, sweeping the apartment with his eyes like some low-budget secret service agent on high alert.

"You must excuse Boris. He is quite paranoid about things sometimes," Valentin says, his tone smooth, almost amused.

"Yeah, all of that isn't necessary. I have your money right here," I respond, reaching behind me.

But I don't make it far.

Boris lunges—fast and heavy—knocking me to the ground. Before I can even react, I'm flipped onto my stomach, my face pressed to the carpet as his massive hands pat me down with zero restraint. He yanks up my shirt, finds the envelope, and tosses it casually toward Valentin like it's just another package.

"Boris, get off him. Let him up—*let him up*," Valentin instructs calmly, thumbing through the bills with practiced precision.

Boris grunts in response, then grabs my arm and lifts me to my feet like a doll, brushing off my shirt and straightening my collar with a too-wide grin. I slap his hands away.

"It's all there. Are we done here now?" I growl, my patience thinning fast.

Valentin gives the envelope a final glance before tucking it into the inside pocket of his coat. His expression doesn't change. Still composed. Still calculating.

"Yes. We are done here. Boris, let's go. We have other business to attend to, my friend." Valentin's voice remains smooth, but there's a finality in it that makes the air feel thinner. "Tommy, it was a pleasure doing business with you. It's always good to deal with someone who does what they say. Good day."

Without waiting for my response, they turn. Boris steps backward, keeping his eyes on me like I might suddenly reach for something sharp. He opens the door and exits, then gently pulls it shut behind them with an exaggerated sense of calm.

No sooner has the latch clicked than I hear it again—the knock. That same *Shave and a Haircut* rhythm, this time against Tricia's door.

My stomach twists.

The bile rises, hot and bitter, as I sit back down. I hate that I had to hand over that much cash to those low-rent enforcers. Hate that they walk around my building like they own the place. But most of all, I hate that it was necessary—for her.

Tricia's been scarce ever since Thanksgiving, her laughter and soft presence missing from the hallways. I didn't think much of it at first, but now... now I'm sure the Russians have their claws in her too. Maybe deeper than I ever realized.

I should be angry with her—for keeping secrets, for hiding this part of her life—but I'm not. I can't be. Because somehow, despite everything, despite the danger and the lies... I think I'm falling in love with her.

(12:05 PM, Saturday)

The sun hangs high overhead, casting a sharp glare off the scratched surface of a gas station payphone. My finger hovers over the metal keypad as the line rings again. Seventh time now. I'm ready to hang up when—finally—he answers.

"Yeah?"

"Hey. What's up—it's Tommy. We still good for the gaming today?"

"Oh, umm... yeah man. I just gotta clean up a little. What time you thinking? And why you calling me from a payphone?"

"My battery's low," I lie, "so I had to go the primitive route. What about two or three o'clock? And who cares about your damn house, man? I'm coming to game, not to rate your feng shui."

He snorts. "Whatever you say, man. Make it three p.m. though. You know how to get here?"

"Yeah, I googled your address from work. Looks pretty easy from where I'm at. You need me to bring anything? I'm by a few stores."

"Yeah, um... get some chips and shit. And some soda maybe."

"That's it? What kind of soda—grape?"

Silence. Then a dry chuckle. "Was that supposed to be your attempt at a racist joke? 'Cause I got some jokes for you." He laughs harder. "Dr. Pepper. And bring your controller, 'cause my other one don't work. My cousin was over the other day, eating cheese puffs and shit. Got the buttons all sticky and nasty."

"Alright bro, I got it. See you in a bit."

"Cool! Prepare to get that ass whooped. I got some tissues ready for you." *Click.*

———

(3:02 PM)

I pull onto a crumbling street off 27th and Burleigh—one of the rougher stretches of Milwaukee's North Side. The pavement is cracked, the sidewalks empty except for a few windblown chip bags and forgotten dreams. Out here, gunshots don't make the news. They're background noise. Sirens, routine. It's a place where life doesn't feel protected—it feels hunted.

And I stick out.

My pale skin glows like a neon sign that screams *wrong neighborhood.* I glance at the fuel gauge—still decent—but if Old Blue breaks down here, I know better than to expect help. White guys don't get a warm welcome in places like this. They get stripped, robbed, and maybe worse.

Derrick's house is easy to spot. Not because it's different, but because three large men are posted up outside his front door, thick arms crossed, watching traffic like hawks. One of them notices me and nudges the others. All eyes swing toward me like gun barrels.

There's no way I'm walking through that lineup. No telling if they're friends or gatekeepers, or something worse.

I keep driving and loop around the block, deciding to take my chances with the alley instead.

I pull up beside Derrick's garage, easing into a spot where the cracked concrete meets patches of brittle grass. The air back here smells of oil and smoke and city dust, but there's something more comfortable about it—less exposed. Safer.

Derrick's already outside, tossing a heavy black trash bag into his dented bin with a grunt. When he spots me, his eyebrows shoot up.

"Why you pulling in back here?" he laughs, brushing his hands on his jeans.

"Better parking?" I reply, half-heartedly.

"Bullshit, Tommy. You ain't foolin' nobody." He chuckles, then gestures for me to follow him toward the back door. "You ain't never been to the hood, huh?"

"I've been to the hood plenty of times," I say, trying to mask the tightness in my voice with confidence.

He gives me a look—eyebrows raised, lips curled like he's sizing up a poker hand. "Bet you ain't never been to a hood like this though. This is *Burleigh*," he says it like a warning wrapped in pride, his grin growing like a challenge.

"I live close to the hood," I mutter. "I kinda know what goes on."

"Right!" he scoffs, stopping abruptly and spinning around to face me. "Let me ask you somethin' then. If gunshots go off in your neighborhood, I bet y'all duck down in the living room and call the cops, huh?"

"So..."

He points at me, already laughing. "*So*, around here when gunshots go off, everybody runs outside—tryin' to see who got shot, or askin' who did the shootin'. That's the hood."

He shakes his head, smiling. "Man, let me tell you. You gotta be careful around here. Especially your fluorescent, skinny, white butt. And *you* know it too—that's why your ass came 'round the back."

He swings open the creaky screen door. "Come on upstairs."

I follow him into the entryway as he begins unlocking his fortress—one bolt after another. Five in total, plus a single chain that rattles loose with a clink.

"Why so many locks?" I ask, eyeing the thick wooden door behind us.

"Are you serious?" he says, halfway through twisting the final lock. "You saw them big Negroes out front, right? I keep things locked down tight—and my *shotty* by the bed, just in case."

"Shotty?"

"Shotgun. *Shotty*. Same thing." He points up the narrow wooden staircase. "Gone upstairs. Don't be scared. Ain't nobody up there."

I glance back. Another staircase leads down into a shadowy basement, the kind that feels like it watches you.

"Oh yeah, your wife and kids are gone this weekend, right?" I ask, stepping cautiously upward.

"Yeah."

"That's too bad. I was hoping to get to meet her sometime."

"Psh," he scoffs. "You don't wanna meet her, man."

"Why not?"

"Well for one, she ain't too fond of white people. Two, she don't like *anybody* in her house when she's not here—*especially* white people. And three... did I mention she don't like white people?"

"Yeah," I say, smirking. "I think I caught that part."

But as I cross the threshold at the top of the stairs, I freeze. The room before me isn't what I expected—not even close.

It's spotless.

Immaculate.

The living room looks like something pulled from the pages of a high-end catalog. Not a speck of dust on any surface. Every item—every knickknack—placed with intention. The rich, chocolate brown leather couch and love seat gleam beneath the soft light from a nearby lamp, perfectly paired with a shag rug that swirls vanilla and mocha together in elegant contrast. Matching picture frames line the end tables. And mounted on the far wall is a sixty-five-inch flat-screen TV, hanging like a centerpiece in a gallery.

The faint scent of potpourri floats in the air, delicate and calming.

I hesitate to sit, afraid I might crease the cushions or scuff the rug.

How the hell does someone who walks around in a shirt stained with God-knows-what keep a place this pristine?

Derrick catches my lingering gaze and grins.

"My wife decorated the living room. You like it?"

That explains the immaculate setup. "Yeah, it's nice. This is really nice, man," I reply, still taking in the pristine surroundings. I drop my bag and sink into the couch. "That TV though. That's even nicer! Hell, what are we waiting for? Let's get to it! Where's the gaming system?"

He laughs. "Man, let's go. We ain't playing nothing on that, please! Let me take you to the dungeon and show you what's up. Grab your stuff."

He opens the bedroom door, revealing a gamer's paradise. Black gaming chairs, every current game system neatly arranged beneath two seventy-five-inch LCD flat-screen TVs. Both screens display the menu for the new video game "Drafted," with music booming through the surround sound.

"One television for you and one for me," he smiles. "Now, you ready to get down?"

"You kidding? Hell yeah, man!" I exclaim, moving toward the chair on the right.

"Um no, get yo ass up. That's my side. You can sit over there," he says, pointing to the identical chair and system on the left.

"What's the difference?" I ask.

"For gamers, that's like sleeping on my side of the bed. I'm just more comfortable over here, that's all."

(6:11 PM)

"I'm out of bullets—I'm out of bullets!" Derrick yells, tilting his controller and frantically pressing buttons as he defends against our enemy.

"Hold on; I'm on the way. Just go behind the building and camp for a minute. No—no, the warehouse building!" I instruct.

"Which warehouse building? There are three warehouse buildings! Can you be a bit more specific? Dude, they're on my ass, and all I have are melee weapons."

"The one in the middle! Go-go-go!" I exclaim.

"Awe damn!" Derrick says, slamming his controller in his lap as his character falls dead from a headshot. "Damn, I hate snipers!"

"That's the third match we've lost in a row. Let's hit a different room; these kids must sit on this game all day and night to be this good."

"Right!" Derrick replies, navigating through the menu.

"Hey, your downstairs neighbors don't get mad with you playing your system at this volume?"

"I usually play with my headset on, so nobody hears anyway. The downstairs is being remodeled by the landlord. Nobody has lived down there for a couple of months now."

"Oh, well that's good for us then. You got a bathroom?" I ask, standing and grabbing my backpack.

"Do I have a bathroom? Of course, I have a bathroom, man—that's a stupid question. Down the hall to the right. If you are taking a shit, flush after every drop. The suction doesn't work that well, and I'm not trying to plunge your nasty ass doo-doo!"

"No worries. Maybe you should practice a little bit more while I'm gone. I'm tired of losing to these little kids online," I say, backing down the hallway.

"Drop and flush—drop and flush!" he yells.

(6:34 PM)

It's getting dark outside, and the only light in the house is the flickering flashes from the television screen as Derrick guns down an unsuspecting group of enemy players huddled in a building.

The room is cloaked in a soft, flickering glow, the only illumination emanating from the twin screens that dominate the space. Derrick is engrossed, his fingers dancing over the controller, tongue peeking out as he concentrates. He's oblivious to my presence, unaware that I stand mere feet behind him, cloaked in black nylon, the fabric whispering with each subtle movement.

In my right hand, I cradle his prized possession—the double-barreled shotgun he so proudly mentioned. Its polished wood gleams even in the dim light, the metal cool and unyielding beneath my fingers. I trace the rim of one barrel absentmindedly, fingering the barrels, my thoughts a tempest of betrayal and retribution.

Memories surge: the financial ruin orchestrated by him and his father, the smug glances, the feigned camaraderie. Each recollection fuels the fire within, my grip tightening on the weapon. He leans forward, engrossed in his virtual battlefield, completely unaware of the real danger looming behind him.

Without hesitation, I raise the shotgun, the butt poised. With a swift, decisive motion, I bring it down upon the back of his head. A dull thud resonates, and he collapses forward, the controller slipping from his grasp as he crumples to the floor.

Silence envelops the room, save for the game's ambient sounds. I stand over him, heart pounding, the weight of my actions settling in.

CHAPTER 18

TIME OFF

(8:36 PM)

I pull the string hanging from the basement ceiling, and a weak, yellow bulb flickers to life overhead. The space around me breathes decay—thick with dust, dampness, and the sharp tang of mildew. The walls are etched with age, and nearly every pipe, corner, and narrow window frame wears a crown of cobwebs, undisturbed by time.

I wrestle his limp, narrow body into position, propping him up in an old metal desk chair that creaks beneath his weight. After securing the final knot around his thin wrists behind him, I loop the remaining rope tightly around the backrest. He won't be going anywhere.

In the far corner, I stack two stained, full-sized mattresses to form a crude barrier, then drape them with rumpled bed sheets I scavenged from the dryer. It gives the illusion of a wall—a grim little stage for the performance to come.

As I shift him deeper into the makeshift enclosure, facing the corner like a child in time out, the light above gives a final buzz and dies, casting the room into sudden darkness. The moment swallows me whole. I pause, letting my eyes adjust, then take my place a few feet to his left. I raise my flashlight and click it on. The narrow beam cuts through the gloom and pins him beneath its glare, as though he's center stage beneath a theater spotlight.

I lower myself to the cold concrete floor, leaning back against the wall. The furnace kicks on, humming quietly behind the silence, a distant mechanical sigh.

As I wait for him to stir, my mind drifts backward—through blood-stained moments and buried secrets. The trail of bodies, the careful steps to erase my footprints, all of it plays back like fragments of a dream. I think of my mother and father—how gentle they once were. Maybe, if they hadn't been taken from me so soon, things could've been different. Maybe those people would still be alive.

But I don't feel guilt. Not even a whisper of it. That, I suppose, makes me unwell in the eyes of most. Still... how would madness feel, to the one who's mad?

While lost in thought, I let the flashlight's beam drift downward, casting a pool of light beneath the chair. I shift it back up—he's still slumped forward, his chin resting on his chest, unmoving.

Restlessness sets in. I start clicking the flashlight on and off, slowly at first, then faster—until the basement pulses like a dim strobe, the effect eerily hypnotic. A silent slideshow, trapped on a single frame.

Then a rustle behind me breaks the trance.

I whip the light toward the sound—just in time to catch a small mouse skittering along the edge of the wall before it vanishes through a crack. I sigh and pivot the beam back to Derrick.

He's awake.

His eyes glint in the light like a cat's, glassy and unblinking. The sudden reflection catches me off guard, and I instinctively switch off the flashlight, plunging us both back into blackness.

"Who is that!?" he shouts, panicked. I hear the ropes strain and twist as he fights against them. "Hey, what the hell is going on? Let me loose!"

The chair scrapes slightly against the concrete. His legs are spread and anchored—ankles bound with duct tape to the chair's legs. He can barely touch the floor. I used nearly a whole roll just for that. His torso is lashed tight with rope, locked against the backrest.

"Thorpe!? Hey, Thorpe!?" he bellows.

My eyes haven't yet adjusted, but I can hear him shifting, attempting to scoot the chair backward. It tips slightly but doesn't go over.

"Hey, man, who's there? Where the fuck am I?" His voice trembles now. "Answer me! I know somebody is there!"

The longer I let his questions dangle unanswered in the dark, the more frantic his voice becomes, each plea more strained than the last. Eventually, he grows quiet. Maybe he's passed out from the panic—or perhaps he's just conserving energy. The furnace gives one final mechanical sigh before falling silent, its cycle complete. The hush that follows is thick and heavy, broken only by the sound of Derrick's breathing—long, loud pulls of air through his nose, desperate and rhythmic. He's trying to orient himself, no doubt piecing together his reality through muffled echoes and the soft press of mattress padding hemming him in.

"Would you like some music?" I ask, my voice calm and even. "I've found that music sometimes calms me down when I'm excited or confused."

"Tommy?" he says, tentative.

"Music allows me to think more clearly—keeps me focused. None of that mindless noise people cling to nowadays, with lyrics that twist and cloud their thoughts. I mean real music. Instruments. Pianos. Cellos. Violins. Things that speak without words," I explain as I swipe through my phone, scrolling the playlist I've built for moments like this.

"Hey Thorpe, what's going on? Cut me loose, man. Cut me loose now." His voice grows more urgent, his chair scraping the floor as he struggles against his restraints.

"How about this one?" I say. "This is Ludovico Einaudi's *A Fuoco*. It's one of my favorites now."

A soft melody begins to play from my phone's small speaker, the delicate piano notes trickling into the air. But his shouts begin again, frantic and loud, echoing against the walls and swallowed by the mattress barricades. The sound of his voice claws at the music, unraveling its purpose before it can settle.

I grit my teeth. The music is being ruined.

Annoyed, I reach into my backpack and retrieve one of the knives I'd forged from an old railroad spike. Its steel gleams in the faint glow of my flashlight, a reflection of cold intent. I cross the short distance and gently press the tip against the soft skin of his throat. His eyes snap wide open, pupils huge in the dim light.

"I'm gonna need you to listen right now, okay? And keep quiet. You'll love this music—trust me." He leans his head back as far as the chair will allow, just enough to pull away from the point.

"Wha—what did I do to you, man?" he stammers. "What could I have possibly done to you for you to set me up like this?"

"Don't play stupid, Derrick," I reply, my voice rising. "You know perfectly well what you've been doing to me this entire time. The real question is: what have *I* done to *you* to deserve being treated like this?"

My grip tightens on the handle.

"I earned everything I have, fair and square. I never asked for more than I deserved. And still, you and your father scheme behind my back. You think I wouldn't notice? You plotted against me. You stole from me." I yank the blade away and slap the back of his head with the flat of my hand.

"What the hell are you talking about, Tommy?"

"You know damn well what I mean," I hiss. "You took my hard work and pocketed what I was owed. You had that smug bastard of a father of yours rework the route so I'd get stuck with the non-paying, bottom-of-the-barrel clients—the very ones you trained to disrespect me. You sabotaged me."

"What? No—listen. You got it all wrong, man!"

"Oh really? How could I possibly have it all wrong?" I say, and then I stop the music and open a recording on my phone. The familiar voices of Derrick and Mr. Gibbons begin to play, filling the silence with cold, incriminating truth.

"Tommy—man, listen to me, I—"

"No. *You* listen." I raise the knife to his throat again, steady this time, while I use my free hand to set the phone behind his chair, the audio still playing.

As the words continue, each one damning, I take a breath. A new distraction rises—I need to pee. The corner would suffice, but that would be careless. DNA, evidence, a mistake I don't plan to make. I should've handled that before all this began.

I sigh quietly and climb the basement stairs, leaving Derrick alone in the dark with nothing but his conscience—and my recording—to keep him company.

Standing above the toilet, I glance down and curse under my breath. I can't believe it—there's no damn fly on this ridiculous outfit. I hadn't noticed before, too caught up in the layers and zippers just trying to squeeze into the thing. It was already a pain to put on. Now here I am, needing to take a leak with no easy way to do it.

No time to undress—not now.

I figure I'll slice a small hole in the front and be done with it. Reach for the knife—

Where the hell is my knife?

Suddenly, a deafening crash echoes from below.

My heart skips. Instinct kicks in, and I bolt for the basement, my boots pounding the steps two at a time. I spot the flashlight on the floor, still casting faint shadows, and snatch it up as I sweep the beam toward the corner.

But Derrick is gone.

The chair's toppled sideways, rope coiled like shed skin, the knife beside it, and my phone blinking dumbly on the floor.

Panic surges.

I whip the flashlight around the room, the beam darting from one shadowed corner to the next. I search beneath the stairs, behind the table—anywhere he could be hiding. My breath is tight in my throat as I creep toward my knife. Every movement feels slower now. Deliberate. I crouch, reaching down carefully, my ears straining for the slightest sound behind me.

A sudden noise snaps through the air. I lurch back, colliding with the cold wall, the flashlight jerking up like a weapon.

The furnace hums back to life.

I let out a sharp breath—just that. Nothing more.

But then—footsteps. Fast. Coming straight for me.

I twist, but it's too late.

He crashes into me, knocking me onto my back. My flashlight slips from my grasp and spins across the concrete, whirling like a bottle in a game of fate. Each rotation tosses out a broken glimpse of the basement—and Derrick—before the light slows, and he disappears into the darker recesses once again.

"Stop hiding, Derrick. You coward. Come out where I can see you."

"You got it all wrong, Tommy! All wrong!" His voice trembles through the dark. "I told Dad not to do it, but it was too late—he already had."

"That's bullshit!"

"It's not bullshit!" he cries out, then falters with a gasp. "Wait... it was you!? You killed those people on your route, didn't you?"

"Way to figure things out. What took you so long?" I say, my voice dripping with sarcasm as I crawl toward the flashlight. "I mean, what gave me away?" I grasp the light just as it rolls to a halt and turn its beam toward the shadows. "Why don't you come out so we can talk about this?"

"Kathy May? You killed Kathy May too?"

"That?" I scoff. "That wasn't my fault. She had it coming—her and that sick bastard she was hiding in the hotel bathroom. Derrick, you don't know pain until you've had a nine-inch dildo rammed up your ass. But that's beside the point."

"You're a sick motha-fucka, man—*sick!* All this because you were mad at Gibbons for shuffling your route? People lost their lives for that!?"

"There's *much* more to it than that, Derrick," I say, standing slowly, sweeping the flashlight through the thick dark. "It's a messed-up world—divided between the people who pay and the people who get paid. Full of liars. Thieves. People who break promises and cut throats to climb higher. People like *you,* who take advantage of people like me. People who just want to work hard and survive."

I step cautiously, my voice calm, almost reverent.

"*Leviticus 19:11* — 'You shall not steal; you shall not deal falsely; you shall not lie to one another.'"

From somewhere beyond the beam of my light, his voice rises, sharp with disgust. "You killed innocent people so you could get on top. How does that make you any better than anyone else, man?"

As he speaks, his voice echoes from different corners of the basement, bouncing off concrete walls and low-hanging pipes. He's keeping his distance, circling like a wary animal. I reach up and pull off my mask, letting it drop beside me. My vision sharpens without the barrier, and my eyes begin to adjust better to the shifting shadows. It doesn't matter anymore—he knows who I am. There's no reason to keep hiding.

"All men have their breaking point," I say, my voice steady but laced with heat. "All damn day we've got supervisors breathing down our necks about stats, about punctuality. Wanting us to kiss every customer's ass—while they curse us out, call us names, treat us like we're the scum on their boots. Like we don't feel anything. Meanwhile, we sit behind a screen with their whole lives at our fingertips, and they still act like we're nobodies. Weak. Replaceable. Just punching bags for their frustration."

I pace slowly.

"We're just doing our jobs," I continue. "Calling to collect on what they *promised*—to the company *and* to us."

"People have lives!" Derrick shouts from somewhere deeper in the shadows. "Who are you to play God and take that away—just because stuff ain't going right for you? Sometimes things happen, and people can't pay. So I cut them some slack. I grew up out here in the hood, man. I *know* how it is to be broke."

I sneer into the dark.

"Don't give me that hood sob story crap," I spit. "If you can't afford something, you don't buy it. Simple. But no—you've got people like you and Gibbons, who lie, steal, screw over your own co-workers—stealing money straight from our paychecks. Money we earned. Why? So you can go buy video games?"

There's a pause.

I spot the glimmer of my knife lying near the base of the stairs and quickly snatch it from the floor, fingers curling tight around the hilt.

"You're fucking nuts, man! Why didn't I see that before?" Derrick yells. His voice comes from farther away than I expected.

Then—*creak.*

The wooden step betrays him.

I kill the flashlight instantly and lunge through the dark.

I catch him by the ankles just as he scrambles up the stairs. His feet slide from beneath him, and he crashes forward, his chest slamming into the steps. My flashlight tumbles from my hand and rolls back down to the floor, spinning lazily, casting erratic beams that flicker like a dying strobe across the chaos.

I straddle him, trying to pin him in place, but he twists beneath me and turns onto his back. He throws a wild right hook. It misses my face but knocks the knife from my hand—it clatters down the steps and disappears into the shadows.

His next punch comes faster. I block it, grab his wrist, and pin it to the step. Then I unleash three solid punches to his jaw, each one harder than the last.

But he's stronger than I expected. He surges upward, breaking my grip, and we both tumble backward off the steps, crashing hard onto the cold concrete below. He lands on top, dazed but determined, reaching desperately for the knife.

I slam two fists into his gut. He hunches over, groaning—and I seize the moment.

I grab the collar of his shirt with both fists and yank him down into a brutal headbutt. *Crack.* Then another. *Crack.* And another. *Crack.* He reels from the blows, eyes glassy, lips slack.

I twist us over and mount him, pressing my knees into his arms to pin him to the floor.

We both breathe hard, sweat mixing with dust and blood between us.

He looks up at me, eyes bloodshot, a crooked smile splitting his busted lips.

"Stickman, huh?" he croaks, voice rasping around the blood in his throat.

"Yeah," I mutter, wiping sweat from my brow. "It works."

His grin widens, smeared with red.

"Y-You know they're gonna catch you. If not... God will." Then he spits, blood and saliva splattering across my cheek.

"Yeah, I thought about that. I've thought about it a lot." I lean in and reach past his head, fingers brushing the cold floor until they wrap around the handle of my knife once more. "I've also noticed that under all those baggy clothes... you're pretty damn skinny yourself. Almost as skinny as me." I grin as the blade catches the faint gleam of light.

"What the fuck does that have to do with anything?" he snaps, his voice teetering between rage and fear.

"Well, you see," I say, casually turning the knife in my hand, "after I heard that little conversation between you and your father, I took the liberty of calling out on your route for the past week." I give a slow, deliberate nod. "I also took the liberty of ridding your route of a few liars and non-payers."

"You did what!?"

"Yeah. Remember that first shuffle—when I got stuck with all those deadbeat accounts? Turns out, some of those people were from *your* original route. That's when everything started to click." I rise to my feet, savoring the way confusion twists across his bruised, bloodied face. "But then I wondered—what if there was a way out?"

I pause, letting the question hang, watching him try to puzzle together the meaning behind my words.

"I remembered something," I go on, stepping back slowly. "That day you lifted your shirt to sniff that God-awful stain... that disgusting shit smear. You didn't realize it, but you exposed your midsection—and you build is an awful lot like mine."

His eyes widen.

The tension in his jaw deepens. He knows. He *knows* where this is going.

"You're not gonna put this shit on me!" he roars.

I don't answer—just offer a crooked smile as I ease back toward the wall, fingers reaching behind me. The cool, familiar curve of the pipe I spotted earlier greets my hand. Just as I get a firm grip, Derrick charges with all the fury he can muster, arms outstretched like a battering ram.

I sidestep with ease.

The pipe whistles through the air and connects with the back of his skull with a dull *crack*.

His body goes limp mid-stride, collapsing face-first onto the floor.

(11:06 PM)

My backpack is cinched tight across my shoulders as I take one last walk-through of the house. Every surface I've touched has been wiped clean—no fingerprints, no hair, not a trace of my DNA left behind. I double-check each room. The basement is just as I found it, the mattresses back in place, blankets neatly folded. I even swept the floor to erase any trace of the struggle—no prints from him, none from me.

Before I leave, I pay one final visit to the gaming room.

Derrick is there—unconscious, propped in the chair like a puppet waiting for its cue. I crouch beside him, inspecting the water-soluble thread I took from Gram's kitchen cabinet. It's taut, looped tightly around his neck and threaded carefully down to the trigger of the shotgun. The stock is wedged between his thighs; the twin barrels stretched wide into his mouth, testing the limits of his jaw muscles. His thumb rests inside the trigger well, twitching faintly.

If all goes as planned, instinct will kick in. The moment he comes to and panics, he'll try to pull the barrels free. That movement will yank the twine and trip the trigger. Or—maybe he'll come to confused and squeeze the stock with his thumb before he knows what he's doing. Either way... it ends.

Satisfied, I draw back both hammers of the shotgun with a final *click*.

This is it.

No more killing after this.

I glance down at the clean nylon outfit—still pristine—and tuck it neatly into my backpack, along with my knife. Then I slide the pack halfway under the bed so it's just visible, a breadcrumb in the story I've staged.

Last, I place the suicide letter—typed on his own computer at work, left unlocked and unattended—gently beneath his thigh. A simple document, saved to a folder on his desktop.

The letter reads:

I'm sorry. I'm so—so sorry for the things I have done. My family... my God, my family. I love you so much. It's only a matter of time before the police catch up with me. I don't know how I could ever face my family's disappointment—or the grief in the eyes of those I've wronged. The loved ones of the people I have killed. So many people. I couldn't help myself. The temptation was overwhelming, and the pressure... unbearable. The online video games were my escape, but even that stopped working. It wasn't enough. I felt like there was a demon inside me, controlling my hands, my thoughts, my desires. The only way I can silence him—the only way to stop him—is to end me. I'm sorry. Forgive me, Derrick.

I sit hunched behind the steering wheel of my frost-covered truck, staring through a smeared patch I'd wiped clear on the windshield with the sleeve of my coat. The engine is off—too loud to risk right now—and the cold air creeps into the cab, fogging the windows from inside. But I don't mind the stillness. Not yet. Not until it's done.

A half-eaten bag of chips rests in my lap, forgotten between chews as I keep my eyes locked on the upstairs window where Derrick sits—silent, waiting, wired just right.

I crank the window down a few inches for a clearer view, the cold biting at my face.

Then—*boom.*

The twin thunderclaps of the shotgun erupt in an instant, followed by the sharp tinkling shatter of glass. A crimson mist sprays against the inside of the window—then bursts outward like a bloom of red dew. Tiny shards of broken glass and blood splatter onto my windshield, clinging in flecks and rivulets.

I wasn't expecting the mess.

I flinch, fumbling for the keys already waiting in the ignition and turn them. The engine groans, but won't turn over. The truck coughs and falls silent.

Panic pricks my spine.

Motion draws my eyes—porch lights flick on behind the house. Then another flickers to life across the alley. Doors open, the sound of curious neighbors stirred by the echo of violence in the dark.

I twist the key again. Nothing.

A third time—still nothing.

I slam my foot against the gas pedal, pump it hard, and turn the key again. The engine sputters, coughs—and finally catches.

The tension in my chest doesn't fade, but I stay calm. I throw it into drive. No tires screech. No engine revs. Just a smooth pull into motion, headlights off, slipping away from the scene as fast—and as quietly—as I can manage.

One thing's for sure: Derrick wasn't lying about what happens in the hood when gunshots ring out.

———

(11:44 PM)

The low, steady hum of my engine becomes a lullaby as I head down the dark stretch of highway. Fatigue sets in. My head nods forward. I jerk awake with a start—horn blaring to my left as I drift into the next lane. A pair of glowing eyes and high beams whip past me. The driver throws up a middle finger before speeding off into the night.

I shake my head and reach for my phone, unlocking it to find something that'll keep me alert. Music. Anything to keep my eyes open.

I dig out the old tape-deck adapter and plug it into the phone. As I scroll, my thumb accidentally brushes the wrong icon.

Instead of music, a familiar voice, Mr. Gibbons, blasts through the speakers.

"Well, I am going to have to break this horrible news to my office. Is there anything else that I can do for you fine officers?"

Before I can stop it, the phone slips from my hand and disappears beneath the seat, just out of reach. The voices continue.

"No sir, but here is my card. If you have any information, please don't hesitate to call us."

"I will, officer. Thank you."

A brief pause, then the muffled click of a door closing.

Almost immediately, it opens again.

"Hey Dad."

"Yeah, come in."

"About that route..."

"What about it?"

"Well, I thought about it, and I don't want to shuffle it."

"That's all fine and dandy, but not much we can do about that now."

"Why?"

"'Cause I've already shuffled it."

"Damn it, can you switch it back?"

"Nope. It's irreversible."

"Why do we keep doing this? I just don't feel right doing that anymore. I should earn mine like everyone else on the floor. I'd feel better about myself. Besides... Tommy seems like a cool dude, not like you thought. He actually looked out for me when I had something going on with my appearance. Other people would've just laughed."

"What did he do?"

"Doesn't matter now. I just think it's best that I do things on my own. I want to prove to you and my family that I can be a better man. Hell... I don't have many friends, as you know. Tommy may be the first in a while."

"Sounds good to me."

There's the faint sound of movement—papers rustling, a chair creaking.

"Is this your phone under the desk?"

"No, it's probably Tommy's since he just left. He must've dropped it."

"I'll get it to him. Thanks, Dad."

The recording cuts off with a final click, and silence settles inside the cab like a fog. I blink, slowly realizing where I am. Somewhere between the rhythm of the road and the weight of the words, I must've slipped into autopilot. I'm parked in my usual spot, engine still idling, headlights casting soft beams across the driveway. I hadn't even noticed the turn onto my street.

Maybe I moved too fast with this one. Maybe I should've waited—planned it better.

I want to feel *something*. Guilt. Regret. Even just a flicker of shame. Anything to prove there's still a thread of humanity in me, buried deep beneath all the chaos. But there's nothing. No ache in my chest. No pinch in my conscience. Just the steady thrum of satisfaction... the rush, the pleasure—the *thrill*—of what went down tonight.

When I crack open the door, a gust of icy air sweeps inside, wrapping around me like punishment. The warmth of the truck retreats, chased out by winter's breath. A shiver crawls across my shoulders as I swing my legs out and plant my boots on the pavement.

That's when I see it.

Down the block, parked just shy of the corner, sits a dark blue vehicle. Government-issued. The same make and model driven by Detective Bedwell.

His headlights blink on, and the vehicle eases into motion, reversing slowly into the intersection behind him. My stomach sinks. The chill in my body deepens—not from the cold, but from the creeping realization.

Was he tailing me all night?

How long has he been on me?

He makes a quiet right turn and disappears down another street, swallowed by the darkness.

No... my night isn't over yet. Not by a long shot.

Chapter 19

PEST CONTROL

(12:25 AM)

Luck seems to ride with me tonight. I take a gamble on which direction Detective Bedwell might've gone after slipping out of view from the parking lot—and I win. There he is, paused at a red light, one car idling behind him. I coast to the curb just ahead, careful not to draw attention.

Without warning or signal, he makes a sharp right. I don't hesitate—I swing out and follow.

My gut tells me to stay with him, and I obey it without question. We head southbound on I-94, the lights of the city blurring in the distance. I keep at least two car lengths behind, matching his speed, which is already pushing ten miles over the limit. The highway feels like it's holding its breath.

I'm not sure what exactly I plan to do, but whatever it is, I know it has to happen soon. I can't risk him reporting anything—not after what happened at Derrick's.

We veer east onto I-794, the glowing stretch of Hoan Bridge rising ahead like the spine of some sleeping beast. It's quiet now—no cars behind me, and only one far up ahead. Just the three of us, alone with the cold wind rushing over the harbor.

I press my foot down hard. Old Blue roars in response, tires shrieking slightly from the sudden torque. I surge forward, pulling up alongside him. He glances over with that damned smug grin of his—waves like he'd known all along I was back there.

I let off the gas briefly, slipping behind him—then slam it down again.

I close in fast, tight to his rear bumper. His head jerks as he reaches for his radio.

Not today.

I clip the back of his car with a jarring bump. His body jolts forward, and the cruiser swerves violently in both directions. But I stay locked to his flank, stalking him like prey.

As we crest the high point of the bridge, I see the fear building in his reflection—his face twisted in the side mirror, no longer cocky, but tense and panicked. Both hands grip the wheel like it's the only thing keeping him tethered to this world.

I smile.

Then I floor it.

Old Blue lurches and connects—hard—with the rear passenger-side bumper. His car jerks sideways, the nose lifting, momentum carrying him like a bullet toward the edge.

Metal screams against concrete. His tires lose grip. The vehicle vaults up over the crumbling barrier, suspended for a breathless moment—then disappears into the black abyss below.

Gone.

(5:47 PM)

I sit at Gram's dining table, the scent of baked cheese and garlic thick in the air. A steaming plate of lasagna sits untouched in front of me—two thick, heavy chunks she'd portioned with love and fuss.

But I can't focus. My mind keeps circling back to Derrick... and Bedwell.

I'd seen what was left of Derrick in the faint morning light—blood sprayed across my windshield, bits of skull tangled in the wiper blade. No doubt there.

Bedwell, though... he lingers. Did he survive the plunge into the icy Milwaukee River? Or did the dark water swallow him whole?

"Suga, I went through a whole lot of trouble to make that food. Now *eat*," Gram says, her tone soft but firm—unyielding in that way only grandmothers can be.

I blink and stir, coming back to the moment. My hand moves automatically to the fork.

"I'm sorry, Gram."

She watches me for a beat longer. "What's wrong with you? Are you okay?"

"Yeah, I'm fine. Just been busy a lot lately, that's all."

"Well, I'm glad you found time to come spend with me. I was beginning to think you were on that reefer." She squints. "You're not, are yah?"

"Reefer? What!? No, Gram, I don't do that stuff."

She throws her head back with a laugh that rattles the dishes in the china cabinet. "Seems like a lot of kids doing that stuff nowadays. When I was your age, it was just weed—a joint. You rolled it, ya smoked it. Now they got all kinds of crazy names and mess they done put in it, make ya see things that ain't there." She shakes her head, her expression twisted in a mix of disgust and disbelief. "With all this stuff going on—murder, drugs, war, and these crazy politicians—this world is definitely gonna burn in hell. And Donald Trump's holding a fist full of matches."

"Yeah."

"*Yeah?*" she repeats, giving me that sharp-eyed glance over her glasses. "I say all that and all you can say is, 'Yeah'? Where's that pretty girl you had over for Thanksgiving? You should've brought her with you."

"I haven't spoken to her for a few days, Gram. She's probably kind of busy with her Customer Service job."

"Well, okay," she sighs. "I think it's time for some news. Just put your plate in the sink. And don't let me hear you in here washing any dishes, young man, *ya hear?*"

"Yes, ma'am."

My appetite's almost nonexistent, but I force down a few bites to keep her from worrying, chasing the heavy mouthfuls with cold lemonade. Each swallow feels like a stone sinking into my gut. If I try for more, I know I'll lose it all.

"Gram," I murmur, pushing the plate away, "I'm gonna wrap this up and take it home. I'm not feeling too well. I'm gonna take your advice and get some rest."

"Okay, sweetie!" she calls from the living room. "Just take that whole pan with you. I'm not gonna eat all of that. Just leave me a couple of sections on a plate."

"Okay."

"Oh my goodness!" she suddenly exclaims.

I freeze mid-step. "What? What's wrong?"

"They found a young man dead in his apartment this weekend. Committed suicide with a shotgun in his home..." She trails off for a breath.

"Now they're saying he may have something to do with the Stickman Murders."

"Stickman murders?" I ask, masking the weight behind my words.

"Yeah, it's been all on the news, Suga. Where have you been?"

"I don't know..." I shrug, eyes shifting to the muted television. "Well, I'm gonna go, Gram. Do you need anything else before I do?"

I bend and kiss her warm cheek, her skin soft and faintly powdered.

"No, just be careful," she warns gently. "Been watching this news, and people out there are crazy, *Suga*."

On the screen, the news anchor from 12News cuts to a live shot of a crane hauling a vehicle from dark waters. The image freezes me for just a moment. The twisted frame of Bedwell's car dangles midair, dripping and defeated. His picture flashes beside it, framed by bold letters across the screen:

"DECEASED LAW ENFORCEMENT OFFICER IDENTIFIED."

The volume is still muted—Gram had hit the button during our conversation—so I can't hear the details. But I don't need to.

(8:31 AM, Monday)

The office is quieter than usual—eerily so. Only a scattering of reps have shown up today, most keeping to themselves, heads low, eyes tired. I settle into my station, pull up my programs, and start scrolling through yesterday's report like nothing's changed.

Routine. Clean. Controlled.

After a while, I open up the skip-tracing software, the one that gives us access to a frightening amount of personal data. Next of kin. Last known addresses. Cell numbers. Places they thought they could disappear into.

Tools of the trade for anyone hunting down those who've fallen off the grid—or simply chosen to vanish.

Out of habit, I plug in a few familiar names—some people I know. Even toss in my own, just to test the accuracy.

Then... I type in *Valentin.*

The results scatter across the screen like a shuffled deck of strangers. Dozens of entries. But only one catches my eye—*light blue eyes, fifty-four years old, Milwaukee.*

I click the print icon, watching the paper feed begin, then return to my report without missing a beat.

(9:42 AM)

The heat in the office is thick and drowsy, like a blanket stitched from the hum of tired computers and stale air. The silence, paired with the soft flicker of fluorescent lights, makes it nearly impossible to stay alert. My focus slips. The lines on the screen blur, and before I know it, my eyelids surrender to the weight behind them.

A sudden staccato of fingernails drumming on the metal edge of my cubicle wall jolts me awake. I blink up into the soft, familiar face of Kimmie, peering down at me from her side with a half-smile. There's a quiet sympathy in her tone, like she knows the kind of exhaustion that goes deeper than sleep.

"Hey Tommy, how you doing?"

I rub my face with both hands. "I'm just tired... and blown away at the same time."

"Yeah, me too. That whole Derrick thing has gotten the entire office disturbed. I can't believe *he's* the one that's been doing all of these killings."

"That just freaks me out, to be honest." I lean back in my chair, the worn cushion creaking beneath me. "Sitting here right next to a serial killer, all this time. And I considered him to be a good friend, despite our differences with the route and all. Just goes to show—you never really *know* someone."

Kimmie folds her arms on top of the cubicle wall and rests her chin there, her eyes distant. "I feel bad for his poor wife and baby. Can you imagine? Maybe that's why he was coming in so late."

I glance across the room. "Where's Gibbons?"

"I heard he's gonna be out for a while," she says, adjusting her glasses. "He's got to take care of his daughter, of course... after finding out her husband *was* a serial killer."

She leans in slightly. "You need to get some rest, Tommy. You should see your eyes from where I'm standing."

"What's wrong with them?"

"They're so red I can barely see your pupils. You should've called off today. A lot of people did. That's probably why it's so quiet in here."

"I'll just tell the front desk I'm sick and going home for the day. You're right—I do need to rest. I can't focus on anything. Hell, I haven't even printed my report yet."

"You have any PTO left?"

"Yeah... a few days. I should probably use them before the year's out anyway."

Just then, movement catches the edge of my vision. A young male detective walks into the office, flanked by the president of the company.

Their footsteps are confident, direct. Jessica leads them, pointing... in *my* direction.

My stomach drops.

My pulse kicks up so fast it's like thunder in my ears. I watch as they draw closer, my muscles tightening with every step. Jessica's heels click lightly behind them.

"Good morning," the detective says in passing, but he doesn't stop. Instead, he turns toward Derrick's workstation.

My hands are trembling. I can't hide it. But maybe I don't need to.

I tap Jessica gently on the arm as the others become absorbed in their task.

"Hi Tommy, what's up?" she asks, tilting her head.

"I'm not feeling too well," I murmur, keeping my voice low. "I think I'm going to take a PTO day. I honestly feel like I'm going to throw up."

"Oh my God, *don't* do that," she says, taking a quick step back and forming a playful cross with her fingers. "I'm kidding. Yeah, you don't look so great. Are you going to be okay?"

"I'll be fine. Just need some rest, I think."

"Sounds good."

As I begin gathering my things—shutting down my computer, organizing my desk—the detective bends over Derrick's workstation. I can't stop watching. He pulls the cord from the back of the machine and begins wrapping it up. His movements are methodical. Cold. Professional.

My gaze shifts to the photo frame beside the monitor. It's a picture of Derrick and his wife, wrapped in each other's arms, smiling in the sunlight of some forgotten park.

A moment later, the frame vanishes—plucked up and tossed into a cardboard box with everything else.

Just like that... erased.

"Tommy?" Jessica's voice pulls me back, her hand waving gently in front of my face.

"Oh. Yeah?"

"Go home and get some rest. You definitely need it."

(1:36 AM — Wednesday)

I wake on my couch, the static flicker of *Freddy's Nightmare* replaying its main menu over and over on the TV screen. The glow casts long, ghostly shadows across the room. I blink the sleep from my eyes and grope for the remote, shutting everything down in one silent command.

As the apartment settles into stillness, I catch the soft, broken sound of a whimper just beyond the door—followed by low, furious mumbling.

My body tenses.

I move quietly to the door, peer through the peephole, and see Tricia's door slightly ajar. The voice that spills out into the hallway—sharp, cutting—is Valentin's.

"You ungrateful bitch, you answer the damn phone when I call you. Do you understand?" A sickening *crack* echoes out—then three more in rapid succession. "Answer me, you..."

Rage rises in me like a tide breaking against rock. I turn and march to the kitchen, snatch one of the long knives from the countertop, and head back toward the door with my jaw clenched and grip tight.

I slip into her apartment, easing the door shut behind me. The living room is dim, lit only by a lamp in the corner. Valentin is hunched over Tricia, who lies on the floor beneath him, her face bloodied and swollen, her breath coming in sharp gasps.

"If you don't get off of her now, I'll slit your fucking throat," I growl, the words pushed through tense lips, my voice calm but laced with fury. The knife stays hidden behind my back.

He pauses.

Valentin glances over his shoulder at me, then slowly turns his gaze back to her before rising to face me fully.

"Just get the fuck out of here. Leave her alone."

"Tommy, go home. Just go home, I'm okay!" Tricia shouts through her pain.

"I'm thinking maybe you should take her advice, my friend," Valentin says, brushing off his sleeves. "Go home. This business is none of yours."

I bring the knife out, turning the handle in my palm until it fits snugly, ready. The tension in the room thickens.

"Tommy, no!" Tricia cries out, panic in her voice.

"Oh—oh, what do we have here?" Valentin grins, stepping forward slowly. "Are you going to cut me, my friend? For something you don't even know about? What is driving you right now? Is it love? Does she provide you with good sex without my knowledge or payment? What is it? *Friendship?*"

He takes another deliberate step toward me.

"I'm just telling you to leave. Trust me—I won't have a problem cutting you."

"I understand," he says softly. Then lifts a finger. "But if you cut me, *he* shoots you."

A chill shoots up my spine.

Behind me—*click.*

I feel the unmistakable pressure of cold steel at the back of my skull.

Boris.

How could I forget about Boris?

"Drop the knife. Now!" he barks, voice like gravel, gun pressed firmly to the base of my head.

But I don't.

I tighten my grip, my thumb twitching. My jaw clenches, and I bite my bottom lip.

Valentin watches with amusement, folding his arms. "Boris, our friend Tommy here is motivated to help his bitch from being beaten. This is his motivation to risk his life. He has no idea how to mind his own business. He lets his anger drive him, yes?"

He pauses, his smile hardening.

"Like your father before you."

My chest contracts.

"What!?"

"I said—you are an angry hothead, like your father before you. It is this same temper you inherited from him... that made him kill *my son* years ago."

The world lurches.

My hand opens. The knife clatters to the floor.

"What? What are you saying? You don't know my father."

"Well, I didn't exactly know your dad. I knew *of* him." Valentin's voice turns low, measured, the edges brittle with something far more dangerous than rage. "I do remember faces, though. And when I saw the photograph from the last time we met, I recognized him immediately."

He takes a step closer, the floor groaning beneath his foot. There's something dark flickering behind his eyes now—something wounded, ancient.

"You see, Tommy," he continues, his voice trembling at the edges, "I have a drive too. After finding my son... murdered—beaten to death in his own apartment—I had the drive to find out who could do such a thing to a beautiful boy. *My* beautiful son. My only son."

His breathing turns heavier, each inhale sharp and uneven, as if the memory is pulling him under. Then, with a deliberate breath, he takes another step toward me.

"So I had some friends look into it, of course."

"Please go home, Tommy," Tricia cries behind him, her voice splintered by fear.

Valentin flings his hands up, frustration flashing like lightning. "Shut up, you fugh..." He stops himself, jaw tightening as he closes his eyes and breathes out slowly. "Let me finish my fucking story."

Another step.

"My friends started their investigation with a movie ticket they found in my son's pocket. Then they reviewed the footage—surveillance cameras from the entrance and parking lot." His voice grows quieter, colder. "That's where they saw your father. He was clearly very angry. He sat in the parking lot of the theater. And he waited. When my son came out... he followed him."

"I remember that night," I mutter, chest heaving with the weight of what's coming. "Your son started everything. He was an asshole who probably de—"

In a blur, Valentin lunges.

He snatches the gun from Boris's hands with stunning precision, cocks the hammer in one swift motion, and presses the barrel—silencer and all—tight against Tricia's temple.

She gasps, then breaks into panicked sobs. "Oh my God please—please—please, no!"

"I fucking *swear*," Valentin snarls, "if you say my son *deserved* it, my friend... I cannot be responsible for what my anger will empower me to do when—and *if*—those words leave your lips."

The room tightens like a noose.

Boris circles around with deadly efficiency and drives his fist deep into my side. Pain explodes in my kidney, and I collapse to my knees, choking on the impact. Before I can recover, he shoves me down, grinding his knee into the back of my head, pinning me against the floor like a nailed-down secret.

Valentin, unshaken, continues like a man reciting gospel.

"So as I was saying, before you *rudely* interrupted... when my son left the movie theater, so did your father. Coincidence? Maybe. But then we check the security cameras at his apartment, and guess who they show, entering the building in a fucking *rage*?" He spreads his arms slowly. "Your father. Not a coincidence."

He slips the gun back into the holster at the small of his back, as calmly as if he were putting away a spoon.

"A normal person—well, they might call the police. With the evidence we had? Sure. But in *my* world, in *my* line of work, we don't like to involve the law." He leans forward, voice barely more than a hiss. "So of course, I want to kill the man who took my son's life."

He paces now, letting the weight of his story settle over us like smoke.

"I find out, through my associates, your father was a Navy SEAL. Frogman. Some kind of Special Forces type. Lots of medals. Very impressive history. Obviously, I cannot beat him in a fight... so I had something arranged."

Despite the pressure on my skull, I spit the words out through clenched teeth.

"Sounds like you missed your opportunity, 'cause they died in a plane crash."

"Yes! A plane crash, *that's* it," Valentin exclaims, his voice filled with bitter triumph. "Missed opportunity? I think not."

He begins to pace again, slow and deliberate, like a man rehearsing his monologue before the final act.

"You see, I have friends in very high places," he says, gesturing upward as if speaking to invisible puppeteers. "The plane your parents were *supposed* to take had a rather long layover. So, my friends offered them a ride—a single-engine plane, straight to their destination. Your parents accepted. Quickly, eagerly."

He lets out a sharp laugh—too loud, too amused.

"This is the funny part, so listen closely. The plane was meant to bring your father *to me*. But the engine had... problems. And down it went."

He shakes his head, eyes gleaming with what might've been grief, might've been madness.

"Yes, *that* was a missed opportunity," he admits. "I wanted to bury a knife deep into his chest. To look him in the face... and tell him, *'this isn't even close to the pain you've caused me.'* Then... watch his life drain from his eyes."

He waves a dismissive hand. "I had no concern for your mother. She would've had to die too—collateral. But still, I was robbed. Even lost a good friend—the pilot of that plane."

As he continues, my breath catches. The floor is cold beneath me, and Boris's weight still presses against my back. But I feel it—the familiar shape of the knife handle, wedged just beneath my hip. He hasn't noticed.

Valentin's voice softens into something darker, something resolute.

"But now... I see it differently. My opportunity wasn't lost. It was *delayed*. Because here you are, his son—standing in front of me. Threatening me. Interrupting my business. That's more than enough reason for me to *finally* get the justice I was denied."

"What are you going to do?" I ask, my voice low, coiled.

He looks back at Tricia, who remains crumpled on the floor, trembling.

"She's lost my trust," he says coldly. "No value. I'll rid myself of her. Maybe sell her to a place overseas. Somewhere they'll bleed every penny from her body, while their customers screw her until she dies."

Then, his icy gaze returns to me.

"For you... well, that should be obvious."

My fingers tighten around the blade's grip. I slide it free with the care of a surgeon, the metal cold and reassuring in my hand.

Valentin turns his back, stepping toward Tricia with intent in his stride.

I act.

With a sharp breath, I drive the blade deep behind Boris's knee. A sickening crunch and tear. He screams—howls—and collapses, clutching his ruined leg.

Valentin spins, already reaching for his gun.

But I'm faster.

I launch myself at him and we hit the floor hard, the weapon knocked loose and skittering across the room. We thrash, fists and limbs locked in desperate motion. His breath is hot with panic. Mine is fire.

Behind me, Boris is still screaming—but his voice begins to fade, lost beneath the roar building in my head. I think of my mother. My father. Torn from the world by this man's cruelty and the toxic bloodline he serves.

I punch him. Once. Twice. My knuckles split.

I wrap my fingers around his throat, pressing down with everything I have, leaning into him with my full weight. He thrashes beneath me, clawing at my shirt, his nails scraping flesh. I slam his head against the floor again—and again—until those glacial eyes begin to drift.

Then... silence. Boris's cries stop.

Still straddling Valentin, I let the fury take full control, pounding his skull against the floor with a primal rhythm. All thought dissolves. There is only rage—centuries old, passed through bloodlines and sealed in bone.

Then, a presence.

Tricia.

She stands beside me now, her hands trembling as they grip the silenced pistol. She points it at Valentin's face.

He raises his hand, a final, useless defense—his fingers spread wide in surrender.

The shot is almost silent.

The bullet slices through his palm and into his right eye. His body stiffens once—then collapses like a puppet with cut strings.

Valentin is dead.

I scramble off of him, breath heaving, ready to take care of Boris.

But there's no need.

He's already down.

A single, precise hole sits dead center between his eyes. His expression is frozen in that final moment of surprise—mouth slightly parted, eyes wide, lifeless. I hadn't even noticed her doing it. She's quick.

Tricia stands above Valentin, breathing heavily, her chest rising and falling in jagged waves. The gun trembles in her grip, her eyes locked on his corpse as if it might still move.

Then—*crack*. Another shot.

And another.

The silencer coughs two more quiet rounds into his skull, each one making his body jolt violently with a sickening twitch. I lunge forward, grabbing the weapon from her shaking hands before she can fire again. Her fingers release it with a ghost-like looseness.

Her eyes, wide and dazed, meet mine.

"Too much noise," she says in a hushed, trembling voice. "You guys were making way too much noise. The neighbors would hear."

I nod, gently setting the pistol on the floor. Then I hurry to the front door, easing it open.

Empty hallway.

Still and quiet.

I dart across to my apartment, shut the door tight, and slide back into hers, locking it behind me. Every sound feels too loud. Every breath amplified.

(3:52 AM)

We coast down the alley behind Gram's house with the truck lights off, nerves sharp and skin crawling. The world is quiet and asleep. The kind of silence that presses against your eardrums, reminding you just how wrong everything is.

I slip out first, creeping to the window to peek inside.

Gram's curled on the couch in her nightgown, lost in a peaceful dream, the television casting a soft blue glow over her silver curls. Safe. Unaware.

With Tricia's help, we unlatch the bed of the truck. The sound of shifting metal seems too loud in the early dark. We begin dumping the dried branches I'd promised to burn weeks ago, letting them tumble to the ground until the grim shapes beneath them are exposed.

Two forms, swaddled in black sheets like offerings.

Valentin. Boris.

We stop and look at each other. A long, hollow silence passes between us. We both know we've crossed a line that can't be uncrossed.

I head for the shed and return with a shovel, its handle damp with morning dew. Tricia stays back, arms folded, a cigarette trembling between her fingers.

Her silence says more than words could.

I dig.

And dig.

The earth is thick, damp, resistant. But eventually, the hole is deep enough. I grab Valentin by the ankles and pull him in first, his body heavy and limp. Then Boris, the sheet slipping slightly from his shoulder.

A full can of gasoline rests by the wall. I douse them both. The acrid fumes sting my nose, burning sharp in the back of my throat.

"Finish the job you were supposed to do for your Gram and use the sticks," Tricia says softly, her voice hoarse.

"Right. Good thinking."

We stack the branches quickly, layering them in a haphazard pyre. Time is short. Dawn isn't far off, and Gram sometimes wakes before the sun.

I reach for her cigarette, still glowing at the tip.

"Hey!" she snaps. "That's my last one."

"You probably should quit smoking anyway," I say, then flick the ember into the pit.

The fire takes quickly—racing up the wood, consuming everything beneath with a low roar. The smoke curls into the sky, black and alive, vanishing into the stars.

We stand there together, staring at the blaze. Watching our sins turn to ash.

Tricia huddles under my arm, her body cold, her heart still rattled.

"So what now?" she asks.

I hadn't thought that far ahead—not until now. That apartment... it's cursed. Tainted by blood, secrets, and ghosts that won't sleep easy. And worse, Valentin's "associates" might come sniffing around, looking for what was left behind.

We can't stay.

There's only one answer.

"We move."

CHapTer 20

TWO PEAS

May, the following year

(6:30 AM, Monday)

The harsh, pulsing shriek of my alarm yanks me from sleep. My face is buried in the pillow, limbs tangled in the blanket like a net I forgot I was in. Groaning, I stretch an arm out and blindly slap at the alarm clock until silence returns—along with the soft crash of my glass of water spilling to the floor.

I yawn deeply, and the warm, familiar scent of pancakes and melted butter drifts in from the kitchen, sweet and nostalgic. Someone's been up early.

A smile tugs at my lips.

I throw off the covers and head down the hall, where Tricia stands at the stove, just finishing a pan of scrambled eggs. A stack of pancakes towers proudly in the center of the dining table, steam curling up in soft tendrils.

"Good morning," she says, smiling over her shoulder. "How did you sleep?"

I wrap my arms around her from behind, kissing the soft curve of her neck. "Like a rock. And you?"

"Once I got past your snoring, I was fine," she laughs, elbowing me playfully. "I figured you might want some breakfast before your first day back on the phones."

"Oh yeah. You're awesome."

"Yeah, well... they're nothing like your Gram's pancakes. I might be cooking in her kitchen, but I definitely don't have her magic."

"You've been doing a damn good job since she left us to be with Grandpa. She'd be proud of you."

"You think so?"

"Yes. She taught you just about everything she knew."

Gram passed away quietly earlier this year, slipping from the world in her sleep. The doctor said her heart simply stopped. Peaceful. Gentle. The kind of passing she always said she wanted. She left the house to me in her will—along with a little money that I now share with Tricia, Tilly, and Rocky.

Rocky's Tricia's new ferret—one of those classic-looking ones, with a dark body and a little black mask across his eyes. He and Tilly, my tabby, have bonded like lifelong companions. I've never seen her so energetic, so playful. It's like they were meant to meet.

(7:25 PM)

Tricia walks me out to Old Blue, the fading light catching in her hair as she presses a kiss to my cheek and hands me a paper bag lunch—like something out of an old sitcom, the kind with perfect lawns and piano theme songs.

"Looks like your veggies are coming up great, babe," I say, glancing at the neatly kept garden just beyond the porch.

"Yeah, I saw that," she smiles, hands on her hips. "They shot up pretty quick, didn't they? Must be something about that soil."

I chuckle.

The garden grows right above what remains of Boris and Valentin—ashes buried beneath rows of beans, tomatoes, and squash. I tried to convince her to start it somewhere else, but she was certain this was the perfect spot. Something about giving life where death once lay. I suppose, in a twisted way, she's not wrong.

I kiss her on the lips. "Bye, babe. Have a good day."

***

(7:41 AM)

The drive to work is smooth, the traffic gliding along without the usual choke points. Morning talk radio hums softly through the speakers, the news anchor's voice riding the rhythm of the road.

Not much has surfaced lately about the Stickman murders. Every now and then, a report questions whether Derrick's gunshot wound was self-inflicted, speculating about the leftover string tied around the trigger. Nothing conclusive. No suspects. Just speculation and recycled intrigue, designed to feed the curiosity of viewers and keep the story alive a little longer.

The media's appetite is endless.

I handed in my two weeks' notice not long after Derrick's death. I blamed it on stress. Too much happening. Couldn't focus. The truth was, I just couldn't stomach walking back into that office and pretending everything was normal.

Kimmie disappeared without warning, no goodbye. Word eventually spread that she got married in the Bahamas. She and Greg settled in Miami, wrapped in sunshine and fresh starts.

Good for her.

Quite a few representatives had walked away from E.A.A.C., unwilling to be tied to the storm of bad publicity that came down on us like a slow-building fire. No one wanted their name whispered alongside the word *murderer*, no matter how far removed they were from the truth. It became the first hurdle of every shift—one we all learned to expect.

The moment we'd ask a customer about their past due balance, we were met with the same tired, sarcastic line: *"I'll pay, just don't kill me, please."*

It stopped being funny after the third time. Now it just burned.

I remember standing in line at a department store not long ago, the dull hum of conversation buzzing around me. The woman in front of me clutched her phone to her ear, voice lowered into a pleading whine as she begged someone—apparently a furniture store manager—for a grace period on a missed payment. Her cart, meanwhile, was filled to the brim with unnecessary purchases: scented candles, designer accessories, and a brand-new laptop perched on top like a cherry on a sundae of lies.

Her friend stood beside her, eavesdropping shamelessly, then chuckled and nudged her.

"Girl, you better pay that damn bill before the Stickman pays you a visit," she joked.

They both turned, eyes flicking to me—just a glance—and then back to each other as they burst into laughter.

"Too late!" her friend giggled.

I forced a polite smile, but deep down, I was boiling.

Derrick got the credit. *He* became the story. The boogeyman. The Stickman. And all because of that damned suicide note.

At one point, 12News had even said, "If it weren't for the suicide and confession letter, the Stickman murders would have possibly gone unsolved."

A legacy... handed to the wrong man.

With Gram's savings now long gone, I was left to start over. Again. I put in an application at another call center—collections, of course—and somehow landed the job. Three weeks of training passed like molasses, but today marks the beginning.

Day one.

———————

I arrive early, settling into my assigned cubicle. It's sterile, bland, filled with the soft hum of quiet tension. I glance to my left where a woman with chestnut hair and a no-nonsense air sits tapping furiously at her keyboard.

"Good morning!" I offer with a half-smile.

She quickly covers her mic and glances at me. "Morning," she whispers, then points at her headset and rolls her eyes upward in exaggerated agony, signaling she's stuck in a particularly rough call.

"How's your day going?" I ask.

She taps mute and leans back slightly. "Well, we've got a monster queue. It's non-stop this morning. Mondays are always like this." She gives me a tired but friendly smile. "Welcome to the team. Customers tend to be *bitchy* at the beginning of the week. They blow through the money they were supposed to pay us with... sometime between Friday night and Sunday morning. I'm *definitely* looking forward to my lunch."

"Hopefully it slows down some," I reply, arranging my notepad and headset as I slide aside the list of customers in my portfolio.

She groans quietly. Then, without warning, she yanks her headset off, tosses it onto the keyboard, and mashes the release button with a scowl. She rises and does that little dance women do when adjusting tight jeans—a combination shimmy and hop.

"I need a break," she mutters, snatching a pack of cigarettes from the desk and striding off without another word.

I exhale, log into my phone and payment systems, and get everything ready. The screen glows cold and familiar, like an old wound that's scarred over but never quite healed.

I take a breath.

And then I smile.

Today is a new day. A new start.

From the corner of my eye, I catch movement—my supervisor, seated in a larger cubicle across the floor, watching me. He taps his wrist with an index finger. A silent nudge.

Time to get to work.

My finger hovers just above the ready button—the one that will send the first call surging into my system like a current. *Am I really ready for this?*

I pause.

One more breath. In through the nose, out through the mouth—just like they taught us in training. I steady my hand and press the button.

The screen flashes to life, the details of my first account spilling across the monitor. The phone rings. Once. Twice.

"Good morning, may I speak to Joseph Bankman, please?"

"This is," he answers, voice clipped and already edged with irritation.

"Hi Joseph, my name is Tommy Thorpe, and I'm calling you about your balance with an account you have in our office. Mr. Bankman, this is an attempt to collect a debt and any information obtained may be used for that purpose. Now Mr. Bankman, I—"

"God *dammit*, you people again!" he erupts. "Haven't I told you before that I'm not going to pay, and have no intentions of paying? I'm so sick of you people calling my house about that *funky ass* sixty-five dollar account! You guys call here at least six times a day, and it's ridiculous. Don't you have larger balances or bigger concerns, rather than calling me every day?"

I don't answer immediately. Instead, I pull in another long breath and curl my lips into a trained smile—like our instructor said, to help temper the tone, to keep the edges smooth.

"You there?" he barks.

"Yes, sir, I—"

"What, you got nothing to say now?" he cuts in, steamrolling right over me. "I'm an *attorney*, and I *know* the law. This is harassment. Against the law. You hear me? I make a ton of money with my firm, so it's not like I *can't* pay. I just *won't*. Your company digs people like you up from the streets to call people like me. You people are beneath me."

His words keep coming—fast, sharp, cruel. Each one lands like a slow drip of acid. I try to focus, try to sound composed, but inside, my frustration churns. I pick up my pen and begin to doodle on the corner of my report, trying to anchor myself to something other than the rising heat in my chest.

I draw a circle. Not much of an artist—never was—but I keep tracing it, round and round, darker and darker.

"Are you even listening to me?" he jeers. "You probably can't even *comprehend* what I'm saying, can you?" He laughs. A mean, hollow sound. "You know what? Get me your supervisor. I'm getting nowhere with you."

"Sir, why do you need my supervisor? We can handle your dispute right here over the phone." My voice is level, but I'm still circling—still pressing ink into the paper like I'm trying to burn through it.

"Because you're *just* a rep," he sneers. "You have no power. I want someone who can *actually* get rid of this situation. I don't want to waste another second talking to a bottom feeder like yourself."

My hand goes still.

I drop the pen and glance down. The dark circle I'd been obsessively carving into the page now has long stick arms and long stick legs. My jaw tightens, teeth clenching as the blood in my ears begins to hum.

I reach, slowly and deliberately, for my highlighter—my fingers steady now, purposeful.

His voice continues in my ear, some new variation of the same tired rage. I'm no longer listening.

I raise the highlighter.

And with the softest *squeal* of ink on paper, I draw a single, bright line through his name.

THE END

ABOUT THE AUTHOR

TERRENCE DAMON SPENCER is an Amazon bestselling author known for his gripping horror and mystery novels, crafting chilling tales that have captivated readers since 2007. A veteran of the U.S. Marine Corps, Terrence shares with his wife a deep fascination for exploring haunted locations—experiences that often find their way into his eerie narratives.

Terrence's journey as an author began gradually, after years of spontaneously entertaining his wife and children with vivid, imaginative stories during long family road trips. However, it wasn't until one unforgettable day at the movies—when a trailer mirrored one of his impromptu tales so closely that his family's jaws dropped in disbelief—that everything changed. In that pivotal moment, his wife finally dared him to write his first novel, setting him on a path he never expected.

Since then, Terrence Damon Spencer's novels—including fan favorites such as *Premises* and *Strong*—have gone on to grace the shelves of his local Barnes and Noble, where they continue to captivate readers with spine-tingling suspense and unforgettable characters. Beyond his writing desk, Terrence enjoys delving into supernatural mysteries and spending quality time with his loved ones. Together with his five adult children, two grandchildren, and their loyal Mastiff/Dane, Tank, he finds inspiration and comfort in their home nestled in Pueblo, Colorado.

www.ingramcontent.com/pod-product-compliance
Lightning Source LLC
Chambersburg PA
CBHW020658110726
47901CB00001B/232